"There's something about a good book
ing. I'm pulled right into the story line,
ters. *The Sound the Sun Makes* is that kind of story. The plot kept me turning pages, staying up far past my bedtime, trying to figure out what would happen next. Best yet, Storm didn't write a fast-paced tale at the expense of characterization. He peopled his story with fully realized, nuanced, authentic characters. Do yourself a favor. Grab a copy of this book and get ready for a read that you won't want to put down."

SUSIE FINKBEINER, author of *The Nature of Small Birds* and the Pearl Spence novels

Praise for Buck Storm

"Lives change in unexpected and hilarious ways in this novel about love, forgiveness, and Elvis's ghost. Populated with quirky, memorable characters, Buck Storm's novel spins a laugh-out-loud tale perfect for a lazy day. . . . But don't be surprised if, after all the laughter, there's some water in your eyes by the end of the story."

THE BANNER

"[One of the] unique literary voices of our day. Infused with humor, imagination, and poetic beauty, Buck's writing is an absolute delight. I've read all his books, and his characters have taken up permanent residence in my memory. They come back to me at unexpected moments and invariably leave me smiling."

ANN TATLOCK, novelist, blogger, and children's book author

"A writer whose gifts only get richer and more compelling with each new story he brings to life. Buck paints such masterful word pictures that his characters breathe and their world becomes yours."

RANDY STONEHILL, singer-songwriter

"I've never read a phrase from Buck Storm that wasn't time well spent—and worth reading again. A topflight storyteller."

RANDALL MURPHREE, editor of the *AFA Journal*

THE SOUND THE SUN MAKES

THE SOUND THE SUN MAKES

BUCK STORM

Published by Kregel Publications, a division of Kregel Inc., 2450 Oak Industrial Dr. NE, Grand Rapids, MI 49505.

The persons and events portrayed in this work are the creations of the author, and any resemblance to persons living or dead is purely coincidental.

Library of Congress Cataloging-in-Publication Data
Names: Storm, Buck, author.
Title: The sound the sun makes / Buck Storm.
Description: Grand Rapids : Kregel Publications, [2021] | Series: Ballads of paradise; 2 | Description based on print version record and CIP data provided by publisher; resource not viewed.
Identifiers: LCCN 2020047811 (print) | LCCN 2020047812 (ebook) | ISBN 9780825477300 (epub) | ISBN 9780825446863 (paperback)
Subjects: | LCGFT: Novels.
Classification: LCC PS3619.T69274 (ebook) | LCC PS3619.T69274 S68 2021 (print) | DDC 813/.6--dc23
LC record available at https://lccn.loc.gov/2020047811

ISBN 978-0-8254-4686-3, print
ISBN 978-0-8254-7730-0, epub

Printed in the United States of America
21 22 23 24 25 26 27 28 29 30 / 5 4 3 2 1

CHAPTER ONE

May 25—Valle Del Viento,
just outside of Paradise, Arizona

Some people say the desert makes a person feel small. But it never had that effect on Early Pines.

Out here, alone in the empty, he always felt bigger than he did in town. Out here, where he could see all the way across the valley to the Chiricahua mountain range, his thoughts bounced off the sky so hard they rattled his skin. And this morning, sipping black coffee on the back patio of his little adobe, they echoed back with particular intensity.

He did his best to ignore them for a while. Or maybe longer than a while, because when he sipped his coffee again it was cold. He set the cup on the ground next to his chair. He could, he told his body, go inside for a refill, but his legs disagreed so he kept sitting. And kept bouncing thoughts.

He flexed his fingers and winced. The thing most people don't know about punching somebody: it hurts your hand about as much as it hurts the guy's face. A week and Early's knuckles were still swollen.

A week . . .

He needed to get up and do something.

Anything.

But he didn't.

It wasn't like him. Or it hadn't been. But these days, mornings on the patio tended to last longer than they used to.

A flicker of movement out in the sage. The coyote was back. The thing came around so often Early ought to give him a name. It slunk a few steps closer and squatted on its haunches. Yellow, serious eyes.

"What?" Early said.

The animal's tongue lolled out of the side of his mouth.

"One time, amigo. I fed you one time. It's over between us, all right? You know what they say, it's not me, it's you. Beat it."

The coyote didn't beat it.

Early sighed. "Fine, but don't get too comfortable."

The coyote lowered onto his belly and blinked.

Past the coyote, far out across the desert, a dust devil danced in the bright shimmer. No roads out that direction. Not much of anything besides a handful of forgotten mines and dehydrated dreams.

Early lifted his cup to the coyote. "Here's to a little peace and quiet, huh? God's country."

The creature rose, backed up a few feet, then sat down again and resumed his one-sided staring contest.

Early's place sat on a rise about five miles outside of Paradise, Arizona, a little backwater town tucked into the foothills of the southeastern corner of the state. Most people who chose to live in Paradise either stuck close to city limits or had homes farther up in the mountains where pine trees and cooler summers were the order of the day. Not Early. He was a creature of the flat. He'd bought the ancient adobe some years ago, back in his rodeo days, from a distant Navajo cousin for practically nothing. Early wasn't even a quarter Native himself, but even a little *Diné* blood was plenty to supply a few cousins in this country.

He'd spent the better part of a year hunting and hauling flagstone for the back patio he sat on now. Built it western facing for the sunsets though he'd found he enjoyed watching the first fingers of the rising sun touch the valley just as much, and maybe even more. At the moment, those sun fingers were hours gone and Old Man Sol had begun his work in earnest. Early sighed, rose, unbuttoned the top button of his shirt, tossed his coffee dregs into a stand of sage, and headed in for a refill, letting the screen door bang shut behind him.

He was rinsing the cup in the sink, having opted for a Mexican Coke instead because of the heat, when he heard tires popping gravel. Sound traveled out here. It'd be at least a few minutes before the truck arrived. He didn't go to the front of the house to look. Didn't need to. Only Jake would make the trip out here now. Everyone else knew Early was in a mood. They'd steer clear. But not Jake. Never Jake. Early walked back out onto the patio and sat, long legs stretched out, ankles crossed. He took a pull from the Coke bottle. The coyote was gone.

More gravel popping. Out front now. A truck door slammed and the front door of the house banged open without a knock. Boot heels scuffed. A cabinet creaked. Jake emerged through the back door, steaming coffee cup in hand.

"Help yourself," Early said.

Jake sipped, his eyes pulling in the distance. He didn't say anything, but that was Jake.

"If I told you I wanted to be alone, would you leave?" Early said.

Jake sipped again.

Early sighed. "Well, don't just stand there all Jake on me. You might as well sit."

Jake dragged a wooden chair over with his boot and lowered himself onto it. He took off his old cowboy hat—same one he'd had since their rodeo days—and set it upside down on the floor next to him. Tilting back, he rested his dark, sweat-matted hair against the mud brick. The dull thrum of a distant plane challenged the breeze. Far out above the mountains, sunlight glinted off metal and a gleaming vapor trail cut a horizontal slash in the blue-blanket sky.

"How you doing, Early?"

"I'm just fine, Jake. How are you?"

"I'm serious."

"I know you are. You're always serious."

"Haven't seen you in town."

"Me and the coyotes have a lot to discuss. So you can understand I've been busy."

"That what you're doing out here, talking to the wildlife?"

"Better than talking to myself."

"I'm not sure that's even a little true."

The vapor trail slowly dissipated to wispy white threads. Early tried to pick the plane out but couldn't now. He uncrossed his boots, then crossed them again. "Matthias send you out?"

"Nope."

"He should have. Shoulda sent you to tell me to come back to work."

"Nope."

"Why nope?"

"He's only doing his job. He's all right. You know that."

"A police chief is supposed to have his detective's back, man. Not put them on leave for something they had to do."

"That what you're telling the coyotes?"

"They agree with me. Lee had it coming."

"As far as I can see, all Lee did was not cross over to the other side of the street when he saw you."

"Exactly what I mean, he had it coming."

"Look, I'm not going to tell you how long you should carry your Lee baggage around, but you can't just knock a guy out on the sidewalk and blame your boss for putting you on the shelf. You know that, you're not stupid."

"It's been a week, man. How long will this go on?"

"Till they decide it's done, I guess."

"Lee knew what would happen if he didn't avoid me."

"Did he? You and Lee have existed in the same town for years. You never hit him before."

Early sipped and shrugged. "I was in a bad mood."

"You put the man in the hospital, Early."

"He got out, didn't he? He's got a head like a brick. Trust me, I had to ice my hand for days. And I'd hit him again. I'm not gonna apologize for hitting a wife beater."

"How many years has it been?"

"Not enough by a long shot."

"All right. But the council thinks he might sue the city, and you, so you can see Matthias's position. He has to wait and see."

"You saying you wouldn't have done the same if you were me? Never mind, don't answer that. Saint Jake would've greeted the guy with a holy kiss."

"Take it out on me, fine. But you need to get a little perspective here, amigo. This isn't going away no matter how long you hide out here with the coyotes."

"I'm not hiding."

"That's exactly what you're doing."

"C'mon, Jake."

Jake looked out toward the Chiricahuas. "You wear a badge, Early. I didn't personally hear the oath you took to do that, but I imagine the words 'protect and serve' were in there somewhere. That includes Lee."

Early said nothing.

"Plus, I'm not sure it's even about Lee."

"What's that supposed to mean?"

"That bad mood you mentioned? Since Gomez Gomez died you've been walking way out on the edge. And I know you, the edge is the last place you need to be."

"I'm fine."

"Tell that to Lee."

Another glint. Another vapor trail on the horizon. A bird flitted in the sage.

Early let his head fall back and hit the wall with a gentle thump. "I don't know, man, maybe you're right about the Gomez Gomez thing."

"It's been known to happen from time to time."

"But mandatory leave? Matthias should—"

"Mathias should've done exactly what he did. Stop lying to yourself."

Early picked at the label on his Coke bottle with his thumbnail. "People saying I was drinking when I hit him?"

"Since when do you care what people think?"

"Not often. But the drinking thing—it's in the past. Kinda bothers me people might think it wasn't."

"You're three years sober. Everybody knows that."

"Three years and forty-one days."

"And I'm proud of you. But sitting out here with nothing but sky and coyotes would test anyone's resolve."

"Are you my sponsor now?"

Jake half smiled. "I've been your sponsor since kindergarten."

Early set his empty bottle down.

Jake stood. "I'm gonna get some more coffee. Get you another Coke?"

"Nah. I'm good."

The screen door creaked and banged. After a minute Jake came back out and took his chair again.

Early scuffed his boot against the flagstone. "You ever think about him?"

"Lee?"

"Gomez Gomez."

"All the time. I miss him as much as you do."

"Three of us rodeoing all over the place all those years. It's weird, him being gone. Like there's a hole in the world where he used to be. Like a star's missing or something."

"That's exactly right. I feel it too."

"Everybody says he's with Angel now. Like that's supposed to make it all good."

"He loved his wife. With her is the only place he'd ever be happy. I'd be lying if I said it didn't make me feel better thinking about it."

"He's dead, man. How's there any comfort in that?"

Jake didn't answer and they sat in silence for a few minutes, the way friends who've seen miles together sometimes do.

"Let me ask you something," Early said. "You remember when Gomez Gomez said he could hear the sun scraping across the sky?"

"I remember."

"Why do you think that was?"

"I don't know, the liquor tore him up pretty bad those last years."

"Yeah, but he was always a little off. Beat of a different drum and all that."

"You know what they say—you've got to be either crazy-brave or crazy-crazy to ride bulls."

"He was a whole bunch of both."

"Probably. Yeah."

"Thing is . . ."

"The thing is what?"

"Man, Jake . . ."

"What?"

"I'm not drinking."

"We've established that."

"I'm starting to hear it too. The sun scraping. I swear some days it sounds like somebody's dragging a ten-ton bag of gravel. So loud it hurts my ears. I think I'm losing it like Gomez Gomez."

Jake studied him. "You hear the sun?"

"It never stops, man. It's crazy, I know. But all this extra time with nothing to do. All this . . . space. Mandatory leave? For hitting stinking Lee? What am I supposed to do with myself?"

Jake stood. "Not sit out here listening to the sun and talking to coyotes, I know that much."

Early leaned forward, elbow on knee, rubbed his temples with thumb and forefinger. "You got a better idea? Because I'm seriously losing it."

"Yup. I didn't come out here to listen to you whine. Go pack a bag."

"Why?"

"Why does a person usually pack? We're going on a trip."

"What trip?"

"A rodeo trip. Quit asking questions and let's go."

"What about Honey?"

"She's visiting that hypochondriac aunt of hers in Phoenix. Won't be back for a few days at least. The house is too quiet. So you'd be doing me a favor if you'd hoist your long, lazy carcass out of that chair and pack your things."

Early didn't move. "This a rescue mission for me or for you?"

Jake lifted a shoulder. "Let's call it combined necessity."

"For me then."

"If the boot fits."

"What rodeo? Tucson was in February."

"Agua Prieta."

Early couldn't help barking a laugh. "You want to go down to Old Mexico? You remember last time we were in Agua Prieta? I spent a night in jail, amigo."

"That night tequila was your amigo, not me. And now you got three years and forty-one days in your pocket. You're a changed man."

"Yeah, but Old Mexico?"

"Not to be confused with New Mexico. It's a good rodeo."

"It was good for you, if I remember right. You won some money there. More than once."

Jake put his hat on. "Got lucky. Drew good horses."

"All I won was a busted face, I think."

"Bulldogging'll do that to a guy."

"*Life* will do that. Tequila too, I guess."

"If you're not careful."

Early finally stood and stretched. "All right, Jake Morales, sponsor and travel agent. Agua Prieta. But we're taking my truck."

CHAPTER TWO

THEY DROVE SOUTH.

Because south has always been the way for men on the run. Whether it be from the law, too-quiet-wifeless houses, or mandatory leaves and overly noisy suns. Early pushed his battered 1972 Chevy pickup as fast as the gravel road would let him, leaving a half-mile-long dust trail to mark their passing. They could have cut west and caught the highway—there was actually a pretty good road down to Agua Prieta—but Early had never been the highway kind. At least not when he could help it. Which was why he'd wanted to drive in the first place.

Jake leaned back, pulled his hat down over his eyes. "You're sure you know where we're going?"

"I got an internal GPS."

"What is it with you and back roads?"

"Life happens on back roads, brother."

"Uh-huh. You know, if I'd known you were going to wear that hat, I wouldn't have brought you."

"I always wear this hat."

"It's a rodeo."

"So?" Early leaned over and glanced at himself in the driver's side mirror. His trucker hat—white front, red bill—said *Kiss Me, I'm Baptist.* He pulled the brim low against the wind coming through the open window. True, he was less than a quarter Navajo but, with his sun-weathered face, he looked more. Dark hair to his shoulders. His nose angled a bit to the left. A fine scar tracing up from the edge of his mouth almost to his eye courtesy of a stubborn steer and a wire fence. The broken nose, close as he could figure, he'd gotten in a parking lot fight behind an Amarillo bar, though his memory of the event was more than a little foggy. "What's wrong with my hat?"

"Where do you want me to start? You're not a Baptist, for one."

"The Baptists gave it to me so I'm at least Baptist approved."

"Was that before or after you gave them your speech about religion being the opiate of the masses?"

"I wanted the hat, man. It makes me laugh. I wouldn't mess that up with a speech. But even you have to admit the communion wine's laced with something a little heavier these days, pontiff."

"Baptists use grape juice."

"That's because Baptists tend to keep their sinning polite and mostly unnamed. They only think white-dove thoughts. Unless they're playing softball, then they get all hard-core. Which is another reason I kinda like the hat."

Jake hung an arm out the window. "I'm just saying you could've scrounged up something else."

"I like to stand out."

"You're six five without your boots on and you're made of wood and leather. Trust me, you don't need a hat to stand out."

Early relaxed in his seat and breathed in the desert. He searched his brain for a white-dove thought or two, but those power lines were vacant. *At least I'm moving.* It was a step in the right direction.

Jake dozed. Or at least he might've dozed, Early couldn't be sure. Jake could be quiet like that, especially on road trips. They'd seen a lot of miles, the two of them. The three of them when you included Gomez Gomez. And it felt good to be seeing a few more. The sun climbed and the temperature with it. Not even close to noon and already a shade over a hundred degrees. Early didn't mind. Heat kept the desert empty. And a desert should be empty. A private place for hawks and lizards and kangaroo rats and him.

A crossroads loomed and he backed his foot off the gas. The intersecting road was paved. On the corner, a ramshackle building with a rusty metal sign proclaimed the Chiricahua Trading Post occupied and open. Early rolled to a stop on the gravel in front of the shop and killed the engine.

Jake sat up, tilted his hat back, and looked around. "You lost?"

"Never lost. I told you."

"Where are we?"

"Smack-dab in the middle of where we are. I'm gonna get something to drink. Rodeo doesn't start till tomorrow. You in a hurry?"

Jake opened the passenger door and rolled out. "Nope."

Rambling adobe and corrugated metal. A low wooden porch fronted the place. Above the entry, a semi-neatly painted *yah ta hey* offered a canary-yellow traditional Navajo greeting. Early stomped the dust off his boots and stepped inside, Jake behind him. Low drum and flute music drifted. Racks of T-shirts. A display of brightly colored wool blankets, pottery, and a long jewelry case. An acne-scarred but pretty teen sitting behind a checkout counter appeared to be the sole occupant. She tore her eyes from her iPhone long enough to give them an I-wish-I-were-anywhere-but-here smile. "Yah ta hey. Hello. Greetings. Aloha. *Privet.*"

"What's privet?" Early said.

"Hello in Russian, I think."

"Yeah?"

"Uh-huh. You impressed?"

"Yeah, actually."

She shrugged and went back to her phone.

A coyote stared at him from the front of a black T-shirt. He pointed at it. "I got one looks just like that who hangs around my place. Fed him once and now he won't go away."

Her dark eyes shifted up from her screen without moving her head. "You shouldn't feed him. Everyone knows Coyote's a trickster. It's a bad omen to have him around."

"You believe in that stuff?"

"I don't know. I got an uncle who used to tell us stories about skinwalkers and stuff. How they can turn themselves into animals. Look like something they're not. Always gave me nightmares. Still does sometimes. Coyote's the same way. If it were me, I wouldn't feed him, but whatever, do what you want." Eyes back to the phone, subject apparently closed.

Early fingered the T-shirt, flicked the coyote on the nose. "I already got trouble, so get in line, pal."

At the cold-drink case in the back of the store he pulled a couple water bottles from a cooler, tossed one to Jake, and opened another. Jake headed back outside, but the swamp-cooled air felt good so Early lingered, stretching his legs. He walked the aisles, his boots loud on the plank floor. He checked out some pottery and blankets, then looked out through the fly-specked window. Unhindered by civilization, the desert rolled off to the horizon. Distant mountains, red and jagged, jutted up against the endless sky. You could always see mountains in the desert distance. Years ago, and several times since, he had rodeoed through the Midwest with its flat plains and unbroken space. He had always found the place unnerving. Mountainless, and without stick or stump to slow the tumbleweeds and dust-bowl ghosts. No, thanks. A man needed something out there to corral his soul.

A cobweb danced in the fan breeze. Out in the parking lot, Jake leaned against the hood of the truck and wiped his water bottle across his forehead. Past him, a decrepit tractor pulling a trailer piled with hay bales popped and jerked as it made slow progress along the side of the road. Early walked back to the counter where the girl gave one-handed change without looking up.

"See ya around," he said.

"Adios. Goodbye. Sayonara. *Proshchay.* Have a nice day."

"You oughta work for the United Nations. Your talents are wasted here."

"True story."

A chime sounded from somewhere in the back as he pulled open the door.

"Hey," the girl said as he was stepping out.

He turned. "Yeah?"

"Watch those coyotes, huh?"

"Will do."

Back out in the heat, he climbed in the truck and turned the engine over.

"Making friends in there?" Jake said.

"Yup. She told me Coyote was gonna eat me."

"It'd be a pretty desperate coyote."

"Let's go to a rodeo."

Jake leaned back and pulled his hat down. "I never argue with Baptists. Drive on, amigo, Old Mexico's calling."

They pulled out and turned right. The road was paved now. The sun high and bright, heat waves dancing on the horizon. Windows up, the old air conditioner complained but blew coolish air. They'd gone a good forty miles when the truck lurched slightly right and a rhythmic thump sounded.

Jake sat up. "Flat tire? Are you kidding?"

"Sounds like it." Early pulled the truck off the road and both of them got out. Sure enough, the driver's side rear rested on the rim. Early took off his hat and wiped his brow. "It's gotta be a hundred and ten. This'll be fun."

"You wanted to take your truck."

"Only because you wanted to go to Old Mexico."

"Yeah, all right. Where's the spare?"

"Mounted under the bed. Get it and I'll grab the iron." Early dug behind the truck seat until he came up with the tire iron. Jake was squatting behind the truck as he rounded the back of the bed.

"Problem," Jake said.

Early stopped. "Don't say the spare's flat."

Jake stood. "All right. I won't say it."

CHAPTER THREE

EARLY LEANED AGAINST THE TAILGATE, arms crossed. Jake stood a dozen yards away in the middle of the road looking down at his phone.

The asphalt shimmered.

The sun scraped and laughed.

"Nothing?" Early called.

"Nothing."

"Keep walking. If you don't pick up a signal, you'll at least hit Phoenix eventually."

Jake started back, shaking his head. "A flat spare. How does that happen?"

Early shrugged. "Rock coulda bounced up. Coulda been anything."

Jake slipped his phone into his jeans pocket. "You and your back roads. What now?"

Early pulled his duffel from the truck bed and slung the strap over his shoulder. "We start walking unless we want to spend the night out here. Which I don't."

Jake pulled his own bag out. "How far do you think One Horse is? Been a while since I've been through here."

"Can't be more than five or six miles. We can at least get to a phone." He opened the driver's side door and grabbed an old blanket-covered canteen from behind the seat.

A corner of Jake's mouth lifted. "Early Pines, a man with extra water but no spare tire."

"Somebody'll come along. I doubt we'll have to walk the whole way."

Jake hitched his bag higher and glanced up at the sun. "Five miles."

"Maybe not even that."

"Let's get to it then."

A mile into the trek, Early was sweating hard. Two miles and his faded denim shirt had turned dark blue. They passed the canteen back and forth occasionally but spoke little, both too hot for their usual banter.

Early did the math in his head. What had it been, twenty-eight years now? Since they were five or six. Jake, quiet and serious even as a kid. Always old for his age. But the kind of guy who had your back no matter what came. Childhood had been wild and rough to say the least, most of the blame for that landing squarely on Early. As adults, they'd hit the various rodeo circuits. Jake, Early, and Gomez Gomez. Seen a lot of the country. Even New York City one time. Madison Square Garden. Jake had been a better-than-good saddle bronc rider. But even had he been average, mere participation in that particular event placed a cowboy among the rodeo elite. Gomez Gomez, thin, wiry, and Teflon tough, rode bulls. Early, mainly because he had the size for it, had bulldogged. A dainty little sport that involved dropping off a full-out running horse and wrestling a six-hundred-pound steer to the ground by its horns.

It had been a good time, even with a broken bone or three, until Jake had been in the car accident that had killed Angel, Gomez Gomez's wife. It had all spiraled down then. Gomez Gomez retreating into a haze of alcohol, and Jake running—albeit temporarily—to the Catholic priesthood of all things, cowboy hat and all. He still ran the historical museum at the mission, when he wasn't breaking the odd horse or two. That all was a long time ago now but it seemed like yesterday. Time was tricky like that. That season of years had eventually passed, but time still marched. Six months now since Gomez Gomez had followed Angel into the next life.

Everything changes. Early looked off toward the distant mountains. *Except the desert.* Maybe that's why he liked it out here so much.

An hour and a half later, a handful of sun-faded buildings emerged from the heat waves. Another half mile and they found themselves in downtown One Horse. Early did a slow three-sixty, his boots scraping in the still afternoon. A gas station that looked like it hadn't seen paint since the fifties, a handful of crumbling adobes, and a sagging wooden tavern with a sign that said *Bob's Place*.

"Better than nothing," Jake said. "At least I see phone lines."

"A real cosmopolitan wonder." Early eyed the gas station. "I don't see a tow truck, though."

"Might as well ask." Jake headed for the open roll-up garage door on the other side of the pumps.

Inside, the place smelled like grease and dead socks and was, if possible, even hotter than the blistered and cracked asphalt outside.

"Hello?" Early said.

"Closed," came a muffled reply.

"Where are you?" Early said.

A hacking smoker's cough. "I said I'm closed. Go away."

"Your door's open," Early said.

"So? It's a free country last time I checked. Door's my business. Go away." Another cough.

The voice, it turned out, belonged to a couple of grease-soaked coverall legs sticking out from beneath a Ford Tempo sedan, sun-bleached to the point of being colorless.

Early knelt. "We got a pickup with a flat about five miles up the road. Can you help us out?"

A wrench banged, the legs twitched, and an impressive and inventive string of expletives flew. "Japanese junk! What part of *closed* are you not understanding, amigo? Beat it. I'm not gonna tell you again."

Early glanced up at Jake, who shrugged.

"I guess he's closed," Early said.

"Seems to be the case."

Early shook his head and took a greasy ankle in each hand.

"Hey!" the legs said.

Early pulled.

Wheels on the mechanic's dolly squeaked.

The body belonging to the legs, no surprise, turned out to be equally filthy. Frizzy gray hair ringed an otherwise bald head and melded with a week's worth of stubble on a fleshy, flushed face. Thick black-rimmed glasses doubled the size of blinking eyes. "What the—?"

"Look at that, you just opened," Early said. "Lucky us, right, Jake?"

"Does seems like good timing."

Early expected blustering and threats but the man surprised when he offered a slow grin. "You really just do that?"

"I told you, we have a flat," Early said.

The man struggled to his feet, grabbed an oily rag off the hood of the Tempo, and attempted to wipe his hands. "Piece-of-cat-feces car has me spitting nails. Says Ford on the grill but they made 'em in Japan. I keep telling her to buy something else. I'm a mechanic, not a magician, for crying out loud. What kind of truck you say?"

"Seventy-two Chevy."

The man pulled a pack of Marlboros from the pocket of his coveralls, shook out a cigarette, and tapped it on the hood of the Ford. He lit it with a Zippo, clacked the lighter closed with a flick of his wrist. "Standard tires? 75R15s? Or are you one of those bigger-the-better guys?"

"Just stock," Early said. "You got a tow truck? Or can you patch it out there?"

"Got a truck out back. I'll take care of it."

"How long will it take?"

"Couple hours."

Jake looked at his watch. "It's four now. So six? We could still make the border tonight."

The mechanic shook his head. "Not tonight. Tomorrow."

"You said a couple hours," Early said. "That makes it six o'clock."

"I said it would *take* a couple hours. That couple of hours will happen tomorrow morning when and if I decide to get out of bed. And I ain't an early riser, *comprende*?"

"No, I don't comprende," Early said. "We need the truck tonight."

The mechanic blew out a stream of smoke in Early's direction, then walked over to a sink and started scrubbing his hands and forearms. "Listen, pal, you're a giant, I get it. Super scary and all that. Yanked me out from underneath a car. Good for you. But the Diamondbacks are playing the Dodgers in about an hour. So you could beat me to a bloody mess right here and now and I promise you I'll rise from the dead and my butt will be parked over on one of Bob's comfy barstools with a cold beer in front of me come first pitch. I don't miss the D-backs ever. Not even for giants."

"What are we supposed to do until tomorrow, stand here?" Early said.

The cigarette bounced on the mechanic's bottom lip, somehow stayed on. "They got some rooms they rent out back of Bob's. They're cheap and clean. Go ask. Plus they're having a big wingding tonight. Don't happen very often. Got a band coming in and everything. Lotta people'll come out for it."

Early looked out the big roll-up door. "What people exactly? You and Bob?"

The mechanic blew dual streams of smoke through his nostrils and pointed, dipping his head a little. "Desert can be deceiving. There's people out there sure enough. Come a long way when something outta the ordinary's happening."

Early glanced at Jake. "What do you think?"

Jake shrugged. "Rodeo doesn't start till tomorrow. Rooms can't be as bad as El Paso that time."

"A gulag couldn't be as bad as El Paso that time. I'm still emotionally and physically scarred from that place. I guess we're watching baseball and hearing a band."

Jake took off his hat and mopped his brow. "Go Diamondbacks."

The mechanic's greasy red face grinned and the owl eyes blinked. He stubbed out his cig on the workbench. "Good deal. You guys'll buy the first round. Least you can do after yanking my legs."

CHAPTER FOUR

Bob's Place surprised. The sun-beaten, crumbling exterior ended at the door. Inside, it was clean and well-kept. A jukebox thumped Flaco Jiménez accordion. Only a few bikers in the place this time of day, and none at the bar where a big flat-screen television had the Diamondbacks pregame show on mute.

"You want to ask about rooms? I need to hit the restroom," Jake said.

"Try not to get lost."

"Might be tough without your internal GPS."

"All you can do is your best, pal. Everybody gets a trophy and a juice box anyway."

An old man so short only his head and shoulders showed leaned behind the bar reading a paperback. He didn't look up when Early took a stool.

"You Bob?" Early said.

"Nope," the man said.

"All right. You got a name?"

"Yup."

Early offered his best winning smile. "Is it private information?"

The old man glanced up, then went back to his book. "It ain't Bob."

Batwing doors behind the bar swung open and a woman entered. Dark eyes took in Early with a cool glance. Her black hair hung straight, halfway down her back. She was tall. And not just because

It-Ain't-Bob was so short. Close to six feet at least. She was also the most beautiful creature Early had ever seen.

"Hey," she said.

"How's it going?" Early replied.

"Jube taking care of you?"

Early pointed to the little man. "If the bookworm's Jube, then so far he's done a fantastic job of telling me his name's not Bob, but that's about it."

"Jube," she said.

"Yeah, I know," the little man said without looking up.

"He must be in a good part. He'll be right with you." She busied herself wiping and putting away beer glasses at the far end of the counter.

Jake appeared and took a stool. He glanced at the woman, then at Early, who was still staring at her. "You gonna live?"

"I'm having my doubts."

The woman approached, looked at the little bartender, nose still deep in his book, and shook her head. "I give up. What are you boys drinking?"

"A beer for me. Something Mexican if you have it," Jake said.

"We're forty miles from the border, something Mexican is about all we have." She pulled a bottle of Dos Equis from a cooler beneath the counter, cracked it open, and slid it in front of Jake. "Glass?"

"No, thanks."

"How about you?" She eyed Early's hat. "Or are you going to take up a stool and not drink because you're some kind of Baptist?"

"I'm not Baptist."

"That mean I don't have to kiss you either?"

Early grinned. "I might've just become a little Baptist."

She eyed him. Didn't smile. "You want something or not?"

"You have Mexican Coke?"

"Coke? You serious?"

"Serious as a Baptist on Sunday morning."

She filled a cup with ice, popped the top off a bottle, and poured. "You a straw guy?"

"Definitely not."

"Nah, you don't look like a straw guy. Okay, let me know if you need anything else." Then she was gone, back through the batwing doors.

"You want to pick your jaw up off the bar now?" Jake said.

"Can I just say one thing?"

"What's that?"

"That, without doubt, was definitely not Bob."

"And you didn't ask if they had rooms, did you?"

"I forgot."

Jake sipped his beer. "Yeah, you forgot."

A stool squeaked and the mechanic slid up next to them. Clean now. He'd even shaved. Gone were the greasy coveralls, replaced with faded Wranglers, old running shoes, and a khaki shirt with a sewn-on name tag over the pocket that said Ray.

"That your name? Ray?" Early said.

The man smiled. "All my life. At least once I could shake loose of Raymond. Ray's a lot shorter and sweeter, like me."

On the flat screen, two announcers discussed the finer points of baseball in silent animation.

"Hey, Jube, grab me a cold one, will ya?" Ray said.

"Grab it yourself."

Ray rolled his eyes but slid off the stool and rounded the bar. He fished in the cooler and came up with a Dos Equis. He lifted a caterpillar eyebrow at Jake and held up a bottle. "Another?"

"Just started this one. Thanks, though."

Ray eyed Early's Coke, shrugged, then took a pull of his beer before coming out from behind the bar and climbing up on his stool again. "Jube, unmute the TV, will ya?"

The barman, eyes never shifting from the page, reached under the counter, came up with a remote, and slid it to Ray. "Wait till this song's over. I like it."

Ray mumbled something about lousy service and unmuted. He pressed the volume button until Bob Brenly's sportscaster baritone drowned out the Texas Tornados. Jube muttered his displeasure but put down his book long enough to walk over and turn off the jukebox.

Early kept an eye on the batwings but it wasn't until the second inning, Diamondbacks down by two and Ray cussing a blue streak, that the dark-haired woman returned, drying her hands on an apron. She stopped in front of Early and Jake. "So I hear you boys are marooned."

"News travels fast," Early said.

"Fast, slow—in One Horse it doesn't have far to go. I'm guessing you're needing a room?"

"Two if you have them." Early jerked a thumb toward Jake. "He snores."

"I have them. Only ones in town. We also have the only food in town, so I guess you'll be eating here too."

"A regular monopoly," Early said.

"Are you hungry now? Be better to eat sooner rather than later. Having a band tonight, so it'll get busy."

"Any time that's convenient," Jake said. "Early's always hungry."

The woman fixed her dark eyes on Early. "What kind of a name is Early?"

He searched deep for a reply that might impress but came up blank.

Jake rescued him. "The inaccurate kind. He's usually late."

Early took off his hat, ran his fingers through his hair, and put it back on again. "He exaggerates. I'm usually pretty close to on time."

"And always hungry?" she said.

"He doesn't exaggerate about that. I'm a growing Baptist."

"Uh-huh." The woman turned to the little bartender. "Jube, put a few burgers on. Better make it two for the big one."

The little man gave Jake and Early the stink eye, then put down his book and shuffled off through the batwings. Pots banged.

"I think your bartender got up on the wrong side of the bed," Early said.

"Sleeps on a cot shoved up against a wall in the back," Ray said. "Only one side to get up on. He's all right once you get past the crust. He dotes on Calico here."

"I don't know if I'd use the word *dote*," the woman said. "I don't think Jube dotes on anything but his books."

"Calico?" Early said. "That's your name?"

"Calico Foster," the woman said.

Early grinned. "I had a very strong feeling you weren't Bob."

Her face hardened, little lines on her forehead. "Nope, I'm not Bob. I'm going to help Jube with the burgers."

Early watched her go. "I thought not being Bob would be a compliment. Brother, that's some thick ice to chip through."

Ray's focus remained on the game. "And it just got a lot thicker. You screwed up, buddy. Bob was her dad."

"Was?"

"Died three months ago. Cancer. Calico runs the place now."

"I'm an idiot," Early said.

Jake set his beer down and patted his friend on the shoulder. "Since kindergarten, amigo. It's a comfort to know some things don't change."

Early took a pull of his Coke and blew out a breath. "Idiot, idiot, idiot."

"Yup, yup, yup," Jake said.

Ray leaned back on his stool and gestured at the TV with both hands. "C'mon! Take him out already! We're getting crushed here!"

One of the batwings pushed out and Calico stuck her head in. "Jube'll have your burgers out in a few minutes. He'll set you up with rooms. Just ask him if you need anything else."

Early'd already formed an apology in his mind, but she was gone before he could speak.

Ray's gripe must have transmitted through the screen. He picked up his beer as the game went to a commercial break for a pitching change.

They watched an inning or two without conversation. Jube pushed through the batwings, walking backward, a plate piled high with burgers and fries in each hand, and slid them in front of Jake and Early. He ignored their thanks and went back to his book.

The sixth inning or so, the front door banged and a slim, bearded man in jeans and a faded Harley Davidson T-shirt shuffled in lugging a bass case. Another man followed with an amp in one hand and a guitar case in the other. His battered cowboy hat worked all right with the trucker mustache but wrestled with the shimmery Saturday Night Fever disco shirt and gold chains. After him, a biker pushing a cart loaded with more equipment.

"Gonna get kicking soon," Ray said.

Early, food long gone and bored with the game, reversed on his stool, propped his elbows on the bar behind him, and watched the band set up. Cowboy John Travolta appeared to be the lead singer. A stick-thin, buzz-cut Native kid in a Lakers tank top thumped and tuned a drum kit. The bass player plugged into an amp and fiddled with the knobs. The bearded, neck-tatted biker picked up an electric guitar and worked through something sounding like a cross between Hendrix's "Purple Haze" and "Feliz Navidad."

"These guys actually make music?" Early said.

"I guess, but who cares? They're here, so they'll bring a crowd. Came over all the way from Wilcox," Ray said.

"They got a name?"

"Lost Prophets was what the poster said. Which is fitting, seeing as you have to be pretty lost to wind up in One Horse."

Ray had been right about the crowd: the bar was filling. Most of the tables and seats were already taken, especially the ones closest to the dance floor. There was the usual Southern Arizona mix of ranchers and desert rats along with a big group of suburbanites that might have driven out from Tucson. A long table in the back was packed with leather-vested bikers and their women. A hard-looking bunch, the women maybe hardest of all.

Calico came in, beautiful in a black dress and heels. She walked up to the stage, talked with Disco Shirt for a bit, then nodded, shook the man's hand, and found a place by herself in a shadowed corner at the far end of the bar. Early tried his best to make eye contact but he might as well have not existed.

Half an hour later the band kicked off their first song to a standing-room-only crowd—Rolling Stones' "Miss You," Disco Shirt doing a very passable Jagger. They dove straight into Johnny Cash's "Folsom Prison Blues," then the Doobies' "China Grove."

Early leaned over to Jake's ear, shouting to be heard over the thump of the bass. "I wonder if they know any slow stuff?"

Jake glanced down the bar toward Calico. "She doesn't look to be in the dancing mood, amigo. I wouldn't go there."

"The only people who don't succeed are the ones who never try, man."

"Your funeral."

"Or my wedding."

Jake shook his head. "Early, you could sell underwear to a nudist colony, I'll give you that, but I got five bucks that says you're not dancing tonight."

The Lost Prophets started into "When a Man Loves a Woman." The skinny drummer took lead vocal, nailing it so perfectly, Percy Sledge would've held up a lighter.

Early grinned. "Five bucks. You're on, brother. Watch the master work."

"Can't wait."

Calico looked up as he approached. "You really need a different hat, man. It's Early, right?"

"You remember my name. That's a good sign. This could be the start of something beautiful."

"Don't get your hopes up. It's just not a name you hear every day, that's all."

"Neither is Calico."

She lifted her glass. "Here's to inventive parents. Now, save yourself the embarrassment and go back to your stool. Easier on everyone if you don't ask me."

"Ask you what?"

"I hope you don't play poker with that face. Whatever you and your buddy bet on us dancing, just go pay him and get it over with."

"How do you know we bet?"

She turned her black eyes on him. "I own and operate what's basically a biker bar on hell's back porch. And, if you'll check, I'm still alive. That makes me a student of human nature the hard way. You bet your friend you could get me to dance. Am I wrong or right?"

"Five bucks. But that part was his idea. All I wanted to do was dance with you."

"Wow, all I'm worth is five bucks?"

"Hardly. Also I'm sorry about saying you didn't look like a Bob this afternoon. I didn't know about your dad."

"I take it Ray told you about my dad."

"He did."

"Nothing's private in a small town, is it?"

"I guess not. Anyway, I'm sorry."

"You didn't know. Don't worry about it. But the answer's still no. Go pay your friend and get it over with."

"He said you wouldn't do it."

"Smart guy. I'd keep him around."

"Believe me, even if I had a choice, he sticks to a person like a cold. He's a saddle bronc man. Even a bad horse can't shake him. C'mon, give me a break. Prove him wrong on this one. Guy thinks he's always right."

"Is he?"

Early considered. "Pretty much, yeah. Probably what makes him so irritating."

"Hate to tell you, but he nailed it tonight. I'm here as a spectator. And a bar owner. That's it."

"What, you have two left feet and you don't want to embarrass yourself?"

She didn't smile. "I dance sometimes. And when I do, believe me, there's nothing wrong with my feet."

"Just not with Baptists?"

"I thought Baptists didn't dance anyway."

"They don't, but I'm a free agent in the religion department. That being the case, you don't have to kiss me. But a dance couldn't hurt, could it?"

"Look, it's not gonna happen, okay? Sorry."

He smiled. "You don't sound all that sorry."

"All right, I kinda lied about the sorry part. Sue me."

Early leaned against the bar, looked at the band. They were tearing through "(Hey Baby) Que Paso" by the Texas Tornados. "Man, I didn't even make the eight second buzzer, did I?"

"You never made it out of the chute, pal. I told you not to try." Her eyes softened, but only a little. "Don't feel bad. Brad Pitt couldn't have gotten me out there tonight."

Early touched his hat brim. "All right. But you don't know what you're missing. If you change your mind . . ."

"Tell you what, if I do, Brad Pitt'll be the first to know."

Early felt a tug on his sleeve and turned but didn't see anyone. Another tug and he looked down. A minuscule woman, couldn't have topped five feet, smiled up at him. Blonde pixie haircut. Her denim dress floor length with tiny silver boot toes sticking out from beneath it.

Her eyes crinkled. "Dance, cowboy?"

Early grinned back. "I guess we could try, but would it be physically possible?"

"We put a man on the moon, didn't we? I think we could manage this."

"You got a point."

"Early, Ingrid. Ingrid, Early," Calico said.

"Ingrid as in Bergman," the little woman added.

"Early as in Early," Early said. "You really want to dance?"

"You shy or something?"

"Ingrid as in Bergman, I'm about as not-shy as they come. All right, lead on. We'll let Calico Foster sit here and wait for Brad Pitt, show her what she's missing."

Ingrid proved herself to be quite the dancer, even if she was so far down there Early was afraid he might step on her. He found himself having a good time. For a little while the mandatory leave order and even Gomez Gomez's ghost faded into the bar smoke and bass thump. They danced for several songs, fast and slow, until the band announced they were taking a break. Ingrid hugged his waist and promised to find him again later. He waved as she scooted off.

Jake was still perched on his stool. He slid Early a fresh Mexican Coke. "That, my friend, was a sight I'll never forget if I live to be a hundred and ten. I truly thought you were going to bust her nose with your knee."

"Don't knock Ingrid as in Bergman, it's dangerous. She teaches kick-boxing down in Patagonia."

"Yeah?"

"No joke. Now pay me my five bucks."

Jake pushed his hat back on his head. "How do you figure that? Calico turned you down exactly like I said she would."

"And I quote, 'Early, you could sell underwear to a nudist colony, but I've got five bucks that says you're not dancing tonight.' Am I wrong?"

"Sounds about right."

"Well, brother, I was a dancing fool. And I got a blonde elf who's hands are registered as lethal weapons as a witness."

Jake pulled out his wallet and flipped Early a five. "Accent on the fool. Anyway, the spectacle was worth every penny."

Early pulled off his hat and wiped his brow. He picked up the Coke. He was mid swallow when Jube stopped in front of him, scowling up.

"Heya, Jube, book get slow?" Early said.

"Ray said you was a police detective. He lyin' or is that true?"

"I'm a detective with the Paradise Police Department. Why?"

Jube grunted something Early took to mean approval in Jube-speak. "All right then. I'm goin' out back for a smoke. Bring your Coke. I gotta talk to you about somethin'."

CHAPTER FIVE

CALICO PACED THE LITTLE APARTMENT she'd called home since she was twelve. Two bedrooms and a bath. The end unit in a block of six motel rooms. Her father had built the motel addition and swimming pool just after they'd come, convinced it would attract more of the desert tourists and add to the income.

The tavern had been her father's dream. He'd always claimed he craved the empty space the desert provided, that Phoenix's urban sprawl had been too confining, though Calico strongly suspected what he really wanted was to escape the shadow of his wife's memory. Funny how every corner of such a huge city could be so utterly haunted by a single spirit. Even so, Bob Foster's had been a stubborn and eternal optimism, making his dreams contagious by nature. *Unless you're the one who has to pick up the pieces.* Bob's Place had been to Bob Foster what the Magic Kingdom had been to Walt—a dream that had become reality that had become everything.

True, he'd been alcohol addled, a sometimes grifter, and an always hopeless dreamer who was far better at talking than doing, but he'd loved his children in his own way. And Calico had loved him, even if the roles of parent and child too often blurred and flipped. Maybe that love was why Calico was still doing her best to keep his dream alive. *More like, what else am I going to do?* But she did love One Horse in all its backward, sunbaked glory. And she'd come to realize she loved the bar too. *And now I'm going to lose it all. How can this be happening?*

Even worse, losing Bob's Place wasn't her biggest problem. Reflexively, she checked her phone. Nothing from Charlie. No text, no call, no Charlie. Her brother the phantom. She tossed the phone onto the couch, walked to the window, hugged her arms to her body, and looked out at the darkening landscape. It was that magical desert time when the whole world turned to silver and soft shadow. A faraway-so-close moon hung low on the horizon. The same moon that had whispered comfort to her soul for as long as she could remember. But tonight she was light on the silver and heavy on the shadow. The pool lights threw blue ripples on the saguaros. Beyond the pool, the long-fallen sun left a vague purple memory above the mountains. She'd always loved the desert, even as a kid. All the sky and space—this was her home.

But it was never enough for Charlie.

Not that the two hadn't been close back in the day. They had been, even though he was younger than Calico by four years—now twenty-five to her twenty-nine. But with her father's attention often elsewhere she'd too often been forced into the role of mother rather than sister. It also didn't help that Charlie had inherited his father's penchant for the "next big thing."

In Charlie's mind, the next big thing had meant only one big thing—California. Specifically, Los Angeles. The promised land, nirvana, and utopia all rolled into a shining tangle of beaches, movie stars, convertibles, and possibilities. The day before his eighteenth birthday, Charlie had shaken their father's hand, kissed Calico's cheek, pointed his old El Camino west, and let the tires spit gravel. Left his family with nothing but the memory of a smile and a loose agreement to keep in touch. Surprisingly, he actually had for the most part.

Charlie, where are you?

A knock on her door pulled Calico from her reverie. Had to be Jube. Something wrong in the bar. Which was unusual because Jube was a man who would rather lose a limb than ask for help. She shifted the curtain a bit and looked out. Not Jube. Early, still wearing that stupid *Kiss Me, I'm Baptist* hat. The guy never gave up. She walked over to the door and cracked it, leaving it chained. After all, this was her personal space. The only one she had. "Sorry, I'm off. Can I help you with something?"

He looked even taller standing out there in the glow of the porch light. He was lean, muscular, and one of the few men she'd ever encountered who made her feel short at her six feet. She hadn't noticed in the bar, but he had a scar angling up from one corner of his mouth nearly to his eye. He was dark, like her. Sun, definitely, but something else too. Maybe Hispanic. Or some Native. His face looked angular and hard in the one-sided light.

He pulled a billfold out of his back pocket. "I know you're off work. I don't mean to bother you. It's just that Jube sent me."

"Jube? Is something wrong?"

"No, not really. He told me you were having some trouble and might want someone to talk to. Thought I might be able to help."

Her face heated and she was glad she was shadowed. "Jube said that? Why in the world would he think I'd want to talk to you?"

He flipped the billfold open and held it up. The porch light gleamed off an official-looking star. He passed it through the door crack.

She looked it over, then studied him. "You're a policeman?"

"I'm a detective up in Paradise."

"You don't look like a detective."

"Congratulations. You're the millionth customer to say those exact words. You just won a knife set and a year's supply of Bisquick."

She handed his identification back. "Jube doesn't usually talk so much. I think I like him better that way. Did he tell you what my trouble is? Or troubles?"

Early scratched the side of his neck. "Look, can I come in? I promise I'm mostly housebroken. Or if you're uncomfortable with me in there, we can find somewhere out here to sit and talk. Might be easier to communicate if it wasn't through a chained door."

She hesitated. The guy wasn't exactly what you'd call safe looking. But the badge and ID looked real enough.

A corner of his mouth turned up. "I'd say trust me, but you don't seem like the trusting type. Which I understand. You can't be too careful these days."

She sighed, pushed the door closed, unchained it, then swung it open. "I guess if you're an ax murderer you might be a blessing in disguise."

He followed her in. "Can't be that bad. Thanks, I kinda thought you'd leave me out there."

"I would've, but I liked the way you danced with Ingrid. I figure you can't be all that horrible. Except for your taste in headwear." She turned, and he'd removed his hat and held it in his hands in front of him. His dark hair hung almost to his shoulders. Cheeks flat, pocked with old scars. The wildness about him much too big for her little apartment. Her instinct told her to take a step back, but she stayed put. "Why aren't you working? Are you on vacation or something?"

"I'm on mandatory leave."

"Mandatory as in you're in trouble?"

"Usually."

"Is that supposed to impress or scare me?"

"Neither. It's just the truth."

She thought about that for a second. "Well, I guess I should offer you a beer or something, right? That's what people do."

"I'm fine."

"That's right, you're the Coke guy. You and alcohol don't mix, that the deal?"

"Let's just say as long as I stay a Coke guy, the world is a much happier and safer place for all concerned."

"Now that I understand. I've seen my share of ugly drunks."

"In your business, I'm sure you have. Good news is I'm beautiful when I'm sober."

"Is that thing on your face supposed to be a win-me-over grin or something? Does it actually work on people?"

"Once in a while."

She pointed to a chair. "All right then, Detective Early Pines, sit."

He eased his frame onto a chair, stretched out his long legs in front of him, and crossed his ankles. He wore a faded blue pearl-button shirt and boot-cut jeans. Both had seen better days. His boots were scuffed, one with a hole almost through the sole. He appeared completely at ease, and Calico got the feeling this was a part of him that wouldn't change no matter the environment, be it her living room, a rodeo chute, or a Manhattan penthouse.

She lowered onto her couch, facing him. "Okay, since we're here and Jube'll never let me hear the end of it if I don't talk to you, how much did he tell you?"

"Only that you were having some trouble with your brother out in LA."

"That's all he said?"

"Pretty much. But I could tell he's plenty worried about you."

She stood, walked to the fridge, and pulled out a bottle of Perrier. She held it up. "It's not Coke, but . . ."

"No, thanks. And it won't bother me if you have a beer."

"I don't drink. Just keep a few beers in the fridge for guests. Which I never really have so they've been in there for a while." She twisted the cap off the bottle, sipped, then set it on the counter. She didn't sit again. "I don't want to waste your time. I honestly don't see how a detective from Paradise, Arizona, would possibly be able to help with my Los Angeles problems."

He shrugged. "I might not, but try me. You never know." That grin again. She noticed he had a crooked incisor tooth. For some reason she couldn't put her finger on, it made her feel a little more comfortable with him. She looked down at her hands, then back at him. "My brother's name is Charlie. He dropped off the face of the earth about three weeks ago."

"You have regular contact with him?"

"Every few days or so. A week at the longest."

"Three weeks isn't that long not to hear from someone."

"Long enough if you know Charlie. Something's wrong."

"What do you mean, if you know Charlie?"

She considered him. This all felt way too personal. Then again, maybe it'd be good to talk about it. It might help her sort some things. And the guy was a stranger. She'd probably never see him again, so why not? "Charlie's the kind of guy, well, if you put him in an empty room, he'd find a way to get himself in trouble. Set it on fire or something. And of course it's never his fault. I love him, but that's the way it is."

"Los Angeles is a very big room. And it's definitely not empty."

"Exactly."

"Is his phone on?"

"It rings, so I think so. I've called and called, but nothing."

"How about the police? Have you talked to them?"

"I tried."

"What did they say?"

"I called them after about the first week. They said they'd look into it. I haven't heard anything since. And the woman I talked to didn't inspire a whole lot of confidence by her tone. Lousy bedside manner you detectives have."

"Yeah, sometimes. But to them your brother is one more guy missing in LA. And he'd only been off the map a few weeks. They've probably got a very long to-do list."

"Okay, but that doesn't help me, does it? Or Charlie."

"Does Charlie usually call you, or do you call him?"

"Does that matter?"

"Maybe. You never know."

"I call him every once in a while, but he calls mostly."

"Tell me more about him."

"We moved out here from Phoenix with our dad when we were kids."

"Just the three of you?"

"My mom died not long before that."

"How?"

"That's a little personal."

"Fair enough. Sorry."

She picked up her Perrier bottle but didn't drink. "The official cause of death was breast cancer. But I'd add a terminal case of disappointment to that diagnosis. That's what really did her in." He didn't say anything, and the silence made the room feel too close so she went on. "My dad always had a plan, always on the verge. I think my mom finally just got tired."

"I'm sorry."

"It's all right. When we came, I was twelve. Charlie was eight. We were chasing my dad's latest dream—a desert oasis for the masses. The next Palm Springs. The whole world was gonna flock to us and lay hundred-dollar bills at our feet." She waved a hand. "And here it is in all its glory."

"It's not so bad."

"No, and I didn't mean it that way. I actually love it here. But Charlie never wanted Palm Springs. He wanted bigger, even as a kid. So he moved out to Los Angeles seven years ago."

"What'd he want to do in LA?"

"I don't know, have the world notice him? I think deep down he was just tired of being bored. He wanted to get out of here and be somewhere things happen. He said he might try acting, but every kid headed west says that, right? You never really expect them to do it. Funny thing is, I don't think he'd been there a week before he landed a part in a commercial. Then a few more. Then a string of bit parts in some B movies. He called every few days and gave us updates. Sometimes he asked for money. Usually he didn't. He was always on the cusp of a big break. Always sounded at least sort of happy. I was just glad to hear he wasn't doing drugs or getting into anything else that might hurt him."

"Are drugs a possibility?"

"I honestly don't think so. But then again, it's Charlie. I don't want to be the person that buries her head in the sand."

"He like to push people's buttons? Get in fights?"

She did smile now. "I can't picture Charlie in a fight. He's pushed a few buttons in his life, most of them mine, but I wouldn't say he did it out of malicious intent. The thing about Charlie and trouble . . . he's not the type to go looking for it, it seems to find him on its own. And when it does, he doesn't try all that hard to get out of the way. If you'd met our dad, you'd understand. Charlie's the proverbial chip off the old block."

Early nodded. "I do understand. Guy like Charlie in a big city, a lotta things could go wrong. I see why you worry. I'm sure you've racked your brain—do you have any thoughts at all about what might've happened to him? Maybe something he said leading up to this that sounded unusual or off? Even a feeling?"

"The only thing I can think of is, a few months before he died, our dad took out a good-sized second mortgage on Bob's and loaned it to Charlie. A hundred thousand dollars. Charlie had some kind of business opportunity in the works and said he'd have the money back within a month. Two peas in a pod, Dad never even asked questions. Not even when the money didn't come back."

"What kind of opportunity?"

"All I know is, Charlie said it was a sure thing. He talked to Dad about it, but I never heard details. They'd never tell me anything like that because they knew I'd be against whatever harebrained scheme it was. I was always the wet blanket. Then again they never considered how the lights stayed on and the AC kept working."

"So nothing about the deal?"

"Dad said Charlie had figures and charts, the whole thing. He acted like he was as excited about whatever it was as Charlie."

"But the sure thing wasn't so sure after all."

"Are they ever? Either way, I never heard. Charlie said it wasn't any of my business."

"Except for the pesky fact that now the money's gone and you're the one stuck with the loan."

She shrugged. "It's a good-sized payment every month and I'm struggling to make the bills. I've cleaned out the savings. I'm about done. So enjoy the room while it lasts."

"Unless Charlie coughs up the money he borrowed."

"Yeah, unless that. But now he's in who knows what kind of trouble. And I have no idea what's going on or what to do. Still glad you knocked, detective?"

He showed that crooked incisor. "Beats television."

"The thing is, when Charlie came home for Dad's funeral, I asked about the money. He thought it should be considered his inheritance. I told him fine, then he could also inherit the debt to the bank, because I sure didn't want it, and I was the one here grinding it out every day, even though technically he owns half of the place. He gave some speech about how it takes money to make money, and I gave him a speech back about how I was about to knock his head off. We made up, but he left straight from the memorial. After that, whenever I brought it up, he'd make excuses, give me some runaround, and promise he'd pay off the bank any day. But guess what? It's been a lot of days and I'm still making payments."

"Anything else?"

She studied the bottom of his boots. "Yeah. I may want to wring his neck, but I'm also worried sick about him. When the police didn't do anything, I found a private investigator online that worked cheap. I thought I could afford him. At least for a few weeks."

"And?"

"He poked around for exactly two days, then called and said he'd done all he could. He asked me to pay for what I owed and that was that. I asked him if he couldn't keep at it a little longer, that it didn't seem like enough time. But he was adamant, couldn't get off the phone fast enough."

"You think he found something and didn't want to tell you?"

"All I know is it didn't make sense. One day he was all over it and the next he was history."

CHAPTER SIX

EARLY PULLED HIS FEET BACK, sat up, and leaned forward, resting his elbows on his knees. He'd known a hundred guys like this brother Calico described. Trouble finds them, sure, but trouble doesn't usually walk through walls; it looks for open doors. Charlie sounded like an immature, selfish piece of work. Still, he'd taken the time to call home on a regular basis. That was something. And Calico, tough exterior notwithstanding, was clearly and truly troubled. That stirred something in Early. Something he hadn't felt in a while.

"How deep are you in the hole financially? I know it's a personal question. You don't have to answer if you don't want."

"Hey, I'm in this far, right? I'm not sure how I can keep my head above water for even another month."

"There was a good crowd tonight. It must've helped a little."

"*Little* being the operative word. Bands help, but bands also cost."

"How is business otherwise?"

"Steady enough. It's the second mortgage that's killing me. That and picturing Charlie lying dead in the Los Angeles River or something."

"Don't think like that." He picked up his hat and worked the brim. "Tell you what. I know a guy out in Los Angeles who could ask a few questions. Check on things. Would that be all right?"

"What would it cost?"

"He's a friend and he owes me a favor. No cost."

"You're sure?"

"I'm sure."

"Honestly, it sounds a little too good to be true. Especially these days."

"Maybe you're due for some luck."

Her body visibly relaxed. "All right then. I know this isn't your problem. You're probably thinking One Horse was a lousy place to get stranded."

He hesitated. "I have to be honest, I'll call my friend, no doubt about that, but your brother sounds like the kind of guy who—let's just say if he got himself into trouble, maybe you should let him get himself out."

"I know what he sounds like. And I know what he is. But he's still my brother. I'm responsible for him."

"Are you?"

She took a drink from her bottle. Pushed at the label with her thumbnail. "I need to know he's okay. I can't help how I feel."

"Fair enough. I'll need Charlie's particulars. Address, description, phone number, anything else you can think of. Oh, and the name of the PI you hired. I'll have my guy check on that too."

Calico went into the little galley kitchen, pulled a notepad and pen from a drawer, scrolled through her phone and jotted. She tore off the page and handed it to Early. "That should be everything."

Early scanned the piece of paper, then folded it and put it in the breast pocket of his shirt. He paused by the door. "I'll let you know what I hear. See you in the morning."

"Lucky you, tomorrow breakfast is on the house for Baptists."

"Most important meal of the day."

The stars were out in force as he made his way to his room. Jake's window was dark. Wouldn't be in bed yet so he must still be in the tavern. Early dropped into a rusty deck chair in front of his room and listened to the night. He took off his hat and dropped it onto the ground next to an ashtray filled with some previous pilgrim's cigarette butts. Still hot out. Not a breath of wind. Venus bright in the sky, decked out in her best cocktail gown. Gomez Gomez said he used to hear her sing. Early almost wished he could.

What are you doing, man?

But he knew. As sure as he was sitting here, he knew.

Out in the dark a coyote yipped and another replied. Stealthy feet padded out past the pool lights. Early saw the animal then, next to a clump of brush. Bigger than the one back home. Alpha male. Yellow eyes watching, studying. Early met the animal's gaze. The yellow eyes blinked. He watched it until it backed away a step or two, then turned and faded into the night.

With a sigh, Early scooped up his hat and put it back on. He stood, unlocked his door, and entered his room. A table lamp with a miniature wagon-wheel base cast a warm glow across wood-paneled walls. The twenty-first-century illusion of comfort. A tiny man-imagined hedge against a spirit world beating its wings against the desert neon. A place where coyotes played tricks and skinwalkers shook the shadows. He stretched out on the bed, hands beneath his head, feet hanging off the end. Without rising, he kicked off his boots and lay there, thinking.

A long time later he heard footsteps coming down the sidewalk. The knob turned and the door swung open. Jake walked in and dropped into a chair by the window.

"Come on in," Early said.

Jake smiled and propped a boot over a knee. "You ought to lock your door. Dangerous characters around."

"Only the coyotes and you. Where you been? The band stopped playing a long time ago."

"Turns out One Horse's only and best mechanic plays a heck of a chess game."

"Ray?"

"Uh-huh."

"You win?"

"Let's just say Ray could give Kasparov a run for his money."

"I have no idea who that is, but I take it you didn't win."

"Kasparov was probably the greatest player who ever lived. No, I didn't win."

"Good. Keeps you humble."

Jake scraped at something on his boot. "Jube told me a little about the Calico thing."

"Uh-huh."

"Told me about her brother."

"For a guy who doesn't say much, Jube sure says a lot. You notice that?"

"So what's the story?"

"Kid's been MIA for a few weeks and she's worried. There's also a little issue of a hundred thousand dollars he talked their dad into borrowing against the bar for him. She's on the hook for it. About to lose the place. She hired a PI to track him down, but he bailed out without explanation after a couple days."

"Ah."

"Ah, what?"

"Ah, Early Pines never bails out. I'm suddenly getting the strong suspicion Agua Prieta's off."

Early sat up and dropped his feet to the floor. "There's always next year for Old Mexico."

Jake stood. "There is. Although I feel very sorry for Los Angeles when you show up."

"What would you do? If I don't go, she'll wind up going herself. I can see it in her eyes. Not so much for the hundred thousand, but she's worried about her brother. Sounds like she pretty much raised him."

"Tell you the truth, when she first walked into the tavern this afternoon, I had a feeling plans might change."

"I thought I'd give Monte Shaw a call. See if he can poke around a little before I get there."

"Monte? That name takes me back. He'd be the guy for it."

"I'll drop you back at Paradise soon as the truck's ready."

"Yup. See you in the morning then."

After Jake left, Early pulled on his boots and walked back down to Calico's room.

She opened the door a few seconds after he knocked, drying her hands with a dish towel. "Everything okay?"

"I've been thinking."

"About what?"

"I think I'm gonna take a drive out to LA. Poke around a little."

She opened her mouth, closed it again. "Look, Detective Pines—"

"Early."

"Yeah, Pines. I appreciate it, I do, but you hardly know me. And I definitely don't know you."

"I know you don't. And I know it's coming out of left field, but there it is. I'm not asking you for anything. I just want to help if I can. It's something I feel like doing."

"What if I say no?"

"Are you saying no?"

"Maybe. I don't know."

"Listen, you're the type of person who doesn't accept help easily. I understand that. I'm exactly the same way. But sometimes a little help can be a good thing. Like I said, I'm not asking you for anything. I don't have expectations. I just feel like maybe I can be of use here. And that's something I haven't been in a while."

"I'm coming with you."

"That's not what I meant. It would probably be better if—"

"I started packing right after you left. I was going to leave in the morning."

"What about Bob's?"

"Jube can run the place with his eyes closed."

"And you were planning on taking that car of yours?"

"What's wrong with my car?"

"I saw it at Ray's. Yeah, he told me it was yours. It wouldn't make it ten miles. If you really want to go, we'll take my truck."

"You're serious about this?"

"Yeah. I'm serious."

"Why?"

"I don't know. Maybe you just caught me at the right time."

"Even though you know I can't pay you?"

"Did I not make myself clear? I wouldn't take it if you could."

Her eyes drilled him. "Okay, but here's the deal. If we go, I don't want you to get the wrong idea. I'm not some teenager to swoon over a white knight in a stupid hat. You understand that?"

"I know I'm irresistible, but I'll try to fend you off, all right? Are you going to give me a break here? I've got no agenda but to help. I've got some time on my hands right now and I could use something to do. I don't have any jurisdiction out there obviously, but I do know what to ask. And I'm pretty good at reading people."

"Yeah? What am I thinking right now?"

"That when a crazy-handsome man shows up at your door offering to help you with your problems for nothing, you should fall on your knees and thank your lucky stars?"

"See? You're not that good at all."

"Was I close?"

"Who told you you were handsome? Your mom?"

"The woman had twenty-twenty vision. Don't knock her."

She pursed her lips, thinking. "Can I ask you something?"

"Sure."

"What did you do to earn this mandatory leave? And don't lie to me. Or whitewash it."

"I hit a guy. Pretty hard."

"Why?"

"Because he should've crossed the street to avoid me and he didn't."

"That's a lousy reason."

"You wanted me to be honest."

"That's all he did?"

"He's a wife beater. I don't like him."

"Did you hurt him bad?"

"Bad enough. He was in the hospital a while."

"Do you regret doing it?"

He looked out at the desert, then back. "I've done a lot of things. A whole lot of them were stupid. But Lee? I'd hit him again right here, right now. So there it is. Unwhitewashed enough for you?"

"Mandatory leave, huh?"

"As mandatory as it gets. Possibly permanent."

"You want a cup of coffee? I was just going to make a pot."

"Subject closed then?"

"Subject closed."

"No, thanks. I'm going to get some sleep. I'll call my guy in LA first thing in the morning."

"When can we leave?"

"Soon as the truck's ready."

She didn't close the door as he walked away. "Pines?" she called when he was almost to his room.

He turned. "Yeah?"

"I still don't like your hat."

"That's okay, I like it enough for both of us." He started walking again.

"Pines?"

Another turn. "Yeah?"

"Thanks."

"You're welcome."

CHAPTER SEVEN

May 4—Three weeks earlier,
Hollywood Boulevard, Los Angeles

CHARLIE DIDN'T USUALLY HATE TOURISTS. Most times they were good for a buck or three. But right now, threading his way up the Walk of Fame at a dead run, he wanted to shoulder-ram every one of the red-cheeked, sandal-wearing, flyover-country hillbillies.

What had happened? Man, he'd had it all worked out. Gone over it in his mind a hundred stinking times. The pitch had been spot on. Bait swallowed whole. The website was perfect and should've kept Parsons satisfied for at least a year. By then phase two would've been in place. Businesses fail, right? Bummer, man, better luck next time. But somehow something had gone wrong. And then Roxy's guys showed up in the middle of *The Price Is Right* and a decent cup of coffee to pound on Charlie's door. Thank the good Lord for bathroom windows.

But they must've had someone watching the back.

And now here he was, running like an idiot up Hollywood Boulevard.

No bueno, Charlie. No bueno at all.

He zigged and zagged through a group of Asian kids peace-signing as they posed for a pic in front of Madame Tussauds. Then almost had a head-on with a guy in a Cornhuskers visor and *I'm With Her* T-shirt rounding the corner off of Orange Drive. The Husker yelled when he lost the top scoop off his ice-cream cone. *Hey, man, a little pistachio's a small price to pay for a good story to take back to Dorothy and Toto, so be grateful.* Charlie dodged a toothless, stumbling meth-head and vaulted over a guy in a business suit passed out on the sidewalk next to a brown-bagged bottle. He scanned his surroundings as he ran, looking for a place to get off the street, anywhere he could hide.

Behind him, someone shouted his name. How could they be that close already? Half a block back at most.

That's when he saw the Roosevelt Hotel shining like the pearly gates.

The hotel was across the street, kitty-corner from him, and definitely not bad for an only choice. He'd never been inside but it had to have endless places to hide. He was due for a little luck. He ignored the crosswalks and cut the intersection diagonally. A Mercedes locked up its brakes, the driver leaning out the window and shouting. Charlie patted the guy's hood and offered a wave as he passed. Ten seconds later he strolled into the Tinseltown-glory-days lobby of the Roosevelt like he owned the place. He whistled through his teeth. Gleaming floors, carved ceiling, old Spanish arches, lots of deep leather furniture. His kind of joint. He'd have to make a point of coming back here sometime. That is, if Roxy didn't kill him first.

A big placard on an easel read *The Continuum Conference: Blossom Ballroom*. An arrow pointed the way. Several people drifted that direction and he joined them. Rule of thumb—always hide in plain sight. Second rule of thumb, if there's an option besides plain sight, take it. At the ballroom entrance, he readied himself to smooth-talk his way in, but the woman behind the table simply asked him his name. When he answered, she smiled, printed CHARLIE FOSTER in neat block letters across a stick-on name tag, and handed it to him. He grinned back at her, peeled, stuck, and shuffled through the archway with the herd, fighting the junior high urge to moo out loud.

The ballroom presented the same opulence as the lobby. No shortage of glitz here. Without a clue in the world about what this whole Continuum deal was, but happy to be momentarily free of Roxy Parsons's muscle, Charlie took a chair near the front. He kept close to the aisle just in case. Seats filled steadily. A big African American guy Charlie was pretty sure was an ex-NFL linebacker squeezed in next to him, nodded, but didn't say anything. Ten minutes that seemed like ten years later, after Charlie had checked the entrances for the millionth time, the lights went down. He breathed a long sigh of relief and relaxed into his chair.

Classical music swelled. A wall-to-wall bank of flat screens blinked to life showing the word *Continuum* floating in infinite blue space. The music dropped, and a man walked out from behind the screens. No spotlight, just a silhouette against the blue.

"Good afternoon." The voice resonated through unseen speakers, clear and calm. "And welcome." Murmured response washed the room. "Do me a favor, would you please? Close your eyes. Closed? Good." This was obviously a well-known monologue. The crowd began to speak with him in perfect unison. "Now imagine, if you will, a continuous line of pictures. One that stretches for miles and miles. Do you see it?"

"Yes!" the room said.

"Good. Now, the first picture, and the second, and the third are practically identical. The naked eye sees no difference at all. The line of pictures continues like this. The thousandth picture and the one next to it are practically identical. The two thousandth and the ones on either side . . . The millionth and the one next to that—the same. But go back to the first and then straight to the millionth and you see two completely different pictures. Completely different scenes. How can this be? Easy. What you see with your mind's eye right now is a continuum, a continuous sequence in which adjacent elements are not perceptibly different from each other, although the extremes are quite distinct. You understand?"

"Yes!"

Spotlights burst to life. No surprise, the guy was big and matched his voice. Blue smoke curled up from a cigar in his right hand. "Of course you do! You're intelligent, bright people. Otherwise you'd be sitting in Starbucks staring at your phones and computers rather than being here." Laughter.

Charlie didn't understand at all, though he found himself nodding like everyone else. A nonfat vanilla latte with whip actually sounded kinda good at the moment.

The man stepped off the stage and started up the aisle. He had that way some people do of making everyone in the crowd feel like he made eye contact with them. When he passed Charlie's row, Charlie could've sworn his eyes lingered for the briefest second, but he moved on. "I'm so glad you're all here to share this with me. What you're about to see on these screens, this little clip of film, is really a tiny continuum. A series of still pictures, each almost exactly like the next—almost—but the beginning radically different from the end. Like our lives. Because, when you consider, our lives are really only a series of snapshots—moments—that shape us into what we are. This is the miracle. This is yesterday. This is now. This is eternity. This is art. I am art. *You* are art. Don't ever forget it."

"Don't ever forget it!" the room said.

Charlie looked around at the rapt faces and smiled to himself. The dude was a real pro.

The music rose and the wall of screens faded from blue to . . . what? Charlie leaned forward in his seat, trying to make it out. A picture, then another, then another, faster and faster until they became a moving scene. And when they did, it was alive. Charlie couldn't account for it, but he could smell it, hear it breathe. It crashed over him like a wave. Filled him. Overwhelmed senses he never knew he had. Vertigo pressed. His breath became shallow.

Then he flew.

He knew in his mind he never left the ballroom. Never even left his chair. But, man, he flew.

Then it was over. The man was gone. The bank of monitors back to peaceful blue. Logo floating where it had been. The room erupted in applause as the house lights swelled. Charlie looked around him. Many of the faces were tear streaked. Euphoria hung in the air so thick you could almost smell it. What had happened? The clip couldn't have lasted more than a minute or two. And yet Charlie knew he couldn't have taken another second of it. It would've killed him for sure. What was this? Who were these people?

No one spoke to each other as they began to disperse. Each seemed lost in their own thoughts. They'd been to church. Been to the mountaintop. Now they clung to the experience with white knuckles.

Pulling himself back to reality with effort, Charlie considered his position. How long had he been in here? No more than fifteen minutes, certainly. Not enough by a long shot. The guys outside were determined.

Someone touched his sleeve and he turned. The name tag lady smiled at him.

"Charlie?"

He looked down at his tag, then at her. "Yeah?"

"I'm Liz."

"Okay. Hi, Liz."

"Come with me please." She started off without waiting for a reply.

He followed. Hey, anywhere would be a safer option than the lobby or street. "Where are we going?"

She glanced back, that smile still on her face. Charlie had the feeling it might always be there, like a tattoo. "Mr. Lamont would like to speak with you. Come please."

Charlie had to trot to keep up. Chick moved fast for such short legs. Like one of those little Scottish dogs. "Cool. Who's Mr. Lamont?"

They rounded the bank of screens and exited the ballroom through a double doorway. She stepped into an elevator and held the door for him. Once he was in, she pushed the up button.

He put on his best Charlie charm. Leaned against the wall, crossed his arms. "Looks like we're headed up to the expensive real estate. That was some film you guys showed down there. I still don't even know what I saw. It was crazy, man."

Her electric tattoo smile didn't fade a watt. A short ride and long hallway later, she opened a door to a room and beckoned Charlie through.

Inside, he stopped short, taking in the decor and sheer size of the place. "Wow, yeah. This is the expensive real estate all right."

"The Gable-Lombard Suite," a male voice boomed. The man from the ballroom strolled into the room, a white terry cloth robe stretched across his considerable girth. He patted his hair with a towel. Mid fifties maybe? Hard to tell. Bags under his eyes made them look smaller than they were. A thick gray beard framed his face, probably to hide jowls. "That's Clark Gable and Carole Lombard, for the record. They actually lived here for a while. Can you imagine? Thirty-two hundred square feet, three levels, a rooftop patio with a view of the Hollywood sign you wouldn't believe." He approached, tossed the towel onto a couch, and extended a hand. "I'm so glad you took the time to come up and see me. I'm Hammott Lamont. And you're Charles Foster. I saw your name tag down in the ballroom. That's why I asked Liz to bring you up."

Charlie took the hand. "Charlie, actually. Well, Charles on my birth certificate, I guess, but I always hated it. You were the guy on stage, right? It was pretty dark, man. How could you see my name tag?"

Lamont waved Charlie to a couch and took a seat in a chair opposite. He lifted a hand. Liz approached and placed a cigar in it. Lamont lit it, pulled, and blew out a billow of smoke. He leaned forward, using the cigar to accent his words. "Charles, I could tell you the name on every tag in that room today. Would that surprise you? In my position, it pays not to miss even the slightest detail. You, for instance, aren't a member of the Continuum. You don't know anything about us. Yet there you were. Tell me, what did you think of my film?"

"Tell you the truth, I thought it was the most incredible thing I've ever experienced. What was it anyway?"

"Art, Charles. That was art. I don't exhibit often, and I never ever announce it, but somehow people find their way to me. Like you did. And I'm glad. I don't believe in accidents or coincidence, do you?"

Charlie glanced at the woman, then back. "I'm not sure."

"Always be sure, Charles. That's a must in this world."

"It's Charlie. I have to say I'm a little confused, Mr. Lamont. What exactly am I doing here?"

Another smoke stream. "Well, for one thing—a very big thing, I would imagine—you're not getting beat up or killed by Roxy Parsons's thugs. For the life of me, I don't understand why he keeps them around. It's so 1972-mafia. So unpolished. But, then again, so is Roxy."

The room tilted. Charlie forced himself to stay calm. "How do you know about Roxy Parsons?"

"Roxy Parsons is a legend, Charles. A behind-the-scenes mover and shaker in this town. Not because he's made any particularly good films, mind you, but because he's a survivor. He's a shark in the Hollywood pond. I've found it pays to keep tabs on the sharks. In fact, I make it my business to know everything there is to know about sharks. Sharks are unpredictable creatures. You never know when they might bite. Or when they might come in handy, for that matter. As far as knowing his men were chasing you, we know them, and I always have people stationed around a conference, inside and out. You weren't exactly discreet when you ran across the street."

"Look, man, I'm sorry. I didn't mean to crash your movie or whatever. I just needed somewhere to hole up for a minute or two."

"Oh, don't apologize, Charles. Like we've established, I don't believe in coincidence. You might have thought you were running from Roxy's men, but I can assure you the universe had a greater purpose for you being in that ballroom today. There's no doubt about it. Now, what did you do to Roxy?"

"What?"

"Don't be obtuse, Charles. They weren't chasing you for exercise. What did you do? Steal something?"

"No! It was a business deal, that's all. A misunderstanding."

"Ah, you tried to con him."

"I'm telling you—"

"Don't worry about it, Charles. As we know, sharks are unpredictable. Also, you're young, and young people are prone to mistakes. It goes with the territory."

Charlie felt the ridiculous need to salvage a little of his dignity. All he could come up with was, "My name's still Charlie. And I'm not that young actually."

Lamont stretched his legs out and laced his fingers behind his head. "Charles, have you ever seen *Citizen Kane*? The film?"

"Dude, it's *Charlie*, don't you listen? *Citizen Kane*? I don't know, maybe—"

"No maybes allowed, Charles, remember? You've either seen it or you haven't. I imagine it was this same indecisive manner that made such a mess of things with Roxy Parsons."

"Then I haven't seen it, all right?"

"Orson Welles directed it. The greatest director and filmmaker of all time, bar none. I'm a great student of Welles. More than a student actually. An expert, you might say."

"The name sounds familiar. Listen, I—"

"*Citizen Kane* was his first excursion as a movie director. He'd done theater, of course, radio—he literally terrified America with his brilliant narration of *The War of the Worlds*. Do you remember?"

"I—"

"Imagine, the police actually came to the radio station studio he was broadcasting from. They knew what was happening was incredibly dangerous—panic had ensued—but had no idea who to arrest. Think about it. This was the genius of Welles. And that was only his voice! He hadn't even filmed one frame yet."

"Okay . . ."

"Charles, something tremendous has happened today. Can you guess what the lead character's name is in *Citizen Kane*?"

A memory swam up out of Charlie's subconscious. He was in a pool. He must've been very young because he hadn't learned how to swim yet. And his mom was still alive, he distinctly recalled her reading a *Sunset Magazine* on a lounge chair. They were probably at a motel on one of his dad's incessant road trips, but that part was hazy. Charlie could still feel the smooth concrete beneath his feet as he edged toward the place where the shallow end started to slope down to deep. He'd hopped up and down on his toes, head angled back. Just to the edge of the slope, that was all.

Then the floor was gone and he was sinking.

That was the same sensation he had now, sitting with this very strange bearded dude in Clark Gable and Carole Lombard's love nest. The vertigo feeling from the ballroom returned. The walls closed in. "I honestly don't know what the lead character's name was in whatever movie you just said. Listen, Mr. Lamont, this has been great and all, but I've got—"

"Charles Foster Kane. His name was *Charles Foster.* Do you know what that means?"

"I get the feeling you're gonna tell me."

"It means this was meant to be, Charles. Not an accident. Not a coincidence. Meant to be."

"Meant to be because I have the same name as some dude in an old movie? I don't know, there are probably a lot of Charlie Fosters out there."

"Charles, don't you see? The universe brought you to me!"

"No disrespect, man, but this is getting a little out there for me."

"The thing is, Charles, *Citizen Kane* was a great film. A stellar achievement. The greatest to date. But it isn't the greatest of all time. Not by a long shot. Because there is more time to come. The greatest has yet to be made. But—and here's where you come in, Charles—I'm going to make it."

"Where I come in how?"

Lamont leaned forward and put his hands on his knees. "Where are my manners? Would you like something to drink, Charles? I'm going to have a whiskey. The Balvenie Fifty Year Scotch to be exact. Have you had it? It's excellent. Nectar of the gods."

Charlie didn't want anything to drink. He wanted to leave. The guy was freaking him out more than a little. Especially him somehow knowing about Roxy. But Roxy's guys were down there, and they wouldn't give up easy. He sighed inwardly. *Okay, Charlie, let it play out, man. Keep your head in the game.* He took a deep breath and felt better. Lamont was definitely out there, but he obviously had money.

Maybe there'd be an angle Charlie could exploit. He relaxed into the couch with an effort of will. "I'm really not much of a whiskey guy. Do you have any beer?"

"Of course. Liz, will you please get Mr. Foster a beer? And a whiskey for me, please."

The woman had been standing in the corner so quietly Charlie had completely forgotten she was there. He smiled at her. "You can call me Charlie."

She said nothing as she moved into the next room.

Lamont leaned back. "A sign. Yes. I do love signs."

No more than thirty seconds later the woman came back with a whiskey and a tall glass of dark beer. Charlie took a long drink. Then a second.

Lamont sipped, gave a satisfied sigh and an exaggerated lip smack. "Thank you, Liz."

Something chirped. Lamont slid his hand into the pocket of his robe, pulled out a phone, and examined the screen. "Ah, my apologies, Charles. I need to take this. It will only be a minute. Relax and enjoy your beer, yes?"

Charlie shrugged. "Sure, man. Take your time." *Please.*

Lamont stood, phone to his ear, and exited the room. Liz followed.

Charlie drank again. He looked around. The place was definitely posh. Movie star ghosts knew how to live. He thought about checking out the Hollywood-sign view Lamont had mentioned but his legs felt weak. In fact, his whole body was tired. Wet-rag tired. *Stress, man.* He drained the last of the beer, set the empty glass on the coffee table, and watched a couple pigeons bob-walk out on the patio. He was about to drift off when Lamont came back.

Charlie's words felt heavy in his mouth. Hard to push out. "Man, I hate to admit it, but I sure feel that beer. I guess I haven't eaten much today."

Lamont grinned down at him. "That's fine! You just sleep for a while, Charles. Dream a little. Dreams can be good for the soul." He winked. "See you on the other side."

"It's Charlie," Charlie mumbled through lips that had become way too thick.

The pigeons on the patio fluttered and flew off, leaving the shimmery, ethereal personages of Gable and Lombard waving goodbye in their jet wash.

At least that's the way Charlie-not-Charles Foster remembered it right before he lost conciousness.

CHAPTER EIGHT

May 26—A second-floor Laurel Canyon apartment,
Los Angeles, California

MONTE SHAW HAD ALWAYS BEEN an early riser. This morning was no exception, even though he'd stayed up a little later than usual last night watching the Dodgers obliterate the Diamondbacks. He lay sprawled in his recliner, an hour and a half deep into the *Lonesome Dove* miniseries and it wasn't even seven. Monte loved *Lonesome Dove*, and not just because he'd wrangled for it back in the day. C'mon, what a cast. Tommy Lee Jones and Robert Duvall? Plus a lot of it had to do with Texas, Monte's home state before he'd relocated to Los Angeles a million years ago in the seventies. They didn't make 'em like this anymore. Great film.

Which was why he ignored the ringing phone. *What kind of an idiot calls this early anyway?*

To Monte's way of thinking, whoever invented that invasive little piece of annoyance called the cell phone should be strung up by their thumbs. The thing followed a man everywhere he went, even into the john. Lucinda, his wife, saw to that. Made him take it in there in case he had a heart attack. She'd preprogrammed 911 on it and everything. Monte might have a heart attack, but he sure as heck wasn't going to have it in the john.

The phone rang again. Monte gave it a dirty look, picked up the TV controller, and turned up the volume.

Lucinda had bought him the whole *Lonesome Dove* series on DVD at Walmart. Monte's Christmas present last year. Which actually cost him money, because with cable and streaming channels, who owned a DVD player anymore? But she'd been excited, so he'd gone down to Pick and Pawn and found a decent working unit. Only problem was, Lucinda took this as license to buy every yard sale disc she saw. You could get 'em for a buck. Sometimes less. And LA was a yard sale town. Good weather year-round. The stacks in their little apartment living room were growing like weeds. Even worse, she'd started picking up VHS tapes, which you could get for even less, so he'd probably have to make another trip to the pawn shop for another dinosaur machine.

The phone rang again. Monte sighed, leaned his head back, and stared at the ceiling, willing it to stop. Didn't work. Loud, old-school ringtone so he could hear it better over background noise. He hated freezing Gus McCrae mid pontification, but he hit the pause button on the remote with a muttered expletive, grabbed his phone off the TV tray where it sat next to a half-eaten bowl of Cheerios—low-fat milk courtesy of Lucinda—and eyed the little screen. Arizona area code. Monte didn't recognize the number. He killed the call, rubbed a hand over his gray buzz cut, scooped a mouthful of Cheerios, and chewed as he un-paused Gus.

The thing rang again.

With a gravel-laced grunt he stabbed the screen to answer. "If you're selling something, I swear to Buddha I'll cut your ears off and feed 'em to the neighbor's dog. He likes ears and yours wouldn't be the first."

A chuckle on the other end of the line. "Didn't your mother ever tell you not to talk with your mouth full, Monte?"

"Who is this? You're interrupting my show."

"And yet I find myself curiously unmoved. No guilt at all as a matter of fact."

"Wait a minute, is this Early Pines?"

"Give the man a silver buckle."

"I'll be danged, big old ugly Early Pines. What're you up to, kid? Not still jumping off perfectly good horses onto horned animals, are you?"

"Not recently. I'm a detective with the Paradise Police Department."

Monte barked a laugh. "Yeah, and I'm running for president of the US of A."

"I'm serious. Been with the department for a while now."

"No kidding? You know what? Come to think of it, you'd be a good cop at that. Good for you, kid. How long's it been since I seen you? Five years? More?"

"Seven, I think. That bar out in Indio, right? I kept you from getting your head bashed in by a couple Harley jockeys."

"Yeah, you did. You definitely did. Man, those were good days. I miss 'em. All I do now is sit around popping Geritol and swigging prune juice."

"Give me a break. What are you, seventy?"

"Sixty-four, thank you very much. Although you can probably add five to that for all the bones I broke. Point is, I like taking it easy. I'm what you'd call a relaxed soul. Semiretired. Watching TV as we speak with no plans to do much else."

"You're not wrangling anymore?"

"I help train bolters down at the Santa Anita track once in a while. And I still take the occasional movie job if it's one of the big studios. They ain't using horses much these days, though. They're all doing that superhero CGI stuff. All starts looking the same to me after a while, just different color tights. There ain't no Tom Mixes or John Waynes anymore, that's for sure."

"True story. How about the other stuff? Investigations?"

"Nah, not really. I wouldn't have called it real investigating anyway. Mostly just picking up extra cash poking around for people."

"I remember you were working on something before that Indio thing. Missing girl, I think."

"Oh yeah, daughter of a friend. Wound up tracking her down at a trailer park out in Victorville. Couldn't have weighed more than eighty pounds when we found her. They got her into rehab. Last I heard she was married with a couple rug rats. Got lucky on that one."

"Uh-huh. What if I asked you to un-relax for a day and do a little poking? You up for it?"

"I don't know, Early. I do enjoy my downtime."

"What if I reminded you your downtime is made a whole lot more relaxing by the fact that your head is still attached to your body? Which, considering Indio, is kinda thanks to me."

"I'd say, 'Thanks for the good times.'"

"You're welcome. Help me out."

"Ain't no such thing as a free lunch, is there? Ah, I was kidding anyway. I'm bored. As long as you're not selling insurance or wanting to discuss my nonexistent college loans, what and where am I poking?"

"It's not a big thing. I need you to check on a guy. Go to his apartment, knock, see if he's there. Take a little look around."

Monte slurped another bite of Cheerios and chewed, thinking. "What kinda guy? This a criminal thing?"

"I don't think so, but to tell you the truth, I'm not sure. I doubt he's dangerous. He's just missing. And possibly annoying."

"Cowboy, this is La-La Land. You could throw a rock and it'd bounce off one missing knucklehead and hit another. Who's the guy anyway?"

"His name is Charlie Foster. He's the kid brother of a friend."

"I assume you've talked to the locals?"

"Police aren't giving it much of a look. Like you said, a lot of missing people out there. And he's an adult."

"How long's he been in the wind?"

"Three weeks maybe."

"Hmm. Young guy in Los Angeles? Three weeks could mean missing, or it could just mean a decent hangover."

"Yeah, but his sister has a feeling something's wrong."

"Sister? It's all coming into focus now. She that good-looking?"

"Knock it off. Humor me, Monte. You've been in California since the Mexicans owned it. I need somebody who knows the territory."

Monte laughed. "Since the disco days anyway. Must be some girl. All right, does this Charlie Foster have an address? And please don't tell me he's out in Riverside or Palmdale or some other godforsaken place outside the civilized world."

The sound of paper rustling, and Early relayed the address.

Monte grunted satisfaction. "Nice. I'm up in the Canyon. Hollywood's right down the hill from my place. You're making it easy. Do me a favor: I got nothing in front of me to write on, text the details to me. I'll run down and bang on his door. Rattle his drunk hind end out of bed. We'll have coffee and read the paper together. Put sis's feeling to rest. You'll be a hero and we'll be even for Indio."

"I honestly hope it works that way. One more thing. His sister hired a PI but the guy bailed after only a few days. Wouldn't give a reason. If you don't find Charlie, maybe you could give him a shout."

"What's his name?"

"Bryan Fishman. That's Bryan with a *y*."

"Why a *y*?"

"How should I know? I'm not the guy's dad. I didn't name him."

"All right. I'll give Bryan with a *y* a shout too. Put it in the text."

"Thanks. I'm down by the border waiting on a truck repair."

"You're coming out?"

"Yup, if you don't find him this morning."

"Because of the sister's feeling?"

"That's right."

"Okay. I gotta shower and get dressed, then I'll head down. I'll call you in a couple hours."

"Thanks, Monte. Adios."

"Good to hear your voice, kid. Kind of hope this brother's not at his place, it'd be good to see you."

Monte hung up and picked up the remote and switched off Gus McCrae.

Lucinda appeared in the bedroom doorway. She'd been to the gym. Strong Pilates, she called it. A New Year's resolution she'd managed to keep. Then again, Lucinda was stubborn like that. Leopard-patterned leggings and a pink Dri-FIT tank. Thick red hair pulled back into a pile and starting to frizz around the periphery. It wasn't exactly a color you'd find in nature, but he'd never actually seen her dye it either. All part of the beautiful mystery that was Lucinda. Fifteen years his junior, forty-nine to his sixty-four, she'd been Monte's housekeeper until five years ago when somehow—the details were still foggy—he'd found himself in a rented tux standing in front of a Cheshire cat–grinning Las Vegas preacher. Thirty minutes later, he and Lucinda were sitting at a blackjack table as Mr. and Mrs. Monte Shaw, the single life and milk with a fat percentage higher than two a thing of the past. They'd won enough at that table to pay for a nice honeymoon. Monte didn't consider himself the sharpest knife in the drawer, but he knew this—Lucinda Brown-Shaw was the best thing that ever happened to him.

She crossed the room and picked up Monte's phone. She looked at it, then raised an eyebrow.

"Early Pines," he said. "Friend from back in the day. He used to rodeo through here every year. We got a little history."

When Lucinda signed, her hands became creatures independent of the rest of her. Had a life of their own. Graceful dancers seamlessly weaving silent words. His own pathetic attempts often brought laughter, but they made it work. And she read lips as accurately as most people heard words. Or better.

Her hands painted her question. "What did he want?"

"He's looking for someone here in LA. Asked if I'd go down to Hollywood and knock on the guy's door. See what the deal is."

Her mouth turned down and her eyes narrowed.

Monte set the remote on the TV tray. "No, it's not dangerous. Just a favor for a friend. That's all. I owe the guy."

She eyed him, then handed his phone back.

"I promise I'll be careful, all right?"

For an answer, she plopped onto his lap, her hip bones digging into his thighs. She kissed the top of his head, then moved her mouth to his ear and kissed that too. He grinned. Yeah, Lucinda Shaw was the best thing that ever happened to him.

CHAPTER NINE

Early was sitting on an old church pew in front of Bob's, watching the day heat up, when Monte called back. The morning spread out, wide and blue and still. A dove cooed from a utility pole across the street.

"Hey, Monte, what's the word?"

"Word is, no Charlie. Knocked and no one answered so I went in."

"Unlocked?"

"It was, after I unlocked it. Very untidy living space. Hope you don't mind me saying, but the guy's a pig."

"So what's the story?"

"Bunch of junk mail on the floor inside the mail slot. Bills. Note from the apartment manager that the rent's past due."

"Nothing else?"

"Nothing that'd tell us anything other than he hasn't been there in a while. And I went over the place good."

"That's disappointing."

"Yup, but Bryan with a *y* turned out to be another story altogether."

"Yeah?"

"Got him on the first ring. He's a local operator, sure enough. Legit but no office. Works out of his apartment in Van Nuys. I mentioned Charlie's name and he snapped shut like an oyster around a ten-thousand-dollar pearl. Said it was client privilege and all that. I told him I was representing his ex-client, so spill. He said he'd rather not get into it. I said I'd rather he did, or I was on my way over to have the conversation in person. After a little more back and forth it finally got interesting. Guy says if I really want to stick my neck in the noose, I should talk to Roxy Parsons."

"You say Roxy Parsons like I'm supposed to know who he is."

"Roxy Parsons is a sort-of movie producer. Been making mob movies since the eighties. Organized crime minus Pacino or De Niro or anyone else you might've heard of. Made for late-night cable stuff. Thing about Parsons is, he's got a reputation even outside the industry. I've never met the man myself, but the word is life sometimes imitates art. You know what I mean?"

"You're saying, along with making movies, Roxy Parsons is in the Mafia? In LA?"

"Nah, not the real Mafia or anything. But this is Hollywood. It's hard to separate fact from fiction sometimes. People tend to invent themselves. Anyway, I Google Roxy's office number and give him a call. A guy answers and I ask to talk with Mr. Parsons. He says, What's it regarding? and I toss him the name Charlie Foster to see what the temperature of the water is. It's cold, but the guy asks me who I am, says my voice sounds familiar. Funny thing is, I was thinking the same thing. Turns out the phone answerer's an acquaintance I know from Hollywood Park. Guy's absolutely addicted to betting the ponies. We chat a minute or two and then I tell him Charlie Foster's missing and I'm representing an interested party. He asks, What interested party? I say Charlie's sister. He gets quiet and says, 'Look, Monte, if this sister wants to find Foster in one piece, she'd better hurry.' I ask why and he tells me Charlie stole an even half million dollars from Roxy and split the scene."

"A half mi—"

"Yeah. That's a fairly big number. And according to my guy, Roxy Parsons wants it back, and he wants it yesterday."

"And your friend has no idea where Charlie went?"

"This is where it gets strange. He says Roxy's guys went to his place to shake him out—and he shook right out the back window. So they chased the little weasel up Hollywood Boulevard. Charlie ran into the Roosevelt. That's a hotel. Old Hollywood. Anyway, Charlie winds up holing himself up in a Continuum conference."

"Okay. I think I got the Roxy Parsons part, now what's a Continuum conference? Los Angeles apparently has a fairly steep learning curve."

"That's what I wanted to know. After I hung up, I did some more digging. The Continuum turns out to be an organization run by a man named Hammott Lamont. Whole thing's very shadowy."

"Who has a name like Hammott Lamont?"

"I don't know, who in the world has a name like Early Pines? I guess Lamont's another filmmaker. Or artist. Or something. I can't figure it out. Not much information out there about the guy. What I do know is he sounds like a strange individual. There are whole internet threads about his work, but I can't find anything he's actually made anywhere online. He's a recluse. Only ventures out into the public for the occasional unannounced conference like the one Charlie ran into. They only last minutes. He shows one of his weird clips and leaves. To make a strange deal stranger, Charlie went in there but he never came out. And Roxy's guys had every angle covered."

"He never came out? This friend of yours is sure about that?"

"Acquaintance. I didn't get the feeling he was lying."

"So Charlie somehow stayed with this Continuum group."

"Smart move too. Probably the only thing kept him from getting his head busted open by Roxy Parsons."

"Hammott Lamont."

"Yup."

Early watched as the dove flew off the light pole in front of Bob's and faded out of sight. "All right. That's a lot of information for one morning, Monte. I'm impressed. How can we get in touch with Lamont?"

"Already tried. Like I said, he's reclusive. But the Continuum has a website set up for donations and such. Real professional. Looks high dollar. Had to dig but I finally found a phone number. The girl who answers the phone cheerfully says she's never heard of a Charlie Foster and insists I have a very, very nice day. Thing is, I'm pretty sure she didn't give a rat's behind if I had a nice day or not. I pressed but she didn't budge. Tell you what, that gal is in the expert class at giving the runaround. And she was lying about Charlie. No doubt in my mind."

"I don't get it. Why would they lie about him?"

"Exactly my question. Makes no sense at all. You got me curious now. And happily unbored. I'd kinda enjoy doing a little more poking. Like you said this morning, I've been here a while. I know a few people."

"Still no budget for it."

"And I'm still in. You coming out?"

"Yup."

"Cool. Drive safe. Watch out for tumbleweeds."

"See you when we get there."

"We?"

"Sister's coming too."

"The one with the feeling?"

"Yup."

"In that case, watch out for more than tumbleweeds."

CHAPTER TEN

THEY WERE DELAYED WHEN RAY had to send to Tucson for the right tire for Pines's truck. Although Calico, impatient, suspected what Ray really wanted was a few more chess games with Jake. They finally pulled out of One Horse late in the afternoon on the second day of the men's stay and arrived at Pines's place, where Jake had left his pickup, just before sundown. Calico climbed out, stretched, and glanced around. Like its owner, Pines's adobe looked like it had been carved out of the desert.

Jake said his goodbyes and Calico was surprised to find herself mildly disappointed. She'd only known Jake a couple days, but she wished he could tag along. The relationship between the two men was obvious. Jake's quiet, cowboy, Gregory Peck-esque presence had a certain calming effect on Mandatory-Leave Early Pines. And she got the distinct impression a calming influence on Pines might be a good thing every so often. Still, if she had to pick between the two as far as turning a city upside down to find a missing brother, Pines was her clear choice.

Jake waved as he drove off, taillights shining dull red through the dust. A minute or so later, the crunch of his tires faded, and the night became quiet.

And, she realized with a late-to-the-party wave of trepidation, she was alone in the middle of nowhere with this man she hardly knew.

The whole thing was getting very real.

She hugged herself, though she wasn't cold.

"You all right?" Pines said.

She pulled herself out of her mind. "Just thinking about Charlie. It's quiet out here. Even quieter than One Horse. What time can we leave in the morning?"

The hard-slanting sun gave them both hundred-yard shadows and showed tiny streaks of gold beneath the brown of his eyes.

"I'm still packed for Agua Prieta. Everything's in the truck. I was thinking, why not now?"

"Now?"

"Yeah. Get a jump. We'll drop down to I-10, drive a while, get as far as Phoenix or maybe even farther. That way we can hit LA tomorrow morning and meet with Monte. Get our bearings and see what's what."

She pulled in a deep breath, let it out. "I'd like that. I think I'm too keyed up to sleep anyway."

"You need anything first? Restroom? Something to drink? I don't have fancy water, but I can scrounge up something. I got Mexican Coke for sure."

She looked at him, standing there in the evening gold. "Let me ask you something, Pines. You ever been to Disneyland?"

"Is this a trick question?"

"No. You ever ride Space Mountain?"

"No and no."

"The line's usually long. And every once in a while you come to a place you can chicken out. Chicken exits, you know what I mean?"

"Uh-huh, I know exactly what you mean. Have we come to a chicken exit?"

"I wouldn't hold it against you. Let's be real. You don't know me and I don't know you. It was one thing to talk about it back in One Horse, but dropping your life and actually driving to Los Angeles? It isn't your problem. We both know that."

"If I ever go on Space Mountain, I'll see it through. What about you?"

"You know I have to go."

He walked to the old Chevy and opened the door for her. "Problems are heavy things to carry by yourself, Calico. I told you I was going and I'm going. Let's find your brother."

His eyes held hers. At length, she nodded and climbed in.

The truck's headlights mingled with the dusk, the road gravel for a while, then Early turned right onto a paved two-lane. They rolled on, both lost in thought, through the kind of quiet that always comes with empty roads and dying-sun deserts. After a while Pines reached over and pulled something out of the glove compartment. He pushed it into the dash with a click and turned the stereo volume low as Johnny Cash began singing about missing someone.

Calico raised a brow. "Are you kidding me, man? Is that an actual eight track?"

"You have a problem with eight tracks?"

"Only that I didn't know they still existed. You got a woolly mammoth somewhere in here too?"

"Stereo's original to the truck. Still works. Why change it? What's in your car?"

"CD player. But even that's old. It's all Bluetooth now, right?"

His eyes were fixed on the road ahead, west, out toward the point where the last slim glimmer of color was turning black. "Nah, sometimes it's still eight track."

She rolled down the window and let the desert blow her hair. "I guess you're right. At least out here it is. At least tonight."

"That's why I like it."

"Me too, Pines. Me too."

Stars poked through. The moon rose over the hills, and she wondered if Charlie could see it. At least she was moving. Doing something other than wearing a path through her apartment floor.

She stole a glance at Pines. The dashboard lights lit the flat planes of his cheeks, accented his sloped, crooked nose. She'd been serious when she offered him an out and had half expected him to take it. She wouldn't have blamed him a bit. But here he was, and she couldn't figure the guy out. He'd been mouthy and flirtatious at Bob's, but he was quiet enough out here on the road. The former she could handle. The latter put her on edge. Still, the whole situation brought an odd hope—and a yearning to trust. But trust was tough, especially alone in a truck in the middle of the night with a man she hardly knew. She closed her eyes. *What are you thinking?*

She squared herself on the seat. "Hey, Pines?"

"Yup?"

Her voice harder than she meant it to be: "We're getting two rooms wherever we stay tonight. I hope you know that."

He looked over at her. "You have enough on your mind to worry about. Don't add me to it."

"Really?"

"Really."

She breathed and watched him drive. Big hands on the wheel, mouth tracking along with the occasional Cash line. She wanted to believe him. She felt like she could. But then again, so did all those women on those true crime shows. Johnny Cash wrapped up a song about stealing car parts. The truck tires whined, reeling in the broken white line with monotonous determination.

The silence got too loud for her again. "Don't you talk?"

"Some would say I talk too much."

"Some haven't been on a road trip with you then."

He smiled a little. "I was just thinking, that's all. You caught me in a rare mood."

"Pensive."

"What?"

"The word is *pensive*."

"Yeah, I guess I'm feeling pensive."

"Why?"

"Just am."

"All right, tell you what, let's talk about your hat."

"Why?"

"You say why a lot, don't you?"

"What about my hat?"

"I don't think you need it."

He glanced over, then back at the road. "This hat's been verbally abused since I put it on my head. It's to the point now I feel sorry for it. It'd be wrong to send it out into the cruel world by itself."

"I'm just saying you don't need it."

"*Need*'s a strong word."

"But it's the one I used."

He shook his head. "Okay, I'll play. Why do I need it?"

"I don't think you need it, I already said that. I think *you* think you need it. I think you hide behind it."

"You think a lot, don't you?"

"Yeah, you hide behind it. Definitely."

"That's very deep, doctor. You should have a call-in radio show."

"See what I mean? You hide behind words too."

"You know this for a fact?"

"No, but it's a good theory and fun to talk about."

"I like my hat."

A mile or so of silence, then she said, "So Jake used to be a priest? Is he still religious?"

"I don't know if that's the word he'd use, but yeah."

"What about you? I mean, you have the hat for it, right?"

"I'm now officially making this hat off-limits for conversation."

"Good luck with that."

"Is that what religion is? A hat?"

"The pope's is impressive."

The corners of his eyes crinkled. "That's true. What is it about night drives through the desert that always inspires conversations about either God or UFOs?"

"You want to talk about UFOs?"

"Not really."

"Then you're stuck with my question, are you religious?"

"I can't really stake my flag on any moral high ground."

She thought about this. "And you think God expects you to?"

"You think he doesn't?"

"I don't know. If he does, then seriously, who can?"

"Okay. What about you? You religious?"

"I don't think so, but I believe in God for sure." She pointed through the windshield at the stars, out in full force now. "I mean, it's stupid to think all this happened by accident. And that you and I are sitting here having a conversation. Thinking and reasoning. How can intelligent thought just accidentally come from nowhere and nothing? That's stupid. So yeah, I believe."

"Lot of people out there who disagree with that viewpoint."

"It's a free country. That's their problem."

Pines rolled his head in a neck stretch. "I guess it is. Gas station up ahead. Don't need gas yet, but you want to stop for anything? Restroom?"

"No, thanks. I'm fine."

No light or stop sign, still Pines slowed the truck as they passed the little intersection. A closed post office on one corner, the gas station on another. A grizzled old man stood by one of the pumps, putting diesel into a Dodge Ram in the yellow glow while a woman held a dog on a leash. The mini-mart behind them was dark with the exception of a neon Pabst Blue Ribbon sign. The whole thing flashed by like a quick and strange scene from a movie, then the desert night swallowed them again.

"Why aren't you married, Pines?"

He laughed. "We're off God now and straight into marriage? Skipped right on by UFOs?"

She smiled. "It's a long drive. What can I say?"

"There've been a few women here and there. Maybe more than a few. I guess none of them saw me as the settling-down type. Then again, they never asked my opinion about it either."

"So you were the settling-down type?"

"Maybe I was. Once or twice, I think. But that was a long time ago and it obviously didn't work."

"Didn't or couldn't?"

"Either way . . ."

"Never married?"

"Nope."

"You should've taken off the hat. That would've helped. Let them see the man instead of the schtick, maybe."

"I didn't even have the hat back then."

"Oh, you had it. You might not have known it, but I bet you had it." She watched him as he considered this.

"Some hats are easier to wear than others," he said. "That's all."

"Exactly my point."

"What about you? Ever married?"

"Not even close."

"Why not?"

"Maybe I'm waiting for a guy with the right hat."

"What would it say? *Kiss Me, I'm Not Really Religious but I Believe in God Because Not to Is Stupid*?"

"Maybe."

"I just might consider having one made."

"Don't waste your time or money."

"You know what I think? I think you're trying hard to resist me, making fun of my hat. You're like a school kid with a crush."

"And I think one of those UFOs we haven't talked about must've sucked your brain out."

"Have I told you yet that you might be the perfect woman?"

She half smiled. "Shut up, Pines."

They talked more, UFOs this time. A few hours of wide-open night later, they hit I-10 and headed west. The same way Charlie had gone all those years ago. He'd taken that freeway all the way to its termination at the Santa Monica Pier. Taken a picture of himself, blue Pacific in the background, and texted it to them. Calico had gotten the height. Charlie was shorter. Had kind of a Johnny Depp thing going on. She could imagine him in movies. There were no boundaries and no horizons in the picture, only ocean stretching out behind him. Perfect, because that was Charlie, all right.

She leaned her head back against the seat and closed her eyes.

After a while, Pines ejected the eight-track tape and caught an AM station out of Nogales. With Mariachi nylon-string guitar playing low, they made their way through the lights of Tucson. They stopped for gas and truck-stop coffee at a travel plaza on the west end of the city, grabbed some food, and spent a few minutes sitting in the parking lot eating lukewarm hot dogs and watching Big Gulp–toting truckers and minivan families ignore each other. Funny how people could be from the same planet yet track along in completely different orbits.

Calico checked herself in the side mirror and wiped some mustard from the corner of her mouth. "I think I'll use the restroom before we get back on the road, okay?"

"Take your time. We'll find somewhere to stay in Phoenix. Not much farther."

Cool air washed over her as she pushed through the glass door. A fat-faced trucker in line at the counter blew her a kiss but she ignored him. She knew the type. She'd dealt with a thousand of them at Bob's. She walked back through the beef jerky and chips aisle, past a flip-flop-wearing, dad-bod guy rifling through a rack of paperbacks, cut around the made-in-China straw cowboy hats, and pushed open the door to the women's restroom, amazed at how big they made these places now. She could fit her whole apartment in here.

She had the room to herself. Empty and quiet. A long line of empty stalls. She chose the one farthest from the door. When she'd finished, she stopped to wash her hands and shook her head at her reflection, wondering again what she was thinking, getting in a strange truck and driving through the night on what would probably turn out to be a fool's errand. She wasn't Charlie's mother, for crying out loud. But who else did he have? She stuck her hands under the faucet, one of those sensor-activated ones. What would they think if she put these things in at Bob's? She splashed cold water on her face. She was beyond tired and looked it. She pulled a paper towel and was drying when she heard the door swing open.

Then a man's voice, bright and cheerful. "Hey! My lucky day. Or, I guess, my lucky night."

CHAPTER ELEVEN

CALICO SET THE PAPER TOWEL on the counter. Her pulse slowed a bit—but only a bit—when she saw the voice belonged to the dad bod from the paperback racks. She'd expected the trucker. "Sorry, man, this is the ladies' room."

"Oh, wow. Sorry about that." But he didn't leave. He crossed his arms and leaned against the wall, watching her.

"Happens to all of us," Calico said. "But you should go. Now."

"My mistake. But I gotta say, the company in here is much better than in the men's room."

She tossed the paper towel in the trash, irritation tugging. "Listen, I'd really like a little privacy if you don't—"

He sauntered to the counter. Stuck his hands under a faucet. Much too close, smiling at her in the mirror. "Bathrooms these days, huh? Everything so wide open. Men in the women's, women in the men's. Why have signs at all? I mean, who needs them? We're all human beings. Anyway, I was hoping to catch you alone, and here you are."

Her heart beat heavy in her throat, making it hard to swallow. Time slowed. There were some initials scratched into the wall next to the towel dispenser she hadn't noticed before. A streak of lipstick on the mirror. Would anyone hear if she called? The restrooms were in the far back of the building. She had nothing to use as a weapon. And at that moment she would've gladly stuck a fork in the creep's eye. She started to turn away, but he leaned in, his thick body pressing her against the side wall.

He laughed. Smelled like peppermint and cologne and mildewed laundry. "Oops."

Bigger than she'd first thought. Taller than her by at least an inch. His cheeks pink and freshly shaven. Tiny veins connected the pores on his nose. He was very heavy. Too heavy.

"Back off." She pushed with everything in her.

He didn't budge. "Oh, come on. I saw the way you looked at me when you passed me out there. You might as well have sent an invitation. Why be all cold now?"

"I never looked at you. Leave. Now."

He laughed again. "What? I just—"

The door swung open and Pines walked in.

Dad Bod took a half step away from her. Still smiling but eyes alert and feral, reminding her of the coyotes who slunk out of the desert every evening to sniff around Bob's dumpster.

"You, out," Pines said.

Dad Bod found his composure quickly. He squared, grinned even bigger. "Hey, man, we were just talking. Give us some privacy, cool?"

"Out," Early repeated.

"Or what?"

"Or I'll hurt you. Probably bad."

Dad Bod's face flushed. "You're making a mistake, friend. We were only trying to have a conversation here. I wasn't—"

"You leaving or staying?"

Dad Bod kept smiling but was far from happy. "You know what? Maybe you should know I teach Brazilian jujitsu, kickboxing, muay Thai, tae kwon do, bunch of stuff. I've had like ten cage fights, man. You should walk away before you embarrass yourself."

Pines waited.

Dad Bod's pink cheeks got even pinker. "Who do you think you are? This is private!"

"No, it's not," Calico said.

Dad Bod snorted a laugh. "Oh please, I know what you—"

Pines hit him then. So fast Calico never saw it coming. Dad Bod's head snapped, then Pines had him by the back of the shirt and seat of his Dockers khakis. He pulled him deeper into the restroom and slammed him into a stall so hard the door came off. The man groaned and stayed down.

Calico stared at the guy's twitching leg. "Wow. I guess they don't have bathroom stalls in cage fights. You want a bouncer job at a place called Bob's?"

"He could've left," Pines said. "I gave him a chance, which was more than he deserved."

"Way more, if you ask me. What took you so long?"

"You okay?"

"I think so."

"We should go."

"Shouldn't we report this or something?"

"And say what? He'll just say he made a simple mistake by walking into the wrong bathroom and I came in and assaulted him."

"Yeah, and then I'll tell them what happened."

Pines sighed and pulled out his phone. "You're right, we should. But I have a feeling this isn't going to help the mandatory leave thing."

The police showed up within minutes. A uniformed officer asked Calico a long stream of questions, then she waited in the truck while he talked to Early. A few minutes later, a stocky trooper pushed handcuffed, stumbling Dad Bod through the glass doors and to a waiting patrol car.

Pines's head did a slow swivel tracking the guy, then he walked over and climbed into the truck. "I got lucky. The guy had some priors. Peeping and domestic battery. A real pillar of society."

"So you're okay with the police?"

"I'm fine. You're the one who had to deal with it. How are you?"

"I'm okay. He didn't have a chance to do anything more than push me against the wall."

"Still, a thing like that can really mess with a person."

"I own a bar, remember?"

"Yup. And I want to know if you're okay. No tough act."

"I am."

He nodded, started the truck, dropped it into gear, and headed for the freeway entrance. His hat was pulled low and she couldn't see his eyes. He didn't touch the radio. None of the usual banter.

"How about you?" she said.

"What about me?"

"You don't look so good. You okay?"

"I'm very good. Which is the problem."

"How does that translate to English?"

A muscle worked in his jaw. "My dad used to go after my mom bad when I was a kid. So when I see a man trying to take advantage of a woman, I kinda go back there. It doesn't take much for me to get heavy-handed. I didn't have to shove that guy into the stall door. But I have to admit, it felt good."

"Did you ever get heavy-handed with your dad?"

"As soon as I was big enough to make it stick, I threw him out the front door."

"What happened to him?"

"After a while he wound up getting remarried. Stayed in Paradise. I never talk to him and we have a clear rule that he avoids me or takes what comes." He went quiet again, index finger lightly tapping the wheel.

"And he abides by it?" she said.

"Yeah, until recently."

"What happened recently?"

"He saw me, didn't cross the street, and I put him in the hospital."

"Wait, are you talking about the mandatory leave guy? That was your father?"

"It was."

"But you called him Lee when you and Jake were talking."

"He stopped being my dad and became Lee the day I threw him out of our house."

"I'm sorry, I had no idea."

"Why would you? I never mentioned it."

"Anyway, thank you for . . . back there. Whether you enjoyed it or not."

"You don't have to thank me." Headlights from the oncoming traffic played across his features.

"Since it's highway confession hour, to tell you the truth I'm still shaking a little bit."

He reached over and patted her hand. She let him, understanding intuitively he only meant to comfort. The last thing she wanted right then was to be alone in a quiet motel room, and he must have sensed it. He blew through Phoenix without stopping. Lights of the city behind them, desert dark avalanching, his body seemed to ease, and he started talking again. Rodeo road stories mostly which, even if she didn't completely believe them, made her feel better. She even caught herself smiling once or twice. They hit the border at Blythe, the big *Welcome to California* sign stirring both hope and unease in her. It wasn't until they passed Palm Springs with the bourbon-soaked spirit of Sinatra whipping around the tires that Early pulled into a Hampton Inn, parked the truck, and killed the engine.

"I'm beat," he said.

"I'll bet."

"You gonna be okay?"

"I think that's about the tenth time you've asked." She held her hand out. "Look, not shaking anymore. All's well in Calico land."

"All right," he said. "We'll hit a lot of traffic tomorrow, but if we get an early start, I think we can make Hollywood by midmorning."

"That's where we meet your friend Monte?"

"Yeah. Then we'll decide where we go from there."

They stood by the truck, road weary, stretching. It was still hot out, over ninety degrees for sure. Pines grabbed her suitcase, slung his duffel over his shoulder, and she followed him inside. True to his word, he got two rooms. He led the way down a first-floor hallway, opened her door for her, and held out the key card. "All yours. I'll be right across the hall if you need anything."

She took the card. "I'm tired enough to sleep for a week."

"Good. It'll keep you from thinking too much."

"Do you really think we can find Charlie?"

"Tell you what, we'll pick Los Angeles up by the boots and shake it until he drops out. I promise you that."

She stood there while he unlocked the door to his own room across the hallway. "Thanks again," she said, just before he stepped inside.

He looked back. "I'll make you a deal. I'll stop asking you if you're okay if you stop saying thanks."

"I don't just mean for what happened at the truck stop. I mean for everything. I don't know if I've really said it yet."

"You might've been too busy insulting my hat."

"Can't help it, it's an easy target."

"We'll find Charlie, all right? It'll work out."

"Just so you know, I don't believe half your rodeo stories."

He grinned, flashing his crooked incisor. "They say truth is stranger than fiction."

"But somehow I believe you when you say we'll find Charlie."

"I'll see you in the morning."

"Hey . . ."

He turned again.

"Don't stop asking me if I'm okay, okay? I kind of like it."

"I wasn't going to."

CHAPTER TWELVE

May 6—two days after Charlie's unfortunate beer

CHARLIE WORKED HIS TONGUE, TRYING to dislodge the cotton in his mouth, but the stuff wouldn't budge. And then there were the dinosaurs. Those flying kind. What were they called? Terryclothtowels or something like that. They kept roaring by, screaming, messing with a good nap. Nah, terryclothtowels wasn't right. But something like that.

And it was hot, man. Crazy, brutal hot. The kind of hot he'd left back in the desert years ago.

The dinosaurs roared again, and he covered his ears with his hands. He opened his eyes. He'd been asleep? Since when? A few minutes ago, he'd been having a drink with Gable and Lombard in their suite at the Roosevelt. No, that wasn't it. Not Lombard—Lamont. Yeah, Hammott Lamont. Weird dude. He must've fallen asleep on the guy's couch. Stress, man—it could do that to you.

He tried to focus but it was too bright. He shifted his hands from his ears to his eyes. What was it with the lights in this place? He cracked his fingers. Blue. The ceiling was blue?

Wait . . .

He sat up. Yeah, it was blue, because the ceiling was the sky. A brilliant, cloudless blue sky. And it was hot because the sun shone down out of that sky like a stinking . . . sun. He struggled to his feet and blinked. Hot like the desert because it was the desert. And not just any desert, this was the *desert*, man. A drop of sweat ran down his ribs. He looked down at himself. A suit. He was wearing a suit. Tie and everything. But no shoes. Only some thin, leather flip-flop-style sandals. His head spun. His stomach knotted and he almost vomited. It had to be a dream. He pinched himself but the pinch didn't wake him. It only hurt.

He cupped his hands and shouted. "Hello?"

Nothing.

A low rumble sounded in the distance. The dinosaurs coming back. The rumble grew to a roar, and then screams, as four military fighter jets wailed past, looking close enough to touch, kicking great billows of dust off the desert floor.

"Am I in hell, man? Did I die? Hello?"

A slight whirring sounded behind him and he spun. Blinked. "What the . . . ? What are you supposed to be?"

A small vehicle, much too tiny to hold a human being, stared up at him through an unblinking lens. The whirring sounded again, and the thing moved back a couple feet. The lens—some sort of camera surely—adjusted, rising an inch like it was searching for a close-up of Charlie's face. He tried to approach it, but it whirred backward and readjusted again.

Charlie knelt. The unblinking lens lowered. He squinted at it, fighting off the sun glare with an upheld hand. "Hey. Who are you? Somebody can see me, right? Mr. Lamont? Is that you? Can you hear me? What's going on, man?"

The machine whirred and shot backward, stopped when Charlie didn't follow, then continued when he did. They moved along like that, Charlie occasionally stumbling on the rough ground, the sand and rocks hot through the sandals. The little robot had no problem at all, its beefy all-terrain wheels managing the topography with ease.

Half a mile into the trek, Charlie's brain focused a bit and his anger rose. "Where we going, man? This is kidnapping, you know that? Answer me, you little piece of junk!" He reached for the robot but it whirred out of reach. "Is this some kinda punk survivor show or something? I never agreed to it. I never signed anything. I never—"

Implacable, the robot spun on. Charlie tried to swallow but his mouth was too dry. He tried to ignore his thirst, but the more he did, the more it raged. Anger faded and tears breached. Tears turned to sobs. He dropped to his knees.

"I'm thirsty, man. Seriously, I feel like I'm gonna puke. This is freaking me out! You win. I lose. Keep the million bucks or whatever. I give up. What do I need to say to make this stop? Is there a bell to ring or something?"

He heard the roar of the fighters again, and a few seconds after they blew by every bit as low as before. He wiped a string of snot from his nose.

A half mile later he followed the robot up a low rise and stopped. The elevation gave him a nearly three-sixty-degree view. His stomach cramped and this time he really did puke. Hands on his knees, he vomited what little was inside him, then dry heaved for a good minute. Groaning, he straightened and scanned the horizon. Nothing. No roads, no buildings, no nothing. Only emptiness as far as the eye could see. And from his position he could see practically to the ends of the earth. Or at least to the distant mountains. Yeah, he was going to die out here. All under the watchful, unblinking gaze of this little freak of a mechanical cyclops. Charlie knelt again, looking the thing in the eye. He got within six inches. This time the machine held its ground.

"You want to watch me die, huh? No way, man. I swear I'll bust this thing to pieces with a rock first. Somebody better talk to me. I'm thirsty. I'm sick. I want to go back to LA. I'll even take my chances with Roxy Parsons. Just make this stop. You hear me, whoever you are?"

At this, the robot spun back, lens still on Charlie, and disappeared around a big boulder. With nothing else to do but lie down and die, Charlie followed. The robot whirred to a stop next to a canvas backpack. The machine swiveled its lens to the bag, then back to Charlie. Charlie studied the bag before reaching for it. "What is it, a bomb?

A sack of scorpions?" But what choice did he have? He picked it up, feeling the lens's gaze. The sack was heavy. He unzipped the top. Several bottles of water and a package of protein bars. Hands trembling, he uncapped a bottle, spilling a little on the way to his lips. He sank to his knees as the liquid saturated his body and bones. It was warm, almost hot, and the most wonderful thing he'd ever tasted. The boulder offered scant shade, but he scooted into what there was and finished the bottle. Then another. Then, though his stomach still knotted, licked a mostly melted protein bar off the wrapper. He felt better when he was done. He tossed the wrapper and watched it bounce away on the breeze. Momentarily satiated, happy to be alive, he turned his attention to the robot. The thing was actually kind of cute when he thought about it. Reminded him of that lamp that came on the screen before Pixar movies.

The sun hung high. It had to be about midday. He took off the suit coat, draped it over his head, and closed his eyes. He heard the jets coming again but this time he put his fingers in his ears and didn't look up. The exhaust from the things yanked his coat and kicked dirt, stinging his hands and face. He cried a little, not caring that the robot watched. He slept again. The robot woke him, bumping his leg over and over until it got his attention.

Charlie lifted the edge of the coat and cracked an eye. "What?"

The thing whirred back and forth a couple times. Then started off down the hill.

"Good riddance," Charlie mumbled. Then, thinking about it, got himself to his feet, slung the pack over his shoulder, and hurried after the machine. What else did he have?

Early evening now, the sun a huge red ball six inches above the horizon. The robot whirred with purpose on a straight track. An hour they traveled. The evening cooled. A star broke through, then more. Charlie worked his way through another protein bar and bottle of water. Four bottles left in the bag. He'd better conserve. With this thought in his mind, he killed another.

Without warning, the desert floor broke and dropped into a wide sandy wash. *Thank God. At least it's something different.* The robot buzzed down the bank, somehow remaining upright. Charlie scrambled after. The machine stopped next to a tangle of boulders. A couple green desert gourd vines. A circle of stones and a stack of firewood. A camp. The robot's camera locked onto him and he could see it either zooming or focusing behind the lens.

"So it's a campout, huh? You and me are a couple of Boy Scouts? How am I supposed to light a fire? You got matches in your pocket? Oh, right, you don't have pockets."

The robot didn't move. With the dying light, cute was becoming creepy. Charlie examined the backpack again, found a compass in one of the outer pockets, then a lighter. He tossed the compass on the ground, then thought better of it—after all, he'd seen *Naked and Afraid* enough times. You never knew what might come in handy. He put it back in the pack, though he didn't have a clue how to use it, and went to work on the fire. It took an hour, and nearly all the fluid in the lighter, but he finally got the thing lit. Darkness pressed now, black as a domino but certainly not empty. A million desert stars danced. A meteor shot almost horizon to horizon.

Charlie eyed the robot. The camera lens reflected firelight. "Shooting star. You got a wish, man? No? I do. It's God, please don't let me die out here with this wannabe R2-D2."

Nothing from the robot. Maybe it was asleep.

Charlie stretched out on the sand, surprised to find it somewhat comfortable. "Snakes don't bite robots, so you got that going for you. I probably won't be so lucky. You'll find my bloated black corpse in the morning. Give you something fun to look at." Another star fell. The others shimmered their applause. "Better dying of snakebite than thirst, I guess. Although, then again, maybe not." He sat up and added a stick to the fire. No snakes to be seen yet. "I read this story one time about this dude who went to sleep in the desert and woke up with a rattler coiled up on his chest. How am I gonna sleep with something like that running through my brain? At least the jets stopped. And, by the way, I remembered—it's pterodactyl, not terryclothtowel. That's *pterodactyl* with a *p* but the *p*'s silent. I know because I got it wrong at a spelling bee when I was in eighth grade. Embarrassing, dude. But why would anyone put a silent *p* on a perfectly good word? It's just mean to kids. Anyway, I'm never gonna be able to sleep with all the snakes." He felt tears rush again. Curled into a ball, he cried for a minute or two.

Then he slept.

CHAPTER THIRTEEN

May 29—Hampton Inn,
Palm Springs, California

Despite the long drive the night before, Early and Calico were in the breakfast room off the hotel lobby by six a.m. By six ten, Early was sopping up the last bit of gravy on his plate with a piece of biscuit while Calico toyed with her uneaten fruit. Early eyed her while he chewed. He took a sip of his weak coffee. He'd made a promise, and he'd tossed and turned half the night because of it.

Lesson for the books—it's easy to promise things to a beautiful woman in a Hampton hallway when Los Angeles is still ninety miles and a night's sleep away. But this morning, sun shining through the plate glass, looking at the perfect curve of her cheek and the way her hair fell over her eye, his confidence suffered. LA was a big place. A huge place. And even with Monte's help, Early was an outsider.

Then again, it wasn't like he had nothing at all to go on. The kid had rattled some cages. There was Roxy Parsons. And then this Hammott Lamont and the Continuum. Hopefully Monte had had some luck in his poking-around efforts and could suggest the best place to start. Monte was an old dog, and even if the old tricks in his doghouse were a little dated, they were well used and proven.

Traffic on I-10 moved along at a fair clip for several miles, but the inevitable commuter grind into Los Angeles proper started around the inland city of Riverside and dug its heels in hard. Early people-watched, braked, gassed, and ground his teeth. To say crowds—and especially traffic—weren't his thing would be an understatement for the ages. And *crowds* was the word that came to mind when he thought about Los Angeles. Everywhere you went, people thronged. "And every single one of them has to be driving this morning," he muttered.

Calico glanced at him. "What's that?"

He shrugged. "Just remembering how much I love freeways packed full of cars."

"It's definitely not One Horse. Or Paradise. How do you think they do this every day?"

"The price you pay for living here, I guess." He looked down at his cell on the seat and the little blue arrow creeping along the nav screen. Most of the freeways were lit up red to indicate traffic. "Interstate 10 to US 101, it's saying. That'll take us through Hollywood. Been a while since I was here. And Jake usually drove."

"Charlie says if you're from here, you don't call it Interstate 10, just the 10. Or the Santa Monica."

"Yeah, I vaguely remember that."

She looked out the window. "I just pray this whole thing isn't hopeless."

"It isn't." Early hoped he sounded more confident than he felt.

"I had a dream last night. Probably the stress. It was all muddled. I don't know how to explain it. Like laying a bunch of colors over one another until there's no color at all. You can't make out the picture even though you know you have to."

"Dreams are funny that way."

"You were in it."

Early glanced at her. "Yeah? Good or bad?"

"I don't know. Good, I think."

"You think?"

"Hey, you were there. Don't complain."

"Right, I'll take what I can get."

"I'm not explaining it well at all. But that's because I can't. I mean—"

"The colors are mixed up."

"Yeah." She turned to him. "Pines, what if we find out Charlie's dead?"

"Was Charlie in the dream?"

"No, just you."

"Navajos will tell you if you dream of a dead family member, it's a bad sign. That they're calling you to the other side. So maybe him not being in the dream is good."

"You believe that stuff?"

"If it helps."

"You were in it. What does that mean?"

He grinned. "Maybe it means—"

"Never mind. But what if you get hurt somehow? We don't know anything about this Continuum. And Roxy Parsons the fake Mafia guy, seriously, what's that? This isn't even your problem, you know? A couple of days ago you were just a guy on your way to a rodeo."

He tried to offer a reassuring smile. "Don't overthink it. It was a dream. And probably stress, like you said. And even so, I've been hurt more times than I can count. You didn't put a gun to my head. It was my own decision to come. We don't know anything yet. Let's cross one bridge at a time."

She sat up a bit. Pushed her shoulders back. "Yeah, you're right. Okay."

The sun slanted down over the San Gabriels and heat waves shimmered on the blacktop as Early finally merged onto the 101. Traffic thinned with the change of freeway and he was able to get up to a decent speed. They passed signs for Chinatown, Angelino Heights, East Hollywood—the place was never ending. Five hundred square miles of city doing its best to lick up the last drops of the Colorado River before it hit Mexico.

Calico shifted on her seat. "Tell me about this Monte guy. Who is he?"

Early checked his mirror and switched lanes to get around an appliance delivery truck. "He's kind of a legend out here. He worked as a wrangler for the movie studios."

"What's a wrangler do?"

"Handles the horses. Monte's pure magic with them. He grew up on a little ranch down in West Texas. Got hired on with a movie crew that was shooting down there back in the seventies and loved it. Came out to Hollywood and he's been here ever since. Worked on tons of stuff. He knows the town and the players. Which is why he kinda naturally fell into helping people with the investigation thing on the side. He's already been a help to us. And if he doesn't have any more information yet, we'll figure something else out."

She rubbed her palms on her jeans, spoke without looking at him. "You know what? I'm glad you hit Lee. I mean, he has the right to walk on whatever side of the street he wants, but I'm glad you hit him."

"Yeah? Why?"

She did look at him now. "Mainly because it got you mandatory leave. And that got you here."

"It's definitely saving me from sitting out there on my porch feeling sorry for myself."

"You wouldn't be sitting on your porch. You'd be at a rodeo."

"The rodeo was Jake's way of distracting me. He thought that I needed it."

"Did you?"

"Probably. Either way, you're a lot prettier company than Jake."

"Thanks, but I'm officially ignoring that statement."

Their exit loomed, and a few minutes later they found themselves driving west on Hollywood Boulevard. Grauman's Chinese Theater, the Walk of Fame . . . Early marveled not only at the sheer amount of people but the wide spectrum of humanity. Clothes from business suits to stuff out of a Mad Max film. At a stoplight, a bearded man in a filthy Led Zeppelin T-shirt slept on the sidewalk next to a skinny pink-haired girl who couldn't have been more than seventeen. The girl sat cross-legged, smoking a cigarette. She smiled at Early when he looked over. When he touched his hat brim, she started to get up, eyes full of hope and maybe something else, but the light turned green and they moved on.

After several blocks, they turned right and drove along treed residential side streets before winding up the hill into Laurel Canyon, where the nav deposited them into a small, crowded parking lot in front of an old brick building. A rusty sign said Canyon Country Store. Lots of spray-painted art. Lots of old metal.

Calico leaned out through the window. "I thought your friend was a cowboy. This place looks more hippie than horse."

"What'd you expect, a saloon?"

"I don't know. Not this."

"It's a place to meet. Monte's a little of everything, I guess. Definitely a breed of his own."

They walked around to the front of the place. Tattered umbrellas sagged in the sun over a handful of patio tables. Monte's familiar gray buzz cut gleamed in the sun. Not a big man. Five eight or nine by Early's recollection. But his confidence made him taller. Old jeans and boots. Clean-shaven, sun-weathered face. White T-shirt stretched over a whipcord frame. Early pointed. "There's our date. Ain't he a gem?"

Monte was getting ready to attack a deli sandwich the size of a small child and a can of Dad's root beer. A woman sat next to him. Mid forties maybe. Her bright red hair clashing mightily with her pink blouse. A necklace made of colored beads the size of walnuts hung around her slim neck. Earrings to match. A multitude of bracelets on both wrists. Her features, taken separately, wouldn't have been considered attractive but somehow bundled into a package, worked together to form something approaching pretty. There was a wounded distance about her, but a kindness too. The combination won Early over on the spot.

Monte waved as they approached. He stood at the sight of Calico, his capped teeth white against his tan. He held out a hand to Early. "Early Pines, as I live and breathe. Welcome to the Ritz-Carlton. Grab yourself a chair if you can find a clean one and park your butt."

Early shook, introduced Calico, and they both sat.

Monte put a hand on the redhead's shoulder. "Don't believe you've met my wife, Lucinda. Lucinda, this ugly green giant is Early Pines. The pretty one with poor taste in traveling companions is Calico Foster."

The woman paid close attention to Monte's mouth when he talked. When he'd finished, she turned, smiled, and gave a small wave.

"Lucinda's hearing-impaired," Monte said. "Hate the way that sounds. Like there's something wrong with her, which is the furthest thing from the truth. She's a hundred-percent perfect, unless you count the fact she coddles me like I got one foot in the grave."

"Then again, you're no spring chicken, amigo," Early said.

Deep lines on Monte's face when he smiled. "Nah, I'm a stringy old rooster. But hey, I still kick around and crow pretty good. What's with the hat, Pines? Because I don't care if you're Baptist, Buddhist, or praying to Richard Nixon, I ain't kissing you."

"Good, I was worried."

Monte shifted his bright eyes to Calico. "That thing work on you?"

Early answered for her. "Not so far."

"We have a traveling agreement," Calico said. "No ulterior motives allowed."

"Beauty and brains, best combo there is," Monte said. "Hold your ground."

Early looked around. "Interesting place, Monte."

"Canyon Country Store's an institution. We got us a little apartment just up the hill. Always liked Laurel Canyon. A lot of movie people live up here. Have since there's been movies, I guess. Musicians too. Whole community of 'em back in the sixties and seventies. Some of 'em still here." He pointed. "Joni Mitchell's over that way. I like that 'Big Yellow Taxi' song. Back in the day, Harry Houdini had a mansion here. And you'll like this one, cowboy—Tom Mix had himself a big log cabin."

"Tom Mix, no kidding?"

"Him and Wyatt Earp used to hang out right here in this building. Called the Bungalow Inn back then. They say one time Earp got hot at somebody and shot his pistol into the wall. Bullet's supposed to still be there somewhere." Monte turned to Lucinda. "Early used to be a bulldogger, though I never thought it was fair. Guy like that gets down off a horse and them steers just naturally curl up in a ball and start sucking their thumbs. No sport in it."

Lucinda smiled.

Early shook his head. "If that were true, I would've come out of the whole deal with less broken bones and a whole lot more prize money in my pocket. Jake was that guy."

Monte grunted a laugh. "How is old Jake?"

"Married. Found a nice girl and they're still in Paradise."

"Good for him. What about that other kid you guys hoofed around with? Scrappy little Mexican. The bull rider."

"Gomez Gomez."

"That's the one. Two names the same. Man, he was a character."

Early let out a breath. "He died last year. Kind of a hard deal."

"Aw, no! Not a bull, was it?"

"Snakebite, believe it or not."

Monte studied him. "That's rough, Early. He was a good, tough kid. I liked him. How are you doing with it?"

"I'm fine."

"Yeah? The muscle twitching next to your eye doesn't make you look so fine."

Early watched a delivery truck rumble by. "He went through a rough patch there at the end, but he was coming out of it. I guess I just don't understand the universe sometimes."

Monte looked at him for a second or two, then shifted his eyes to Calico. "Early tell you about a time down in Indio he cleared out a whole bar full of Hells Angels to keep my carcass in one piece?"

"No, he didn't," Calico said. "Which surprises me because he's told me every other story about his life from kindergarten to the present. It was a long drive."

"That's our boy. If there's one thing he's not short of, it's words."

"It wasn't a bar full," Early said. "And they weren't Hells Angels.

They were a couple of knuckleheads who thought boots and two wheels made them tougher than they were."

"There was six of 'em at least," Monte said.

As Monte relayed the story, Early found himself watching Lucinda. With her husband's attention engaged elsewhere, she pulled his sandwich away with a pickpocket's stealth and slipped it into a nearby trash can. In another single, clean motion, she dumped the root beer into a potted plant and refilled the can from a water bottle she pulled from her purse. She slid the can back into place and dropped a plastic baggie of carrots where the sandwich had been. The whole exercise took all of ten seconds. Early raised an eyebrow in her direction. She returned the gesture and focused her attention on Monte.

"Anyway, that's the way I remember it," Monte said. "Early saved me a trip to the hospital or worse." He took a drink of water from the root beer can, then picked a carrot stick out of the baggie and munched it without batting an eye.

"It sounds like he's mastered the art of the rescue," Calico said. "I've experienced it myself."

Monte picked up another carrot. "Yeah? Do tell."

Early leaned forward onto his forearms and changed the subject. "Monte, you find out any more about Hammott Lamont?"

"Guy's got walls around him ten stories high and twenty feet thick. But I think I mighta got lucky. When I called up the Continuum office, I musta shook something loose. Got a call last night from a woman named Jackie. Said she was near the front desk and overheard the call on their end. Got my number when the receptionist was in the john." This brought a poke to the ribs from Lucinda. Monte winced. "My apologies—when she was otherwise occupied. Turns out Jackie's one of Lamont's personal chefs. Also turns out Lamont talks a bit. From her tone, I'm guessing she doesn't always like what she hears. She didn't want to go into detail on the phone. Sounded a little paranoid, to tell you the truth. She suggested we meet instead. She definitely knows something about our Charlie."

"Can we call her now?" Calico said.

"No need. She's on her way." Monte glanced at his watch. "Should be here any time." He took another drink from the Dad's can. Early waited for a reaction. Nothing but a satisfied sigh. "They got decent food here. You two want anything?"

"I'm not hungry yet. We ate at the hotel," Calico said.

"How 'bout you, Early? Corned beef's the best around."

"Yeah, I might have—"

The guttural boom of Harley pipes shook the store windows and a motorcycle rolled to a stop on the street. The rider dropped the kickstand, pulled off a helmet, and surveyed the four of them. "One of you guys Monte?"

"Guilty as charged," Monte said around a mouthful of carrot. "One of you Jackie?"

The woman hopped off the bike and set the helmet on the seat. With the bike, Early'd expected leather and tattoos. Skull earrings or something. But Jackie surprised. No biker boots or ink. More like a diminutive soccer mom. Her hair a nondescript brown, cut short in no particular style. Eyes the same noncolor behind rimless glasses. Skinny jeans and a pink pastel hoodie. Could have been on her way to pick up her kids from school. She swung a backpack off her shoulder, dropped it, pulled over an unused chair from another table, and settled into it. "Yeah, I'm Jackie. Good to meet you."

Monte shook her hand and made introductions. "You hungry? Early and I were just discussing the gastronomic delights of corned beef."

"Tempting as a heart attack sounds, no thanks. I had a protein shake earlier." Jackie's focus shifted to Calico. "So you're the sister?"

"I am. What can you tell me about Charlie? Is he all right?"

"As far as I know, but what I know isn't much. I'm a chef for Mr. Lamont at the Santa Barbara compound three times a week. More if he requests. Anyway, I was checking out at the front desk—you have to check in and out—when I heard Liddy, the receptionist, talking to Monte on the phone. I got enough to figure out Charlie's sister was looking for him, and I could tell Liddy was giving the runaround. Not unusual, I think that's ninety percent of Liddy's job description. Made me mad. I have a little brother too. We're super close. I'd hate it if I couldn't get in touch with him because of an egomaniac like Hammott Lamont. So I snapped a pic of the number while Liddy was—"

"Otherwise occupied," Monte said.

"Exactly. Liddy's full of it. Hang around the Continuum compound more than five minutes and you'll absolutely hear the name Charles Foster. I'm guessing that's Charlie."

"I can't imagine him letting anyone call him Charles," Calico said.

Jackie bent to the side, unzipped her backpack, and pulled out a magazine—*Hollywood Reporter*. "Talking to Monte got me thinking. See, Mr. Lamont has this thing about Orson Welles. Even looks like the guy. He's really into Welles's movies. Especially *Citizen Kane* and what he says are all the genius scenes in it. Angles and stuff. I tried to watch it once and it bored me to sleep. Thing is, the main guy in that movie's name is Charles Foster Kane. So it wouldn't be a stretch for Mr. Lamont to call Charlie 'Charles.' He'd see it as a sign. That's another thing he's really into, signs."

"But why? What's Charlie doing with him?" Calico said.

Jackie lifted the magazine. "This might tell you. Just out today. The *Reporter*'s the insider entertainment rag around here if you're not familiar." She thumbed through the magazine, opened to a page, and tossed it on the table in front of Calico. "It's just a guess on my part, but what do you think? That look like your Charlie to you?"

CHAPTER FOURTEEN

May 7—The desert,
three days after Charlie's unfortunate beer

CHARLIE WOKE IN THE CHILLED silver light of the desert dawn, still curled up in a ball. He sat up and checked his limbs and torso. No snakebites. Good, now he could die of thirst in peace. He'd decided in the night that thirst would be better than snake anyway. The thought sent him to the backpack for a bottle of water. He drank half. Only two more when this one was gone. No sun yet, but hazy, colorless light hung above distant rocky peaks and the stars had faded to three notches below blinding.

The robot whirred, clicked, and drilled him with its mono eye.

"Good morning to you too. You coulda put a toothbrush in the pack, man. My mouth tastes like a cat died in it."

The robot moved down the wash several feet. It paused when Charlie didn't follow.

"What?" Charlie said. "I'm tired. We walked all day yesterday. At least I did. And I'm hungry. For something other than cardboard pretending to be a candy bar."

The machine came back, bumped Charlie's leg, and started off again.

"No way. I'm not going anywhere until I get some answers. I'd rather die right here." Charlie held up the backpack. "Two bottles left, then the angels sing. Few days, or however long it takes to kick it from thirst, and I'll be a dried fig. A memory."

The robot's miniature tires spat sand as it whipped a fast three-sixty, lens coming back to settle on Charlie.

Charlie kicked at it but missed. "Is that a temper tantrum, lame-o? You gonna go? Go."

At this, the robot charged and bumped Charlie's leg again. Harder this time.

"Ow, man! Leave me alone."

Another bump.

"Ow! No!"

The unblinking eye stared at him. Charlie had the strangest feeling the little machine was thinking. Finally, it spun and started up the wash on a quick roll.

"Yeah?" Charlie called. "Beat it then! I won't miss you." He settled back onto the sand and watched the robot disappear around a bend. "Little freaky freak. Good riddance. I thought you'd never leave."

Then again, what was he going to do now? Really die?

He looked around at his piece of the desert. Right here? This was where he was going to buy the farm? Not how he'd pictured it. In his mind it was always in a nice, clean hospital. And he was at least a hundred and thirty. Yeah, and he'd be surrounded by family and friends. He'd tell them a story or two about the old days before he punched out. Give 'em a laugh to remember him by.

He stared in the direction the robot had gone. "Hey!"

Nothing but silence and sky. The thing had actually left him out here to the snakes and scorpions and heat. Speaking of which, the sun had cracked the hills now and the air was already getting hotter.

"Stupid, stupid robot." He got to his feet, brushed the sand off his suit, and started after the machine. Easy to do with the deep tracks it left. The sand grabbed at his flip-flops and got stuck between his toes, a feeling he had always hated. At least the ground wasn't too hot yet.

He found the robot waiting for him just around the bend, smug eye staring.

"Really?"

The thing whirred and started off.

Charlie followed. "You even know where we're going? I know what happened, I'm in hell, man. Roxy Parsons killed me and I'm in hell. My punishment is to trail after you for all eternity. All the religions in the world got it wrong. Hell is really a never-ending episode of *The Twilight Zone*. Which, when I think about it, makes total sense. I mean, why not?"

A mile or more they followed the wash, then the robot climbed a shallow spot in the bank. For an hour . . . two . . . three, Charlie verbally went at the little machine. The water bottles were empty now. Protein bars gone. The sun climbed. He took off the suit coat and draped it over his head, tied his tie around his forehead to hold it in place. The sand burned his feet through the sandals.

Still they continued. He rubbed at a cramp in his thigh. He should at least be able to see a road by now. Telephone poles. Dust from a car. Something.

And then he did.

A shape began to take form out in the heat waves. Charlie blinked, hardly daring to hope. A hundred yards farther and he knew he wasn't hallucinating. A building, sure enough, solid and substantial, standing alone out on the wide valley floor.

Charlie pointed. "I don't know about you, dude, but I'm headed for that. At least I know there's some form of civilization left in the world. I was starting to think this was some sort of apocalypse. Maybe they even have AC."

The robot seemed to have the same idea. It whirred on in a straight line toward the structure. As they got closer Charlie could make out details. The building wasn't large. A low-built thing with, of all things, *Snack Bar* above it in sleeping neon. No cars around. No telephone or electrical lines. On the front wall of the building, there were two doors at opposite ends. One said *Entrance*, the other *Exit*.

Charlie bumped the robot with his toe. "This part of the show? An abandoned snack bar in the middle of hell when I'm dying of thirst and hunger? Torture me, right? Great footage, man. That was sarcasm, by the way." With a what-the-heck headshake, he headed for the entrance door. He was surprised when the knob turned in his hand and the door swung in. More surprised when a gust of icy air from inside hit him in the face. And stunned beyond words when an acne-faced teen in a vintage uniform smiled at him from behind a well-stocked counter and said, "Hi, sir! What can I get you today?"

CHAPTER FIFTEEN

May 29—Canyon Country Store,
thirteen feet from Wyatt Earp's lost bullet,
Laurel Canyon, Los Angeles

CALICO LEANED FORWARD AND STUDIED the picture in the magazine. She blinked. It was Charlie, no doubt. A little longer hair than last time she'd seen him. The beard too. A desert landscape behind him. Face aglow with golden sunlight, every whisker and pore accented by the photo's sharp focus. His eyes were red, weary. And the fear—no actor could pull that off. He wore a suit, the tie loose and hanging. Never in her life had she seen her brother in a suit. Charlie but not Charlie—Charles. The photo was a glossy full-page ad for a project "As Yet Untitled." A film by Hammott Lamont and featuring Charles Foster, slated to begin production shortly.

She felt Pines's eyes on her.

"It's him," she said. "He looks . . . different, but it's him." She looked up at Jackie. "I don't understand. All of a sudden Charlie is Charles and he's in some kind of movie?"

"Not just a movie. *The* movie, according to Mr. Lamont. It's all secretive and hush-hush around there. But you know how it is, especially in closed environments. Secrets are the things people talk about the most. This project is Mr. Lamont's big thing. It's been in the planning stages for years. I'm sure your brother got caught up in his whirlwind. Most people do. I heard someone up there this morning talking about the new spread in the *Reporter* and checked it out. I had a feeling."

"So little brother landed a role," Monte said. "Good for him."

Calico's eyes fell to the ad again. "But why not call me? Why not answer the phone? It's not like him. I'd be the first one he'd want to brag to about something like this."

"Not if Mr. Lamont didn't want him to talk to anybody," Jackie said.

"Why wouldn't he want him to talk to his sister?" Pines said. "Is the guy that controlling?"

"He can be. He doesn't just hire people, he owns them. But he always has his reasons. Especially when it comes to his art. That's about all I know. I'm just a worker. Seen but not heard, if you know what I mean."

"You're his personal chef, is that right?" Pines said.

"More like his impersonal chef. I do the job and get out. I mean, whatever, right? The money's good. Anyway, I'm only one of several. Mr. Lamont is serious about his food. It's a team effort. No one is supposed to talk to each other. You sign a contract to that effect when you start. I'm breaking every rule talking to you right now, but like I said, I have a brother too."

"What's his name?" Pines said.

Jackie stared at him. "What?"

"Your brother, what's his name?"

"Do you think I'm lying?"

Pines lifted a shoulder. "You make it sound like Lamont has puppet strings attached to everybody around him. Why not you?"

"My brother's name is Jessie, all right?"

"Pines, c'mon," Calico said. She turned back to Jackie. "So, outside of this ad, you don't know anything else? You've never actually seen Charlie there at all?"

"You sure about your taste in friends?" Jackie said.

"He's just being protective," Calico said.

"Okay, whatever. Look, I only know what I told you. Honestly, your brother might be there, or he might be anywhere. The Santa Barbara compound is a definite probably—the place is huge. But the Continuum has places in LA, Palm Springs, Hawaii. Maybe others too. I'm lucky to know what I know. Even luckier to have overheard Monte's call."

"This is crazy," Calico said. "All I want to do is talk to him. Make sure he's okay."

"It's Los Angeles," Monte said. "We got our own particular brand of crazy here. Lamont's another crackpot cult guy in a long line of crackpot cult guys."

Jackie frowned. "I feel for you. I do. I don't know if you'd call it a cult, but at the Continuum it's Hammott Lamont's world. He makes the rules and that's that. If your brother was told not to contact you or anyone else outside, he won't."

"It can't be that bad," Calico said. "The guy isn't God."

"No, he's not," Jackie said. "But don't tell him that."

"What else can you tell us about the Continuum as a whole?" Pines said.

Jackie narrowed an eye at him. "You? Nothing."

"Me then," Calico said.

Jackie sighed. "It's not the barefoot, white-robed, hippie sort of thing you're probably picturing. It's kind of hard to explain. Mr. Lamont is an artist, you know? A visionary. Lofty stuff, from the way it's described. Way over my head. He calls it higher art infused and intertwined with spirituality. He doesn't put things online. You might find something pirated off a phone video recording or something, but it's not from Mr. Lamont. He only shows clips on rare occasions at unannounced and undisclosed locations. But somehow the word gets out and people show up. Celebrities even. I think they want to be associated with something avant-garde. Something bigger and brighter than the typical Hollywood movie mill. Then again, he also talks about the environment sometimes. The Hollywood set loves that. To tell you the truth, though, I suspect he might only do that to pull in money donors. I mean, his Santa Barbara place is huge. Then there's the helicopter and about a zillion cars. He's a regular Al Gore when it comes to carbon footprint. If he gets a sniffle, he even has a concierge doctor on retainer he flies in from Reno on a private jet. How into saving the environment can he be? But Mr. Lamont's a planner. Always a few moves ahead. So who knows?"

"I saw one of those pirated clips online," Monte said. "Bizarre stuff. It made no sense to me."

Jackie pulled off her glasses and wiped them with her hoodie. "Art is different things to different people. Eye of the beholder and all that. Mr. Lamont's mystery is a big part of his appeal."

"I still don't get it," Pines said. "The guy's a citizen like anyone else. He shouldn't be able to tell anyone who they can and can't be in contact with."

"It seems like we could go to the police now," Calico said. "Isn't this kidnapping somehow?"

"Is it? Or is Charlie there of his own free will?" Jackie said. "How can you know? I know what Mr. Lamont will say. Charlie too, if Mr. Lamont tells him to say it."

"We can still try," Calico said.

Jackie shrugged. "Seriously, what will you tell them? Your brother hasn't called? It's a free country. No law that says you have to report everything you do to your big sister. And besides that, I doubt you'd get much help from any authorities. At least around SoCal."

"Why not?" Monte said.

"Mr. Lamont has friends in high places. I mean other than celebrities."

"How high?"

"He took a phone call from the governor once when I was there. At least I'm pretty sure it was the governor. And I'll tell you this, Mr. Lamont was the alpha dog in the conversation."

"What do you suggest then?" Calico said.

"Honestly? Leave it alone. You know what he's doing now. And no one's going to hurt him or anything. That's all I wanted for you, to ease your mind. He'll call you eventually, right?"

"So, that it?" Monte said. "Sounds like the mystery's solved. Early, you two want to stick around for a day or two? We could show you the town."

Early watched Jackie, said nothing.

Lucinda pulled the magazine over and studied the photo.

"It's not right," Calico said. "I can feel it."

"Feel what?" Monte said.

"I don't know, but something."

Lucinda poked Monte, signed something, and pointed to the magazine.

Monte looked down at the ad, then nodded. "Lucinda doesn't think Charlie's acting in this picture. She thinks he's really suffering, and he's scared. I'd believe her too. Never known her once to be wrong about facial expressions and body language."

Pines stood. "I've heard enough."

"What are you thinking you're gonna do about it?" Monte said.

"I'm going to Santa Barbara to get Charlie."

"Waste of time," Jackie said.

"She might be right," Monte said. "It's private property. And these guys obviously don't want to be messed with."

"Or she might be wrong," Pines said.

"I'm not wrong," Jackie said. "Believe it or not."

"Either way, I'm gonna rattle Charlie out of that compound," Pines said.

"Sounds like we know what's next then," Calico said.

Jackie stood and pushed in her chair. She zipped up her hoodie. "I highly doubt that. Only Mr. Lamont knows what's next. It's like a rule of the universe. It sucks, but it's true. But, hey, you can keep the magazine." She glanced at Pines. "And maybe find a cooler traveling companion."

CHAPTER SIXTEEN

May 29—Several miles north of Earp's lost bullet

CHARLIE SIPPED AN ICED COFFEE—light ice, just the way he liked it—and took in the view from the window of his little cottage. Gold and green hills rolling down to the absolute perfect blue of the Pacific.

"Crazy how far that water goes, isn't it? Seriously, it blows my mind. All the way to China, right? Russia, Japan . . . Even Hawaii's like a trillion miles out there. Kind of freaks me out, all that water."

Isabella, the maid, smiled and nodded. Man, he dug that dimple in her cheek. Isabella hailed, as close as Charlie could tell, from Honduras and spoke somewhere between none and zero words of English. Which made her the perfect person for him to dump his thoughts on. And these days his brain was chock-full of thoughts. He was also, when he really considered it, sure he was more than a little in love with her. At least as in love as a guy could be after only a week or so of companionship with a person who spoke a completely different language.

He sipped again and gave an exaggerated satisfied sigh. "Anyway, like I was saying, I woke up in the desert, man. Not a soul around anywhere. Just a freaky robot dude and a backpack with some water and protein bars. And serious desert hot, you know? Honestly, I'm proud of how I handled the whole thing. I think a lot of people would've freaked if something like that happened to them, but I kept my cool. Stayed strong the whole time. I bet old Hammott didn't expect that."

He'd told her the story a dozen times. But she had no idea. And he liked getting it a little better with each telling. He'd probably write about it someday. Or somebody would. He'd found he liked to pronounce the name Hammott with a posh British flare. Mr. Lamont didn't have an accent, but Charlie had been working on his British lately, and the way Hammott rolled off his tongue made it an easy target. Plus he kinda hoped something in his cavalier-bordering-on-disrespectful attitude toward the man that was his host and Isabella's boss might break through the language barrier and impress her. She had to recognize the guy's name if nothing else. And he must've been right because Isabella smiled again. Man, that dimple.

Charlie finished the coffee, set the glass on the dresser for Isabella to collect when she got around to it, plopped on the freshly made bed, and laced his fingers behind his head. "You ever spent any time in the desert? I grew up there, so I knew how to handle myself. *Survivor* stuff and all that. You've probably seen that kinda thing on TV, huh?"

Isabella gave her usual *no comprende* shrug.

"Exactly. So I knew from experience I needed to save my energy. In the desert, keeping your head can make the diff between life and death and all that. So, I got up and started moving, little *Freaky Friday* robot tagging along behind me the whole time like he was scared I was gonna leave him. Figured I'd eventually hit a road. Guess again, man. Nothing, nada, zilch. Sun started going down, so I made camp. You're probably thinking *snakes,* right? They don't like fire, so I made one out of rubbing sticks together. You know what? I grew up with desert stars, but I've never, *never,* seen anything like that sky. Like it was alive or something. Wild sunrise too. Red, orange, a couple of stars still hanging up there. Walked most of that day, still no road. And then I saw the building. A snack bar, can you believe it? Out there all by itself. Crazy Hammott, right?"

Another shrug and dimple.

"And then the kid behind the counter. Full-on vintage. I ate like two whole pizzas and drank a gallon of everything cold they had. Felt like I'd died and gone to heaven, thinking the whole time I'd gone to hell. Then this huge helicopter drops out of nowhere and guess who? Yup, our dear old boss, all smiles and how-are-yous and you-passed-the-tests. Crazy Hammott"—British accent again—"drugs my beer and I wind up in the middle of nowhere. Ha! Crazy Hammott. He said I could call him that, by the way. I mean, I guess the dude's some kind of genius. Knew what he needed to see in a screen test. I had no idea that's what it was, but he dug it and I got the part. Probably because I know the desert and all that." Charlie rolled up onto an elbow. "Although I'm still waiting for a script and I've been sitting around this bungalow for a couple weeks. Probably gonna film in the desert. That'd make sense. But I'd like to get a look at that script. I think I'm kind of a method actor, you know?" This got him another dimple. "I need to prepare. Get myself way deep into the character. But it's developmental stuff, I guess. They're probably fine-tuning everything now that they've got their lead actor. Every film has to go through it."

Isabella straightened a towel on the rack, then moved toward the door.

Charlie stuck out his bottom lip. "You really got to go?"

Another shrug.

"I'm gonna miss you. Don't forget the cup on the dresser."

She smiled again and left the cup. When the door closed behind her, Charlie laid back, stared at the ceiling for a while. He'd fought the whole Hammott thing at first, but then there was the helicopter ride back. With champagne, man. Hammott was a smooth dude, top to bottom. And now here Charlie was in a private bungalow looking down at the ocean with a personal maid and everything he could ever want and a leading part in a film on top of it. And the cherry on the cake—he was pretty sure Roxy Parsons didn't have a clue what had happened to him. Well, old Roxy could drop dead. What could he do now? Hammott Lamont had a *private helicopter*, man. A big one. Guys with stuff like that were untouchable. And Charlie was all safely tucked up in Hammott Lamont paradise, wherever that was.

A knock at the door. It swung open and, speak of the devil, Hammott poked his head in. "You decent, Charles?"

Charlie grinned. "Not usually, Hammott." No accent this time.

"A joke. Good man. I came out for the day. Thought I'd check in on you. Plus I've got something to show you."

Charlie sat up. "Yeah? The script?"

Hammott tossed a magazine onto the bed. A paper clip held it open to a specific page. "Better than a script. Recognize anyone?"

"Are you kidding? Is that me?"

"Great shot, don't you think?"

"Is that from your midget robot?"

"That 'midget robot' cost twice as much as most people's houses, Charles. But, yes, it's a shot from the CD10000. The light was perfect. We released this a few days ago."

Charlie examined the page. "I've been thinking about my sister. She's kinda my only family, you know? Probably freaking out. I'd love to show her this. Maybe send her a pic? I don't have to talk or anything."

"We've been over this. No contact with anyone whatsoever. For the project. But it won't be long."

"All right . . . yeah. Wow, this is really happening, isn't it?"

"Oh, it's happening, Charles. It's definitely happening. We'll change the world together, you and I. This film will be perfection. And nothing must stop it."

"Cool, man. When can I see the script?"

"Are you familiar with Orson Welles's work, Charles? Have I asked you before?"

Only about eighty times. "Not really, but he was a genius, yeah?"

"He was a great filmmaker, yes. His last attempt, *The Other Side of the Wind*, might have been a masterpiece had it ever been released. Oh, yes, they've put it out now on streaming sites, but not his own edits. Glorified smut, really. Not his final voice. No, the system would never allow that. Because that's what the system always does with true genius, with real vision, do you understand? But we, Charles, we're different.

We haven't made the same mistake Welles made. We aren't owned, you see. And don't owe anything to anybody. We're free, Charles. Above the fray, if you will. The studios are stuck in a never-ending cycle of pandering to the masses. What happened to art, Charles? What happened to da Vinci? Where is our Beethoven today? Our Hemingway? Our Proust? Our *Welles*? Where, for that matter, is our Christ? I'll tell you where: they're recording their music in bedrooms for no one to hear. They're self-publishing and losing their souls to the white noise of the internet. They're making home movies on iPhones because that's the only outlet available to them! They are at best scoffed at and at worst ignored. But not us, Charles. No watered-down scripts required to get greenlit by the studios. We are the captains of our own ship, my boy. And we will create greatness together."

Charlie sat riveted and not a little stunned by this speech. Hemingway sounded vaguely familiar. Da Vinci as well. Proust he'd never heard of at all. Still, the names and the passion Hammott said them with . . . It all gave Charlie wings. Plus he'd seen the clip at the Roosevelt. He'd flown. Here was something great. Something bigger. And Charlie had never been bigger before. He shook his head. "Man, Hammott. When do we start shooting? What do I need to do?"

"Do? You're doing it, Charles. Stay out of sight. Build the mystery. Relax, enjoy, be merry. I'll let you know."

Charlie nodded with sincere seriousness. "Be merry. Relax. You got it. I'm actually kind of an expert."

"I know you are, Charles." Hammott tapped the magazine. "Everything, boy. It will be *everything*."

CHAPTER SEVENTEEN

THE 101 FREEWAY—A TRUE piece of California Americana. Sun-drenched by day, moon-drenched by night, it's been the inspiration for movies, songs, and innumerable hippie road trips. It's hosted James Dean's Porsche, O. J.'s Bronco, and billions of other metal boxes stuffed full of souls.

And today, a 1972 Chevy truck with Arizona plates.

Early and Calico drove north. Leaving behind the eye-shadow sky and inversion-layer stink of the LA basin, they wound through city and suburb before dropping down the steep grade from outlying Newbury Park toward Camarillo. The buildings thinned and the sky cleared. Here and there, strawberry fields edged the road. The air became cooler, tinged with the thick tang of ocean salt. Twenty miles later, just past the coastal city of Ventura, the Pacific pressed in. A seagull tracked along with them for a few seconds then veered off. A few scattered surfers bobbed on the water. On the right, the hills shone brown and gold in the California sun and a stiff ocean breeze rippled the chaparral. The landscape stayed close to the same for almost another half hour. Then oaks thickened and the nav system announced their impending exit.

Montecito, a Santa Barbara suburb, proved to be a hillside community made up of, as far as Early could tell, hedges, towering oaks, thick walls, and the occasional glimpse of impressive Spanish architecture.

"Wow," Calico said. "If Charlie's here somewhere, he's not slumming, is he?"

"Montecito. Home of the rich and famous."

"You've been here before?"

"Not here exactly, but Santa Barbara, yeah. Decent rodeo. Montecito's kinda Santa Barbara's rich aunt, from what I remember. Connected but not connected at the same time."

Calico put her hand out the window, palm open to the wind. She leaned back, eyes closed, and breathed deep.

"You all right?" Early said.

"I'm nervous. It's stupid. I don't even know why."

Early studied her profile, which brought on a few nerves of his own. "Because you care. And don't stop. Baptist's orders."

Calico saluted. "Aye, aye, Reverend Pines."

They wound through tree-lined streets, higher and higher up the mountain, until the nav system ordered a hard left between a couple of towering eucalyptuses and they found themselves on a narrow, paved lane.

"I never would've seen this," Early said. "Not even a sign."

"Jackie wasn't kidding the guy likes his privacy."

Before long, they broke out of the trees. Brown brush spread in both directions. Occasional oaks in the distance. A few miles later, the lane ended at a wide gate, the robotic woman on the nav announcing with cheerful optimism that they'd arrived at their destination.

Early looked back over his shoulder. Far below the Pacific stretched to an endless horizon. "Wow."

"I've never seen another view like this," Calico said.

"I don't think there is another view like this."

Beyond the gate, a brick road, split down the middle by a manicured berm, curved into the distance, but no building could be seen. Early leaned out of his window and pushed a button beneath a speaker set into a solid granite post.

"Welcome to the Continuum." The woman's voice sounded young. "What can I do for you?"

"We'd like to see Charlie Foster."

"I'm sorry, there's no one here by that name, sir."

"*Charles* Foster, then."

A long pause, then, "I'm not authorized to allow compound visits, sir. I'm sorry."

"So he's here?"

A longer pause. "Again, I'm very sorry. That's privileged information. And even if it weren't, visits and tours aren't being allowed at this time."

Calico leaned over. Early felt the heat of her body against his arm. "My name is Calico Foster. I'm Charlie's—"

"Yes, Miss Foster, I know who you are. But still, what you're asking can't happen. It's impossible to see any of our members at the moment."

"Excuse me? How do you know who I am?"

"I'm really very sorry. That's all I can say. But please, have a nice day."

"Can we speak to someone in charge?" Early said.

After several seconds of no reply, Early pressed the button again.

"Yes?"

"Look, clearly Charlie's here. We're going to speak with him whether you like it or not. We're not leaving until we do."

Slight static, then, "None of our members are available at this time. I'm sorry. Now please—"

"No," Early interrupted. "I don't want to have a nice day. I want you to put Charlie on and let him tell us himself he doesn't want to talk to his sister."

"I'm not authorized to let that happen, sir. Please drive safely on your way back down the hill."

"Wait." Early reached for his billfold and badge. "I'm a detective, and I'd—"

"Detective Early Pines. Paradise Police Department in Arizona. Yes. Please leave immediately or I'll have to call security. And I really don't want to do that. I'd hate it, in fact. We're a peaceful facility."

"How do you know who we are?" Early said.

The speaker stayed mute.

"What now?" Calico whispered.

Early shook his head. "Who are these people, the CIA? This is crazy." He opened his door and slid out of the truck. Punched the button. "Hey, let me talk to Hammott Lamont. Right now."

A bird fluttered in the brush.

Early pushed again. "Hammott Lamont. Now."

"Pines, look," Calico said.

From the other side of the gate, a van approached. Light blue and sparkling clean, *Security* on the side. It pulled to a stop at the still-closed gate. The door opened and a man climbed out. Khaki shorts and a golf shirt the same color as the van. Not your usual tough-guy-security type. Early had known plenty over the years, most ex-military. This guy looked to be maybe in his mid forties, average height, scruffy beard, thinning, longish sandy hair. Aging surfer rather than mercenary. He smiled a very crinkly, un-bouncer-like smile. "Can I help you folks?"

Early walked up to the gate. "Are you security?"

"Much as we got, I guess."

"Anybody ever tell you you're not all that intimidating?"

The man laughed. "We're not about violence at the Continuum, Detective Pines. The very opposite, in fact. I don't want any trouble." He reached through the bars of the gate and extended a hand. "I'm Wayne, by the way."

Early, caught a little off guard by the gesture, shook hands. "All right, Wayne, then you won't mind letting us in so Calico Foster can see her brother."

The smile never left the man's face. "Look, I'm not here to run you off. I mean, look at you, how could I? I'll tell you what I'm going to do. Let me see if I can get you in to see Mr. Lamont. It won't be for at least a week, but I think I can make it happen. I'm sure he'll be able to explain things better. Now, I wouldn't be able to do it if Miss Foster weren't Mr. Foster's sister, you understand. But since she's family, I'm betting we can work something out."

Early met the guy's grin. "That sounds great. Thing is, there's really nothing to work out. Miss Foster would like to see her brother right now, not in a week. So—and this is so simple it's beautiful—all you have to do is open this gate and take us to Charlie. Problem solved."

Sympathetic concern replaced Wayne's smile. "Man, detective, I wish I could help, I really do. But Mr. Lamont's the only one who can greenlight something like that, and like I said, I'll try to get to him as soon as I can. As you can imagine, he's incredibly busy."

The pickup door slammed, and Calico appeared at Early's side. She held out her hand. "Hey, Wayne. I'm Calico."

The guard took her hand. "Hi, Calico. Like I told the detective, I'll do what I can for you. I really will."

Calico nodded. "The thing is, Wayne—"

Tires crunched gravel behind them and Early turned. A sedan, police department insignia on the door.

An officer, not as tall as Early but with shoulders every bit as wide, got out and walked over. This one wasn't a smiler like Wayne. Early met him halfway, stopping by the tailgate of the pickup.

"Hey, Tony, thanks for stopping by," Wayne called from behind the closed gate. "No problem or anything, just some curious guests."

"Not guests," Early said. "Guests wouldn't be standing out here. This woman's brother is inside, officer. We'd like to speak to him. Make sure he's all right."

The man nodded. "Better get back in the truck and pull out, sir."

Early reached for his badge but the officer stopped him. "No need, Detective Pines. I've been informed who you are. And even if you weren't on mandatory leave, you'd still be way out of your jurisdiction. You know that. Please, just get back in the truck and move on." He held out a hand. "Officer Tony Peterson. I'm not here to give you a hard time. But cop to cop, the best thing would be for you to go, understand?"

Early looked the guy over. "How do all you people know who we are?"

"Please do what I tell you, detective. There are more patrol cars on the way, and trust me, you don't want to be here when they arrive. They won't be so accommodating."

Early shook his head. "Answer my question, Officer Peterson. How do you know me?"

The man took a half step forward. He spoke low enough not to be heard by Wayne. "Look, I understand your frustration, all right? And to tell you the truth, I one-hundred-percent respect your point of view. If it were my brother in there, I wouldn't be happy either. These guys, you know? But the lady will spend a night in jail just like you if you're still here when those other cars arrive. Mr. Lamont will make sure of it. He's very connected, I'm not kidding. The guy's no joke." He shot a glance toward Wayne. "Out of respect, I'm trying to give you a chance here."

Early looked at Calico, then back at the officer. "Jail for what?"

"Detective Pines," Wayne said, grinning again. "Better do as he says. We really don't want trouble. In the meantime, I'll see what I can do. I promise. With any luck, a week at the most. Maybe sooner."

"Put us in jail then," Calico said. "We haven't done anything but ask a couple questions. How will you explain that?"

Early stared at the guard, then pulled open the door and slid into the pickup. "C'mon, Calico."

"No! I don't care! I'll let him arrest me."

"I know. That's why I want you to get in the truck."

Her eyes flared and she started to argue, then closed her mouth and climbed in, shaking her head.

"You have my word, Miss Foster," Wayne called. "I'll figure something out with Mr. Lamont."

"Yeah? If you need us, we'll be the ones holding our breath," Calico said.

The officer pushed Early's door shut. Quiet again, he said, "Detective Pines, I hear you're a guy who doesn't mind bucking the odds. Likes it even. And it appears you have quite the bookend sidekick in Miss Foster. But listen, leave this alone. Your best bet is to head back to the desert, trust me. You can't win here. You've seriously got zero room to maneuver, understand?"

Early started the truck. "Officer Tony, the desert's hot right now.

I think I'll stick around. Enjoy the ocean breeze. Maybe have a little seafood."

The edges of the officer's mouth turned down. "I wish you wouldn't say that. Because if you do stick around, the next time we meet won't be good."

Early dropped the truck into gear. "No, it probably won't. But *bad* can mean a lot of things, Tony."

He swung the truck around. As he pulled away, in the rearview Wayne still stood there. And he still smiled.

"Did he just call me a sidekick?" Calico said.

"Yup." Early hit the gas and headed down the hill.

CHAPTER EIGHTEEN

FROM THE FLOOR-TO-CEILING WINDOW OF the private penthouse apartment in downtown Los Angeles, Hammott Lamont looked down on the hunting ground. Downtown to Burbank to Beverly Hills and beyond. An endless metropolitan savanna, predators padding through concrete canyons, prey shuffling with numb repetition along their well-worn trails. They called it the City of Angels but there were devils here too. Angels and devils and God and tissue and bone all boiling in a massive cauldron of smog and beauty and art.

Hammott loved every square inch of it.

After all, what could be better than a coming together of the filthy human and the glorious divine? Most often a messy proposition, yes. But art at its best was always messy. There was tremendous beauty in the cacophony if you knew how to see it. Violence, for instance, could be lovely. And love violent. Take Shakespeare's *Romeo and Juliet.* Or Welles's *The Immortal Story.*

Yes, there was beauty down there. You only had to look. Had to have vision.

He put his hands against the glass, spread his fingers. Hands fascinated him. Capable of so many things. The full spectrum from loving caress to flat-out disturbing hurt. He'd never met his mother, had no idea what genetic attributes he'd inherited from her, but he had his father's hands. Long fingers. Strong. He shuddered and smiled.

Hammott remembered his father's hands perfectly. What they

looked like lighting a cigar, unlocking a door, reprimanding a maid, pulling his belt when Hammott made the mistake of being heard as well as seen. They were whiskey and violence and smoke. His father had been a force of nature, a tornado. Something to be both studied from a distance and avoided.

Still, in a way, his father had been instrumental the day the world had changed. Hammott's thirteenth birthday. He'd spent the morning mostly alone in his room, then walked down to the beach and swam in the afternoon. But that evening the summons came. He'd entered his father's study on trembling legs, dried wet palms on his pants. His father had nodded at him. Then, of all things, he invited Hammott to take a seat on the deep leather couch. Then poured him his very first glass of whiskey which Hammott choked on, said happy birthday, switched on the big television set built into the bookshelf to *Three's Company*, then disappeared with one of the maids.

Alone in his father's world for the first time, Hammott hadn't had a clue what to do. He had no interest at all in cheesy sitcoms, so he'd rifled through his father's VCR collection. He had plenty of time. With that particular maid, his father would be hours. A tape caught his eye. Mostly black-and-white cover. A man at a podium, something powerful about him. Another man's mustached face massive on a wall behind him. The title of the picture bold, red, and—for a reason Hammott couldn't explain at the time but later came to realize had been the very voice of the universe calling—irresistible.

Citizen Kane.

Hammott removed the tape from the cover, pushed it into the VCR player, and tried another sip of whiskey.

And then . . . *everything.*

Orson Welles's *Citizen Kane* in all its glory—one hour and fifty-nine minutes that forever changed Hammott's life.

Ironically, his father died on that very same couch watching *Charlie's Angels* before Hammott saw thirteen years and one week. But the loss hadn't mattered one whit. The stars had already shifted. Planets had aligned. Orson Welles, with his brilliant floor shots, his hard lighting, his flow-of-consciousness approach to story and art and life, had made sure nothing in Hammott's world would ever be the same. That night, numbed by whiskey and attention, baptized in wondrous black and white, Hammott Lamont had not only known what he wanted to do with his existence but who he was destined to be.

Hammott watched and studied everything Welles had filmed or worked on a hundred times over. Memorized every interview, book, and commentary on the director's life and work. Through Welles, Hammott first understood the freedom an outsider possessed. He gained the confidence to walk above the common man. He made his first attempts at films in high school. Generic trash, really. Psuedo-artistic dribbles and dreams. But a person had to start somewhere. UCLA film school was the next rung on the ladder, though he knew Welles would never have approved. And he would have been right. UCLA, as it turned out, had no interest in real art. The classes were bland, two-dimensional, colorless, mute.

So he dropped out. Then, free of convention and expectation—and flush with trust money—he set to work writing, scripting, and shooting a film about a sculptor who falls in love with his model, a woman twice his age. He rented equipment and hired a crew—cameras, operators, actors, runners. Once he rented an entire hotel to get one shot. But why not? It had to be right. In hindsight, he'd gotten excited, carried away. But hadn't Orson done the same more times than not? The world would see Hammott's brilliance. His star would rise high and burn bright.

Six months later he screened his masterpiece for the public—all fifty-three of them who bothered to show up, twenty-two if you didn't count cast and crew—in a little Santa Monica playhouse on an autumn night thick with Pacific Ocean mist.

Like the fog outside, like the world it blanketed, the reaction was bland, colorless, mute.

And the worst part—they were right.

It took months to admit it. Hammott had fumed, blamed, pointed fingers. But, in the end, all fingers pointed right back at him. There was no escaping it. His inexperience, combined with his eighteen-year-old ego, had produced a pretentious piece of very expensive refuse. But it wasn't the fact that the film was bad that bothered him so much. Bad he could have handled. No, what cut him to the bone was that it was inconsequential. Nothing. Forgotten even as those first viewers walked out of the theater.

On top of it all, the project nearly drained his trust fund. Now he was both broke and unimportant. Two things that were unacceptable. But hadn't Orson been the same? Always on the fringe, like most geniuses. Hollywood's pockets had closed. So he'd made his own way. And in doing so, maintained his integrity in a landscape awash with mediocrity.

Hammott determined in his mind to learn from Orson's example.

As the universe would have it, it turned out he had a particular and peculiar knack for making money. It was like art: one simply had to think outside the box. He realized immediately the power of "cause." The common masses were made up of seven and a half billion suckers. A small nonprofit to help the homeless addicts downtown quickly became a cash cow. The right place at the right time and a suggestion—some might have called it blackmail had they known the details, and were it not serving higher art—brought a rising actress and her very famous and very still-married costar amour to help pass out meals on Thanksgiving Day. The press went wild. Money poured. After that, a string of similar enterprises took him to New York, Philadelphia, Kansas City—almost wound up in prison that time, Midwesterners have so little imagination—Miami, and eventually back to Los Angeles and civilization.

Then, with more money than he could spend, Hammott started making art again. *Real* art. He cultured connections. Built mystique. Gained traction. Even more money. Made some films. Played, created, experimented.

And now, at last, it was time. This piece would be the jewel in his crown. It would be what art had cried out to be from that first day the stars had sung.

Maybe it had been the ghost of Welles who had brought Charles Foster. Hammott liked the thought. But then again, this was bigger than even Orson. Call it fate, God, karma—Charles had been delivered. No doubt about it, this was meant to be.

And now, though Hammott wasn't yet sure how they fit into the piece as a whole, Early Pines and Calico Foster. A surprise, yes, but not an unwelcome one. He'd known about their search within minutes of Monte Shaw's phone call. Nothing escaped his attention, especially anything to do with Charles and the project. Early Pines, with his mouth and temper—Hammott's research department was as thorough as it was quick—had real possibility. The man had punched his own father, knocked him out in plain and public sight right on the sidewalk. Explosively predictable—beautiful colors to paint with, and Hammott was already making strokes on his mind's canvas. Calico was sharp and reportedly beautiful, though pictures had been hard to come by. The universe had left her as a bit of a mystery, but her purpose would no doubt unfold.

Anyway, as tempting as it might be, it was nonproductive to formulate too early. After all, true art had to remain fluid. Always fluid. It couldn't—shouldn't—be boxed or contained. The universe wouldn't have it. When she brought you players, you let them play. And, best of all, you played with them. No doubt more would come to light when he sat down with them. Face-to-face he could pluck their soul-strings, listen to the sound, tune what needed to be tuned.

Hammott let his hands drop to his sides. A trash truck worked its way along the street below. Its operators no bigger than sand fleas from up here. In the building across the street, someone watched TV, their apartment window shimmering with anesthetized blue delusion. A beautiful night. Even some stars poking through the cloud layer. Later he'd head up to the roof and watch the planes on the flight path in and out of LAX. The meaningless and blind comings and goings of the simple, common souls always calmed him.

He picked up his whiskey glass off the credenza and sipped, then slipped his phone from his pocket. He started to dial, then stopped.

No, not quite yet. Let them wait. Let them wonder. Let it build. Maybe later, up on the roof.

He smiled at himself in the window, sipped whiskey, didn't choke.

Because he was an artist.

A *real* artist.

His father could rot in hell.

Orson would have been proud.

CHAPTER NINETEEN

Monte had a buddy who owned a block of apartments across from the beach in Santa Barbara, and in exchange for a couple of Monte's almost-never-miss horse racing tips, he'd agreed to rent Early and Calico a vacant two-bedroom unit cheap for a few days.

Calico stood, arms crossed, in the middle of the living room squinting at the wallpaper. "What's that pattern, do you think?"

"Retro beach maybe? I can't tell. Kinda gives me a headache. Price is right, though."

She closed one eye. "You know what it makes me think of? Those posters that they used to have that looked like nothing at first but if you stare long enough you start to see something. You remember those?"

"Yeah. I won one at a fair once popping balloons with darts. Yuma, Arizona."

"Who was the lucky girl?"

"Who said anything about a girl?"

"You remember the exact town. And guys don't throw darts at balloons unless there's a girl. Everybody knows that."

"Baptists might."

"Not even Baptists."

"She was a rodeo queen, if you have to know."

"Wow, you sound so proud."

"You asked."

"Then again, why wouldn't you be proud? Not every Joe Schmo gets to date royalty."

"She might've been second runner-up to the rodeo queen. Maybe third. And I'm pretty sure she tossed the poster as soon as I dropped her off. Saw her again the following year and she acted like she didn't know me."

"Broke your heart?"

"I cried for a full minute or two."

"I doubt that." She took a step back, staring at the wall. "I don't see anything. Wait, maybe a dinosaur?"

Early looked around. "I have to hand it to Monte, the place isn't bad."

Calico flopped onto an overstuffed couch. "You shouldn't have made me get in the truck, Pines."

"Have we not gone over this fifty times already? Get over it."

"He called me a sidekick. I can't get over it."

"Besides, I didn't make you get in the truck. You didn't want to go to jail and you know it."

She opened her mouth to reply but sighed instead. "All right, I didn't want to go to jail. But that stupid cop didn't need to know that."

"I think he was duly impressed by your tenacity. How about you let it go now and stare at the wallpaper."

"What if I don't want to let it go?"

"You're mouthy for a sidekick, you know that?"

"Shut up, Pines." She laughed a little and it warmed him. She stood, crossed the room, and slid open the patio door. "Man, check this out." The black bulk of the Pacific lay beyond the road and wide beach. Anchor lights bobbed. An oil rig shone in the distance. She stepped out and sank into one of the two chairs crowding the tiny deck. Early followed and took the other. To the right, a pier stretched seaward, bright beneath the starless sky. Strings of lights sent shimmering trails across the water. Thin surf out past the traffic noise.

Early propped his boots up on the rail and leaned back. "I bet we missed a million-dollar sunset from here tonight."

"The beach actually faces south. I saw it on the nav."

Early squinted off to his right, what he figured to be west.

"I read somewhere once that sunsets are God's finger paintings," Calico said. "I always kinda liked that."

"Uh-huh."

She surveyed him. "What?"

"What, what?"

"Something's bugging you, I can see it."

"Nope. I'm good."

"C'mon, Pines. We'll have a moment together."

"Sarcasm. Great."

"Relax, man. What are you thinking about?"

"You gonna keep bugging me?"

"Absolutely."

"My friend Gomez Gomez said he could hear Venus singing. And he could hear the sun crossing the sky."

"That's weird."

"Yeah, pretty weird."

"And that's what's bugging you?"

"When I say this, you're gonna want to run back to One Horse."

"Half the time I already want to run back to One Horse, so spill."

"I can hear the sun too."

She stared at him.

"Ready to run?"

"I don't know. You can hear the sun as in you're crazy and might kill me in my sleep, or you can hear the sun as in, man, this guy is really a sensitive soul and needs a buddy right now?"

He laughed. "Neither, I hope. I just hear the thing. It drives me nuts."

"Okay, what does it sound like?"

"Like somebody's dragging a sack of gravel the size of a house over a flat rock. It scrapes and moans. So, yeah, I'm probably crazy."

"There are a lot of things out there we don't understand. They don't make us crazy. Maybe they're God's way of letting us know we're not really in control of things no matter how much we think we are."

"Sounds like true believer stuff."

"Is there another kind?"

"Gomez Gomez used to call himself an imperfect believer. There's that kind, I guess. Fits me better."

"We're all imperfect believers, Pines."

"Some more imperfect than others."

"Uh-huh. You know, on that note, I've been thinking about something."

"Yeah?"

"That God's not Lee."

This stopped him. "What's that supposed to mean?"

"That's what's going on with you, right? You want God to keep himself to the other side of the street."

"I don't think God is Lee."

"Don't you?"

Early put his hat back on. Scratched his neck, fishing for the right words. Came up empty.

"Anyway, I bet that's what Jake would say," Calico said.

"Guy's not even here and he's preaching to me."

"It's a good point, though. I'm a little proud of it."

"Gomez Gomez tried believing, look where it got him."

"Out of pain and reunited with the woman he loves?"

"I guess, if that's your perspective."

"I like that perspective. At least better than yours."

"I'm no Gomez Gomez. And I'm definitely no Jake."

"Nobody's perfect, Pines. Not even Saint Jake."

"Okay, you win. Let's go stare at the wallpaper again."

She laughed, soft in the night. "Early Pines, signing off. Kiss my backside, world, I'm Baptist."

A car honked below. An acoustic guitar played somewhere. Far out on the water, past the oil rig, lights from a passing tanker winked.

"Listen," Early said. "Today was a bust. But we'll get to Charlie, all right?"

Calico pulled her legs up and wrapped her arms around them, eyes fixed on the invisible horizon, or maybe the tanker. "Not a bust. We did something, at least. We tried. I just wanted to talk to him before I went home."

"It'll happen if I have to kick that gate down myself."

Their faces were shadowed. He wished he could see her.

"I can actually picture you doing that."

"And you'd be first through the hole."

"You bet I would."

"I've done worse things. Don't forget, I'm an ugly drunk."

"But beautiful sober," she said.

He pulled a boot back and rested his ankle on his knee. "It's not fair to tease a Baptist in love, you know that?"

"Things just come out of your mouth, don't they? You forgetting about our deal?"

"How can I when you won't let me forget? But you started it with that beautiful-sober comment."

Calico stood. "You know what? I feel like walking for a while. Is that okay?"

"Alone?"

"I don't know, will you leave the hat?" When he hesitated, she shook her head. "Geez, Pines, I'm kidding. Come on."

With little discussion and no particular destination in mind, they drifted toward, and then out onto, the pier. Cloud cover hung low enough to touch. A car drove past, shaking the thick timber planks. Early leaned on the rail and watched the waves wash the sand below. Calico did the same, harbor lights illuminating her features. He'd been more than half serious earlier: he'd happily kick down those compound gates if it would bring her even a little peace.

He spoke silently to the ocean and the clouds and the night. *I don't know if you hear me up there, man. If you can, don't hang up. I know you and I aren't gonna sit down and have beers together, even if I still drank. But this one here, she's different. If you care about her at all, help her out. I don't mind doing the heavy lifting. Just a little direction, that's all. Thanks.*

"What are you thinking?" Calico said.

He eased back from the rail. "Probably nothing that'll do anybody any good."

In his pocket, his cell buzzed. He pulled it out. Matthias, his boss. He sighed, thumbed the screen, and lifted the phone to his ear. "Hey, Matthias, what's happening?"

The NYC in the chief's accent had a way of growing in equal parts with his irritation. "You tell me, Early. What in the world are you doing in Santa Barbara? I thought you were here hermiting in the desert."

Early glanced at Calico. "I'm helping a friend. How do you know where I am?"

"Listen, detective, you have no official capacity out there, you understand that? Zero. And California's a delicate and fragile place. Guy like you is very likely to break something."

"I have no official capacity here, yeah. Then again, I have no official capacity there at the moment either."

Matthias's voice rose. "Look, I know you have a beef with your old man, all right? I get it. And I'm working on it. Because—and I hate to admit this, especially to you—you're the best guy I've got and I'd very much like you back on the job. But you're not helping the situation by going outside your jurisdiction a few hundred miles and bothering people with your extremely big and obnoxious mouth."

"I get it, I'm outside of my jurisdiction."

"Then why are you showing your badge?"

"Who've you been talking to?"

"I have bosses too. Listen, you're poking hives out there. And I know you, poking is only the beginning. You won't be satisfied until you knock the thing out of the tree and step on it. Do everyone a favor, especially yourself and your 'friend,' and get back in your truck and come home. That's an order, detective."

"Is my leave over?"

"You know it isn't."

"Then I'm gonna stay here a little longer."

"How long?"

"As long as it takes. I'm helping look for a missing brother."

"I know what you're doing. Miss Foster's brother isn't missing, he's making a movie. So all you're doing is being annoying and making a mess for me."

"Yeah, he's supposedly making a movie, but—"

"I didn't call to argue. I said get back here. Now."

Early pushed his temper down. "I'm on leave, man. That's your choice, not mine. It's my own time and it's a wide-open, free country."

"Wrong, Pines. Your time is what I say it is. You're bothering people. And it's been made very clear to me these are people who don't like to be bothered."

"So? When has that stopped me before? When has it stopped you either?"

"Look, man, you're swimming in the deep end. And I have a strong feeling being big, mean, and slightly whacked in the head isn't going to keep you from floating belly up out there or getting eaten altogether. I'm not going to say this twice, so listen carefully—this could absolutely mean your job. Permanently."

Early looked at Calico again. "These people aren't the only ones who've had their cage rattled. They're doing their share of rattling too. I'm gonna finish what I need to finish."

There was quiet on the line for a few beats. "As a friend as well as your boss, I'm telling you you're in over your head. Just come home and whatever's going on, I promise we'll figure it out."

"I'm not running away with my tail between my legs because some rich guy knows the governor."

"Early—"

"I gotta go."

"Yeah, you gotta go."

"What did you think I'd do?"

Matthias sighed. "Exactly what you're doing. But I had to try. This time it's going to hurt when you land. You need to know that."

"Maybe."

"Not maybe. Definitely. Your friend, she's worth it?"

"Yeah, she is."

"Then God help you, and God help California."

"Adios, Matthias."

"I can't promise your job, you understand that?"

"You weren't gonna say it twice, remember?"

"You're out of your mind, but what's new?"

"Probably."

"See you when I see you then."

"See you." Early thumbed off.

"Your boss?" Calico said.

"Guy can't live without me."

"You're in trouble for this, aren't you?"

"That's my business, not yours."

"Wrong. It's very much my business."

"Those people pushed me today. I'm not going anywhere."

"Don't be thickheaded, Pines."

"You're about thirty years too late to tell me that."

His phone vibrated again. "Did I not make myself clear to him?" Not Matthias, though. A blocked number. Early put the phone to his ear. "Yeah?"

"Detective Pines? Hammott Lamont here."

"As I live and breathe, the man himself."

"I'd like you to do something for me."

"Yeah? What's that?"

"Go away. Leave my actor and my film alone. Will you do that?"

"Wow, not even a please?"

"All right, *please* go away."

"Tell you what, that's up to you. Miss Foster only wants to speak with her brother. Do we see Charlie or not?"

A pause. "If I say no?"

"Don't say no."

"You're a stubborn man, aren't you?"

"You have no idea."

"Oh, I think I do. I'll tell you what, why don't we meet? The three of us. We'll talk about it."

CHAPTER TWENTY

MORNING SUN REFLECTED OFF THE water. Palms swayed and shook above the Santa Barbara Harbor parking lot, pushed by a hot offshore wind. Early threw the truck into park and swung his door open. "Man, so much for cool ocean breezes, huh?"

Calico pushed her hair from her face. "No kidding. We might as well be back in the desert. I wish he wanted to meet at the compound. After they ran us off, I'm seriously curious about that place."

"So am I, but we'll see what happens here. At least we'll get a feel for Lamont."

"And see Charlie?"

"From the way Lamont sounded, I'm not holding my breath."

"Then what?"

"Planning is overrated."

"Said nobody but you, ever."

"Thing is, sometimes when a bull starts breaking china, things start to happen."

"And sometimes he winds up as barbecue."

"There's always kicking the gates down."

"Good to have a backup plan."

They walked along the harbor's edge. Out on the docks, a diver dropped into the water, bubbles forming above him as he started cleaning the hull of a sailboat. A long, sleek coast guard cutter lay at ease, crewmen scrubbing down her decks. A commercial fisherman backed his boat into a slip with the slow, practiced ease of long repetition. The air thick with ocean and fried fish and diesel. Up ahead, a wave crashed against the far side of a stone breakwater, throwing saltwater rainbows into the morning air.

At length they turned left down a ramp, passed through a gate leading out onto the docks, and followed the main causeway. Several smaller docks jutted off on either side. The sky spread out, cloudless and bright. Seabirds wheeled and dipped. Hundreds of tall masts reflected sun. A buoy clanged out in the channel.

At the end of the causeway, Early pointed out a large boat, maybe eighty feet long, brilliant white and chrome with an occasional teak accent. "Looks like the one."

Magic Trick, the yacht Lamont had described, was berthed on an end slip, tugging gently against its lines in the wind. Wayne, Lamont's little security man, stood on the deck at the top of a set of stairs. Today he wore a light-blue madras shirt, baggy shorts, and worn deck shoes, his thin hair standing at windblown attention.

"Detective Pines, Miss Foster, so glad you could come. Mr. Lamont's eager to meet you." Wayne noticed Early taking in the craft. "You like it? Eight-five feet, stem to stern. Custom made for Mr. Lamont by a private builder outside of Athens, Greece. It was delivered earlier this year."

"Uh-huh. Nice boat," Early said.

"Yes," a voice cut in. "A magnificent craft. We are richly and truly blessed."

A man who could only be Hammott Lamont emerged onto the upper deck and leaned over the rail. White linen suit. White shoes. Small, round sunglasses hid his eyes. He was a big, heavy man. Nose too small for his face. Hair combed straight back. A thick beard that couldn't quite hide sagging jowls.

"Detective Pines and the extraordinarily lovely Miss Foster, sister of my new lead." He turned to a woman standing next to him. "Liz, will you bring us some drinks to start, please?"

Early glanced at Calico as they climbed aboard and followed Lamont up a curved staircase to a wide aft deck. Calico's mouth was tight, posture stiff.

A table, complete with fresh flowers, centered the space. Lamont pulled out a chair for Calico. "Miss Foster, you sit here please." He pushed the chair in for her as she sat, then indicated another. "Detective, you there, if you will."

Early lowered himself. *Guy definitely likes to direct.*

Lamont seated himself. "What a day, isn't it?" He spread his arms. "So, my new friends, I'm glad you're here. How are we today?"

Early plucked a grape from the fruit bowl and popped it in his mouth. "Well, Hammott, if you must know, I suppose we're a little put out at being stonewalled and escorted away from your compound by a police officer. How are you?"

Lamont leaned forward on his forearms. "Detective, compounds by nature are very private places. You have to understand that."

Early shrugged. "Our request was straightforward. All we wanted to do was talk to Charlie Foster, not toilet paper your office. What's the problem?"

Lamont frowned. "Straight talk. All right. I want my property to be peaceful and the people who work for me to feel free from any threat. It simply wouldn't do to allow a man who knocked out his own father with no provocation onto the premises. As you can see, I'm a man who does his homework." His lenses shifted to Calico. "Miss Foster, unfortunately you've made a poor decision as far as companions go. Detective Pines's temper and violent tendencies are unchecked and well observed."

"I think I can decide for myself who my acquaintances are," Calico said.

"It strikes me," Early said, "that if you really believe these things about me, it might not be your best course of action to test me right out of the gate. You have the reputation of being a smart guy too. Or is that inaccurate?"

Lamont's laugh was sudden, as if Early's response both surprised and delighted him. "Really, detective? You make my day. Even better than I'd hoped for. Not more than a minute into our conversation and you threaten me. Yes, I've read the reports on you. Just because I didn't let you onto my compound doesn't mean I don't respect your methods, for lack of a better term. It must be exceedingly hard doing what you do. How can one 'protect and serve' the innocent against a world that's become increasingly violent and evil without stooping a little to that level oneself? Music is the language of angels, but violence the language of men. Am I correct?"

Early leaned back. "I'm sure you think you are. Then again, when you're sitting on your own yacht in a thousand-dollar suit snapping your fingers for drinks, you're naturally prone to have a very high opinion of your own opinion."

Lamont, still smiling, considered. "I do have a high opinion, I'll admit. But look, it's a new day. I've invited you onto my private yacht for drinks and conversation, haven't I? It seems that this should go a long way toward soothing your wounded pride over being turned away from the compound yesterday. What do you say we start fresh?"

"Fine," Calico said. "Mr. Lamont, please, where's Charlie?"

Liz came through a doorway, tray in hand.

"Just set it here, Liz," Lamont said. His eyes found Calico. "On the ship, I always prefer to serve my guests myself. So much less pretention, don't you think? Why stand on formality? It's a yacht after all—a place to have fun and relax." He took a glass from the tray and handed it to Calico. "Iced tea. Two sugars for you, I believe, Miss Foster. I have to tell you—forgive me—you're even more beautiful than Charles described. A real leading lady. Then again, a brother sees through a different lens, doesn't he? It's only natural."

Calico set her drink on the table. Her face went hard. "I've come a long way and it wasn't for small talk. It wasn't to be impressed with your toys or drinks or staff. I came to see my brother. Is he here or not?"

Lamont sipped from a whiskey glass, then pursed his lips. "Miss Foster, you're every bit as direct as Detective Pines, aren't you? That's interesting and a little surprising. I'll tell you what, we'll get to Charles, all right? But drinks first, please. We're civilized people, after all. Mexican

Coca-Cola for you, Detective Pines, correct? Unless you'd like something stronger? Our bar is extensive." He lifted his glass. "Personally, I'm partial to The Balvenie Fifty Year Scotch, arguably the best whiskey on the planet. Whiskey was your poison of choice once upon a time, wasn't it? One never really gets past that sort of thing. What is it they say? One day at a time?"

Early took the Coke and set it on the table. "Okay, you know all about us. You've made your point and we're impressed beyond belief. We have chills. Calico asked about her brother. Where is he?"

Lamont raised a brow. Early could picture the guy practicing the look in the mirror. "Yes, she did. And I didn't answer her, did I? Detective, what's with the hat? I mean, I do want to have a serious conversation, but . . ."

"Trust me, this is a very serious conversation."

Lamont sipped again, squinted at Early's hat. "You know, on second thought, I think I like it. It's a statement. Imagine, a man who can wear a hat like that but still gives the impression he'd tear your heart out with his bare hands for amusement. You are what in the film world we call a character, detective. Yes, I believe I love it actually. *Kiss Me, I'm Baptist* . . . perfectly brilliant."

"I'm glad I entertain you. Where is Charlie?"

Lamont's smile never faltered. "Right. Won't be deterred from the stated objective. And eager to engage. Exactly as reported. Excellent. Really excellent."

Early met the smile. "Keeping to the spirit of direct talk, it's only fair to let you know I'm having an intense and overwhelming urge to toss you over the rail."

Lamont chuckled. "I appreciate your candor, but I do weigh a little bit. You'd find it a challenge."

"Mr. Lamont," Calico said, "I'm worried about my brother. Surely you understand that."

Lamont leaned back and took off his sunglasses, accepted a small cloth from Liz, and began cleaning them. "Miss Foster, I understand your concern. I do. But Charles is fine."

"We have your word for that," Early said. "But we haven't even heard his voice. Enough is enough."

Lamont handed the cloth back to Liz, replaced the sunglasses, laced his fingers and steepled his thumbs. "*I've* heard his voice. Liz has heard his voice. It's an interesting saying, 'enough is enough.' In my experience enough is actually never enough. I learned that from studying Orson Welles. I've made a study of Welles a life practice. I'm afraid his influence saturates every area of my life whether I like to admit it or not. He was a genius, you know. The world is finally realizing it, though they kicked him to the curb enough times when he was alive. But when hasn't the world scoffed at true brilliance? If history teaches us anything, it's that it takes the average Joe a long time—decades, even generations—to catch up. Welles was an expansive man of voracious appetites, be it food, love, art, you name it. And so am I. As with anyone, there's always the inevitable need for more. So enough is really never enough. Am I wrong? Are you a fan of caviar, Calico? Do you mind if I call you Calico? I figure it's okay since Early here seems to think we're on a first-name basis. And I do love your name. It's so musical. I have some caviar on board, and I have the urge to splurge. Ah, a rhyme! Two hundred and fifty dollars an ounce the stuff costs. Can you imagine? For fish eggs? Liz, will you bring it out please?"

"Mr. Lamont . . ." Calico said.

Lamont sighed. "Charles, I know! I just would really like to get to know each other first. Is that too much to ask of guests? You don't see it now, but it's important. For Charles's sake, and the rest of us too. Tell me, what was it like growing up out there in the desert? All that space and silence? I envy you. I really do."

Calico's face flushed. "What exactly is your problem? Where's Charlie?"

"Please, humor me."

"Humor you? The desert is hot, okay? And envy me why? It looks to me like you're doing just fine, sitting here on your million-dollar boat eating gazillion-dollar caviar while you dodge my simple question."

"Please, let me explain something neither of you have grasped yet."

Lamont waved a hand around. "Miss Foster, all this, what is it? What value does it really have? Do you have any idea how much money I've accumulated? Did you know I once supplied three third-world countries with out-of-date US computer cabling technology I purchased for pennies on the dollar and sold for tens of dollars on the dollar? That enterprise alone netted over a billion dollars. A billion! Can you imagine? And it's only one of my little forays. I discreetly mention a polar bear, or a condor, and Hollywood can't throw cash at me fast enough. They have more than they need anyway. What I'm saying is the money part is easy if you have the slightest bit of imagination and a little backbone. But the money is only a means to an end. I don't care about any of it." He waved his hand again. "I don't care about this. It's nice, yes, but it's all fleeting. Chasing after the wind. What I care about is *art*. Only art is eternal. And my latest project, the one Charles is such an integral part of, has very much to do with the desert. The desert, you see, is symbolic in so many ways. The desert is where the children of Israel wandered for forty years. Where Jesus Christ was tempted. Where Peter Fonda tried in vain to work through his issues in Hopper's *Easy Rider*. And—you'll especially like this one, detective—where John the Baptist ate locusts and communed with God, although he didn't have a Baptist hat and I doubt very much anyone ever kissed him. I mean, think of the breath alone. Even Orson Welles himself retreated to the desert in the end for *The Other Side of the Wind*. The point is, Charles, the desert, me, we're all tied together—a multistrand cord. And it must not be broken, do you understand? Of course you do. You must."

"A billion dollars will buy a lot of desert," Early said. "If you love it so much, why are you sitting here on a yacht instead?"

Lamont shook his head. "The yacht, yes, it's one of my fleshly downfalls, I'm afraid. Still, it's not the physical land so much as the spirit, don't you see? *That's* where the art is. The desert represents our suffering, but also our growth. It's our hell and our salvation. It's our crucifixion and our rising up. Pain, suffering: they give birth to life! Ask any mother, they'll tell you. There must be death so that life can burst forth. I dream of the desert. And I don't mean in a wishful sense—I actually do own miles of it. I mean literally. I dream of the desert almost every night. I have for years."

"I honestly don't have any idea what you're talking about and I don't care," Calico said. "I just want to talk to Charlie."

Lamont's wet teeth reflected sunlight. "This is fun, isn't it?"

"Enough." Early said. "No more games."

Lamont's smile collapsed. "Ugh, why are you so boring, Early? There's that word again—*enough.* Although you're right in a way. The line between games and art can be very thin. Even imperceptible. But are you really this dense? I'd hoped for something more stimulating."

Early picked up his Coke. "I might be a little dense, yeah, if by dense you mean I've only listened to about every other word you've said since we stepped on this tub."

"Every other word . . . yes. Would you really throw me in the water?"

"Without hesitation and with joy."

A gust of wind whipped over the ship. Threw stiff ripples across the water below.

"You know, I believe you." Lamont looked out at the mountains beyond the city. "The Santa Anas, they call this wind. It's fascinating. It starts out in our desert. That's why it's so hot. In Arabia they call it a simoom. Did you know, in 1859, a US survey ship here in the channel recorded a Santa Ana wind temperature of 133 degrees? They say it came on so fast, the birds fell right out of the sky. Now there are some people who doubt the story—say it would be impossible for the temperature to climb that high here—but I believe the impossible is only impossible because of our human fear. I enjoy the impossible immensely! I mean, all this is a miracle if you consider. Picture it." He finished the last of his drink and held the empty glass up for Liz, who took it and replaced it with a full one. He sipped and nodded his approval. "Out there in some forgotten valley, God breathes. Can you see it? A tiny tendril of dust stirs from the floor of the desert. God imagines, and the tendril swirls and grows and pulls dust into its vortex. It circles and dips, picks up speed and strength and bits of tumbleweed. It chases a game trail across the valley floor. On and on it goes, bigger and bigger until it bursts into a full-fledged wind, spreads its arms, and tumbles up and over the mountains, bending trees, banging doors, dropping birds . . . It strips us, bares us, even scatters what's left of our lifeless ashes. Just like your friend, Gomez Gomez, eh? All because God let out a little breath. Because God wants it so. Do you believe in God, Detective Pines?"

"Don't talk about Gomez Gomez."

"Why not?"

"Because it's disrespectful and it angers me. Need more?"

"I was simply illustrating my point. Let me explain my little speech, even if you only heard every other word. There's a point to it, and Charles is involved. This wind, this boat, you, me, Miss Foster, everything is a miracle. A little piece of God's imagination. A billion little miracles all making up the Continuum. Do you see? And film, at its purest form, is the same. Because what film is is a million tiny pictures. Each the slightest bit different from the last. The differences aren't visible to the naked eye. But the pictures make up a whole. Every film has a beginning and an end. And so do we. Our life is only a film, yes? A series of a billion still shots, all connected to each other. People are like that too. Connected. Like you were, and still are, to your friend Gomez Gomez. And now you and I and Calico are connected also. As is Charles. We can't help it. I goad you a little and you want to lash out. To throw me over the rail. But there's no point. Even if you were to do it, which I highly doubt you could, what will be will be." Lamont's voice picked up cadence. "Please, follow me here. Every continuum must have a culmination. It's a rule of the universe. We can't control it any more than we can control the wind. Or space. Or Tasmanian devils. Your brother, Miss Foster, is chosen. He's going to play a part in the culmination of my greatest continuum. And to do this, he can't be distracted in any way. *In any way.* He must remain pure. That's why he hasn't been in contact with you. Or anyone else. Do you understand? He can't. This is too important."

"No, I don't understand," Calico said. "He's going to be in a movie, so what? I want to talk to him."

Lamont gave an emphatic shake of his head. "*Movie*, ugh, I hate that word! It's so . . . plebeian. You're not hearing what I'm saying, please. Charles has been *chosen*. He's been cast to play a part in what will be the most important film of my life. Of your lives. And not just a film. A mighty, mighty piece of art. *The* piece of art! One that will ring through the universe as long as time exists and even after. And no matter your opinion of art, or me, that is a monumental statement. What we're talking about here is a marriage between the flesh and the spirit. A melding of God and man. You need to understand this. This is not my decision. The universe has chosen me, and the universe has chosen Charles."

"And the universe happened to tell you all this?" Early said.

"Nothing can stop this, detective. Not even you in all your bull-headed arrogance. All of us, together, are standing on the edge of a precipice. And on this precipice, every little thing is important. Every moment. We must pay attention. This film will be beauty itself. You'll see in the end. You'll understand. You have to."

"Mr. Lamont, I only care about my brother," Calico said.

Lamont leaned forward. "And that's admirable. It is. Orson Welles once said, 'We're born alone, we live alone, we die alone. Only through our love and friendship can we create the illusion for a moment that we're not alone.'" His eyes shifted to Early. "But it's a need in me, this art of mine. You of all people, detective, should understand need, being an alcoholic. The overwhelming *must*. It soaks your body, doesn't it? Floods you. I wonder, do you feel it right now? I bet you do." He lifted his glass. "The Balvenie Fifty Year Scotch. Nearly fifty-thousand dollars a bottle. If the gods drink whiskey, they're passing around a bottle of the Balvenie Fifty Year. If that's not to your liking, I'm sure Liz can dig up something less sophisticated. Maybe some Wild Turkey? Or let's go lower, get down to Early Pines level. Ten High? Old Crow? Do you feel it yet? The need?"

"Yeah, I do." Early stood and started around the table.

Lamont scrambled up and stepped back, palms out. "Early, if you do what you're dying to do right now—if you manage to throw me overboard—what would it accomplish?"

"It'd wipe the smug look off your face. That's about it, but believe me, it's enough. Oops, there's that word again."

"Oh no, there would be more. What else would happen is it would irritate me, and that's something you don't want to do, believe me. I'd make sure you absolutely and permanently lose your job back home in Podunk, Arizona. And here's the real rub, Miss Foster would be no closer to seeing her brother. In fact, the possibility, as remote as it is, would become an *im*possibility. See? A little tendril of wind stirs in the desert, one action leads to another, and look how it winds up. Life is film. Film is life. Everything is art. You throw me into the water and birds fall right out of the sky. One little frame and a whole string of other frames follow."

Early shrugged. "Tell you what, the birds can live, that's up to you. All you have to do is produce a brother."

"Sorry, that's not going to happen."

"Then why ask us here today?"

Lamont's eyes took on an amused glint. "The honest answer?"

"No, lie to me."

"I asked you here because I wanted to see what kind of entertainment the universe brought me when you two showed up looking for Charles. I wanted to see desperation in Calico's eyes and know I caused it. I wanted to taunt you with liquor and see what happened on your face when I mentioned the name Gomez Gomez. Don't you see? You're nothing but playthings to someone like me. Honest enough?"

Early stared at him. "What's the matter with you?"

"Early, I'm the *artist*! And whether the world wants to admit it or not, the greatest artist is also most often the monster under your bed." He spread his arms. "So, my friends, while you—"

Early looked over at Calico. "I can't even hear this guy anymore. I think we should kill some birds."

"Absolutely," she said.

Lamont shook his head. "You wouldn't dare. I swear I'll make you suffer, you have no idea. I'm not a strong swimmer! And you couldn't even lift—"

That was the last thing that came out of his mouth before he hit the water.

CHAPTER TWENTY-ONE

Santa Cruz, the largest of the Channel Islands, lazed on the diamond-sparkle horizon. Beautiful. But beauty was the last thing on Early's mind as he gunned the pickup onto the 101.

"We're really going up there?" Calico said.

"You have a better idea? It might be now or never."

"Without a plan?"

"Plans are overrated."

"I don't think that's actually true, but okay."

"Did you see Lamont's eyes? That whole thing was beyond weird. I thought he was a straight-up con man, but the dude's a true believer. I don't know in what, but definitely something. He's bought in to the voices in his head, which makes him unpredictable. And the Gomez Gomez thing—he's only playing with us."

"And you think he might hurt Charlie." A statement, not a question.

"Guy like that? I don't know. And I don't like not knowing. This morning I thought if you could talk to Charlie, see with your own eyes that he's okay, that'd be enough to put your mind at ease. I mean, he's an adult and he's in charge of his own life. I half thought we'd be headed back to Arizona by now. Now I want to get him away from this lunatic as fast as possible. Hopefully before said lunatic dries out and gets himself back into action."

"Agreed. How do we get Charlie out? What if he says no?"

"I have no idea. I'll carry him out over my shoulder if I have to."

She smiled. "I gotta say, Lamont's face when he went over that rail . . . You do have style."

"Yeah? Have I asked you to marry me yet?"

"Have I asked you to shut up yet?"

Early slowed for the Montecito exit. "See, what you don't understand is that you only fan the flame when you talk like that. Tell me to shut up one more time and I'm gonna buy a ring."

"Go ahead. Just make sure it fits your own hand."

They headed up the hill on a treed side road. Early shifted down. "I kinda wish Jake were here. Lamont fancies he's spiritual with his whole art thing. That stuff is definitely more Jake's department."

"Well, I wouldn't trade."

"No?"

"No."

"But you still won't marry me."

"Wouldn't marry Jake either. Or Brad Pitt. Does that make you feel better?"

Early grinned. "A little, actually."

"Shut up, Pines."

Two minutes later Early hit the brakes and the pickup slid to a gravelly stop next to the Continuum compound gate. Ten seconds after that, Early was seated on the tall stone wall, looking down at a manicured lawn. He turned back to Calico. "Wait here, I'll be back."

"No way." She pulled herself up next to him and swung her long legs over. "You go, I go, Pines. Period."

"I'm serious. If there's gonna be trouble, it'll be better if I don't have you there to worry about."

"I'm supposed to wait out here like some little kid while who knows what happens to you? I'm going, end of argument. And give me a little credit. You don't have to babysit me. I can take care of myself."

Early sighed. "Fine. But I'm going first in case there're dogs. Give it a minute or so."

"Yeah." She pushed off the wall and dropped down.

Early landed next to her, brushed the dust off his hands. "I guess chivalry's dead."

"No dogs. Now what?"

"What if there had been?"

"Wayne said the Continuum isn't about violence. I'd put guard dogs in the violence category. Don't be a baby."

A raptor hung on an invisible draft above them, eyes on some unsuspecting prey out in the brush. Bees buzzed in the still air.

Early scanned the grounds. "I get nonviolence. But this is too quiet. They have to know we're here. They've known everything else so far."

"Probably." She started up the brick road at a pace that forced Early to almost trot. "When you say they might be watching it makes my skin crawl."

"Yeah, not a great feeling."

"It also ticks me off."

"Good. You might need that."

The road topped a rise, dropped into a shallow valley, then disappeared over another hill. They walked at least three quarters of a mile before seeing a building in the distance.

Calico slowed. "This is the compound? It looks like a house. After Lamont's yacht, I expected more."

"Something's not right. Look at it. The landscaping stops. No cars. Nothing."

"I can take Wayne. Even dogs. But this is bizarre."

"You want to go back?"

"Not a chance. You?"

"I've never backed up in my life."

"I'm gonna knock Charlie's teeth out for this."

"I'm gonna hold him while you do it."

Five minutes later, they approached the front of the building. White stucco, red tile roof. Plastic taped over the windows offered no glimpse of the interior. The circular drive in front was dirt, though graded as if in preparation for paving.

"This looks like new construction." Early strode up to the door and looked for a speaker or bell of some kind. Nothing. He knocked instead. No response. He pounded harder. Still nothing. He tried the knob and was surprised when the tall double doors swung open.

"You think everyone left?" Calico said.

Early looked through the open doors. "I don't think anyone was ever here. It's not even finished."

"Then who did we talk to on the intercom? And where the heck did Wayne come from?"

They moved through a big foyer and a front room. Bare, unfinished drywall. Concrete floor.

Calico shook her head. "This makes no sense. What do you think is going on?"

"I think Lamont is playing a bigger game than we thought. But I have no idea why."

Early headed for a passageway to another room. More of the same—nothing. Also the room after that. Dust hung suspended in beams of sunlight shining silent down through skylights.

"The guy gets weirder and weirder," Early said. "If this isn't the Continuum, then what is it? And where is the actual Continuum?"

"And where is Charlie?"

"The million-dollar question."

"Why was Wayne here yesterday? He couldn't have possibly known we were coming. And then that cop got here within minutes. *Here.* This has to be the place. If not, the whole thing had to be staged. Which is impossible, isn't it? I mean, there's no way." She crossed her arms and looked around the room, paused. "Pines?"

Early followed her gaze. On a windowsill, reflecting slanting sunlight, was a bottle topped with a bow. Early walked over and picked up the bottle.

"What is it?" Calico said.

"A bottle of Old Crow whiskey. And a note."

Detective Pines—Wake up, sleeper, arise from the dead. Welcome to the world, welcome to the game. Art is life and life is art.

As I mentioned, you are *entertaining, even if you are completely predictable. Buttons are so easily pushed, aren't they? Can you imagine, I'm leaving this bottle and writing this note before we even meet today. I know what will happen, of course. I'll push your buttons and you'll storm off. If you're reading this, which you will be, then I'm right. Isn't it frustrating?*

Ah, the beauty of art! Granted, beauty can be violent, but I wonder, can beauty ever truly be found within the violent heart? I suppose only you can answer that. We'll see, won't we? If there's one thing Orson Welles has taught me, it's that some things have to be believed to be seen. But you, detective, you're a blind man, nothing more. So is there any hope at all for you? Or should you simply slink back to the desert? If you do, don't forget your bottle. My gift. And it wasn't cheap. Although I doubt you'll be able to tell the difference.

Don't forget to lock your closet doors. You never know what monsters lurk.

Hammott Lamont, filmmaker

Early crumpled the paper and tossed it on the floor.

Calico picked it up, turned the paper ball in her fingers. "What have you done, Charlie? Seriously, how did Lamont do it? And who was the girl on the intercom? Nobody knew we were coming."

Early opened the bottle, poured its contents into an uncovered vent, and pulled out his phone. "Somebody knew." He scrolled through the contacts, then hit a button.

"Yeah?" Monte said.

"Where are you? We need to talk."

CHAPTER TWENTY-TWO

CHARLIE SLEPT TILL ELEVEN.

Got up.

Had coffee.

Had some vanilla yogurt and granola.

Wished the yogurt and granola were biscuits and gravy and bacon.

Watched a show about flipping houses.

Watched two episodes of *The Bachelor*.

Thought for a while about how he'd make a better bachelor than that loser.

Watched another show about flipping houses . . .

C'mon, man, something happen!

Sure, the bungalow was great. Yes, it was cool to be in the *Reporter* spread. He'd looked at the page about a thousand times. But there was only so much lying around drinking club soda and iced coffee he could take. The view outside was okay, but seriously the ocean just laid there. How long could a guy stare at it?

The only thing Charlie found remotely entertaining in the day in, day out routine was Isabella. And her lack of communication drove him crazy. He watched her now as she bustled around the room straightening and picking up. He sighed.

Mr. Lamont had been very clear about Charlie's staying put. He wasn't to leave the bungalow beyond the attached rear porch. He wasn't to speak with anyone until Mr. Lamont himself gave him the all clear. He'd even had Charlie sign a contract to that effect. Which was cool and all—Charlie was supposed to be resting up, preparing. But, man, preparing for what? Where was the script? How was he supposed to prepare with no material? Did they ask Christian Bale to work without a script? Leo? Depp? How could a guy immerse himself into a character when he didn't have a clue what the character was? How could he get into the spirit of the whole thing?

"What do you think?" he said to Isabella's back as she washed up the dishes in the sink. "Don't you think a serious actor needs a script? I bet Clooney has a script right now. I'm as good as Clooney, man. Probably better. Hey, where do you go after you leave here? Because I got all these theories. You have a place close by? Roommates? How many places do you clean a day? Ten, twenty? Do you clean Hammott's place? I don't even know where Hammott lives. Probably lots of places, right? I don't know where anything is around here. Man, I gotta get out. I'm losing my mind. Flipping houses? World's greatest cupcake? Who cares about cupcakes? Although now that I think about it, a cupcake sounds kinda good actually."

Isabella turned to him, drying her hands on a dish towel, said nothing.

"Do you miss Honduras?" Charlie said. "You still have family down there?"

Isabella smiled. She moved to the door, gathering her cleaning supplies in a large bucket. "Adios, Señor Charles."

"Yeah, adios," Charlie said. "Nice chat, man. Do come again."

He stared at the door after it closed. He thought about sneaking out and following her. He wasn't in prison, right? Then a knock sounded. Isabella must have forgotten something. But it wasn't Isabella. It wasn't anyone. Just a garment bag hanging on a hook by the door. He brought it inside and unzipped it carefully. A suit. A nice one. Charlie checked the label. Neiman Marcus. O'Connor base sharkskin two-piece. He whistled. This wasn't Ross Dress for Less. This was the real deal. Charlie noticed an envelope in the front pocket and pulled it out. A note written in a tight, neat hand.

Charles,

It's party time, my friend. You'll find the suit fits. It's tailored to you exactly by one of the best houses in the world. It will be spectacular, and I want you to look your best. Get dressed and Wayne will be around for you shortly.

Believe in great things, Charles. Always believe. I do!

Cheers,
Hammott Lamont, filmmaker

CHAPTER TWENTY-THREE

IT WAS PARTY TIME, ALL right. Charlie did his best to look calm, cool, and collected. Tried to channel his inner McConaughey. The same McConaughey, by the way, who'd given him a polite, fairly stoned nod when he passed by not more than two minutes ago.

Man, what am I doing here? Hammott was right, this is stinking huge.

It was one thing to lie around the bungalow and pretend he was somebody. But here he actually kinda was. Or at least was treated like it. And it blew his mind. Literally everybody who was anybody was at this party. He'd bumped into Bono at the bar. Bono, man! Asking for a Jack Daniel's and not a Jameson Irish. Bono drank Jack—unbelievable. And, since Hammott's full-page ad in the *Reporter*, people here actually knew Charlie's face. Maybe Bono and McConaughey didn't, but a lot of them did. They spoke Hammott Lamont's name in a kind of revered wonder. The word *genius* popped up more than once. No one seemed able to remember anything about Hammott's film work when Charlie tried to make conversation, but still, Lamont was the man. And now the names Lamont and Foster were linked in the minds of these people. Charles Foster, actor. Charles Foster, genius.

The cinematographer yammering away in front of him at the moment wasn't talking about Hammott Lamont, though. Heaven forbid. Talking about someone else would cut into the time the guy needed to talk about himself. He'd been going on for five minutes straight about some period piece he'd been working on in Italy for the last six months and hadn't offered a single verbal pause for Charlie to respond. Come to think of it, to Charlie's best recollection, the man hadn't even taken a breath. The guy being alive at all after being deprived of oxygen for so long was a mystery for the medical books.

Dude's like a parakeet. All he really needs is a mirror.

Even as the words passed through Charlie's brain, mercy smiled. The yammerer spotted Bono's yellow-lensed glasses on the other side of the pool, shouted the singer's name mid sentence, and, receiving a very Bono-ish peace sign, scooted off without as much as a goodbye, adios, or arrivederci.

Fine with Charlie. He needed a break, man.

Moving into the shadows, he let his eyes travel out over the low stone wall, past Beverly Hills, to the shining city skyline beyond. Insane. Charlie Foster was now a king. He was Elvis flying a hundred feet above Beale Street with a brand-new pair of blue suede wings care of Hammott stinking Lamont. The whole thing made him high. Less than a week ago, he'd been running a stupid, small-time con on Roxy Parsons, and now he was hanging with U2. He was about to star in an important film. At least according to Hammott it was important. But important or not, Charlie was a bona fide artist now. Roxy was in the past and the future held nothing but red carpets and starlets and parties where Irish rock stars wore yellow glasses and ordered Jack Daniel's instead of Jameson. Hey, maybe he'd surprise everybody and bring Isabella to the Oscars. Let everybody know he was a guy who hadn't forgotten where he'd come from. A man of the people. Yeah, that's exactly what he'd do. He brushed a crumb off the sleeve of his coat. Probably left there by the yammerer. The man had been holding half a caviar-topped cracker the whole time he talked, the other half caked into the corners of his mouth.

A woman passed. Familiar. He'd seen her in a movie or TV show, he was sure. She offered her congratulations as she walked by. "Hammott Lamont. Nice. He's a genius." Something in her smile. Maybe Charlie would have to rethink Isabella for that first red carpet.

He shook his head. Hammott Lamont, probably the most popular and in-demand man at this party, wasn't even here. Funny thing, though—Charlie could still feel him. Like he was watching somehow. He probably was. Charlie could imagine him having spies here. Maybe even the pretty actress who'd walked by a minute ago. He pushed away the thought and the tug of unease that accompanied it. Thoughts like that ruined a guy's high. And look where he was. Hammott knew how to play this game, that was obvious. So might as well enjoy the ride. Like he'd enjoyed the exactly two glasses of champagne he was allowed to have before switching to club soda. Hammott's orders, right after he'd handed Charlie a sleek cell phone to put in his pocket, inspected him suit collar to pant cuffs, and instructed him on what shoes to wear. Charlie had held up the thin leather flip-flops, still dusty from the desert.

"You're sure about these? It's a nice suit, man. I don't mind a pair of shoes."

"You look spectacular, Charles. You'll be a big hit. Believe me when I tell you people won't be able to take their eyes off you."

Yeah, man . . . absolutely. Elvis on Beale. Blue suede flip-flops, Charlie.

But Lamont had been right. People were watching him. And nobody even mentioned the sandals.

The cell vibrated in Charlie's pocket and he pulled it out. "Hello?"

"Charles, how is the party?"

Charles—he still couldn't quite get used to that. "Just doing what you said, Hammott. Smiling a lot. Listening. Trying not to talk too much. Which isn't hard since most of these people here talk enough on their own."

"Ha, yes, they do. You're doing absolutely perfectly, Charles. You know you're the reason half those people are there, don't you? They want to get a look at you. I've dropped hints about this project for more than a year. And the *Reporter* advertisement gave them a tiny glimpse. You see how it's done? We pull back the curtain, but only a crack at a time."

"Yeah, I get it. Get the mark on the hook, then reel them in slow, right?"

"Charles, I've told you. This is not one of your cheap schemes. You need to understand this. We are spirit and we are man and we are art. What we're doing is like taking Michelangelo's *The Creation of Adam*—God touching man, you understand—to an even higher level."

"Sure, I understand." *Not really, but that's Gigi Hadid over there, man!*

Lamont cleared his throat. "Then no more talk of marks or schemes or reeling in fish, big or small. Agreed?"

"You got it. Absolutely. Sorry about that."

"Apology accepted. Now, mingle a bit more. You'll be leaving soon. Wayne will come for you when it's time."

"All right. You know, I wish my sister could see this. It would blow her mind."

"Charles, we've talked about this. No contact. No leaks. No distractions. You signed the contract and you have to stick to it."

"Yeah, but when do you think I'll be able to talk to her?"

"As soon as we wrap shooting."

Charlie sighed. "All right. About that, on the other films I worked on I had a script in advance. I could review my lines and everything. Get in character like Bale does. That's how I work. At least that's how I think I work. When can I see ours?"

"The first mistake you're making, Charles, is calling those wasted bits of celluloid you participated in films. It's a sacrilege to the art. You'll know what you need to do and say when the time comes. I'm the director and I'll be with you every step of the way. That's the way *I* work. Trust me."

"Okay. Maybe you could just have someone tell Calico I'm cool? That everything's all right?"

"It's already been done. She's well and proud and wishes you the best of luck. Which you won't need because you have me."

"Yeah? Cool, man, thanks. I feel better."

"Of course. Now, excuse me, Charles. I have something I need to take care of. Keep an eye out for Wayne. We'll talk soon."

"Hey, just so I know, when do we start filming?"

"When I say so. Rest up until then. Once we get on set, you'll be a busy man. And remember, not too much talking."

"Nope. No prob. Lips are zipped."

Yeah, Hammott was a trip. Since day one, Charlie had been waiting to see a crack in the guy's facade, but nothing. Cool as a breeze all the time. Charlie finished the last of his club soda, set the glass on a tray in the hand of a passing waiter, and threaded through the crowd to find a restroom. The house was one of those where most of the back wall opened up to the deck and pool. Indoor-outdoor living or whatever. Charlie's house would be like this someday. Maybe soon. He'd have a dozen Isabellas puttering around cleaning the place 24-7. And his own Isabella would live there like a queen. Maybe he'd even learn Spanish, at least a few words. She'd learn English for sure.

The living room was roughly the size of Dodger Stadium. A woman Charlie took to be a maid, but wasn't sure, directed him to a restroom down a long hallway. He laughed out loud when he found it. Who lived like this, man? The guest bathroom was bigger than Charlie's whole apartment. He'd never seen anything like it. All he had to do was pee, how much room did a guy need? He could do cartwheels before he reached the toilet, which, by the way, was in a whole other glassed-in room. A full-length mirror stood in one corner of this one. He walked the three miles over to it and gave himself a once-over. The sandals looked weird, but they did make him feel kinda artsy. The man bun had also been Hammott's idea. Charlie hated man buns, but what are you gonna do? His beard was perfectly scraggly with some kind of product in it. Yeah, artsy. Artsy artist Charlie. Genius. In a gymnasium of a bathroom perched right on the top of the world.

Behind him, the door swung open. He thought he'd locked it. "Hey, man, occupied."

"Hiya, Charlie, what's shaking?"

Charlie spun. Roxy Parsons stood in the doorway.

He swallowed the lump in his throat. Played it cool. "Roxy . . . What's happening, man? Good to see you."

Parsons pulled a pack of cigarettes from his pocket, shook one out, and lit it. He blew a stream of smoke. "Is it? Where's my money?"

"Look, like I tried to tell you, I want my money back too. Everybody does. If you have any ideas, I'd love to hear them. But Wang disappeared. I'm starting to think he scammed us. I'm as mad about it as you are."

"You don't look mad. You look like a schmuck in a stupid ponytail who thought he could steal half a million dollars from me and walk away."

"Man bun."

"What?"

"The ponytail thing—it's called a man bun."

"I don't care what it's called, you idiot. Where's the money?"

Another man stepped in. Big guy. One of the ones who'd chased Charlie that day he ran into the Roosevelt. "Problem, Mr. Parsons?"

Charlie held up his hands. "Listen, I have a part in a movie now. A huge part. I can get your money no prob—"

"Wrong answer, Charlie," Parsons said. "What you have is the momentary and I'm sure fleeting attention of that crackpot Hammott Lamont. Maybe I'm the only one in this town who doesn't buy his line of bull, but I know who he is and what he does. He's a posturing, pretentious fake who's made the mistake of buying into his own press."

"Still, he's loaded. If I ask him for the—"

"No. You took my money, Charlie. And you're the one that's gonna give it back. It's not even about the cash, it's the principle. You're gonna cough it up or start losing fingers. Welcome to grown-up world."

"No, man! I—"

"Bring him and let's go." Parsons glanced at his man. "There's too many people I know here."

Charlie started to protest but closed his mouth when he glimpsed the butt of a pistol under the big man's coat. No one seemed to find it odd that the three of them exited the bathroom together. Roxy returned nods and a few waves as they passed through the living room and then the wide foyer.

Charlie tried to pull away. "Seriously, man, we don't have to—" A hard shot to his ribs from Parsons's man emptied his lungs of air.

Parsons grinned. "Shut up, Charlie."

They stepped through the front door and Parsons sent his man for the car.

"Charles!"

Charlie and Parsons both turned at the shout. Wayne stepped out of a waiting car and approached. "Mr. Lamont is waiting. Time to go."

"Charlie's got other plans tonight," Roxy Parsons said.

Wayne's eyebrows raised. "Plans? I'm sorry, Mr. Lamont explicitly told me—"

"I don't care if Joseph, Mary, or Jesus himself told you. I said Charlie's got other plans."

"And who are you?" Wayne said.

"Roxy Parsons. Make sure you remember the name so you can get it right for Hammock Lame-mont. Tell him Roxy Parsons says hello and that the odds are high his latest distraction here is going to lose a body part or two. So if he needs a pretty face for this masterpiece of his, he might want to call his casting director because the body parts in question are likely to be a nose or an ear. My guys seem to like those for some reason."

Wayne stepped forward. "Listen, I don't know what you think is going on, but Charles is coming with me."

Instead of replying, Parsons placed a hand against Wayne's chest and shoved. Wayne tumbled back into a potted palm and collapsed in a heap of soil and shards of terra-cotta, eyes wide.

At that moment Parsons's man pulled up in a limo. Parsons opened the back door. "Get in, Charlie."

"No way, man. I'm not—"

Stars exploded in his eyes. He put a hand to his nose and pulled it back, bloody.

"Get in. Or go ahead, tell me no again."

CHAPTER TWENTY-FOUR

"I DON'T KNOW LAMONT FROM Adam, so it wasn't me that let him know you were coming," Monte said around a mouthful of fries.

"I know it wasn't you," Early said. "It had to be Jackie. She set us up from the start. Gave us directions and knew full well it wasn't Lamont's compound. He must've pulled her in and put the whole thing in motion right after you called when he realized Calico was looking for Charlie."

"And then when she called me back that night I told her about you too. Stupid me."

"You couldn't know."

"But why do any of it?" Calico said.

Early took a sip of his soda. "Only thing I can think of is that he likes to play games with people. He likes control. He made that clear enough on the boat. And then the note: 'Welcome to the world, welcome to the game . . .' The guy's a bad cocktail of crazy, rich, influential, and maybe bored."

Monte considered. "So? Get in your truck and go home. Let him entertain himself. End of story."

Calico shook her head. "It wouldn't be the end for Charlie. I'm not leaving until he's away from that nut. No way."

"She's right," Early said. "We can't leave him. Guy's not safe."

"Charlie's a grown-up," Monte said.

"In theory. In reality, I'm not so sure," Calico said.

"All right, but where do you go from here? Can't follow the Jackie trail, number doesn't work anymore. Not surprising, I guess. She had to know you'd be looking for her."

"It's crazy, she seemed so honest," Calico said.

"We're in a city full of actors," Early said. "And she was good. No other explanation."

"We still have the Continuum number," Calico said.

"Yeah, and look how much good that's done," Monte said. "For all we know, whoever's answering at that number is in Topeka, Kansas. Or Budapest."

They were sitting in a window booth at Tommy's Burgers. A place Monte had insisted on.

Monte wiped his mouth with a napkin and gave a contented sigh. "Thing about Tommy's is the chili. Without the chili it's just another burger joint, right? But the chili takes it to a whole new level. Whole different plane of existence."

Early eyed the burger on the tray in front of him where it sat proudly next to an equally chili-slathered pile of fries. "You ever had actual chili? Because I gotta say, this stuff looks like it leaked out of a rusty fifty-gallon drum out by Area 51."

Monte took a bite and talked while he chewed. "They got a bunch of locations, but this is the original. Tommy's is a Los Angeles institution, kid. Think of me like a tour guide you don't have to tip. You're welcome."

"I'm welcome? Because I seem to remember paying for all this."

"Yeah, but you never would've had the experience if it weren't for yours truly. Besides, I thought you were supposed to be a tough-guy bulldogger. You're whining about chili? I'm mightily disappointed."

"Chili's supposed to have substance. This looks like warmed-up peanut butter."

"Well, your hat is stupid, what about that?"

"That's the best you got? My hat's stupid?"

"What are you two, in second grade?" Calico said. "You're complaining, Pines, but that's your second burger, so knock it off. I like the chili."

"You own a place that serves food and you're on his side?" Early said.

She narrowed an eye at him. "Yeah, I am, because he's right about the hat." She looked at Monte. "I have a theory. I think Pines is hiding behind it."

"I don't hide from anything," Early said.

Calico ignored him. "I suspect if someone could ever pry the thing off his head, there might be a reasonable adult under there somewhere."

"Not sure I'd go that far," Monte said. "I like this girl, Early. She's smart and she's got gumption."

"She's got something, all right," Early said.

Monte forked a chili-covered fry into his mouth. "So the boat wasn't even Lamont's?"

"The whole thing was a lie start to finish," Early said. "We went straight back there from what was supposed to be the Continuum compound. Only person aboard was a woman wiping down the chrome. She said a company had rented the thing for a meeting because they wanted to impress some important clients. I guess we were the clients."

"What company?"

"Somebody called Amberson and Associates."

"Never heard of 'em."

Early picked up a thick book off a seat and tossed it on the table. "I think I have."

"What's the book?" Monte said.

"It's called *Citizen Welles.* Definitive biography of Orson Welles. Picked it up on the way down. I have to admit, the dude was fascinating."

"What's it for?" Monte said.

"Hopefully a little insight into Lamont's weird game. Jackie mentioned Welles, and Lamont did again on the boat, and again in the note. He's obsessed with the guy. Even looks like him. Check this out, Welles's second feature film after *Citizen Kane* was called *The Magnificent Ambersons.*"

"Amberson and Associates," Monte said.

"Uh-huh."

"What about the cop up in Montecito?" Monte said. "Bribed or what?"

Calico pushed her tray back and leaned on her forearms. "Officer Phony Tony Peterson. We called the Santa Barbara Police and asked about him."

Monte slurped root beer and set the glass down. "Phony Tony doesn't exist?"

"Oh, the man exists," Early said. "He was real, onion breath and everything. But he definitely doesn't serve and protect the good people of Santa Barbara."

"Those are some elaborate mind games, amigo. And expensive to pull off. Takes bodies. Jackie for one. Wayne, Liz, this cop." Monte scraped up some leftover chili with a fry, used it to animate his words. "Still, guy like Lamont gets his hooks in people. Nothing new. Heck, Manson was the same way."

"Manson, that really helps my worry meter," Calico said.

Monte grunted. "Sorry, I didn't mean it to come out that way."

"Monte's right, though," Early said. "I couldn't care less about crawling through Lamont's brain or humoring his weird games. We just need Charlie out."

Monte finished off the last of his burger. "Yeah, maybe."

"Why maybe?" Early said.

"I don't know, lesser of two evils? Kid could be better off where he is. If Roxy Parsons is as upset about getting rooked as I hear he is, he's out for blood."

"I might kill Charlie myself if I can ever get my hands on him," Calico said.

"He does sound like a class-A screwup. No offense," Monte said.

"None taken. Believe me."

Monte shrugged. "Then again, we've all been screwups at one point or another. I ain't innocent of it in my younger days. Probably my older days too if you ask Lucinda." He pointed at Early. "Trust me, this guy has had plenty of moments."

"Thanks a lot," Early said.

Monte eyed Calico. "Had a brother myself once. I had to pull his tail out of a crack more times than I can count. Thing is, Roxy Parsons don't care about your feelings. He don't care if Charlie's related to Joan of Arc or Sister Theresa. He's gonna want his money and his California godfather rep back. That's his bread and butter."

Calico opened her mouth to say something, then didn't.

Monte went on. "That's why I say Charlie might be better holed up somewhere with Lamont's gaggle of whacks. See? Lesser of two evils."

"I don't know," Early said. "Lamont's fixation with Charlie is pretty out there. And it's definitely not healthy."

Behind Early, the door squeaked.

Monte grimaced. "Lord help me."

Lucinda slid into the booth next to him.

Monte eyed her. "Woman, I love you, but if what you're gonna say is about chili, I don't want to hear it. How'd you know where I was anyway?"

A little line formed in her cheek. She pulled her phone from her purse and showed him the screen.

Monte squinted. "You tracked me?"

She smiled.

"They got an app for everything, amigo," Early said. "I saw it on TV once, show about cheating husbands. You're a guilty-as-charged chili cheater."

Lucinda pointed at Early and gave a thumbs-up in agreement.

"I'm not cheating! I'm eating a hamburger." Monte looked at Lucinda. "I can't believe you actually tracked me."

She leaned over, kissed him on the ear, and replaced the root beer cup with a water bottle from her purse.

Monte gave it a dirty look. "That purse of yours never ceases to amaze me. It's like the Mary Poppins carpetbag of all things tasteless. This is Tommy's for crying out loud."

Lucinda winked at him, her red hair collecting piles of sunlight through the window. Monte twisted the cap off the water, sighed, and sipped. "Let's get back to the problem at hand before I'm eating twigs and broccoli."

"What more is there to say?" Early said. "I hate this. Jackie's really our last and only connection. When it comes down to it, we have absolutely no idea where these Continuum people hole up."

"Lamont mentioned owning property in the desert. Is there a way we can search that?" Calico said.

"Maybe," Monte said, "but who knows how many shell companies a character like that is hiding behind?"

"Or if he was even telling the truth about the property," Early added. "So far honesty hasn't been the man's most defining attribute. Still, it's worth a try. Problem is, unless everything's public record, I'm in the dark. If I was on the job, I might have more access. But my boss made it crystal clear I'm on my own."

"Let me make a call," Monte said. "I got a guy at the IRS office over in Little Tokyo who owes me a favor."

"Horse tip?" Early said.

"They get me a lot of favors, what can I say?"

"Worth a try," Early said. "You might look into Amberson and Associates. We know Lamont's used that one."

Monte nodded. "I was thinking that. Wouldn't get my hopes up, though. What are you two gonna do now?"

"I know this much, I won't go home until I have Charlie in a headlock," Early said. "Not only for his sake, but Lamont plain old makes me mad. We'll wait for his next move. I'm sure there'll be one. He didn't go through all this chain yanking for nothing. Meantime, we'll find a place to stay and hope something shakes out with your friend in Little Tokyo. Maybe we can get ahead a move or two."

"I got his number on my rolodex at home. I'll call you soon as I talk to him."

Early laughed. "Did you just say rolodex? Out loud?"

"So what?"

"You know you have an address book on your phone, right?"

"Says the man with an eight-track player in his truck," Calico said.

"Tell you what, I never dropped a rolodex in a toilet. And this is my second phone this year."

"Well, that's just nasty." Early pushed himself out of the booth. "All right then, we'll wait for your call."

"And let me know if you hear anything on your end. I'm seriously curious about this hombre loco."

They all walked out together, the asphalt so hot it sponged beneath their feet. Early fished in his pocket for the truck keys and opened the door to let the heat escape. Monte did the same with his ozone-faded Crown Victoria.

Calico's phone chirped and she pulled it out of her purse. Her eyes went wide.

"What?" Early said.

She held up her phone. "Maybe the wait's shorter than we think. A text from Charlie's number."

CHAPTER TWENTY-FIVE

CALICO STARED AT THE SCREEN, pulse ticking in her temples. "'The Frolic Room 30 mins.' What's the Frolic Room?"

Pines glanced at Monte. "You know it?"

"Yeah. About a half mile up the boulevard next to the Pantages." Monte pointed to Calico's phone. "That sound like your brother to you?"

"Not at all. Especially after not hearing from him all this time. He'd call for sure, not text."

"Another one of Lamont's games," Monte said. "But why not call you? Isn't that what he did last time?"

Pines opened the passenger-side pickup door for Calico. "Lamont hasn't done one thing anyone expects him to do. He fancies himself as smart, which he is, and he's having fun playing with us. Let's go. If it's Lamont he's gonna wish all I did was throw him off a boat."

"You mind if I tag along?" Monte said. "I kinda get the feeling another body in your corner might come in handy. Plus if Jackie conned me, I'm gonna have something to say about it."

"Can't see that it'd hurt," Pines said. "I gotta tell you, though, I have no idea what we're walking into, and whatever it is I'm going in swinging."

"No kidding? I thought you'd take 'em flowers. Let's take my car. There's more room." Monte waved at Lucinda, standing next to a blue Prius with Hawaiian-print seat covers and a lei hanging from the mirror. "Lucinda, darlin', I'll see you at home."

Lucinda narrowed an eye, walked over, and climbed into the front seat of the Crown Vic.

Monte leaned down. "No way. I'm telling you right now, go home."

Lucinda cranked up the window and locked the door.

Monte looked over the car at Calico and Early and shrugged. "She ain't gonna budge. I can tell you that from experience. Looks like you two get the back seat."

"Fine. Let's go." Pines opened the door for her to slide in.

Monte pulled onto Hollywood Boulevard and gunned the big V-8. He rolled down the window and hung his elbow out. "I'll say this for your texter, whoever it is. Frolic Room—he's definitely got a sense of style."

"Why? What's the Frolic Room?" Pines said.

Monte glanced at them in the rearview mirror. "Old Hollywood watering hole. Place is legendary."

"Another stop on Monte's budget Hollywood tour?" Calico said.

"Definitely. The Frolic is Tinseltown noir all the way. Real deal dive bar. Occasional tourists but mostly locals and professional drinkers. Celebrities every once in a while. They filmed *L.A. Confidential* there back in, I think, '97. I knew the stunt coordinator on that one. Bunch of other films too. Sinatra used to hang out there. Oscars after-parties when they had the Oscars at the Pantages. Oh yeah, get this, it was the last place the Black Dahlia was seen alive. Can't remember her name now."

Lucinda poked Monte in the shoulder and signed.

Monte watched her. "Elizabeth Short. 1947. Wannabe actress. Somebody chopped her up and dumped her in a vacant lot. Cops never solved it." He shook his head at his wife. "Why in the world do you know that? It's morbid."

She signed again.

"She says she saw a documentary on Hulu. I don't know why she watches that stuff. Gives me nightmares."

Lucinda smiled and tugged his ear.

"Here we are, the Frolic Room." Monte signaled and whipped over to the curb. "Parking spot right on the street. Our lucky day. We should buy a lottery ticket."

The four of them climbed out. Monte had been right about the noir part. Painted black. Gold trim. Deco neon sign.

"You ready?" Monte said.

"More than." Pines pushed the door open and walked in.

Calico followed, heart in her throat. She blinked, letting her eyes adjust to the room after the Hollywood sun. A man in a dress shirt and black vest stood behind a long bar, giving the polished surface lazy circle swipes with a rag. Sunlight from the doorway caught the milky opaqueness of a glass eye as he nodded at them. Lots of red tuck-and-roll upholstery. A mural—sketches of Hollywood royalty—stretched nearly one entire wall beneath a row of stools.

"You having a private party or something? Place is empty," Monte said to the bartender.

"Is one of you Calico Foster?" the man said.

"I am," she said.

The bartender pointed toward the back of the room. "Then you're the party. He's waiting for you."

A dim, hulking form at the far end of the bar lifted a casual hand. His voice rolled through the room, all cigarettes and gravel. "Yeah, I had 'em clear it out for a while so we can talk private. Come on back. Even saved you a parking spot. Aren't I thoughtful?"

"Who are you?" Pines said.

"Hmm, are you Calico Foster? Because if you are, you're one ugly broad. And if you're not, I wasn't talking to you."

"I don't care who you were talking to. I asked you a question," Pines said.

"And I only have business with a Miss Foster, so shut your mouth or I'll have it shut."

Pines gave a hard-eyed grin. "Now it's starting to sound like a party."

"Yeah, it is, complete with giant clowns apparently."

A muscle worked in Pines's jaw. The same muscle Calico had seen on the boat when Hammott Lamont tossed out the name Gomez

Gomez. Early was a big man with a bigger heart, but the guy was also deeply troubled. And that trouble, dressed up as temper, boiled close to the surface.

"I'm Calico Foster. Where's Charlie? How do you have his phone?"

"Now you I'll dance with," the man said. "Come and sit down and we can talk. If you haven't guessed, my name is Roxy Parsons. Maybe, just maybe, there's an off chance you can do your idiot brother some good."

CHAPTER TWENTY-SIX

Early held Calico back and went first. The smell of stale alcohol and commercial cleaner burned his nostrils, that same old bar stench he'd been familiar with for as long as he could remember. Roxy Parsons wasn't alone. A big, squinty gym rat stuffed into a cheap suit flanked him. The whole scene almost comical, like some bad late-night movie. Still, as far as security went, the rat was definitely more up to the task than little surfer Wayne. Lamont should be here to take notes.

Roxy Parsons was nearly as big as his bodyguard. Tall even on his barstool. Thick and solid as an oil drum. Mid fifties probably. Blue eyes alert. Bottle-black hair heavy and slicked.

"You have Charlie Foster's phone. Where is he?" Early said.

"That message was sent to Charlie's sister, I believe. You, friend, don't strike me as the sisterly type, so butt out. Who are you anyway?"

Early leaned forward. "I doubt friendship's in our future, so let's not play. I asked you how you have Charlie's phone."

Parsons eyed Early. "Are you bound and determined to be trouble?"

"Most of the time."

"You got a gun?"

"Not with me."

"My guy has a gun. So I win."

"You better tell him to shoot me. You're gonna have to."

"What?"

"You heard me."

"Are you crazy?" Roxy looked at Calico. "Is he crazy?"

"Yet to be determined, but very probably. Answer the question. Why do you have Charlie's phone? Where is he?"

Parsons sighed. "Yet to be determined. Why does everything in life have to be so complicated?" He pointed a meaty finger at Early. "Maybe I'll have him shoot you later, pal. Right now I just want to finish my drink and talk with the pretty lady."

"So talk," Calico said.

Roxy's smile revealed a straight row of thick gray teeth. His wheezing laugh had, at some point, been rolled in sawdust and mud. "I can already tell you're a lot tougher than your brother, you know that? Not that it takes much."

"Yeah, I do know that," Calico said.

Roxy nodded. "I like it. You know what I like to do sometimes, Miss Foster? I like to answer a question with another question. Guy told me one time, answer a question with a question and it makes you sound smarter. I don't know if that's true or not, but I like to do it anyway, just in case. So you ask me how I have Charlie's phone. I ask you, how much do you think your little shack of a bar out there in the desert's worth? A hundred thou? Two hundred? Now, if you were to say five-hundred thousand, you'd make me a very happy man."

"How is my bar any of your business?" Calico said.

"Simple math actually. Not that Common Core crap they're mushing all the kids' brains with these days. Least when they're not mushing 'em with iPhones. I'll spell it out. Half a million minus half a million equals zero, which is what I have now. And that equals very bad things for Charlie. Are you allowed to have two equals in one equation? I forget. Anyway, here's the good news—zero plus half a million *plus* interest equals me happy and Charlie whole and almost healthy. I say 'almost' because I'll still knock him around a little on general principle, but he'll likely be able to walk on his own after. Then he can go do screwy Lamont's screwy art picture. Easy math, right?"

"What are you asking me, Mr. Parsons?" Calico said.

He squeezed lime into what looked like a gin and tonic. "Call me

Roxy, please. No reason we can't keep this civil." He snapped his sausage fingers at the bartender. "We need some drinks, pronto. Miss Foster, what's your pleasure? And your friends here, too. Even the big, rude one."

"We're not here to drink," Early said.

"Okay." Roxy jutted a chin at Early. "Let me get everyone straight at least. Miss Foster I now know. Who are you?"

"Detective Early Pines," Calico said.

Roxy lifted a brow. "Detective? I'm sort of impressed. All right, who are Eastwood and the signing deaf chick here?"

"Monte Shaw," Monte said. "That's my wife, Lucinda. And so you know, I'll be breaking one of your fingers before I leave here for what you just called her."

Roxy grunted something between a laugh and a phlegm hack. "Deaf chick? That's what she is, right? You'll be breaking my—" Another hack. "That's funny, man. You know what? I like you people, I really do. First the detective who doesn't mind getting shot and now this guy who's gonna break my finger. And he says it so matter-of-fact. Ha! Monte Shaw, I think I know the name. You've been around. Horse guy, right?"

"Guilty as charged."

"Not much call for horse guys in crime pictures. Probably why we never met."

"I've seen a few of your movies. Not bad work. Entertained me at least."

"Thanks. And you're gonna break my finger?"

"Have to. Matter of honor, you understand."

Roxy barked another laugh. "We got to get together sometime, Monte. I mean outside of this business. You're old-school."

"Maybe I should have a Bud after all then," Monte said. The bartender cracked a bottle and slid it down the bar, and Monte took a sip.

Roxy shifted his focus back to Calico. "Okay, let's get back to the math. Your brother owes me five hundred thousand dollars plus interest. And the interest is substantial and growing daily, only slightly slower than my impatience. You and Charlie own a bar. That's a start. You sign the building and property over to me and at least we're making progress in the right direction."

Calico's expression betrayed nothing. "You want me to sign everything I own over to you because my brother's an idiot? You're serious?"

"Serious as a hand full of broken fingers." Roxy winked at Monte.

"Say I were to agree? You have his phone, but I still don't see Charlie," Calico said.

"Good old Chuck, yeah." Roxy gave a lazy wave. His flanker stepped out a back door briefly then returned, gripping the arm of a man Early recognized from the *Hollywood Reporter* spread as Charlie Foster. Except for a couple black eyes and a pretty good swollen lip, he looked decently in one piece. His build was thin. His hair dark and longish and tucked behind his ears. He had a scraggly beard that hadn't found the guts to grow in right. He also looked like he was about to cry.

"Cali?"

"Charlie? What have you done?" Calico said.

"I'm sorry about all this. I really am. I—"

"Shut up, Charlie," Roxy said. "Calico, about the bar."

"You gotta do whatever he says," Charlie said. "I swear he's gonna hurt me if you don't. He'll do it."

Calico's eyes tightened. "First of all, are you all right? At least for the moment?"

Charlie bobbed his head. "Yeah. They hit me a little but I'm okay."

Calico's nod was almost imperceptible. "Good. Now where is Mr. Parsons's money?"

"What?"

"Where's his money? It's not a hard question."

"Cali! You really think I'd take his money? I got ripped off just like him, man. Everything dad loaned me. Guy named Kim Wang, he's the one. He ripped off all of us. I trusted the guy."

Roxy shook his head. "Nope. I've looked high and low for Kim Wang. He doesn't exist."

"Of course he exists!" Charlie said. "He was the one that first introduced me to Slim Sound. You video-conferenced him! You saw him. I'm not lying, man. I've told you a hundred times."

Roxy pursed his lips. "Yeah, I saw a guy claimed to be named Wang. Maybe he was, maybe he wasn't. Either way, you're the guy that told me where to wire that money and you're the guy that's here now. So like I told your sister, the bar's a start. I take ownership, then you both work off the balance."

"What in the world is Slim Sound?" Monte said.

"Way to melt fat off your body with some kinda sound-wave machine," Roxy said. "Gold mine, right, Charlie? It looked good too. Lots of facts and figures to back it up. Before and after pictures, I love those. Charlie took my money. And a couple days later I get a call from my accountant, says something's wrong. Turns out Slim Sound, along with my money, has vanished into the wind. So the way I see it, Charlie here set me up and absconded with my half million. We're back to simple math."

Charlie whipped his head back and forth. "I'm telling you, Mr. Wang showed me all the research. Doctors and everything. Slim Sound was a sure thing. He just needed investors. Cali, that's why I borrowed from dad, he was into it. And then when I happened to meet Roxy at a party, the subject came up and he got interested. That's it. We both wired Mr. Wang money. He's the one. I swear it!"

Roxy rubbed his temples. "We both didn't do anything. I wired that money on your word. There is no Wang, there's only you. And that's where the proverbial buck stops." He signaled the bartender. "Get me a Wild Turkey, will ya? And a beer back. Leave the beer in the bottle. Every time this kid opens his mouth he gives me a headache. So, Calico, we were talking about the value of the bar."

Calico looked at Charlie, considering. "What if I say no? What's to stop me from just calling the police?"

Roxy's drinks appeared. He sipped the whiskey then took a pull from the beer. "Listen, up to now I've been keeping this whole thing low-key. I got a reputation in this town and getting ripped off by a nobody punk like your brother doesn't read well in my life script. It's embarrassing. But, hey, I'm an easygoing guy. Go ahead and call the blue. Let old Charlie tell his story and I'll tell mine."

Charlie met his sister's eyes and pulled himself erect. "That bar's mine too. I got a say in this as much as you."

Calico stared at him. "Really? Did that really just come out of your mouth? I'm the one who took all the responsibility. I'm the one who's kept it floating. Even after you wouldn't give the hundred thousand back. Where have you been? You'd do this to me?"

"Dad's gone, Cal. And so is his dream. What do you even want that stupid bar for anyway?"

Early did his best to curb his temper. He'd come out here to find Calico's brother, and now he was seriously considering knocking the kid's head off. Still, this was between brother and sister. He clenched his jaw, kept his mouth shut, and focused on ignoring the smoky vanilla aroma of Roxy's Wild Turkey.

"Look, Calico, I'm not the kind of guy that wants to hurt anybody, right?" Roxy said. "That being said, a man does what he has to do. Nobody rips me off, period. It's bad for business."

"Bob's Place is all I have," Calico said. "Seriously. I don't have anything else."

"Then I'll have to be satisfied with it, won't I? At least for now." Roxy looked Calico up and down and something changed in his expression. "Unless you have another suggestion?"

Early shifted his weight forward.

Roxy raised a brow and grinned. "What? She's a good-looking woman. You got something to say, detective?"

"Nope."

Early hit Roxy from his stool. Not as hard as he could have had he been standing, but hard enough that Roxy's eyes rolled back in his big head and he slid to the floor. A stool caught the now-moving bodyguard full in the face—Monte's doing. The man let go of Charlie and doubled over, blood streaming through his fingers. He gave a thick shout and was answered by someone out back.

Charlie's face was white. "They got another couple guys out there, man! We gotta get out of here."

Monte picked up his Bud Lite off the bar, finished it in a long drink, and set it down again. "Thanks for the beer, kid. Take the ladies, huh, Early? I'll be right there."

"Yup." Early took Calico's and Lucinda's elbows in his hands and ushered them toward the front door. Behind him, he heard the distinct and unmistakable sound of a finger bone snapping.

CHAPTER TWENTY-SEVEN

EARLY DEPOSITED LUCINDA INTO THE front seat of the Crown Vic. Calico and Charlie piled into the back. Ten seconds later Monte slid into the driver's seat and fired the engine.

"Everything all right?" Early said.

"You busted his nose good. And he ain't gonna be using his left hand for a while."

As Monte pulled the car onto the street, the door of the Frolic Room burst open, spilling three shouting men out onto the sidewalk.

"Dude's got a gun!" Charlie shouted as he ducked.

Monte hit the gas with a screech of tires.

Early looked back. "They'll probably follow."

Monte checked his rearview. "Yeah, but not fast enough. I'll get 'em tangled in traffic."

Charlie sat back, eyes wide. A green tinge to his pale face. "Who are you people? Cali, who are these people? I can't believe you just punched out Roxy Parsons, man. You know what he's gonna do to you? You're dead!"

Lucinda turned in her seat, fire in her eyes as she signed.

"What'd she say?" Charlie said.

"Said Calico's your sister. You shoulda been the one to hit the guy. Her language was a bit more colorful, but that's the gist of it."

Charlie's head swiveled back and forth between Monte and Lucinda. "I'm sorry, who are you?"

"Somebody who'd just as soon throw you out the window than listen to you," Monte said.

Charlie turned to Calico. "Cali—"

"You're welcome," Calico said. "Now shut up."

"Cali, they're going to kill us! Do you not understand that? Roxy'll take us out and dump us in the ocean, man. Tie chains all around us and sink us like rocks. And that's if we're lucky."

"Maybe we oughta leave you here then. Let you go for a swim," Early said.

Charlie shook his head. "You! You knocked out Roxy Parsons. Who are you, man?"

"Somebody who's helping a sister look for her brother. Which, at this moment, I'm second-guessing. You really thought it'd be a good idea to drag her into your mess? What's the matter with you?"

"How could you offer up the bar?" Calico said. "What were you thinking?"

Monte took a hard left, throwing everyone to the right.

"Are you hearing me at all?" Charlie said. "These guys aren't playing around. It's *half a million dollars.* And the bar's all I got."

"No, Charlie. You don't 'got' anything. I don't care if dad left it to both of us. You left. You never wanted it. And I'm the one—me—who's been paying off the money he loaned you. Money that you now lost. Well, guess what? The bank doesn't care if you lost it. They don't care about me or you or Roxy Parsons or this Wang person. All they care about is that dad borrowed a hundred thousand dollars against the bar and now I'm the one that has to pay it back."

"Look, Cal, if we—"

"There is no 'we'! You took his money, not me," Calico said.

"No, I told you, Wang took the money! All of it. The hundred thousand I got from dad and Roxy's half mil. He conned me, man."

"Sounds to me like you walked into whatever you walked into with open eyes," Early said.

"And a closed brain," Monte added.

"I don't see how any of it's your business," Charlie replied.

"You're saying you had nothing to do with the play itself?" Early said. "If that's what you're selling, I'm not buying it."

At something in Early's tone, Charlie gave in a little. "All right, fine. We were going to play Roxy. But only because he has more money than God and he's a criminal himself. We figured he wouldn't ever go to the police because he's too dirty. Everybody knows it around here. But Wang split with the money! He totally scammed me. I wasn't as smart as I thought, okay? The bar's all I have left. It's life or death, Cali. C'mon."

"I really don't see what's keeping me from letting him get out and walk," Monte said.

Charlie threw himself back against the seat. "Are any of you listening to me?"

Monte swiveled, dropped an elbow over the seat. "Can I just dump him?"

Early glanced at Calico. "As much as I'd like to say yes, the kid's got a point. Roxy's gonna be out of his mind when he comes around. We'll get Charlie out of town, then I'll figure out what to do."

Monte wove through Hollywood streets for several minutes, then worked his way back to Tommy's. He pulled in next to Early's truck.

"Looks all clear here."

"They couldn't have known where we were when they texted, could they?" Calico said.

Early scanned the parking lot and the adjacent streets. "I've been back on my heels since I got to this town. I don't know who knows what. It all feels upside down to me and I'm not taking any chances."

"They couldn't be that smooth," Monte said. "Roxy Parsons strikes me as a guy that moves more like a bull than a panther. If his people were around, we'd see them."

"What now then?" Calico said.

"We found Charlie," Early said. "That's what we came for. I say we get in the truck and drive. Right now."

Charlie looked back and forth between them. "Drive where? Back to One Horse? I don't think so. I got a part in a movie, man. An actual part. I'm not gonna go sit in the desert and let everything I've worked for go to waste."

Early eyed him. "Worked for? All you did was run an amateur con and now your sister's in the middle of it."

"Whatever, man. I'm not going anywhere."

"What do you suggest then, Shakespeare? Stay here and let Roxy give you swimming lessons?"

"This is all your fault, man! You punched him out." Charlie turned to Calico. "And yours. If you just would've worked a deal with him, we'd be out of this right now. I'm going back to Mr. Lamont. He'll keep Parsons off my back. I'm not going to One Horse. No how, no way."

"Don't be an idiot. Hammott Lamont is as bad as Roxy Parsons. He's dangerous. You have to see that," Calico said.

"How do you know?"

"Because I've met the guy. He's crazy. You're not going back there."

"He told you I was fine, right?"

"He's a liar, open your eyes."

"You don't know anything about him. He's a genius. I'm an adult, much as you'd like to think I'm not. I know what I'm doing. I met Bono, man. And McConaughey. What have you ever done?"

"What have I . . . ?" Calico shook her head.

"I'm one million percent going back to the movie. You can't stop me. You're not my mother."

"Charlie, I've always been your mother."

"I never asked you to be. Anyway, you could never understand. I'm an actor, man. I've paid dues to get where I am."

"I have no problem taking him back to Arizona, no matter what comes out of his mouth," Early said to Calico.

Charlie opened the door and climbed out of the car. "Forget it, whatever your name is. Look, I'm trying to be cool here. I still don't know how you know Cali, but I guess you did what you thought was right in the moment, even if you did majorly screw it up."

Early got out of the car. The others followed.

Calico walked around. "Charlie, think. For once in your life. You have no idea what you're doing. There are things going on here you don't understand. Lamont toyed with us for his own entertainment. He admitted it to our faces. And he's got some weird fixation with you. Stay away from the guy."

"You're the one that doesn't understand. Hammott Lamont's a genius. I never asked you to come look for me. So in a way this is on you, man. Sorry to be so blunt but it is."

"Did you think I wouldn't try to find you?"

"No, but Mr. Lamont—"

That's when the back window of Monte's Crown Vic blew out.

CHAPTER TWENTY-EIGHT

Early pulled Calico down with him as he dropped behind the car. Monte had Lucinda down as well.

"Was that a gun?" Charlie got to his knees and started to creep up for a look.

Calico grabbed his shirt. "Stay down."

"Where'd the shot come from?" Monte said. "You see anything?"

"I don't know." Early pulled his phone out and dialed 911. The operator assured him units were on the way and asked him to stay on the line.

"This is your fault, man!" Charlie said. "We could've walked away clean. You had to hit him. Now we're dead."

In the distance a siren wailed.

Less than a minute later two police cruisers were in Tommy's parking lot.

Five minutes later three more pulled in.

Twenty minutes after that they were gone.

"Negligent discharge of a firearm," Early said, walking back from where the patrol cars had been parked. "They think it was a gang thing. Maybe an initiation. I guess there's been a rash of it going on in the area. And since we didn't see a vehicle or where the shot came from, not much they can do."

"And you conveniently didn't mention to them you knocked out an insane gangster today?" Charlie said.

"How deep do you want the police into this? Right now you're lucky to be away from Parsons."

"Show a little gratitude," Calico said. "Your whining is giving me a headache."

"Gratitude for what, making it worse? I'm gonna find Hammott. He'll take care of this."

Early looked at Calico, who rolled her eyes, shrugged, and nodded. He pulled up the number and handed Charlie his phone. "That's the main desk, wherever that is. Be my guest, junior. Good riddance. Nobody's kidnapping you."

"Except for Roxy Parsons," Monte said.

"Good point," Early said.

Charlie turned away from them. "Hi, this is Charlie Foster. I mean Charles Foster. I need to speak to Mr. Lamont right away. Uh-huh. Well, where is he? This is sort of an emergency, man. No, I'm Charles Foster. He'll want to talk to me. I . . . No . . . But . . . Then find him! This is *Charles Foster*, do you understand? The lead in the film. Yeah, I'll hold." Charlie glanced back at Calico then walked away a few steps. "Yeah? What do you mean? No . . . Did you tell him who I was? When will he call? Look, will you tell him someone just shot at me? Does that count as an emergency? What? I don't understand. I *am* the lead role. No! He can't just— Hello? Hello?" Charlie lowered the phone, arms limp at his side.

"What's going on?" Calico said.

"They said he's busy. He's at a casting meeting for the lead in his film. He wouldn't even talk to me. He told them to tell me he didn't know where I disappeared to, but he needs someone stable. That the film is too important." Charlie looked down at the gaping hole in the knee of his pants and the blood on his shirt. "And that I could keep the suit."

"Early," Monte said, "you two got your boy. Hit the road. Get back home. That way at least you're out of Parsons's backyard and in familiar territory. Hopefully he'll back off and let this thing blow over."

"You think so?" Calico said.

Monte's lips tightened. "No. That's why I said hopefully. Hope doesn't cost nothing."

"What about you?" Early said. "He knows who you are."

"Yeah, and he's gonna remember for a while every time he wants to use his left hand." Monte scratched at his ear, glanced at Lucinda. "I was thinking it'd be good for Lucinda to go up and stay with her mother in Redmond for a couple weeks. Let things settle."

This brought a flurry of signing from Lucinda.

"No way, no how. I'm not staying with your mother," Monte said. "You know what happened last time."

More signing.

"I'll be fine here. I got friends. They'll watch my back for me."

More signing.

"Monte," Early said, "how about you both tag along with us? If these guys are playing with guns, you can't keep your head down far enough to stay safe. You said it yourself, I'll be on familiar turf back home. And in Paradise I have jurisdiction. I know Jake would like to see you. Think of it as a vacation."

"Have you ever noticed that when you're around it isn't usually all that relaxing?"

"Maybe, but it's more relaxing than getting shot. You can't stay here right now. And I feel responsible."

"Please, Monte," Calico said. "If something were to happen to you or Lucinda I'd never be able to live with myself."

"I've always been lousy at saying no to a lady. But—"

"Then say yes," Calico said.

Lucinda tugged Monte's sleeve and signed with intensity.

Monte sighed. "All right. You win. Tell you the truth, I hate thinking about being apart from Lucinda anyway. But it'd be a little cozy if we all tried to fit in your truck. We can drop the Crown Vic back at the apartment, then me and Lucinda will tag along behind you in the Prius."

"Sounds good."

"I do appreciate the invite. But here or there, I got the funny feeling this thing ain't over."

CHAPTER TWENTY-NINE

WIND SPILLED DOWN FROM THE eastern peaks, rattling the leaves of the massive oak shading nearly the entirety of Paradise's town square. It swirled along First Avenue and whistled through fences. One particularly big gust banged open the glass door of the Jesus Is Coming Soon Thrift Store, knocked over a hatstand, and scattered a stack of newspapers across the floor. Out past the edge of town, where the world either ended or began depending on one's point of view, pines danced and dipped and tumbleweeds tumbled west toward the desert basin.

Early breathed deep, loving it. This wasn't the disconcerting furnace blast he'd experienced out on the coast. In Paradise, when the wind blew it made sense.

Today it welcomed him home.

With traffic getting out of Los Angeles, along with restroom, coffee, and gas stops, it had been a little over a fourteen-hour drive to Paradise. That made for a long, sleepless night, and at this point Early practically had his eyes propped open with toothpicks. They took First Avenue through the residential neighborhoods and past the scattered industrial parks and wound down the mountain. As they dropped in elevation, pines and scrub oak thinned and gave way to high desert. Eventually the road teed and Early swung the pickup left onto Highway 30.

"We're not going to your place?" Calico said.

Early shook his head. "That's the first place they'd expect if anyone follows us out here. That or One Horse. Addresses aren't hard to find. And we need rest right now. We'll spend a day at the Venus, then decide what we need to do."

"What's the Venus?" Charlie said.

"Motel out here. Been around a long time. It's far enough outside of town we won't be too noticeable."

"Do you really think it's necessary?" Calico said. "We're a long way from Los Angeles."

Early cranked down the window and let the air blow on his face. "Ask Charlie. Half a million dollars is a lot of money."

Charlie yawned and rubbed his eye. "I told you, I didn't take—"

"You need to get something through your head once and for all, Chuck," Early said. "As far as Parsons is concerned, you took his money. That means you go to jail if he decides to go the legal route. Or you at least fight it out in the court system until someone produces this Wang guy. That means lawyers. And who's gonna pay for them, your sister? In the meantime, Roxy's people are obviously not playing around. Just ask Monte's back window."

"Yeah, well, you hitting him didn't help either, so there's that." Charlie crossed his arms and looked out the window.

Early lifted a finger off the wheel. "There she is."

In the distance, a towering neon Venus, still aglow in the growing desert dawn, raised a welcoming hand to the empty highway.

"Pines, she's beautiful," Calico said.

"Now that's old-school," Charlie said.

"1941 old-school," Early said. "Story is it was built by a guy running from the Pittsburgh crime syndicate."

"No bugs, right?"

"If there are, I'm too tired to care," Early said. "They can eat me to nothing and pick their tiny teeth with my bones."

"It's not Hollywood, man, but at least there's a pool," Charlie said as they swung into the parking lot.

Early parked, opened his door, and dropped a leg out. "I'd tell him to shut up, but I'm too tired."

"Shut up, Charlie," Calico said.

Monte and Lucinda pulled up next to them and climbed out of the Prius. "Home sweet home?" Monte said.

"For a minute or two."

In the office, Early arranged rooms for everyone, then stepped out onto the sidewalk and passed out keys. No one talked much as they headed off. In his room, he went face-first onto the bed without taking his boots off. He expected immediate sleep. What he got was an endless stream of road reflectors bouncing off the inside of his eyelids and a skull full of white noise. After a while he gave up, got up, left the room, and walked out to the edge of the parking lot in an attempt to settle his mind. Still early. Not a car on the highway in either direction. The wind rolled across the asphalt, moaned through the towering Venus, and tried to tug the hat off his head. He clamped a hand down on it. He leaned against one of Venus's metal legs and watched the rising sun charcoal shadows out on the valley floor.

Something moved in his peripheral vision, pulling his eye up the highway. A coyote loped in his direction, hugging the white lines in the middle of the road. It didn't even glance over as it passed. Early watched until the thing disappeared into the liquid-silver distance. *Coyote is a trickster.* Well, Early had definitely been tricked. Maybe he should start taking the old stories a little more seriously. Then again, Jake would tell him to pray.

"I thought you'd be sleeping."

The voice startled him. He turned to find Calico watching. "For some reason I can't get the road noise out of my head."

"Me neither."

"You see the coyote?"

"The one with the big bomb chasing the three-foot-tall roadrunner? How could I have missed it?"

"I'm serious. Ran right up the middle of the road."

"Are you all right? You don't look good."

Early stared back out at the desert.

"Pines?"

"I don't think God is Lee, okay?"

"Okay."

"I don't."

"Fine. I heard you."

"Good. So that's it. Let's just leave it alone."

"You brought it up, pal, not me."

He hesitated. "I brought it up because what you think matters to me."

She touched his arm. "What I think is Early Pines is a very good guy who's carrying some bags he needs to set down. I'm glad my opinion means something to you. Yours does to me as well. It really does."

Early felt his shoulders relax. Hadn't even realized he'd been tense. He smiled. "There really was a coyote."

"I know. I saw him too." She looked at him, then up at the Venus. "I like this motel a lot. Very Pines. Very eight-track."

"And that's good?"

"Sure, Pines is good."

"Are we rethinking our deal?"

"You're standing out here by yourself staring at imaginary coyotes. Probably roadrunners too. Not exactly the stability I crave. The deal stands."

"Since when do you crave stability?"

"How's the road noise doing?"

"Almost gone."

"Good. Let's go get some sleep."

He sighed, glanced out at the desert, then down the road in the direction the coyote had gone. "Yeah, all right."

"Come on," she said, taking his arm.

They walked across the parking lot without talking. She gave his arm a light squeeze before she stepped inside her room.

He could still feel it when he hit his bed.

He took his boots off this time but that's about as far as he got. Hours later he woke, chilled from the AC, undressed, and climbed under the covers.

He dreamed then. Dashboard lights and endless deserts. Calico in the passenger seat. But then she was gone and it was Charlie. Then Charlie became Roxy Parsons, holding a bloody rag to his face. He kept trying to take a swing at Early but with the seat angle couldn't get power behind it. Then the coyotes came. Hundreds of them. Leaping up from the side of the road into the headlight beams. Early tried to swerve and miss them, but they smashed into his grill with an even, rhythmic thump, thump, thump that made him sick. He rolled over on the bed and forced his eyes open.

Not coyotes. Someone knocking on his door.

"Early!" Monte's voice.

Early sat up, dropped his feet to the floor, rubbed his face with both hands. He gave his head a hard shake. "Yeah?"

"Open the door, cowboy. You need to come out here."

Early pulled his pants on, shuffled over, and swung the motel room door open. Monte stood in the sodium glow of the porch light, a red-orange sunset smoldering behind him.

Early squinted. "Have I been asleep all day?"

"Unless you been watching *Gilligan's Island*. You'd know better than me, I wasn't in there cuddling you." Monte jerked a thumb over his shoulder. "We got a little excitement out here. Visitors. When's the last time this joint had a helicopter land across the road, you think?"

Sure enough, there it sat, black and massive against the horizon, blades thump-thump-thumping.

"Is it Lamont?"

"Yup. And get this, Parsons too."

"Parsons?"

"Raccoon black eyes, hand cast. It's Roxy," Monte said. "Calico chased Charlie out there, then I couldn't see what happened after that 'cause they were all on the other side."

Even as he said it the big chopper's turbines roared, and the blades kicked dust as it lifted off. Calico stood alone in the wash. She watched the helicopter move away, then, head down, walked over to the Venus sign.

"That don't look good," Monte said.

Early pulled on a shirt and his boots. She was waiting for him when he walked up. He stopped short and stared. Blood roared in his ears. "What happened?"

"I tried to talk Charlie out of it, but he wouldn't listen. Lamont paid Roxy Parsons the half mil back, so Charlie thinks everything's golden."

"You know what I mean. Your face. What happened?"

She put a hand to her deeply bruised left cheek. Her eye was red and watering. "I've had worse. This is about Charlie, not me."

"Not anymore. Who did this?"

"Lamont. After the rest were on the helicopter. It came out of nowhere." She glanced out at the desert, then back at him. "He said to tell you it was for you. Payback for throwing him off the boat. That hitting me would hurt you worse than anything else he could think of."

"He's right."

"Pines, I'm fine. It's over. You've done enough."

"Let's get you some ice for your face."

"I know that look. I said I'm fine."

Early looked in the direction the chopper had gone. "Uh-huh. Let's get you some ice."

CHAPTER THIRTY

Charlie might've enjoyed the helicopter ride had it not been for Roxy Parsons giving him the death stare. Dude had his money back, what was the deal? He could've picked any seat too, but he had to take the one facing Charlie. Man, Early'd done a number on him. One punch and Roxy looked like he'd gone fifteen rounds with a diesel truck. Whole face practically one big bruise. And then Monte and the finger. Well, when it came down to it, Roxy had been rude. And cocky. He kind of deserved it. Charlie would've hit the guy himself for what he said to Calico. He was just about to, even. He was gonna elbow the guy holding him in the gut, then flatten Roxy with a roundhouse kick. Wham, bang, bam! Have a nice fall, pal, see you next spring. At least that's how he remembered it when it played back in his head.

But it was all good now, dirty looks or no dirty looks. What did it matter? Roxy was off his back for the money, Charlie had his part again, and he was in a private helicopter about to be served drinks by a fairly decent-looking flight attendant.

The helicopter flew quite a bit lower than planes Charlie had been on, not that he'd been on many. One, actually, if anybody was counting, when his dad had flown the family back to visit an aunt in Wisconsin one time. Charlie couldn't have been more than five. All he really remembered was an endless carpet of clouds beneath them that looked solid enough to get out and stand on. He'd asked his dad if they could and he'd laughed. Which made Charlie laugh. Charlie always loved the sound of his dad's laugh, especially when he laughed at something Charlie said. Which, come to think of it, made Charlie a little sad sitting here in this helicopter that didn't fly above the clouds. Instead, it flew above the desert floor. Fast too. Like the helicopters in those old Vietnam movies. Swooping in to save the day. They called the Vietcong "Charlie" in those movies. Charlie, the bad guys. Weird. Then again, right now, thinking about the hundred thousand dollars he'd talked his dad into borrowing, and that plane ride, and his dad's laugh, Charlie did feel a little like the bad guy. Which was bringing down his mood.

Snap out of it, man.

Because, hey, it'd all worked out, right? Without that hundred grand Charlie would never have had access to Roxy. And without Roxy he'd never have run into that Continuum meeting. And without that meeting he wouldn't have met Hammott. Without Hammott he wouldn't be an up-and-coming movie star. His dad would be proud.

He pushed clouds and worn-out wars and his dad's laugh out of his head.

Everything happens for the best. Don't stop believing, man. "Don't Stop Believin'"—he started to whistle the song through his teeth.

The helicopter was huge. Thing had to seat at least ten or twelve people, not counting the pilots. Like a private jet inside. Wild, man. Out to the west, the sky faded to a dull glow, turning the mountains jagged and black. It looked like a scene from Dante's *Inferno*. Charlie'd never read the dumb poem, but he'd played the video game. He made it a point to play lots of different video games. It was important for an actor to be well-rounded. He pressed his forehead against the window and watched the hard lines of the mountains fade.

Don't go, Charlie . . .

What was wrong with Calico? He'd accused her of being jealous, said that right to her face as she was trying to hold his arm back, but jealousy wasn't her style. A shiver swept him. Probably the AC. He wished Roxy would quit staring at him.

Sunset on the right, so that meant they were headed south.

He leaned into the aisle. "Hey, Hammott, we going back to Los Angeles?"

Hammott, huddled up front with Wayne and Liz, turned in his seat. "Nope. Good news, Charles. Time to get to work. We're headed to the set."

"We have a set finally?" Charlie said.

Hammott laughed. "You're going to love it, Charles. Just you wait."

"Cool. Hey, how did you know where I was anyway?"

Another laugh. "Charles, if you haven't learned by now, there's very little I don't know. Especially about those important to me. And you're one of those."

Charlie looked at Roxy. "What about Mr. Parsons? He's going back with the helicopter after we get dropped off?"

"The helicopter will stay with us, Charles. So will Roxy. He's going to help with the film. He's an experienced director after all."

Roxy grinned at him. Reminded Charlie of a shark about to take a bite out of a seal. Or out of a Charlie.

"Where's the set?" Charlie said. "I grew up down here. Nothing but more desert."

Hammott flashed his teeth. "Exactly! What could be better?"

The helicopter banked a steep climb, pressing Charlie back into his seat, then leveled again. He looked out the window. Horizon glow gone. Only black now, broken by intermittent flashes of strobe lights against the spinning blades. Charlie dozed. Dreamed about One Horse and Calico. The sensation of sharp descent woke him. A few lights below, but he couldn't make anything out. A few seconds later the craft settled with a gentle bump and the rotor whine lowered in pitch as the blades slowed.

Hammott stood. "Liz, would you escort Roxy to his trailer? Wayne, you can take care of Charles. We'll convene in the morning. Not too early. I'll let you know."

The door swung open, and with a wave Lamont faded into the darkness.

Charlie followed Wayne down the steps. Wayne clicked on a flashlight.

"Watch your step, the ground's rocky."

He wasn't lying. Charlie stumbled and almost went down more than once.

"How far is it?" he asked after they'd walked a good ten minutes.

"Mr. Lamont wants you prepared and in character. You'll be a distance from the rest of us. How you doing, Charlie? You all right with all this? Gotta be a change. With Mr. Lamont, things tend to happen fast. You have to buckle up and hang on."

"I'm getting the picture. But I'm definitely glad to be back in, man. Thanks for calling me Charlie and not Charles."

Wayne chuckled in the dark. "Yeah, that'll be our secret. Mr. Lamont has a serious thing about the Charles deal."

"No doubt. Man, we're still not there? There's not even a light out here. How much farther?"

"Not far. You'll love the place. Trust me."

"By myself? Are you staying out here or what?"

"Nah. I gotta be close to Mr. Lamont. Never know when he's gonna need me. Between you, me, and the doorpost, even walking you out here is kind of a nice break. The guy can be crazy overbearing. But a job's a job, right? And I could never make this kind of dough working for anyone else."

"No? That's cool. You have a family?"

"Not yet. But I got a girlfriend up in San Jose. I'm saving money right now. She wants to get married and have kids. White dress, preacher, the whole deal. We're gonna move to Hawaii, the Big Island, when the time comes. Surf and sand, man. Spend the rest of my life on a beach."

"That sounds cool."

"It will be, if it ever happens and I ever get to see her. Now we're out here in the middle of nowhere for Mr. Lamont's film. Who knows how long it'll take?"

"How long do you think?"

"In the past he's worked fast and furious, but this time I don't know. It all feels different. And he's super mysterious about it."

"Yeah. I haven't even seen a script yet. And I'm supposed to be the lead, right? Are there any other actors out here right now? I don't even know what the movie's about."

"I don't know who's out here besides who was on the copter. That's the way Mr. Lamont works. Keeps everyone separate until he needs them. But he's apparently the genius, right?"

"Sounded a little sarcastic there, Wayne. Trouble in paradise?"

"Did it? Nah, man. Seriously, who am I to say? My favorite movie's *Point Break*. You know it? Keanu Reeves? Swayze? Bank robbers and surfers, got it all. I mentioned it to Mr. Lamont once, but he called it trash."

"Ha. I believe it. How much farther, man? I think I'm getting a blister." The night cooled against Charlie's skin. "We going into a canyon or something?"

"Or something. Be patient."

Something in the guy's voice. Charlie slowed.

Wayne turned and shone the flashlight full in his face. "Pick it up, Charlie. Let's go. I don't want this to take all night."

Charlie held up a hand against the sudden glare. "This is weird, man. Why can't I stay back there with everyone else? It's pitch-black out here."

Wayne started walking again without reply. It was either follow or get left in the dark. Five minutes later Wayne stopped and indicated with the flashlight. "Okay, this is it. You first."

"Me first what?"

"You heard me."

"Why me first?"

"Because I said so. Go."

"I want to go back, man. This is freaking me out."

"There's no going back. You chose to be here. Now walk."

"What do you mean there's no going back?"

"I mean what I said. Now walk."

"Which way?"

Wayne shone the light forward. A cave set back into a rock wall. "Go on."

"Into a cave, man? In the middle of the night in the middle of who knows where? Are you serious? Why are you being like this? I thought you were cool."

"Dead serious. It's not so bad. You'll see."

"You ever heard of snakes and scorpions?"

"Don't be a baby, dude. Walk."

Charlie started forward, tripped on a rock, and went down on his hands and knees.

Wayne shone the light down. "You all right?"

"I don't know. I think so."

"Get up and walk, Charlie. C'mon."

"I'm going, all right?" Hands extended, he pushed his way forward. "Is there a lantern or something? A cot? I mean, I'm a method guy, but this is over the top." Something pricked his neck and he slapped at it. "And there's stinking mosquitoes out here too. Is there a net or anything?" He turned and caught a brief glimpse of the needle in Wayne's hand as it passed through the flashlight beam. "What did you do? Are you kidding me?" He realized with a start he was talking from his knees. Then a wooden thump as he went down to his side.

Wayne's voice came from the other side of the world. "Don't worry, it'll be quick. And they tell me it's painless."

CHAPTER THIRTY-ONE

NOT EVEN NOON YET AND Shorty's Café buzzed. Ranchers, clerks, shop owners—every walk of small-town life filled the place. Carne asada plate, today's special, the word of the hour. Monte and Lucinda, enjoying the getaway, had opted to hang at the Venus an extra day or two. Lucinda had told Monte he was sleeping in whether he liked it or not. But Early was beyond restless; he was furious. The fact that Lamont had played them for fools—for what reason only God knew—was one thing, but hitting Calico was another altogether.

Lamont now owed, and Lamont would pay.

Early wanted a fight, *needed* a fight, but the big black helicopter had faded into the twilight, leaving nothing to punch but air.

He and Calico took a table by the big front window. Outside, light shafts filtered through the branches of the massive oak centering the town square, terminating in bright patches of summer on the grass beneath. The huge tree was large enough that it spread out over the streets on every side. It was surrounded by a low wall made of adobe and iron, a grassy park inside, one of Early's favorite places. The sight usually calmed him. Not today. Today he wanted to drink whiskey, not Coke, and he wanted to hit someone, hard. The first he wouldn't do. The second he couldn't because there was no one to hit.

To add to it, Calico had been quiet since they'd left the Venus. She was worried about Charlie. Worried about the bank loan and losing her bar. And also probably worried about what Early would do when he caught up to Lamont. If that was the case, she had good reason—her face looked even worse today.

The bell over the front door clanged and Jake walked in.

Early kicked a chair out for him. "I had a feeling you'd show up. Have a seat."

Jake did, then took off his hat. When he saw Calico his face clouded. "What happened?"

"Hammott Lamont happened," Early said.

Calico's swollen cheek made her smile lopsided. "Hi, Jake."

Jake leaned his forearms on the table. Looked at Calico but spoke to Early. "Early . . ."

"Lamont hit her. *Hit her.* Out at the Venus. He came in a helicopter. Left the same way."

"Listen—"

"Don't try, pontiff. I know you're thinking the same thing I am."

"Of course I am. But I'm also thinking I'd like to keep you out of prison, if possible. There's a right way and a wrong way to do this."

"He was sending a message to me. He told her that to her face."

"Pines," Calico said. "I'm fine. It's over. No one else gets hurt. I'm not going to give him a pass, but let's let the authorities handle it now. It's not worth you getting into even more trouble."

"It's completely worth it. Lamont made it personal and he made sure I knew it was personal."

Katie Morales, Shorty's owner, stopped at the table and passed out water glasses. Her accent rolled thick. "If it isn't my nephew, the mooch. I suppose you're all starving?"

"Why are you waiting tables, Aunt Katie? Who's in the kitchen?" Jake said.

"Your uncle. Complaining nonstop about it too. When's that wife of yours coming back to work? Every other girl I get flakes. Like today. I gotta handle this place all by myself and I'm too old and fat for it." She looked down at Early. "What's the matter with you, you get your tonsils out or something? This is the part where you tell me I'm not fat,

I'm just party size. And that this much beautiful in any given body is bound to overflow."

"All true, Katie. You know I couldn't live without you," Early said.

Katie narrowed an eye at Calico. "Ah, now I see what's the matter."

"Katie, this is Calico," Early said.

Katie nodded a hello. Then, to Early, "How you gonna kill the guy? You decide yet?"

"Don't throw gas on the fire," Jake said. "It's burning hot enough."

Katie leaned down for a closer look at Calico's face. Gently touched her cheek. "You think I'm joking? Who hit you, honey? I swear I'll take care of him myself."

"It's a long story," Calico said. "But thank you."

"Judging by the look on our boy's face, that story's going to have a short and very painful ending."

"Aunt Katie—"

"Jake, I love you and you're every inch a man, but somebody does that to a woman, I'm sending Early. He'll burn the house down and spit on the ashes. You do it right, Early Pines, you hear me?"

"Absolutely," Early said.

"Good." Katie reached down and took the menu from Calico's hand. "No ordering for you. You're with my boys so you're family now. You eat what I bring. Trust me." She scooted off with her tray.

"She's your aunt?" Calico said.

Jake nodded. "Never lets me forget it. Big family around here. Everybody knows everybody." He looked at Early. "You gonna tell me what happened in Los Angeles?"

"Short story?" Early said. "Threw a fat guy off a boat. Got given the royal, very freaky runaround. There was a small car chase. Guy who fancies himself some kind of mob boss got a broken finger, busted nose, and two excellent shiners. You know, things happened."

"Sounds to me like Early Pines happened."

"In my defense, Monte was responsible for the finger."

Early briefly explained the roundabout Hammott Lamont had given them. Then Charlie's situation with Roxy Parsons, culminating with the blown-out car window, the drive back to Paradise, and Lamont's helicopter visit to the Venus.

Katie showed up with a tray piled high. She slid bowls of chips and salsa onto the table. Then carne asada specials in front of the three of them. "There you go. And don't worry, Jay Silverheels, it's on Jake's tab. He stole my best waitress." She scooted off again.

"Has anyone noticed it's always on my tab?" Jake said.

Early picked up a fork. "Why do you think I eat here?"

"Jay Silverheels?" Calico said.

Early chewed. "Guy who played the original Tonto on *The Lone Ranger*. Katie had a crush on him. Probably has to do with me being beautiful sober." He took a long swallow of Mexican Coke. "Jake, do me a favor? Drive Calico back to One Horse?"

"Why?" Calico said.

"Because as soon as we're done here, I'm headed back to Los Angeles. I'm gonna find him and knock his head off."

"Morning, Early. Guess what? You're not going anywhere." Matthias, Early's boss, flipped a chair around backward and sat with his arms folded across the back.

"Didn't see you come in," Early said.

Matthias stared at him, then held out a hand to Calico. "Matthias Gault. You must be the elusive but much talked about Calico Foster."

Calico shook. "Nice to meet you."

"What happened to your face?"

"Hammott Lamont hit her," Early said.

Matthias looked at the bruise on Calico's face, then at Early. "I need a word."

"About what?" Early said.

"You're absolutely sure Lamont did this?"

"I was obviously there," Calico said. "He did it."

Matthias sighed. "Early, you have to stay out of it. Trust me on this."

"No."

"Early—"

"The answer's no. Fire me if you want."

"That's the thing. You're already fired."

"Why? Lamont?"

"You threw the man in the ocean. Have you lost your mind entirely?"

"You don't know this guy."

Matthias looked back at Calico. "I think I'm getting the picture. Problem is, this guy has very deep pockets. And Paradise doesn't. He also wants more than your job. He wants your head on a pike. He wants to hurt you."

"He's doing a good job so far."

"Look, he assaulted a woman. Here. In my jurisdiction. And we'll write it up, open a case. But you won't be part of it. You've got other issues to worry about. Lamont sent a lawyer out from LA yesterday. He's been holed up with Lee at his place. I can only imagine they're talking about suing you, the city, and anyone and everyone else they might think of. And the thing is, they have a case. You out and out assaulted Lee."

Early scratched his neck, looked out at the big oak, then back to Matthias. "So that's it then? I'm really fired?"

"I've been in with city council for the last two hours. They called an emergency meeting over this. They want you out immediately in the hopes of sticking their finger in the dam. Honestly, man, they're right. In the name of damage control, you have to go. I'm sorry, but that's the way it is. You had to have expected it."

"Matthias, look—"

"You assaulted Lee. You shoved a guy through a truck stop stall door. You punched some movie director in a bar?" The police chief stood and flipped the chair back around. "Miss Foster, I'll need a statement, but it can wait till after you've had your breakfast. I'd also like you to see a doctor so we can make sure everything's official. Early, I'm sorry, I am. You never had much self-control to start with, but at least there was some. But since the Gomez Gomez thing that's all changed. This is just the way it has to be. Come by the station in the next few days and I'll have the paperwork ready." He nodded to Jake, said goodbye to Calico, then was gone with a clang of the bell above the door.

Silverware clattered. Across the room a farmer laughed at something his tablemate said. On the radio behind the counter somebody sang a jangly song about the ghost of George Jones. Life went on.

"Pines, I feel terrible. It's my fault," Calico said.

"It's not even close to your fault. It's been coming for a while and I pushed it. I shouldn't be surprised." He sipped his Coke. "He's right, since Gomez Gomez I've been looking for a fight. When Lee stepped into my crosshairs I should've turned around and walked away but I didn't. My choice. Now I live with it."

"So maybe you should learn something from it and leave Lamont to Matthias," Calico said.

"Listen to her, Early. I'm serious. Think about it."

"I know, pontiff, you're always serious. And you always think about it." Early studied Calico, then leaned forward. "Stop lying."

"Lying? What do you mean lying?"

"You say it's not worth it. You want me to back off and forget it. No way, I know you better than that by now. Tell me something, that woman who turned me down flat when I asked her to dance? The one who fumed over being called a sidekick? The one who fights a smile but doesn't want me to know when I joke about buying a ring? What does that girl want me to do right now? Tell me the truth."

Calico glanced at the ceiling and blinked. Her eyes brimmed, but when they met Early's there was fire in them. "I want you to find him. And when you do, I want to knock his stupid, pompous, fat head off."

Early smiled. "There she is."

CHAPTER THIRTY-TWO

THE TABLE QUIETED.

Calico watched through Shorty's window as Matthias wrote a parking ticket and stuck it under the windshield wiper of a double-parked Dodge pickup. The chief was younger than she'd expected. Sandy hair, weathered face brown from the sun. Khaki uniform shirt tucked into Wranglers. And, above all, he seemed fairly reasonable. For a second she considered going out and talking to him, try to get him to take back firing Pines. Because no matter what Pines said, she did feel responsible. But what could she say? Given the situation with his father, the city's position was hard to argue, even if Lamont had hit her. And, about that, it was his word against hers. He might even suggest it had been Pines. After all, Early had a known history of temper. The whole thing looked like a knot there was no way to untangle.

Katie came around and cleared dishes. "You're all quiet. So what did the chief want?"

"I just got fired," Pines said. "So that's fun."

"Oh, man, Silverheels. Because of the Lee thing?"

"Among others."

"Well, I still love you. I got a waitress position open. How do you look in yellow polyester?"

He laughed a little, no conviction behind it. "Probably great, but I'm not quite that desperate yet. Thanks though."

She patted his shoulder. "It'll work out, kid."

"Uh-huh."

"Hang in there." She scooted off to another table.

Pines stood. "Excuse me, I've got Coke coming out my ears."

Jake watched him as he ducked to fit into the hall leading to the restrooms, then looked at Calico. "Did he just say 'excuse me'? Because that phrase has never crossed his mind, much less his lips. What have you done to him?"

She shook her head. "I feel horrible."

"He's right, though. None of this is your fault. He's been daring God to knock a stick off his shoulder since Gomez Gomez died."

"Pines has a hard head. I kinda like that about him."

"Believe me, I've seen it go through more than a few walls and it wasn't the skull that suffered."

"He respects you."

"He might not realize it, but I respect him just as much if not more. I worry about him," Jake admitted. "He talks a tough game, and he definitely backs it up, but there's a whole lot of pain in there. Has been for a lot of his life."

"It's not hard to spot. I told him I thought God and Lee were the same person to him. I shouldn't have. It's deeper than I thought."

"I met Early in kindergarten and even by then he'd learned to talk and joke his way around his dad's temper. He's still doing it, just not with Lee anymore. When I think about it, you were dead on."

"And now this. He'll go charging off to Los Angeles with a sword in his hand against an adversary he can't beat."

"Maybe. Don't underestimate Early. Lamont's bound to have a weak spot."

"I'm not talking about Lamont. I'm talking about God."

Jake considered her. "You know what? You may be the best thing that's happened to him in a long, long time. He's a one-man rodeo for sure, but please tell me you'll hang in there for the ride."

"Is that how you see it? I happened to him?"

"I don't believe in accidents. And you care for him, that's obvious."

She felt the blood in her cheeks. "We have a deal. It's not like that."

"Isn't it?"

"You have to understand, there's a whole lot going on right now. I have zero extra energy or time to repair damaged men."

"And Early's a lot to handle."

"Exactly."

"But you still talked to him about God and Lee."

She looked out the window. "That's different. It was a long drive."

"I'll bet you've discovered by now that he gives a whole lot more than he takes."

Pines's chair scraped as he pulled it back and lowered himself into it. He looked at them. One after the other. "You know what? I don't even want to know what you were talking about."

"Probably good," Jake said.

The door banged and a small, boisterous group entered the dining room. A few men and a woman, all laughing at something one of them had said. They nodded and tossed out hellos to Jake and Pines as they took seats at a neighboring table and picked up menus.

"When do we leave for Los Angeles?" Calico said.

Pines shook his head. "I'm doing this one alone. No arguments. It's not going to be gentle this time."

"Because last time was a church service?" Calico said. "I'm confused. Which gentle are you talking about, the shoving-a-guy-through-a-stall-door gentle or breaking-Roxy-Parsons's-face gentle? Or maybe Lamont-smacking-me gentle?"

"Calico—"

"I think I can handle a little more gentle if it comes up, Pines."

Early wiped his hands on the legs of his jeans. "I'm just saying—"

"You're saying you want to hurt somebody and don't care what happens to you after. Well, thanks to you, you idiot, I care what happens to you now."

Jake smiled. "The first woman on planet Earth to shut Early Pines's mouth. I like her."

"Good, you can buy her a corsage and take her to the prom. She has the time, because she's not going to Los Angeles."

"Something I was thinking about," Jake said. "You said Lamont came to the Venus in a helicopter?"

"Yeah, a huge one. I've never seen anything like it."

"How do you know they went back to Los Angeles? They could be anywhere."

"That's true actually," Calico said. "Lamont never said anything specifically about where they were headed."

A chair at the next table scooted. A woman turned. She wore coveralls. Her gray hair, thick and curly, pulled into a ponytail and pushed through the back hole of an ASU ball cap. "You talking about a big jet helicopter? Kind that carries a bunch of people? Black?"

Pines shrugged. "Maybe it's a jet. Definitely carries a bunch of people. Landed out at the Venus last night. Took off from there."

The woman nodded. "Not many of those big private jobs around. Too expensive for our neck of the woods. But if you're looking, I saw one like that down on the border this morning. If it was at the Venus last night, I'll bet dollars to donuts it's the same one. Those things are scarce unless they're military or Homeland Security and this was neither. I thought it might be connected to the cartel or something."

"On the border where?" Pines said.

"I flew down and picked up a private fare in Tucson early this morning. Took 'em over to Las Cruces. I did the same flight just the day before and that copter wasn't there then, I'd have seen it for sure. It was sitting out in Valle Del Cielo. Big valley out east of Agua Prieta. Whole crazy lotta nothing out there."

"US or Mexico, Gracie?" Jake said.

"US, but down there it's all a little blurry. Just ask the cartel."

"Could you fly us in?" Pines said.

"Nope. Nowhere to land. Way too rocky for a fixed wing. Only way in is a helicopter like they did. Or motorcycle maybe. Probably a Jeep road in from somewhere but it'd be rough. And you never know if things are washed out or not. That place is like the moon. Or Mars. No reason for anyone to go there. You could try to charter a helicopter out of Tucson, but most anybody I know is going to be leery about landing an expensive aircraft smack-dab in the middle of cartel central. Lotta guns down there. Good chance of not taking off again. Hard to fly shot full of holes. If it was me and I really wanted to get there and keep it quiet, I'd go down and hit up old man Hetter for some horses. He's got the closest place to that valley. Rough mountains in between, but I bet he's no more than twenty miles as the crow flies from where I saw that helicopter."

"If it's still there," Jake said.

"Looked like somebody'd lifted in some trailers. Set up a kind of camp. Something's there."

"The movie," Calico said. "Hammott Lamont said he had a place in the desert. It's got to be the movie set."

"That makes sense," Pines said.

"Listen," Gracie said. "I'm doing the same route again tomorrow morning. Same guy. I can check it out, get a little lower, and give you a shout. Let you know if it looks like anyone's around."

Pines nodded. "Thanks, Gracie. That'd be a help."

"Consider it done. I got your number. I'll call you midmorning." She turned back to her lunch.

Pines stood. "I can't look another Mexican Coke in the eye for at least half an hour. How about you?"

Calico glanced at Pines's empty plate. "You sure you don't want seconds?"

"I could. Especially now that I have a line on Lamont."

She got up. "Let's go before I have to wheel you out."

"Where are you headed?" Jake said.

"Out to my place, I think." He turned to Calico. "That all right? I have an extra bedroom for tonight. Tomorrow we can talk about getting you home."

"Not home."

"Home."

"Early, you okay?" Jake said. "I mean really okay? It's a lot for one day."

"Planning a trip is cathartic, isn't that what they say?"

"If they do, I've never heard it. I'll be out later."

"No need."

"Still."

"I said no need."

"I'll see you out there then."

Pines pulled out a ten and put it on the table for a tip. "Yeah, okay. I'll see you out there."

CHAPTER THIRTY-THREE

CHARLIE MOANED, SAT UP, THEN dropped onto his back again, holding his head in both hands. He groped through his mind for something solid to grab, some explanation as to why he felt like he'd been run over by a truck, but anything approaching a recent memory wriggled out of his periphery and slid into the ink.

Then a glimmer.

Wayne.

Wayne had freaked him out, man. Marched him a hundred miles out into hell's outback and got all *Apocalypse Now*–Brando at the end. Stuck him with a needle! *Everyone's gone crazy, man. Completely out of their minds.*

Charlie cracked an eye, wincing at the explosion of pain the simple action produced. He was still in the cave. Surrounded by rock walls. Wind and water carved, it looked like. Not man-made. Sand beneath him. Cool to the touch though the air was warm. He strained to listen but heard only insects buzzing and an occasional bird chirp. His head spun. He closed his eyes to calm it and wound up sleeping again, dreaming of a towering neon Venus that looked like Calico. The air was cooler when he woke. The bird chirp was gone but the insect buzz was louder. Something moved close by and Charlie snapped his eyes open, thinking of snakes. He sat up. The world had settled and he felt better now. The buzz intensified.

"You've got to be kidding me."

The little robot watched him with its cyclops eye from the mouth of the cave. It whirred and moved closer. Charlie got to his knees, holding up his hands to ward it off.

Which was when he noticed the sleeves of the suit jacket. He looked down at himself. Exactly like that first day. A full suit, thin leather flip-flops.

He crawled over to the robot, got close. "Hammott, c'mon. Not again, man. I don't know what this is about. I guess you're filming, right? But I don't know what to do, okay? I haven't seen a script! What kinda movie is nothing but a guy walking around out in the desert dying? Who wants to watch that?"

The robot whirred and backed up a few feet.

Charlie sank back. "Look, I feel like warmed-over death thanks to Wayne. Seriously, you guys drugged me again? There's no way I'm walking anywhere for a week. Where'd you stash the backpack anyway? I could use some water, dude. I'm totally dry."

The robot didn't move.

"Hello? Mr. Lamont? Wayne? Liz? Somebody? Whatever you stuck me with did a serious number on me."

The sun looked bright outside, but Charlie had no way of knowing if it was midmorning or afternoon. He laid down and stared at the cave ceiling.

"You happy with this riveting footage, man? I hope so, because I'm not moving till I see some water."

The more he thought about it, the thirstier he became. He tried to sleep again but couldn't. After a while he scooted out to the cave mouth. The robot whirred happily.

Charlie glared at it. "I hope you're at least getting my good side."

The cave opened to a wide canyon. A hot breeze blew. As the sun inched along overhead, Charlie realized with a pang he was hungry as well as thirsty. He rolled to his side and looked into the robot's eye lens.

"No food, no water. So what? You're watching me die? Some sort of freak film? That's real world-changing art, man. Here, watch Charlie Foster dry up and die, that'll be twelve bucks."

The robot didn't move.

"C'mon, man, please! I don't know if *you* know, but you don't play around with the desert. I'm serious. Look, I'll walk, okay? I'll follow the camera and you can film me the whole way. I'll stumble and stuff. Act. Is that what you want? Tell me and I'll do it. I'll even *die* for you. Just get me to craft services. Get me to my trailer. Gatorade and a power bar. Anything. Hello?"

The robot didn't seem to be on. Was the battery dead? A wave of panic crashed over Charlie, then receded. After all, they had to know where he was, right? They weren't gonna actually let him die out here. It was just one of Hammott's games, that's all. They'd be laughing about this in an air-conditioned trailer in an hour with Liz bringing them cold drinks. And maybe a steak. With garlic bread. A baked potato. Butter and sour cream.

His stomach growled.

And he thought his tongue might be swelling.

Yeah. It was definitely swelling.

And then the sun was gone. And the robot hadn't taken him to the backpack. It hadn't even woke up. Not a whir or a chirp. And Charlie didn't have a lighter to make a fire. *Two sticks.* That's what he'd told Isabella. What a fat lie. He'd almost believed it himself at the time. But whenever he'd seen them try two sticks on *Survivor* it hardly ever worked. Even when it did, it looked like a lot of stinking work. Charlie was too thirsty and sick to work.

There was a prickly pear cactus near the mouth of the cave. He'd seen a movie once where a guy survived days by sucking water out of a cactus. He took off a flip-flop and poked at one of the thick, pear-shaped pieces until it broke off. He picked it up by a thorn and studied it in the half-light. It was heavy. Definitely moisture in there. It wasn't Gatorade, but this was life or death. He tried to work some of the thorns off with a stick, but the things were stubborn. He flung it a couple times against the rock and that worked better, each time giving him a little bigger spot where he could grip. He smashed one end until it was pulpy.

Here goes nothing.

He spat the first bit of sticky, bitter pulp into the sand. Tried again and gagged. The third time he managed to pull enough moisture out of the thing to ease his aching tongue a little, but it wasn't nearly enough. If he ate the whole plant he'd still die of thirst.

"Mr. Lamont . . . please."

The robot might as well have been an oversize paperweight.

Stars began breaking through.

They blurred as Charlie cried.

He crawled back into the cave.

Somewhere, deep in the night, his tears turned to sleep.

CHAPTER THIRTY-FOUR

Calico slept a perfect, dreamless sleep.

She woke to a room filled with soft morning light and the smell of coffee. It took her a moment to place herself. Pines's spare bedroom. Whitewashed adobe walls, clean-swept stone floor, the brass headboard and Indian blanket on the bed. Her suitcase was open on a chair in the corner. Keeping on the T-shirt she'd slept in, she slipped into jeans and flip-flops. The bathroom was empty. She used the toilet, brushed her teeth, and washed up. She did the best she could with her hair, pulling it up into a loose knot. The bruise on her left cheek was yellowing around the edges. She touched it and found it much less painful than yesterday.

She peeked into his bedroom as she passed—empty, bed made. They'd stayed up late. Then he and Jake even later, sitting out on the back patio beneath the stars, talking long into the night in low voices.

She'd seen a different Pines last night. He'd lost his job and a big hammer of a lawsuit hung over his head. But she knew what bothered him the most was that Lamont had hit her. With the fading light, he'd become quiet, receded into himself. It both pained and scared her.

From the kitchen window, as she poured herself a cup of coffee, she could see Jake's truck was gone. She hadn't heard him leave last night. She stirred in two spoons of sugar and sipped, holding the cup in both hands as she looked out at the desert. The adobe was an isolated place.

Not a building in sight. Both strangely at odds with and perfectly fitting its headstrong owner.

She wondered what Charlie was doing. Filming a scene? Sitting in a makeup trailer? Was he out in the desert like they suspected? Or was he back in Los Angeles? Did he know Lamont had hit her? Would it change Charlie's mind if he did? Sadly, probably not. Charlie would only make an excuse for him because that's what would benefit Charlie. Still, she wasn't ready to give up. If she could get her brother away somehow, she would.

The plate glass living room window looked out at the back patio and beyond. Calico stopped and sank into a chair. Outside, Pines sat with his back to her, a cup of coffee in his hand. In front of him on a low table was a bottle of Wild Turkey 101. He sipped the coffee, bringing the cup slowly to his lips. She wondered at his careful movement, but then she saw the coyote. The animal crouched several feet away beside a scraggly sage, tongue lolling to the side, yellow eyes fixed on Pines. For ten minutes they sat like that, Pines taking slow sips, Calico not daring to move, and the coyote staring, still as a statue.

Then Pines stood.

The coyote's ears came up. He backed away a couple inches, eyes still fixed, then crept forward. It took him nearly a minute of wary movement to reach Pines. Cautiously he reached down and scratched the animal behind the ears. At that moment, the coyote seemed to sense Calico's gaze. He met it, then turned and loped away into the brush. Calico rose and stepped out onto the patio through the open French doors.

Pines sat down again. "Morning."

"I scared him off. I'm sorry."

"Don't take it personally, he's obviously a lousy judge of character."

"Are you okay?"

He looked up now. "You don't need to worry about me. I'll be fine. How's the face?"

"A little better today."

"Monte called a bit ago. He and Lucinda are on their way over."

"Good. I'll make some more coffee."

"Thanks."

She started to turn, but before she could, he said, "You know what Jake and I were talking about last night?"

"Probably about losing your job. And the lawsuit. I know it's a hard—"

"We were talking about you."

His eyes were so intense that she averted hers. "Pines, look . . ."

He sighed. "I know. You don't need to say anything. We had . . . *have* a deal."

"The old line is it's not you, it's me, but think about it, in our case it's both of us. I'm barely treading water in life. And c'mon, you're sitting out here mad at Lamont and God and the universe and your dad and who knows what else staring at a bottle of Wild Turkey. Is there any world where this is a healthy match?"

"I'm not drinking."

"Yet."

"I put it there once in a while to see if I'm strong enough."

"You're the strongest person I've ever met. That's God's honest truth. But sometimes strong isn't enough. I'm not talking about the whiskey. I'm talking about us. And fine, if you won't listen to anything else, we have a deal." She wanted to touch him but didn't. "I'm sorry, okay?"

"For what?"

"For dragging you through all this for nothing. And now you've lost your job and you're getting sued. I wish I could take everything back. I wish you hadn't stopped in One Horse. I wish you'd gone straight to that rodeo."

"That hurts worse than getting fired."

"You know what I mean." On her tiptoes, she kissed his cheek lightly. "I'll go make the coffee."

In the living room, she stopped and looked at his broad back through the plate glass. He bent, picked up the whiskey bottle, and in the same fluid movement flung it far out onto the rocks. It caught the sun one last time before it shattered. He stood there for a minute, then sank into his chair and picked up his coffee mug.

CHAPTER THIRTY-FIVE

CHARLIE'S DAD TOLD HIM ON a camping trip once that the old-time cowboys used to put pebbles in their mouths to keep their saliva active on long, dry cattle drives. Charlie spat out a stone. *Well, Pops, I guess you were never lost in the desert, because this idea is lame.* There were a thousand pebbles within arm's reach, every one of them laughing at him, and Charlie hated all their tiny pebble guts. All he could think of was falling face-first into a cold pool of water right after he wrung Hammott Lamont's hairy, fat neck. He put his hands over his ears. The stars laughed louder than the pebbles. And there were a lot more of them. He sucked some more of the prickly pear juice as he lay in the sand staring at the sky. He was getting used to the taste, but it did about as much as the pebble to take the edge off his thirst. He slept a little, his dreams a blue tangle.

The heat woke him. It had to be well over a hundred, even in the cave. Maybe late morning judging by the light outside. He knew immediately he wasn't alone. It took effort to move his head to the side. A face looked into his.

"Heya, Charlie. You still alive?" Wayne said.

"No," Charlie said.

"Time to get up."

"No."

"You want water?"

Charlie opened his eyes now. "Last time I saw you, you stuck me in the neck. I thought I was going to die."

"You didn't though."

A tiny blossom of something akin to hope bloomed in Charlie's gut. "You're serious? You have water?"

"Gonna have to walk to it though." Wayne held out a hand.

Charlie took it and struggled to his feet. He hurt everywhere. His lips burned. Cracked and bloody he was sure. His skin was dry parchment and felt like it would tear if he moved too fast.

"Hammott getting some good stuff? How's he gonna explain all this to my sister once I'm dead?"

"Mr. Lamont's thrilled actually. He says no matter how this ends for you, alive or dead, your name will be immortal in the film world. I've seen some of the footage and it's crazy, man, even to me. I'm telling you, over the top." Wayne started walking up the wash.

Charlie stumbled after, wishing with everything in him he had the strength left to choke the life out of surfer Wayne. He coughed. "Yeah? Better than *Point Break*?"

Wayne laughed the laugh of the living and the hydrated. "Let's not go that far. You're talking about a classic."

"Well, Hammott's happy. That's what counts."

"Sarcasm doesn't look good on you, buddy. Isn't that what you said to me?"

They didn't go far. After a bit, a path angled out of the wash, climbing along a hill. Steep at first but easing as they neared the top. Charlie blinked as they crested and the blast-furnace sun hit him directly. He hadn't realized how protected he'd been down in the canyon. He held his hand up to shield his eyes and saw something up ahead in the glare. They were on top of a flat mesa as far as he could tell. A massive valley fell away behind the shape ahead, edged by tall, broken mountains in the far distance.

A table . . . Yeah, the shape up ahead was a table. White tablecloth and everything. And on the table a bucket and a pile of rocks. And in the bucket a water bottle. Charlie would have cried if he'd had any tears left in his beef-jerky body.

Wayne stopped next to the table, turned, and stood erect, hands behind his back. The wind gusted across the flat top of the mesa, tugging at his faded cargo shorts, faded Hawaiian shirt, and thin, faded hair. He smiled a faded smile beneath his mirrored aviators. "Looks good, doesn't it?"

Charlie watched condensation drip down the side of the bottle.

"What's with the rocks?"

"Got me, man. Mr. Lamont's orders. They set it all up for you. The shot, I guess."

"He's filming?"

"Cameras are always rolling, Chuck. You should know that by now."

"I don't have a script, man."

"So you've said about eighty times. Go on, drink up."

"What's the catch?"

"Why do you think there's a catch?"

"Uh, I don't know. How about because there's always a catch with you guys? Hey, Charlie, come meet Hammott Lamont. Hey, Charlie, you want a beer? Guess what, Charlie, you get to sleep with snakes and follow a *Twilight Zone* robot all over hell's back porch. Hey, Charlie, hop in the helicopter, you're gonna be a star! Oops, don't mind crazy surfer Wayne and his needle collection."

"Do you see anyone here besides you and me?" Wayne held up his hands. "No needles, dude. It's all yours. Go ahead."

"No catch?"

"All yours."

Charlie reached out a tentative hand, eyes locked on Wayne. He touched the bottle. Wayne only watched. Charlie pulled the bottle from the bucket. No Wayne reaction. He unscrewed the cap with care.

Wayne nodded. "Go ahead."

Hands shaking, Charlie brought the bottle to his lips and sipped.

And gagged.

And spat.

"I knew it! What is this?"

"Vinegar, Charlie. You don't recognize the taste?"

"You said there wasn't a catch."

"I said you can have it and you can."

"It's vinegar! That's a catch."

"I never said what was in the bottle, dude. You assumed."

"You're sick, man."

"I only follow orders. What can I tell you?"

"Lamont's nuts, man. He's killing me to make a movie. That's murder! And not just killing me—killing me in one of the worst ways possible." Charlie sank to his knees, his legs suddenly deciding to no longer support him. He started to cry. "I need water, man. And we need to get out of here. This is crazy and criminal. C'mon, you have to see that."

Wayne took Charlie's arm and helped him to his feet. "Get it together, Chuck. You're drooling. I wouldn't have thought you had enough liquid in you for it."

Wayne led him away from the table to the edge of the mesa, a matter of only a few feet. Charlie looked down and his head spun. The cliff was abrupt and high. He started to crumble again but Wayne held him up.

"It's a long way down there, isn't it?" Wayne said. "A couple hundred feet at least, I'd guess. I don't think anyone's measured."

"What do you want?" Charlie said.

"You said Mr. Lamont wanted you to die in the worst way possible. But that's not entirely true. You have a choice. Not a good one, I admit. And I'm totally glad I'm not you, man. But anyway, it's a choice."

Charlie felt sick. "What choice?"

"You know what choice." Wayne pointed down. "Look. See them?"

Charlie did. A small gathering of people standing around a camera. Lamont was there dressed in white. And Parsons. So was Liz.

"You want me to jump?"

"I don't, no. But put it this way: you jump and the thirst stops. Or you walk back down into your little canyon and experience what I can only imagine would be a pretty horrific way to go. A lot of sun and no water."

"You're all crazy. You're as bad as he is."

Wayne dropped his voice, gave the robot a sidelong glance. "I know you think that, man, but listen, with what I'm getting paid for my part in this carnival freak show I'll be able to buy my own island. Or a place on the North Shore with nothing but umbrella drinks and nonstop perfect ground-swell waves. You understand? I'm sorry for you, dude. But I gotta do what I gotta do. And, just between you and me, I gotta get out of this alive too. With Lamont, nothing's guaranteed."

"Well, I'm not jumping, man. No way."

"It'd be the best thing, Charlie. Lamont's not messing around here. It's art."

Charlie looked down at the white figure. Lamont put something to his ear and music cut the still desert air. Charlie knew the tune, his dad used to sing it. Jimmy Buffett's "A Pirate Looks at Forty."

Wayne pulled his phone out of his pocket and thumbed the screen. "Yes, sir?" He nodded and held the phone out to Charlie. "He wants to talk to you."

Charlie took the phone. "Hello?"

"Charles, your voice sounds terrible. I'm so sorry about this. Just know that you're changing the world. It's going to be unbelievable, my friend. You will be a legend."

"Your friend? You left me in the desert without food or water. I'd hate to be your enemy. What do you want?"

"What do I want? I want what I always want, Charles. I want the most important thing there is to want. I want the shot. Because it's the shot that drives the continuum."

"You want me to jump and die so you can film it?"

"You won't die, Charles. You'll finally live! Don't you see? You will be immortal. You'll never die."

"You're crazy, man. I want water, and I want to go home. I quit."

"There is no quitting. There's only the film. Jump, Charles."

"No. I won't do it."

"Charles, think how much more spectacular this piece will be if you only jump. Think, you'll fly for a second or two and then all the pain will be over. And the immortality will begin!"

"No way, man. You're completely psycho. Get me out of here."

Lamont sighed. "Charles, please hand the phone back to Wayne."

Wayne put the phone to his ear. "Yes?" His eyebrows rose. "You're sure? All right." He slid the phone into his pocket, then reached behind him.

And then Charlie was staring down a gun barrel the size of a manhole. "What are you doing?"

"Lamont. You know how he is."

"What?"

"Jump, Charlie. This thing'll put a hole in you so big you could throw a cat through it. You should see it, I'm serious. It's crazy."

"C'mon! It's a prop, right?"

Wayne shifted. The pistol sounded like a cannon in the still desert air. The smell of gunpowder and a hole in the table the size of a fist.

"I'm a *Point Break* guy," Wayne said. "I don't know much about art. But Mr. Lamont sent me with clear instructions, you understand?"

Charlie held up his hands. Had there been an ounce of moisture in his body he would have wet himself. "No, man, I—"

"Jump, Charlie."

"I can't do it! I can't!"

Wayne stuck out his bottom lip, then dropped the gun a couple inches. "Tell you what, to show you I'm not messing around, how about I take out a knee first? Or any major bone. You pick."

Charlie gagged. "Wayne!"

"Pick, Charlie. Or jump."

CHAPTER THIRTY-SIX

MONTE AND LUCINDA ROLLED UP to Early's place around nine. Monte telling Calico he was curious about what the pilot had to say, and that Lucinda refused to go back to Los Angeles until she knew Calico was going to be okay which, much to Calico's embarrassment, brought tears to her eyes. Jake showed up a few minutes later. Calico poured coffee for everyone and they congregated on the back patio. For once, Jake talked more than Pines, he and Monte lobbing rodeo stories back and forth. Calico noticed, though, Jake kept a careful eye on his friend. She would miss these people. The thought brought a momentary pang of loss.

Around ten, Pines's phone rang. He listened a few seconds, then put it on speaker. "Say that again, would you, Gracie?"

Calico took a deep breath, not sure what she wanted to hear. Or what she would or could do about it when she did.

"Your helicopter's still down in Valle Del Cielo sure enough," Gracie said. "Sitting there like they own the desert."

"There's a good chance they might," Early said.

"There's more," Gracie said. "I was curious how a chopper like that could sit right there straddling the border without raising any red flags with the boys at the good old US border patrol. Things are hot down there these days, you know? So I called a friend of mine with the agency over in Nogales. He says they were notified and know all about it. It's private land and somebody's filming a movie down there. Asked not to be bothered if possible. A request the border patrol would normally ignore. But these helicopter guys apparently have some kind of clout."

"A movie." Pines glanced at Calico. "I appreciate it, Gracie. I owe you one."

"Hey, all I did was look down, then make a phone call. Hope it helps."

"It helps. See ya."

"By the way, sorry about your job, Early. I heard."

"My own fault. I'll survive."

"Yeah, okay. Let me know if I can do anything else, all right? You got my number."

"Will do." Pines thumbed off. "It's them. What do you think?"

Calico stood and looked out at the desert. "I think my brother's an idiot."

Pines touched her arm. "Grab your things. I'm taking you home."

She studied him. "You're suddenly in a hurry to get rid of me now?"

"Yeah."

"Because you're going after Lamont."

"Yeah."

"Down there."

"Yup."

"What do you think you can do?"

"Don't know yet, but I'm going. He doesn't get to punch a woman and just fly away."

"How do you plan on getting there?" Jake said. "Gracie said yesterday the only way in is helicopter or horseback. You don't have a helicopter last time I checked."

"I'll do exactly what she suggested—go down to that rancher Hetter and rent a couple horses."

"You know the guy?" Jake said.

"Nope."

"You think you're just going to show up and a border rancher's gonna give you horses to ride south?"

"I guess I'll find out."

"I know Lou Hetter," Monte said. "Met him a couple times when I was wrangling on shoots down in Tombstone. He used to have a lot of good stock. Probably still does. He's a cantankerous old cuss, but I bet he'd rent if I asked him. A ride sounds good to me."

"Nah, Monte," Pines said. "You should head back to LA and your relaxing. You've done more than enough. And I'm not forgetting I owe you a back window."

"You don't owe me nothing. I'm the one that broke Roxy's finger. And I'm not going anywhere but down to the border with you. You can't put me in the game then bench me at the top of the eighth, no, sir. Don't even think about it. Lucinda can stay here with Calico."

"I'm going too," Calico said.

"No way," Pines said. "You're going home."

"If you're going, I'm going, Pines. That's the way it's been. Why break tradition now? Besides, I'm the one Lamont hit."

Lucinda let go with a flurry of signing. Calico didn't know the language, but the woman's intent was clear enough—she'd not be left behind either.

"Look," Pines said. "This is out of the question. Any way you look at it, it's gonna be a rough ride. And that border country is a long, long way from being the safest place in the world."

"I grew up in border country," Calico said. "Or did you forget?"

"I know that look on Lucinda's face," Monte said. "Might as well throw in the towel."

"Have either of you ever even been on a horse?" Pines said.

Lucinda poked Monte.

"She might not look like it, but Lucinda was born in the saddle. That's one thing I'm not worried about. She'll outride us all and make it look easy."

"I've ridden before," Calico said. "And even if I hadn't, I'm not letting you go by yourself after I started this whole thing."

"I think I'll tag along too," Jake said.

Pines eyed him. "Don't you have work to do?"

Jake lifted a shoulder. "Honey can take care of things for a day or two. And you know her, if I don't come bail you out of whatever tangle you're about to get into—and there will be a tangle—I'll never hear the end of it."

"She loves me, that's true," Pines said. "But I can take care of myself."

"Uh-huh. I'll bring bail money for the Mexican jail."

"That was one time," Pines said.

Jake held up two fingers. "Two times."

"All right, two times. But they were a long time ago."

"Not that long. If I were headed out on something like this, are you saying you'd sit back and watch? I know you and you know me. Plus, my truck's a crew cab. We can all ride down together and still have room for gear."

Pines grinned. "Fine. Tell you the truth, I'd feel better having you along. We can swing into Paradise and grab your saddle and tack on the way."

"It's already in the truck," Jake said. "A few sleeping bags and food too. You're predictable."

"Lou'll most likely have plenty of gear. And he'll outfit us, I'm thinking." Monte held up his phone. "I just looked him up. Didn't even need my rolodex. I'll give him a call on the way down."

"Let's go then," Calico said.

The sun hung mid sky, leaving the desert without shadow as they pulled out. Pines sat up front with Jake, Calico in the back with Monte and Lucinda. Pines had figured it at about a five-hour drive to Lou Hetter's ranch. The day wound on. They talked little, each of them preoccupied with what lay ahead. Pines had been right when he'd said it was a dangerous area they ventured into. The Mexican drug cartels had long used this desolate piece of the Southwestern US border as a personal highway. And not only for smuggling drugs. Flesh, bone, and soul were in-demand commodities as well. There would be no 911 out there. No quick response should trouble come. Pines had strapped on his pistol before they'd left his adobe. Jake had a rifle in the truck. But firepower or not, if this rancher would indeed loan them the horses, they'd be riding headlong into a broken land where only God could protect.

The drone of the tires made Calico drowsy. Plenty of time to worry later. She closed her eyes and dozed. The sun was still bright but pushed farther to the west when a tap on the brake pedal woke her.

"Who is that and what's she doing?" Jake said.

"I have no idea," Pines said.

Calico sat up. She recognized the Chiricahua Trading Post up ahead.

And standing in the middle of the road, light reflecting off mirrored sunglasses, wind playing with wisps of gray hair, an old woman.

CHAPTER THIRTY-SEVEN

Early watched the woman's form take shape. Traditional Navajo attire, ancient as the desert. Heat waves settled and receded around her as the truck neared.

"Is she crazy? Pull in, Jake."

"We could use a pit stop anyway." Jake pulled off the road to the right of the woman and drove into the dirt parking lot. She stared at them as they passed, lined face unreadable. Jake parked, killed the engine, and they all climbed out.

"You all right?" Early called.

The old woman grinned at this, waved, then shuffled off the road and across the parking lot, moccasined feet kicking up tiny clouds of dust.

"What was that about?" Jake said.

The woman sank to her knees next to a blanket covered with rings and other silver jewelry.

"No clue," Early said. "Grab me a water, will you?"

"You're not coming in?" Calico said.

"The lady has me curious."

While the others headed inside, Early walked over and squatted on his haunches in front of the woman's blanket. "Yah ta hey, mother."

Obsidian eyes looked him up and down. "Yah ta hey."

"What's the special today?"

Her face collapsed into a thousand wrinkles when she smiled. "You in the mood to dicker?"

Early pushed his hat up on his head and scratched at his cheek stubble. "I don't think so. I get the distinct feeling I'd lose."

"Probably. You want something nice? For your girl maybe?"

"Unfortunately, as it turns out, it's just the three of us these days—me, myself, and I."

"Too bad. You're a good-looking boy."

"That's exactly what I keep telling everybody."

"How about a ring for yourself? Big man like you should have something on his hands."

Early scanned the blanket. "I don't know. I got big fingers."

The woman cackled a laugh. "Big fingers, big heart. I got all kinda rings for all kinda size hearts." She selected a wide silver band with a good-sized turquoise stone and held it out. "Try this."

Early slipped it on, surprised it fit. "It's not bad."

"Not bad? That's a nice ring."

"Okay, you win. I like it. How much?"

"Good turquiose."

"Uh-huh. How much?"

"Durango silver."

"Give me a number, mother, 'cause I'm about to take it off and put it back."

"Eighty-five bucks. Firm. Now go ahead and make me an offer so I can say no."

"You really want me to?"

"Sure. It'd be fun to watch you crash and burn. My entertainment for the day. It's been pretty slow."

"I'm unemployed at the moment. How about a discount?"

"My heart breaks. Eighty-five."

Early stood and pulled his billfold from his back pocket. He fingered out a hundred-dollar bill and handed it to the woman.

"I don't have any change," she said.

He squatted again. "I didn't expect any."

Another thousand-year grin. "You're really lousy at this. You know that?"

"Uh-huh. Anyone ever tell you standing in the road is a good way to get hit?"

She cackled again. "Never happen. You're the first vehicle I seen in over an hour."

"You been standing out there for an hour?"

"You think I'm stupid? I went out there when I heard your truck. I don't have many teeth inside my head, but I still got real good ears on the sides of it."

"Why did you stand in the road?"

"Why do you care?"

"I don't know, I just do."

"Get you to stop, of course. What do you know? It worked."

A wind swirled, pulled at Early's shirt, lifted a corner of the jewelry blanket.

"That's a tough way to get customers. Especially in this heat," Early said.

She studied him. "Not to get customers. To get you. You've got a troubled face. Do you have dreams?"

"What do you mean 'to get me'?"

"The world's a mysterious place. Get over it. What about your dreams?"

The old woman definitely had a screw loose, but Early felt bad for her sitting out here in the heat. "Everybody has dreams."

"But your dreams are different. Tell me."

He polished the ring on his jeans and looked at it. "If I tell you my dreams, I tell you my path, isn't that the deal? Aren't I supposed to keep them to myself?"

"Depends."

"On what?"

"You're not Native. Maybe a little, huh?"

"My grandmother was Navajo."

"A quarter then. Are you religious in the Navajo way?"

"No disrespect, but not really."

"That's okay. In any way?"

"I think God has a bad sense of humor and I don't like him much. What way is that?"

She nodded as if she'd expected this. "That's what I thought. The running way."

"What's that supposed to mean?"

"Not much, just that you're gonna get tired legs. That's about all the running way gets you. What's it gonna hurt to tell me your dreams anyway?"

Early considered. "I'm not sure. I'm a little Navajo. Maybe, when I think about it, I'm a little superstitious."

"Navajo way says if you dream bad things, you should pray them away before the sun comes up."

"You can interpret dreams?"

"Maybe, maybe not. But sometimes dreams mean something."

"What the heck, you already got my hundred bucks. Sometimes I dream a lot about a guy I knew who died a while back."

"That's why you don't like God's sense of humor? Because this guy died?"

"The guy's only the cherry on the sundae, trust me."

"Boo-hoo, you think you got a patent on tough times? Was this guy a relative?"

"He was like a brother, so what does that mean?"

The bony shoulders shrugged. "Could be bad, could be nothing. Or it could just mean you're nuts. Either way you should slow your legs down and quit running."

Early laughed. "You're a real encourager, you know that?"

"Want encouraged, get yourself a life coach. I tell it like I see it."

"I don't feel nuts."

"So? Nobody feels nuts when they're nuts."

"You sure about that?"

The wind swirled again. Early held up a hand against the dust. The old woman just blinked.

"How did your friend die?" she said.

"Got bit by a snake."

"That's very bad. You ever hear an owl?"

"Nope. And I know all about owls. They call you when you're gonna die. I'm safe on that count. When did this turn into a job interview anyway?"

"Never. I'm not hiring." She pointed to the pistol on his hip. "You're a violent person?"

"I wish I could say no. Sometimes I am."

"You're on your way to commit violence now?"

"With any luck. But the man deserves it."

"We all deserve it."

"You're probably right about that."

"Not probably, I am. You need to let your friend go. And stop being the running kind. And you need to pray."

"Pray to who? Mother Earth?"

"Don't be dense. Mother Earth is a speck of dust. You think a speck of dust can answer prayers?"

"I already told you, me and God aren't friendly."

"Because your friend died? So what? Everybody dies. Seeds can't become trees unless they go in the ground. You want to carry that soul of yours in that body forever?"

"Gotta admit, it's a good-looking body."

"Exactly what a tired-legged runner would say. Show me that body again in fifty years."

The store door clunked shut and footsteps approached. Calico knelt down next to Early, handed him a bottle of water and another to the old woman. Early unscrewed and drank; the woman nodded thanks and set hers on her blanket. She narrowed an eye at Early.

"I thought it was only you, yourself, and you."

"It is. She and I have a rule," Early said. "Apparently four's a crowd."

The old woman sniffed. "Rules are made to be broken. Especially dumb ones like that."

"You've now become my favorite person," Early said.

Calico pointed. "That's a beautiful ring you have on. I've never seen anything like it. Is it Navajo?"

Early hadn't noticed the old woman's ring. Delicate, intricate bands of silver holding a clear sky-blue stone.

"You change the subject, huh?" the woman said. "Smart girl. No, this ring is not Diné. And no, you haven't seen anything like it 'cause it's one of a kind. It's not for sale." She scanned her blanket, then picked up a necklace. Silver, holding a small stone similar to the ring. She handed it to Calico. "For you. Because I can see you're a strong woman."

"It's beautiful," Calico said.

"It's very old. I've had it many years. Been waiting for the right person to give it to."

"Give?"

"That's right."

"I can't let you give it to me. I'll buy it."

The woman waved a hand. "How can you buy a gift? It's impossible. It's yours now."

"You let me buy my ring," Early said.

The old woman cackled. "Do I look like I'm made of money? Besides, I don't like your hat."

"Of course you don't," Early said.

The woman looked past them out at the desert. "Where were you headed before you pulled in here? Where is this violence of yours?"

"Call it parts unknown," Early replied.

"No such thing. Every part is known. Still, you gotta be careful on a trip like that. Remember what I told you."

"Pray?"

"Yup. It'll get you a lot further than that hat. I'd tell you to turn around and go home, but men with bad hats and pistols on their hips don't usually do that."

"This is something I gotta do."

She gave a slow nod. "If you gotta do it, then do it. But those legs aren't gonna last forever." She pointed out toward the desert. "Especially with that guy nipping at your heels."

Early followed her finger. Fifty or so feet away, a coyote sat on its haunches in a little clearing of scrub, eyes fixed on them. "When did he show up?"

"Little before you did," the old woman said. "How I knew you were coming."

"I don't believe that for a second."

A shrug.

Early stood, jerked a thumb at Jake's truck. "Tell you what, if Coyote's chasing me, he'll have to hit at least seventy."

"You'd be surprised what a trickster can do."

"It's not my first rodeo, mother."

She laughed again, eyes shining. "It's not the first rodeo that counts, boy. It's the last."

Early scratched his neck, glanced back at the coyote. "Good point. You got a tip for going the whole eight seconds?"

The black eyes considered. Another gap-toothed smile. "You really want a tip?"

"Why not? I'll take all the help I can get."

"Okay, hat boy. Bend down and let me tell you a secret. Or maybe, if you're lucky, I'll tell you three, one for each of you."

CHAPTER THIRTY-EIGHT

BACK IN THE TRUCK, CALICO entertained herself by counting mile markers. Around number twelve she surveyed Pines's profile.

"You're quiet. What did the old lady whisper to you?"

"If I tell you it won't come true."

"It wasn't a birthday wish, Pines. C'mon, spill it."

"Nope. Between me and the coyotes."

"You're really not gonna tell me?"

He smiled, leaned his head back, and pulled his hat down to his nose. She rolled her eyes and went back to mile markers. After a while she lost count and just watched the desert roll by.

What Pines had estimated as a five-hour drive turned out to be eight, the last four on a teeth-jarring, washboard-gravel road.

To say Lou Hetter's ranch was remote was like saying Elvis Presley put out a popular song or two, but once reached, the property impressed. Calico slid out of the truck with a groan and took a look around. A huge barn surrounded by a dozen or more corrals backed up against a towering black cliff. To the left, the ranch house itself sprawled, a rambling adobe-brick affair. A woman, bent nearly in half with age, worked a broom over the long stone front porch. Another sat in a rocker. A small army of Mexican children played in the yard. Calico had the immediate feeling she'd stepped back in time a hundred and fifty years. It wasn't full dark yet, but the area lay in shadow, the sun having dropped behind the mountains.

A man stepped out through the front door of the ranch house, face deeply lined, hair swept-back and white as bleached cotton. He wore a plaid long-sleeved shirt, stiff new Levi's jeans, and spit-polished boots. He didn't smile but, when he saw Monte ease his frame out of the back seat of the truck, offered a curt wave.

"Monte Shaw," he called out. "What the heck happened to you? You got all old on me."

Monte laughed. "Yeah? Well, you were always old, Lou. Least I can say I got a few good years in first."

Hetter stepped down off the porch and approached. He smiled now, his tobacco-stained teeth a contrast to his white hair. He took in Calico and Lucinda. "Least you brought somebody prettier'n you."

"Not hard to do," Monte said.

"True enough. Come on up and have something to drink, I guess."

Hetter led them up onto the porch. He offered them chairs, but after the long ride no one felt like sitting.

Monte made introductions all around. Hetter leaned over the rail, spat a stream of brown juice, then fixed his blue eyes on Jake. "You're Jake Morales, the saddle bronc rider?"

"Not for a while," Jake said.

Hetter grunted. "You probably rode some of mine. I raise some good rodeo stock."

The woman who'd been sitting on the rocker when they'd arrived backed through the screen door with a tray of iced teas and passed them around. She was dark and round with beautiful, happy eyes. She gave a shy smile when she handed Calico a glass. Calico smiled back and nodded her thanks. The woman gave the last glass to the ancient sweeper, who murmured something in Spanish and creaked her body onto a rocker.

"We're a big family out here," Hetter said. "As you can see, I'm well taken care of. Keep a dozen or more vaqueros on at any given time to work the place." He pointed to several small homes built along the cliff face, then the kids in the yard. "Most of 'em got families and they're all welcome. It's a wild, lonely place."

"Looks to me like a nice way to live," Jake said.

Hetter nodded. "World don't touch us much down here. Cartel gets a little cranky once in a while, but they mostly leave us alone. Border patrol swings by occasionally, takes a look around." He spat again and waved a hand toward the cliff. "There's a defined border down there for sure, but there's also some element of no-man's-land to this country. Gets in the news every time an election rolls around, but most of the time things kinda float along out here, if you know what I mean."

The old woman finished her tea and got to her feet, taking up the broom again. Hetter machine-gunned something in Spanish. She nodded, smiled, and sat down.

"She'd work till she dropped if I let her." Hetter fished out his tobacco wad from his bottom lip and tossed it into a rosebush at the base of the porch. Took a drink of his iced tea, Adam's apple bobbing, then gave a satisfied exhale. He eyed Early. "So, Monte says you want to ride back into Valle Del Cielo. Why in the he—" He glanced at Calico and Lucinda and his neck reddened. "Pardon my language. Why in the world would you want to do that? That country's a hearty slice of hades on earth, no two ways about it."

Pines laid out an abbreviated version of the situation.

Hetter scowled. "Film shoot way out there? Had a couple of 'em here on the ranch over the years. But I don't know what they want with that valley 'less it's some kind of space picture and they want to pretend they're on the sun or something."

"We were told horses would be our best option," Pines said.

Hetter looked thoughtful. "I'd agree with that. Roads would be iffy for anything with wheels. Helicopter would get you there in minutes but everybody and their *hermano* would hear you coming. That might not be the best situation 'less you're bulletproof."

"So we'll need horses to ride and a couple to pack," Monte said. "You game? Our money's green."

Hetter looked at Calico again. "You're all *gente loca*, but I can facilitate you if you're determined. And no charge. Any man who'd hit a woman gets no love from me. That's a fact."

"Much appreciated," Monte said.

Hetter shrugged. "De nada."

"We'll need directions in," Jake said.

Hetter spat again. "I could probably count the times I've ridden back that way on one hand. It's semi-passable, but I ain't gonna lie to you, it won't be easy. I'd suggest heading out before first light. Get as far as you can before it gets too hot, then rest your animals through the worst of it. If there was a tree back there, which there isn't, it'd be bribing dogs to whiz on it. And the trails are crookeder than a box of fishhooks, but I got a couple boys working here that know them pretty good. I'll have somebody draw a map for you. You better follow it close, though. Ain't no help out there. Not by a long shot. Even and especially from me."

"Understood," Pines said.

"Good. Now, Consuela's put together some rooms for you. And she's got food on. You better eat it, or she'll get all bent out of shape and make my life miserable."

"Not a problem there," Pines said. "I'm starving."

Hetter smiled, fished a tobacco can from his back pocket, fingered out a generous amount, and stuffed it down into his bottom lip. "After dinner we'll go pick you out some horses."

CHAPTER THIRTY-NINE

A COUPLE DAYS AGO, CHARLIE would have counted the fact that Wayne hadn't shot him as one of life's pluses.

But that was a couple days ago.

After he didn't jump, and after Wayne dumped him back in the canyon, Charlie pushed himself with the last of his strength into the mouth of the cave. At least he could hide inside from the sun while he died.

And if Charlie knew one thing, it was that he was dying. He'd complained before. Whined about his thirst. But now, day whatever with nothing but cactus pulp passing over his cracked gums . . . this was for real, man. He laughed, a horrible scratching sound in the still desert air. He didn't want to die. But he saw the situation in vivid Technicolor. How could he not have seen it before? Calico had been right to warn him. Hammott Lamont was crazy, bottom line. Even now, the awful little demon of a robot stared at him. Whirring away with its unblinking eye. He thought about taking a rock and smashing it out—that would teach old Hammott, deprive him of his moment-of-death money shot—but Charlie almost didn't have the energy to think it, much less do it.

He heard the footsteps crunching up the wash before anyone arrived. It didn't sound like Wayne, though. Heavier. And unsteady. He didn't care. He was past any sort of caring. He closed his eyes and focused on dying.

A foot bumped his side. He mumbled and tried to wave it off, though he didn't think his hand actually moved.

Another kick. Harder this time.

It took effort to move his head to the side. A face looked down. Blurred, bloodshot eyes. Red flaked skin.

"Roxy?" Charlie rolled over and closed his eyes. "Whatever it is you want, man, just let me die."

The producer's voice came from far away, bounced through a few dried-out riverbeds and across salt flats before reaching Charlie's ears. "Get up, kid."

Charlie rolled back and cracked an eye. "You have water, man? I need water so bad. Where's Mr. Lamont? Where are the others?"

The little robot whirred and rolled close, lens fixed on them.

"What's going on?" Charlie looked at it, then at Roxy. "I don't get this, man. Why is he trying to kill me? And film it? C'mon, I seriously need water."

"Get up," Roxy croaked, the two words seeming to be the only ones he could manage.

Charlie flopped back onto the sand and groaned. "I'm dying."

Another kick to Charlie's side. "Now, Charlie."

Something in the guy's voice. Charlie sat up and looked at him, really looked at him. Roxy was a real mess. Hair matted with twigs, face drawn, eyes sunken.

"You look like I feel. What did they do to you, man?"

Roxy's eyes took on a desperate sheen. "No time for talk. Just c'mon."

"Tell you the truth, man, I don't think I can stand," Charlie said.

"Please." Gone was the mouthy Los Angeles gangster. In his place was a beaten, broken shell. "If I can stand, you can stand." Roxy held out a hand.

Charlie reached up, took it, and let Roxy help him up. Roxy motioned him to follow and he did his best, stumbling after him on wooden legs.

The mesa again.

And Wayne.

"Oh no," Charlie said.

Roxy said nothing.

"Heya, Charlie." Wayne said as they approached. "How's tricks?"

"Shut up, Wayne."

"Now is that any way to talk to the guy who didn't shoot you last time you saw him?"

"Yeah, thanks for that. Feels like Christmas in summer."

The table was there again. Ice bucket and water just like before.

"What's in it this time? Dog slobber laced with cyanide?" Charlie said.

"Nothing but good, old, fresh spring water," Wayne said. "That's a promise."

Charlie snorted. "And no catch, I suppose? Hammott's suddenly feeling giving?"

"Nope, there's definitely a catch this time. But not much of one for you."

"I'm not jumping off any cliff, man."

"Don't have to. Just drink the water."

"And what happens?"

"You live."

"Uh-huh. What else?"

Wayne shrugged and indicated Roxy. "Not much. Roxy dies."

"Dies?"

"Look at him, dude. He's in as bad a shape as you are. Maybe worse because he didn't figure that cactus thing out. So that's the deal. There's one bottle of water and no sharesies. Your call, Chuck."

"You're sick, man. I'm not doing that."

"Not as sick as you." Wayne jerked a thumb at Roxy. "Not as sick as him either. You guys are a mess. Crazy what the desert'll do to you. See why I'm thinking Hawaii?"

"You can't do this," Charlie said.

"I can and I have to. So what do you say?" Wayne said.

"Wayne, I—" Roxy started to say.

Wayne cut him off with a hard hand. "Not your call, dude. I already told you. You live or die on Charlie's word, period. You know the drill. Charlie, I'll ask you again, what do you say?"

"I say this is crazy. Let's just stop, all right? I'm not sentencing somebody to die." Still, he couldn't help his eyes traveling to the bottle of water.

"I know," Wayne said. "I bet nothing ever looked so good."

The little robot whirred over, its single eye taking in everything. Charlie stared at it, then at Wayne. "Wayne, be serious. You can't do this. I can't choose."

"Simple instructions, simple choice, man."

"It's not simple when you've been dying in the desert for days."

"Sure it is. Probably even simpler."

Charlie looked at Roxy. The producer's eyes were on the bottle. His legs shook.

"Listen to me," Wayne said. "They say a human in decent shape can live without water between two days and a week. I would've thought longer, but I'm no expert. Now, those cactus leaves might extend you a bit, but face it, you're tapped, dude. Without this water right here, you're gonna die. No way around it. Think. You've got a future, man. Mr. Lamont is ready to make you a star, right? So let's up the ante. What if I said you can have whatever you wanted? You tried to steal half a mil? You can have a hundred times that. Your own chopper. Your own mansion—mansions—wherever you want them. Anything. The world is yours, all you have to do is pick up that water and live."

"Lamont would give me all that?"

"Let me tell you something. Hammott Lamont is willing to give you every cent, every piece of property—everything he owns—to do this film. He'll even give you his name."

"His name?"

"Think about it. You'd be the genius for once. You'd be the one in the driver's seat."

Roxy made a half-moaning, half-hissing sound, as if someone was deflating him, and sank to his knees, where he started to cry.

"But Roxy has to die?"

"C'mon, chief. If Roxy was in your shoes right now and you were in his, he'd be halfway through that bottle and you'd be on your way back to your cave for the ants to eat you. He hates you, Chuck. So how is this even a decision, man?"

"Because it is! This is insane."

"Nope. It's art, man. The real deal. So think now. You can have it all."

Charlie stared at the bottle. "If I don't drink the water what happens to him?"

"He gets the bottle, goes back to a nice trailer to recoup and rehydrate, then goes on doing his producer gangster gig, I guess."

"And I go back and die."

"I know you, Charlie. We all do. You'll take the water. Come on now, it's hot out here. Heck, nobody's gonna miss Roxy, trust me. They'll be glad the dude's gone."

"He'll suffer."

Wayne shrugged, pulled his giant pistol from the back of his pants, and pointed it at Roxy's bowed head. "What if we solved that problem right now? Make it easier?"

"No, man! It doesn't." Charlie couldn't take his eyes off the bottle. A drop slid down the side. A gust of wind rose and tugged the white tablecloth. He swallowed, his throat raw, his tongue a sock full of hot gravel. He couldn't believe he was even thinking about this. "You'd really kill him?"

"Not me. Lamont. Roxy's a criminal, man. He'd take this gun and shoot you in the face if it'd get him a quarter. That's the truth. I don't want to influence your decision, but don't be an idiot."

Don't go, Charlie . . .

Why hadn't he listened to Calico? She'd actually left the bar and come all the way to Los Angeles just to find him. Then again, when had he ever listened to anybody?

Don't go . . .

And now he'd never see her again. She'd never even know what happened to him unless Hammott actually filmed this.

Don't . . .

She loved him. Though for the life of him he didn't know why. He'd never done a thing deserving of it. And now this. Standing on the back side of hell being played with by a crazy man. He looked down at Roxy's thinning hair. The man's scalp was angry red. Tiny beads of sweat had formed.

Wayne pulled the pistol's hammer back, the click loud in the desert air. "Everything, Charlie. The world is yours, man."

"Hammott's filming? Really?"

"Always. You'll be immortal, man."

Don't go, Charlie . . .

Charlie took one last look at the bottle, then turned and started walking.

"Charlie?" Wayne called. "You can't be serious, man! For Roxy Parsons?"

Charlie lifted a tired hand. "See you, Wayne. I know the way back to the cave."

Calico would be proud of the last choice he ever made.

CHAPTER FORTY

THE RELENTLESS FEELING OF DREAD grew steadily as they rode. Calico did her best to push it away, but the more she tried, the more it pressed.

"You all right?" Pines said, edging his horse alongside hers at a wide point in the trail.

She pulled herself from her mind and offered what she hoped was a confident nod.

He touched her arm. "Hey, seriously, are you all right?"

The fear overwhelmed. "No. Something's wrong. Charlie's not okay. I can't tell you how I know, but I know."

They'd started out before the very first smudge of gray touched the sky. Too dark to see clearly, but Lou had sent a rider with them to get them started. The man spoke very little English, but he'd put them on the right trail and pushed along with them for several miles before turning back with an apologetic smile and wave. Several miles farther now, and late morning brought the heat with it. The path up to this point, when there had been a path, was like nothing Calico had seen before, even growing up in the desert. Black volcanic rock rising in great slabs on both sides, and smaller perpendicular ridges beneath their feet. They'd let the horses pick their own way to protect their hooves from the sharp stone. The occasional gourd plant had been the only vegetation. They saw no footprints of either man or beast.

Through the morning they'd climbed up and into the hills, stopping only once to give the animals water. Calico had been impatient to push on. With every step, every clop of hoof on stone, the feeling grew in her that time was short and getting shorter.

Pines loosed his canteen from the saddle horn, unscrewed the top, and offered it to her. She drank and handed it back. "Can we go any faster?"

"Nope," Monte said from behind them. "We're pushing as hard as we can now. It's not gonna get cooler either. We'll hit that spring Lou's man put on the map in a few miles. We'll have to wait there through the heat of the day. We got no choice, I'm sorry. We kill these horses pushing them too hard in the heat and we most likely kill ourselves too. Like Lou said, there's no help out here. Check your phone. Haven't had a signal since we left Lou's ranch. And it was faint then. These radios will get somebody on the horn, but we're practically impossible to get to out here."

"How soon then, best case?" Calico said.

Monte frowned. "Tomorrow evening, I'm guessing. Good news is the trail Lou's man marked for us should drop us about where Early's pilot friend last saw the helicopter. Which is most likely their base camp. Can't think of any reason they'd move once they were in the valley."

"Tomorrow night . . ." Calico said.

Monte nodded. "That's about the size of it."

They pushed on higher into the rocky crags. The sun climbed. An hour later, the route angled down, the ghost of a trail narrow and unimaginably steep.

Calico's heart went to her throat. "We have to go down that? It's a cliff."

"It's what the map says," Monte said. "There's a spring down there someplace. That's where we'll hole up till the late afternoon."

"Trust your horse," Pines said. "He doesn't want to fall any more than you do."

Calico swallowed. She reached down and gave the animal a light scratch on the withers. He was a big bay gelding who, at the moment, looked half asleep.

"I'll be right in front of you," Pines said. "You'll be okay."

Calico gave a nervous nod. She'd talked a big game back at Pines's place about knowing how to ride. In truth, she'd been on a horse exactly once in her life, and that had been a pony at a birthday party in Phoenix.

But she had to do this.

Lucinda edged next to her, smiled, and signed something.

"She says trust," Monte said.

Calico smiled back.

Trust . . .

Monte leaned out and looked over the edge. "They were right, you'd never get through this country on anything with wheels. Nothin' to it but to do it, huh? You okay, Lucinda?"

The deaf woman nodded and motioned Monte forward. He spurred his mount and the horse tossed its head with initial reluctance but obeyed, starting down. Lucinda followed, face focused.

Pines looked at Jake. "You bring up the rear with the packhorse?"

"You bet. Right behind you."

Pines reached out and ran his hand down Calico's horse's neck, gave it a light pat. "He'll be fine. This is his country. If you need to, close your eyes. He'll get you to the bottom."

"I'm fine. Piece of cake," Calico lied.

"Uh-huh." Pines winked at her, then reined his horse around and dropped down onto the trail.

Stomach churning, Calico followed. The big bay took a careful step. Then another. It felt like the horse's shoulders fell out from under her, but she stayed in the saddle and the animal pressed on. After the initial drop, the narrow trail took an immediate right and angled along the cliff face. Her right stirrup brushed the cliff. Her left hung out in space. She fought to control her breathing.

"You all right?" Pines said, his voice low and even.

"I'll let you know if we get to the bottom," Calico said.

"Oh, we'll get there," Monte said. "One way or another."

"That's not helping," Pines said.

The wrangler chuckled. "We'll have a story to tell, that's for sure."

The trail widened a little and dropped into a steep switchback. Then another. And another, until Calico lost count. It took more than an hour before they reached the floor of the canyon. Monte reined up and they rested for a minute or two. Calico looked back and up at the route they'd descended. She'd have thought it impossible. Pines unscrewed his canteen and handed it to her. She drank, offered a smile of thanks, and handed it back.

Monte glanced up from the map he'd been studying. "We go up the arroyo a distance, then another smaller canyon cuts off to the left. We'll know it by a big rock that looks like a fist. That's where the spring is where we'll break."

They found the canyon offshoot without any problem. A narrow cut that widened as they entered. Fifty yards in, surrounded by towering vertical walls, vegetation sprang up, the air cooled, and the sandy floor dipped hard to the right into a pool of green water. They pulled saddles and gear from the horses and let them drink. Lucinda rifled through the pack and came out with some tortillas and jerky for a makeshift lunch. Calico managed to eat a little, though her restless dread dampened her appetite.

Food consumed, horses picketed on a small patch of grass, the group settled down to rest and wait out the heat. With everything in her vibrating to be back on the trail and headed toward Charlie, she forced herself to close her eyes. Tried to quiet the alarm bells ringing in her mind and soul. Bees buzzed in the brush around the pool. A breeze cooled the sweat on her forehead and arms. She dozed in fits and starts.

She woke to movement around her. The others were on their feet, moving silently. Then a sound. Shuffling footsteps and cloth scraping brush. Early met her eyes and put fingers to his lips.

Someone was coming up the arroyo.

An odd, choked humming accompanied the footsteps. A choppy and unfamiliar melody. Human, certainly, but strained and broken, like nothing she'd ever heard.

With care, she scooted backward into the brush. Monte and Lucinda worked to quiet the horses. Jake leaned against the rock face a short distance toward the canyon mouth, rifle to his shoulder. Pines winked and gave Calico a reassuring smile before walking toward the coming sound.

The picture of calm.

But the drawn pistol in his hand told another story.

CHAPTER FORTY-ONE

EARLY MOVED CAREFULLY ACROSS THE sand and took a position against the canyon wall opposite Jake, far enough ahead of him so as not to get caught in the cross fire if it came to shooting. He'd done his best to look calm for Calico, but his racing adrenaline made him anything but. The dragging footsteps and stilted, singsong humming out here in the middle of nowhere unnerved him, to say the least. He wiped his palm on the leg of his jeans.

This wasn't Los Angeles or Phoenix. Or even Paradise. This was the border country. And as much as the United States and Mexico wished differently, the Mexican cartels ruled the roost down here. The cartels meant drugs. Drugs, in this lost corner of the world, usually meant automatic weapons that spat before asking questions.

Early had been a police officer for several years. In all that time, he'd drawn his pistol in the line of duty twice and never had to fire it. Once as a young man, after a rodeo in Truth or Consequences, New Mexico, he'd seen a man shot in a bar. He wasn't a picky drinker in those days, and it was a rough place. Cinder-block construction, peeling plywood sign over the door. He'd been three whiskey shots with beer backs into the evening, self-medicating away the pain of finishing out of the money in the arena that day, not to mention a couple broken ribs, when the fight broke out. He never knew what started it, and it didn't last long—gunfights usually didn't. Two participants. Words escalating quickly to shouts. One man pulled out a knife, the other a gun. The gun won. Early still had dreams about the blood soaking into the sawdust and concrete on that barroom floor.

And he didn't want to shoot anyone now, but he would do what he had to do to protect someone important to him. He glanced back toward Calico.

The footsteps and weird humming advanced. Drag of shoe against stone.

A man stepped around the corner.

Early stepped out, gun extended. "Stop."

The man, eyes on the ground in front of him, didn't. He kept coming. And kept humming.

"Hey!" Early said. "I said stop. *Alto!* Comprende?"

Early lowered his pistol. Jake the rifle. The man still hadn't heard. And something wasn't right. It had to be over a hundred degrees, even here in the canyon, but the man wore a sun-faded wool beanie pulled down over his ears. His gray khakis were gone at the knees. His paisley long-sleeved shirt unbuttoned over an undershirt that might have been white at one time but now sported an impressive montage of brown tobacco stains.

The man almost ran into Early before noticing him. When he did, he let out an earsplitting screech and scrambled back so fast he landed on his rump with a thud. Crossing his arms in front of his face, shaking his head back and forth with enough force to crank it off his shoulders, he croaked out a string of incoherent sounds, followed by a long moan.

Early held out his hands to show he wasn't a threat. "Señor, tranquillo! Calm down, amigo. Come on now."

The man slowed his rocking and stared at Early. His eyes darted over the others, lingering on Jake's rifle.

"Get up," Early spoke in Spanish. "No one here is going to hurt you."

"I don't think he can hear you," Jake said.

Early studied the man. Not old, not young. Five seven, maybe. Broom-handle thin. Skin nearly black from sun. "Do you understand me?"

The man continued to take in the scene, his face a puzzle. He croaked again, then made a gesture with his hands.

"He's deaf, sure enough," Monte said.

Lucinda left the horses and came forward. She signed something. The man's eyes widened and his weathered hands fluttered in answer.

"What's he saying?" Early said.

"Don't know," Monte replied. "Mexican sign is quite a bit different. Lucinda knows it pretty good, though."

The man and Lucinda went at it for a while, their dancing hands making the canyon even quieter. Finally Lucinda turned to Monte and signed for a full minute.

"All right," Monte said, turning to the group. "His name's Caesar or something close to it. Got him a little sheep ranch up the canyon a ways. Been in the family for generations. Anyway, he says the cartel don't bother him much, but several years ago a bunch of 'em came through one night and decided they'd take Caesar's wife along with 'em. He naturally objected."

"What happened?" Early said.

"Cartel doesn't take well to objection. They took his tongue and ears with 'em. And I don't just mean poked his eardrums out—they did that, yeah—I mean they cut 'em off. That's why he wears the hat. Says he used to be a handsome man until the cartel turned him into a monster."

"They really did that?" Calico said.

Monte nodded. "He figures he still has his eyes so he got off easy. But they fixed it so he couldn't hear and couldn't talk. A little reminder to keep what happens out here to himself."

"What about his wife?" Jake said.

"They wound up leaving her alone. No accounting for the cartel. Probably figured she was too much trouble to take along and they were in a hurry. Who knows? Caesar says she decided she didn't like it here and went back to Nogales some years ago. Just him and his sheep now. Oh, and a burro he was looking for when he came this way and almost got shot."

"He didn't almost get shot," Early said.

Monte grinned. "His words, not mine."

Caesar was on his feet now. Lucinda offered him a tortilla and jerky. He gave a shy smile, nodded thanks, ate the tortilla in four bites, and carefully put the jerky into the front pocket of his pants. He looked around at the group, then signed something to Lucinda. Taking in her response, his eyebrows arched.

"What?" Monte said.

Lucinda explained.

"Okay. He wanted to know what we're all doing out here. Lucinda told him about Lou lending us the horses and about Lamont's helicopter over in Valle Del Cielo. He knows Lou. Has a boy who works for him. And he also knows about the activity in the valley."

"What can he tell us?" Calico said.

Lucinda and Caesar signed some more. Eventually Lucinda said something to Monte. Monte opened his pack and pulled out Lou's hand-drawn map. He spread it on the ground in front of Caesar and the little Mexican squatted and took it in, tracing the occasional line with his finger. He signed at Lucinda, who interpreted to Monte. Then the process reversed. After several minutes, Caesar stood and rapid-fired a paragraph or two. Then Lucinda again.

"Is he sure?" Monte spoke out loud as he signed.

Caesar must have understood this without translation. He tugged Monte's sleeve and nodded with conviction.

"What?" Early said.

Monte looked up. "Caesar says Lou's man draws lousy maps. There's a faster way to the valley."

"How much faster?" Calico said.

"We'd have to leave the horses at his place and go on foot, but if we hustle, he says we could make Valle Del Cielo by tonight."

CHAPTER FORTY-TWO

CHARLIE COULD HAVE DECIDED DIFFERENTLY. He'd dreamed a dozen times last night he had. He'd felt the cold water pouring down his throat and, because it was a dream, watched Wayne pull his cannon of a pistol out and send Roxy to the angels. Or to hell. Yeah, Charlie could've chosen differently. He could be alive right now instead of a dried-out corpse waiting for whatever the next world would bring. But he knew, even now, if the choice was put before him again his answer would be the same. He'd never known how heavy a human life could be until he held one in his hands.

Yeah, his answer would be the same. And somehow, strangely, even in his semi-delirious state the thought brought him comfort. Because really, when he thought about it, choosing Roxy's life over his own was probably the first unselfish act of his whole life. Which in one way was sad, but in another was happy.

At least it's a good way to go out.

And he was going out.

Funny, he didn't feel thirsty anymore. As far as dying went, Charlie didn't feel much of anything really. Maybe a touch of euphoria. Then there was the fact that it was the middle of the day but everything was dark. And there were all the Chinese paper lanterns raining down around him. But that part was beautiful.

A scorpion moved across the sand. Stopped a few inches from one of the lanterns. Scorpions, snakes, none of it mattered now. What could possibly matter when a guy's dead? When he's already worm food? Poor worms shouldn't get their hopes up; they weren't going to get much.

What comes after this? Heaven? Hell? Charlie had never been religious. His dad had a little. Calico maybe some. But Charlie had never had time. Too much to do in this world to worry about the next. He thought about it now, though. Maybe he'd be reincarnated as a scorpion. That'd be something. Sting Hammott Lamont would be first thing on the scorpion to-do list. Snake would be even better. Charlie wouldn't even rattle before he stuck his fangs into Hammott's stupid, fat body. The look on his face, yeah, that'd be cool. He didn't really think reincarnation was a thing, though. Heaven, hell, that made more sense. Pay for the things you've done, right? And Charlie had done his share. The celestial scale certainly wasn't going to tilt in his favor.

He propped his head up against a rock and closed his eyes. *Then again, maybe dying is just going to sleep and never waking up.* Except even with his eyes closed the paper lanterns kept landing all around him. He watched them drift gracefully down the insides of his eyelids. And there were voices too. Singing. But lanterns didn't sing. So that must be part of the whole dying thing. Still, the music was beautiful. Like nothing he'd ever heard. Soaring melody and whispery harmony. Thrumming bass that vibrated his dried-out, guitar-string guts. Maybe it'd be heaven waiting after all. Maybe choosing Roxy over himself somehow weighted in his favor. Put him over the hump. *Nah, that's a big hump, buddy. If it's either up or down, gravity's going to get you on this one. Stupid, man. What did it all get you?*

He thought about his dad then and the hundred grand that had seemed so important. He thought about Bob's and Calico. And how One Horse hadn't really been that bad.

He wished death would hurry.

"Charlie . . ." The voice came from some place far away. Possibly heaven. Or Venus. Or the Andromeda galaxy. Soft and beautiful like the singing. Maybe part of the singing. "Charlie . . ."

He tried to open his eyes but they were dried shut.

"Come on, Charlie. Look at me now."

Not Wayne. Not Roxy. A woman. Unfamiliar voice. Some sort of accent. British maybe? *Hey, man, I've been working on British . . .* He tried to open his eyes again and managed a crack. The sun was back. Lanterns gone, which gave him a sharp pang of loss.

"Charlie . . ."

A figure knelt next to him. Charlie worked to bring it into focus.

"I have water. Can you move at all?"

The word *water* pulled his eyes open to a narrow squint. He blinked. Tried to talk but nothing came out.

Then water.

Only a trickle. But the bottle touching his cracked lips burned, the most glorious pain he'd ever experienced in his life. Water . . . Carefully, he took in more.

"Not too much, Charlie. A little at a time. That's it. You'll be okay."

"Isabella?" he croaked.

"With as much water as you need. Can you sit up?"

Charlie did, the rock wall hot against his back. The little robot was nowhere to be seen. He drank more. Poured water into his hands and washed his face. Let the life soak into his skin.

"Wait, you speak English?"

The girl smiled. "I speak lots of things."

"Why didn't you ever say so?"

"Have a little more water. You're already looking better."

"I don't understand. Mr. Lamont sent you?"

"No, he didn't send me."

"He's letting me die out here. What's wrong with him?"

"Don't think about him right now. You're alive. And you're going to stay that way, at least for a while."

"How long is a while?"

Isabella shrugged. "What's a life in the scheme of things? Half hour? An eternity? The green flash when the sun sets into the sea? All of them? A while is as good a term as any. I have to go now but I'll leave the water. And this." From a bag slung over her shoulder she pulled out a thick plastic-wrapped package. "Keep this safe. Hide it if you have to. I have a feeling you may need it."

"What is it?"

Her head tilted as if she'd heard something. "Drink now. I'm leaving enough water to last a while. You have a chance now."

"Am I dreaming? Or dead? I don't get it."

"You don't need to get anything. Just stay alive. You did a good thing saving Roxy. I was proud of you. Keep your chin up, all right? I have to go."

"Because you're scared of Hammott? Stay with me. We'll get out together."

She bent down and touched his cheek. "You're in no shape for it, pal. But I'll always remember what you did. You proved them all wrong, Charlie. You put them on their ear. You proved yourself wrong too. You'll never be the same."

"Isabella, I might be in love with you."

She smiled and the sun and stars stopped. "Of course you are. How could you not be?"

She gave him a light brush on the forehead with her lips, rose quickly, and started down the arroyo at a fast walk. Charlie wanted to follow her, ask more questions, but his body declined.

She spoke English that whole time?

Bit by bit, the sun lowered. A bird flitted in and out of a creosote bush on the other side of the wash. Charlie drank some more. He felt better. Started to nod off. To sleep this time, not death.

That's when he heard the motor.

CHAPTER FORTY-THREE

CAESAR'S CLAIM OF A FASTER way to the valley proved true but complicated. They wound through so many narrow canyons and cracks, edged so many hills and cliffs, Early lost count. They'd literally put their lives in the little man's hands. If he chose to betray them to the cartel or anyone else, they didn't stand a chance.

But then they were there, gathered in the mouth of a canyon spilling out above the valley floor, evening sun slanting hard across the basin.

Staring at the impossible.

"What in the world is Lamont doing?" Early said.

Calico shook her head. "How did he get all that out here?"

"I have no idea," Early said.

"The man built an entire drive-in theater?" Jake said.

"Look at the cars," Monte said. "They're all sixties and older. That's a whole lot of collecting."

"By Gracie's description, the helicopter should be here at the east end of the valley," Early said.

"If it was, it's gone now," Monte replied. "And I don't see any movement. I don't think anyone's down there."

"They left?" Calico said. "Did we come all this way for nothing?"

Early pulled a pair of binoculars from his pack and did a careful scan of the area. Not a soul. A drive-in theater, complete with old-school speaker posts, a projection building, and at least a hundred vintage cars. The massive movie screen stretched across the base of a low hill. A large marquee edging the entry road was covered with a canvas tarp. Above and behind it, three crosses towered in the fading sunlight.

"No, we didn't come for nothing," Early said. "They might be gone now but they'll come back. I'm going down there and taking a look around before they do."

"For what?" Jake said. "To get arrested for trespassing?"

"What are they going to do, call 911? You're as curious as I am."

Jake took in the scene again. "Yeah, I am. Let's go then."

Caesar, seeming to sense the direction of the conversation, backed away, signing with fast hands, then crossing himself.

"He's going home," Monte said. "I think those crosses on that hill over there got him spooked even more than a run-in with the cartel."

"He's going to walk back in the dark?" Calico said.

Monte shrugged. "He knows this country about as well as it can be known, I expect. He'll be all right."

Early pulled out a flashlight and offered it to the little man, but Caesar shook his head with a strained smile, nodded his goodbyes, and disappeared into the shadows of the canyon.

Early turned to Jake. "You figure we can find our way back to Hetter's ranch on our own?"

"There's always the long way. Still got the map."

"And no horses," Early said.

Lucinda signed.

"Lucinda says she can find our way back," Monte said. "I don't doubt her either. She notices things most folks don't."

Early shouldered his pack. "I'm going down while there's still a little light. You want to set up camp here while I'm gone? Good a place as any. Up here any fire will be shielded from the valley."

"Be happy to, 'cept for the fact I'm going with you," Monte said.

"Somebody needs to stay and look after the ladies," Early said.

"Kid, if you don't know these ladies by now, you're hopeless. They ain't missing nothing."

"He's right," Calico said. "We're all going down. We started this together and we'll keep on."

Early pushed his hat back on his head. "Calico, look—"

"Don't even try, Pines. If you're going, I'm going." She moved past him and started down the narrow trail toward the valley floor.

Early watched her. "You know what? I give up."

Jake gave a half smile. "I've seen you in a hundred tight situations, amigo, but I've never heard you say those three words. Where has she been?"

"One Horse, apparently," Early said.

Jake headed after Calico. Monte and Lucinda followed them. Early brought up the rear. The game trail, when they could make it out, was thin as a wire and faded almost to nothing, forcing them to move single file all the way down. By the time they'd picked their way to the basin floor the sun had eased itself halfway behind the distant hills, turning the valley to gold fire.

"Why does it suddenly feel like I got a visitor's day pass to hell?" Monte said.

The drive-in lay a good half mile away. Early put the binoculars to his eyes. "Still don't see anybody."

"I can't decide if that's good or bad," Monte said.

Calico took the binoculars from Early and looked through them. "I guess we're about to find out."

The valley floor, though rocky, was fairly flat and made for easy walking. They reached the outskirts of Lamont's imagination within ten minutes or so.

"I wonder where he got these cars?" Monte said. "Even in Los Angeles this would be hard to put together. Look at them, they're all the real deal but they look like everyday drivers. Not restored like show cars would be, you know what I mean?"

Calico moved slowly down a row. "I've only seen drive-ins in the movies before."

"This looks exactly like the real thing," Monte said. "Even got the playground under the screen. I remember running up there before the movie started when I was a kid. They'd flash the lights to let us know it was time to go back to our cars. My old pop had a '57 Caddy convertible. Cream inside and out. His pride and joy. Used to reach back and push my head down if there was something he thought I shouldn't see. I can still smell the leather seats."

"How about dates, you ever take them to the drive-in?" Calico said.

Monte glanced at Lucinda and grinned. "I have no recollection of any woman before Lucinda."

Lucinda rolled her eyes.

Most of the cars had metal speakers hanging on partially rolled-down windows, a cord looping from the speakers to a post, one between every two cars. Monte picked up a speaker and looked it over. "Got rid of these back in the eighties, I think. Started broadcasting shortwave and everybody just used their radios. Guy's gone to a lot of effort for period detail."

Color flickered suddenly and a neon *Snack Bar* sign popped to life above the building in the center of the lot.

And the lights above the giant screen began to flash.

CHAPTER FORTY-FOUR

EARLY STARED AT THE FLASHING lights.

"Guess it's time for the kids to find their cars," Monte said. "I'm hoping they show *Lonesome Dove* but I'm thinking this is more of an *El Mariachi* sort of joint."

"Am I the only one who finds this whole thing insanely creepy?" Calico said.

In answer, Lucinda moved next to Monte and hugged his arm.

"Lamont's playing games," Early said. "He knows we're here."

"I don't like it," Calico said. "What can we do?"

"Be ready, watch and wait for him to show. He's here somewhere."

At that moment the lights died. A projection booth above the snack bar whirred and a beam shot out through a small window, lighting the huge movie screen with colored brilliance. A hot dog with arms and legs and horn-rimmed glasses shrugged into a bun and started dancing with a tub of popcorn. A slice of pizza and a box of Milk Duds edged into the picture and joined them.

"Can't hear it from here," Jake said.

"Might as well make ourselves comfortable." Monte walked over to a long, low convertible, opened the passenger door for Lucinda, walked around, and slid into the driver's seat. He cranked up the speaker and thin music gave a rhythmic soundtrack to the dancing snacks.

Early and Calico climbed into the rear and sat up high on the seat back. Jake leaned against the side of the car, arms crossed.

The music shifted to a singsong version of "La Cucaracha." A sultry female box of Hot Tamales dropped a sombrero onto the ground and started dancing around it while a neon sign behind her flashed, *Candy? Arriba! . . . Popcorn? The hotter the butter! Hey, fellas, make sure you take your own hot tamale to the snack bar before the show starts!*

The tamale danced off and the screen went dark. Familiar music cranked up and Bugs Bunny appeared munching a carrot.

"Is he serious? Cartoons?" Calico said.

"Guess so," Monte said.

"I want to know where Charlie is," she said. "And Lamont."

"I have a feeling we'll find out," Jake said. "But like it or not, we're on Lamont's schedule."

"Uh-huh. The fly's also on the spider's schedule." Calico hugged herself.

The trouble in her eyes made Early's blood boil worse that any threat or lawsuit could.

The full cartoon played and another started. Early had no interest in either. Halfway through the second, Jake nudged his arm and spoke low.

"I could use a snack. How about you?" At Early's questioning eyes, he pointed back toward the snack bar. A shadow. Someone moving inside.

Early was out of the car in less than a second.

The building was white-painted brick. A couple weathered picnic tables in front. A plaque that said *Restrooms* with an angled arrow indicating they were around the corner. Separate entrance and exit doors, both propped open and lit from the inside. Early charged in without slowing his pace, Jake behind him, their boots loud on the polished concrete floor. The smell of popcorn. Pizza slices warming in a glass case. A wide assortment of candy displayed beneath glass.

A pimple-faced teenager stood behind the counter. White-collared shirt and black bow tie. His red apron matched the paper hat perched on his head. "Hi, can I get you fellas something?"

Early approached, looking the kid up and down carefully. "Where did you come from?"

Confusion crossed the kid's face. "Home? What do you mean?"

"Where's Hammott Lamont?"

"What?"

"I wouldn't play around if I were you, son," Jake said. "I can tell you definitively my friend here isn't in the mood."

The kid nodded and looked back at Early. "I didn't mean any disrespect. Who did you say, sir?"

"Hammott Lamont. Where is he?"

"I really don't know. That's the truth."

Early started around the counter.

"Early, don't," Jake said. "He's a kid."

The teen backed away, eyes wide, mouth open. "I swear, I don't—"

"Pines," Calico said from the doorway.

Early stopped and turned.

Her face had drained of color. "I . . ."

He got to her in four steps. "What's wrong?"

"You're not going to believe it. I don't even know if I do."

"What?" Jake said.

She shook her head. "Where did they all come from?"

"Who, Calico?" Early said.

She pointed out through the door into the night. "Them. It's impossible, right?"

Early stepped out. His skin went cold in the warm air. Every car had people in it. All watching the screen and laughing along with Bugs and Elmer Fudd.

"What happened?" Early said. "We were inside less than a minute."

Calico gripped his arm. "I don't know. Our eyes were on the screen. There was no one here. And then this. They came out of nowhere!"

Early walked over to the closest car, a dark El Camino, and knocked on the window. A middle-aged man and woman sat inside. They were holding hands. It struck Early as painfully innocent. The woman wore too much makeup, her face glistening in the shifting glow of the screen. The man's thin hair was pasted back and stuck to his skull. The deep farmer's tan on his neck ended in an abrupt line beneath the open collar of his shirt. A cloud of Old Spice wafted out as he rolled down his window. "Can I help you?"

"Yeah, you can help me," Early said. "Where's Hammott Lamont?"

"Excuse me?"

"You heard me."

"Sorry, mister. We're only here to watch a movie."

"Where did you come from?" Early said.

Confusion clouded the lined face. "It's Friday night. Movie night. What's your problem anyway?"

"Get out," Early said.

Sudden fear. "Look, sir, I don't want trouble. My wife has fragile nerves. Please, leave us alone."

Early took a step back. "Get out!"

The man rolled up the window and locked the door, face a tangle of real terror. Early looked around. People were staring. The Warner Bros. theme lifted and fell.

"Early . . ." Jake said. "Look at the sign."

Early turned. The dizziness of impossibility spinning his brain. The canvas tarp covering the marquee was gone. The movie title now visible. Black block letters against brightly lit electric white.

THE SOUND THE SUN MAKES

CHAPTER FORTY-FIVE

THE CARTOON THEME DIED, AND the color faded, deliberate, slow, to black and white.

THE SOUND THE SUN MAKES

A Hammott Lamont Production

Then a hard white blaze of sun burning against a dark gray sky. The picture sharp and perfect. The camera pulled back and panned.

Calico sucked in a breath. "Charlie . . ."

Charlie, all right. Stumbling along glassy-eyed, a suit jacket strapped to his head with a dress tie. Early started for the screen. No one in the cars looked at him as he passed, their eyes fixed on the film in front of them. Charlie walking, then sleeping in the dirt, firelight flickering against his haggard face. Vintage narration boomed, "Welcome our suffering servant. The man who is the brush in the hand of the Great Artist." On and on the voice went as Charlie walked, a close-up of his face, the bleak and arid landscape blurred behind him.

Early stopped at the first row of cars and climbed up onto a Chevy Bel Air, the family occupying it staring up as if an alien had landed on their hood. He looked out over the theater. "Hammott Lamont! Show yourself!"

As if in reply, music blasted. Echoing electric guitar, haunted and melodic, so loud it filled the sky and bounced off the distant mountains. Early turned back to the screen. Charlie still walking, this time silhouetted, the sun a massive ball dropping down behind him. Early hopped down and moved from vehicle to vehicle, staring at occupants. Lamont had to be here somewhere. He knew it. How had the guy pulled this off? Car after car, every single person perfectly vintage Southwest Americana. How? And why? He walked back to the convertible Monte had picked out. His friends had vacated the car and stood next to it instead, their unease at the sudden and unexplainable appearance of a couple hundred people here in the middle of nowhere written clearly across their features.

The electric guitar cut off with such suddenness it gave Early mental whiplash. His heart clenched when his own voice, and then Calico's, reverberated through the unseen speakers.

"We're all imperfect believers, Pines."

"Some more imperfect than others."

"Uh-huh. You know, on that note, I've been thinking about something."

"Yeah?"

"That God's not Lee."

"What's that supposed to mean?"

"That's what's going on with you, right? You want God to keep himself to the other side of the street."

And then Lamont was there. Not in person but forty feet tall, face fleshy above his beard, smiling down from the screen. "God and Lee. Deep thoughts, aren't they, Early Pines?"

"Early? What's happening? How could've he recorded that?" Calico said.

Early stared. "He had to have recorded us in the apartment. The title, he knew about me hearing the sun too."

"I feel like I'm in a bad dream," Calico said.

"I think that's the idea," Jake said.

Lamont went on. "Yes, God as our father, our father as God. A deep thought! But then again, how else are we to see God, really? How but through our own father experience?" He spread his arms. "How do you think our hero, Charlie, sees God out there in the desert? If he sees him at all, I assume he sees him like his own father was, a lost, lovable grifter. To his boy, a gullible genie in a bottle. One who'll cough up a hundred thousand dollars at an irresponsible son's whim."

Lamont faded. Now Charlie lay on the sand in what looked to be the mouth of a cave. The camera zoomed in on his face. Vacant eyes, cracked lips. Calico said nothing but her fingers dug hard into Early's arm.

Lamont's narrative continued over Charlie's features. "Funny though, even as he suffers in this physical world—and believe me, he has suffered—we never hear him call out to God, do we? So maybe, just maybe, the theory is flawed after all. Then again, what good is a hundred thousand dollars when what you really need is water? But let's get back to the Pines men, father and son. Early and Lee. Specifically Lee. Because Lee begs the question—"

The screen changed again. The yacht, and Lamont tumbling over the rail. Then a fade to the Frolic Room and Roxy's nose exploding under Early's fist.

"Ouch!" Lamont laughed. "Yes, Lee begs the question, who are you really after in these scenes, Early Pines? Me? Roxy Parsons? Or, just maybe . . . Lee? Which, according to the beautiful and astute Miss Foster, very well might mean you're lashing out at God. I should really have you on a couch, shouldn't I? I can see it. I could be smoking a pipe and you could tell me all about your childhood pain and mother issues. We're going to have to discuss writing that scene in. It's interesting, isn't it, what happens when we give art its head and let it run? Let it breathe? What started as a great project, the retelling and, indeed, immortalizing of the most famous story in history, was revised and transformed with the arrival of Early Pines. I was pushing, calculating, creating, but the universe knew there was an element missing. *Art* knew! So just like the universe brought us Charles Foster, it also brought us Early Pines. Just think, *The Sound the Sun Makes.* What a title! I think even Orson Welles would be proud."

At the name Orson Welles, applause rose from the people in the cars.

Lamont cross-faded and the film continued. Sometimes black and white, other times oversaturated color. Charlie in many. But Early in others. Practically everything he'd done since arriving in Los Angeles had been captured and edited into a collage of mind-bending images.

The group watched in stunned silence. Scene wove into scene. Emotion into emotion. Charlie. Calico, Early, Charlie again, Hammott Lamont . . . No story line to speak of, but—and Early fought admitting it—there was an undeniable beauty to the flow. So much so that while his anger diminished not one iota, it took the hand of an equally painful and overwhelming sadness. A world of it. A universe. It made him dizzy.

Then Charlie on a windswept mesa, staring at a pile of rocks on a table.

Cross-fade.

Charlie on shaking legs looking over a cliff.

Cross-fade.

Charlie and Wayne in the frame. Wayne speaking, *"What if I said you can have whatever you wanted? You tried to steal half a mil? You can have a hundred times that. Your own chopper. Your own mansion—mansions—wherever you want them. Anything. The world is yours . . ."*

"The temptation of Christ," Jake said. "Charlie is Lamont's Jesus."

"But why?" Calico said.

"The world's most famous story, told through the filter of Lamont's brain. In his own image."

"Ain't any voice I want to hear," Monte said. "And why Early? What's his part in this thing?"

Without warning the screen cut to black. Applause from the people in the cars. Even the snack boy had exited his shack and was clapping.

"Ladies and gentlemen!" A game show–announcer voice shook the stars. "Please say a warm hello to your director, creator, and host . . . Hammoooooooott Lamont!"

Spotlights exploded to the right of the theater screen, illuminating a large flat spot on the hill below the three crosses. There, decked in brilliant white as always, Lamont stood beaming and waving to the crowd, his form mirrored, massive and live, on the drive-in screen. The applause lifted to a fever pitch.

"Finally." Early started forward.

CHAPTER FORTY-SIX

EARLY CHARGED AROUND A PICKUP parked backward to the screen, a Hispanic family in the truck bed. He ran between a Pontiac and a Volkswagen Bug, then a Mustang and a Lincoln Continental, until the only thing between him and Lamont was a fifty-yard stretch of desert.

The crowd still roared. He heard footsteps behind him and knew without turning it was Jake.

Fifty, thirty, twenty yards . . .

And then Wayne.

And a pistol straight out of *Dirty Harry.*

Early pulled up, breathing hard. "Tell you what, Wayne, how about you put that away before I shove it down your throat."

"Sorry, man, Mr. Lamont's call," Wayne said. "And he says the *pistola* stays."

Early looked up at Hammott. The director beamed at him and, of all things, gave him an enthusiastic thumbs-up.

"He's filming this too, isn't he?" Early said.

"Never know when the art's gonna happen, dude," Wayne said. "It's a hard-and-fast rule. The cameras are always rolling. You shoulda seen that on the screen. Not a lot of privacy but you kinda get used to it."

"Fine, film this." Early pulled his own pistol. He walked close enough to the little surfer bodyguard that the barrels touched. "I guess we see who blinks, don't we?"

"Nope. You guys aren't loaded. Crazy, huh? Bet you never saw that coming." He smiled. "The magic of cinema, ain't it grand? I'm around the guy 24-7 and even I don't know how he pulls this stuff off. Misdirection, I guess. I'm telling you, he's like David Blaine or something. It's freaky."

Behind Early, Jake's rifle ratcheted. "He's right, I'm empty."

Early checked his own gun, cursed, then slid it back in its holster. He turned to Jake. "How? I've had this with me the whole time. Somebody at Hetter's place?"

"No, no, a magician never reveals his methods! Everyone knows that." Lamont lifted his arms out to the drive-in crowd. "Ladies and gentlemen, the boys are fresh out of ammunition." Mock surprise. "How did that happen? Hey, how have you enjoyed our little picture so far?"

A vintage-looking *Applause* sign lit to the side of the stage, eliciting claps and cheers from the crowd. Everyone was out of their cars now and moving toward them in a loose semicircle. From somewhere in the throng, Calico called his name.

"Of course," Lamont said, "we still have some filming to do, don't we? That's why we're here. Because every great picture needs its big finish!"

Applause. More cheers.

"Hammott," Early said, "talk to me."

People quieted, an unspoken expectation hanging in the air.

Lamont looked down, eyebrows arched. "Mr. Pines, I'm sorry but I believe you're interrupting. Don't get me wrong, you've been great, and I appreciate your involvement more than you know, but we're working, you understand."

"What is this? What are you doing?" Early said.

"I'm surprised you ask. You've been paying attention, haven't you? Art. Poetry! We're painting the heavens with word and color and emotion and light. We're making music not only with sound but for all the senses. And not only the five senses. We're writing the *eternal story.* Now, can I answer anything else or will you please let me get back to work?"

"What's with the gun?"

"If our project so far demonstrates anything at all, it's that you, Early Pines, are a man of immediate and violent tendencies. Take, for instance, the way you rushed the platform just now. Without the gun, Wayne would be a stain in the dirt, and who knows what you would have done to me. So the pistol is somewhat rhetorical when you think about it, isn't it?"

"I don't hit women."

"Well, you don't know what you're missing, do you? Now, please be quiet."

Early lunged, but Wayne's pistol caught him in the forehead, knocking him back.

"He will shoot you, make no mistake," Lamont said. He lifted his face back to the drive-in crowd. "Where were we, good people? Oh yes, discussing a climax for our story."

Applause.

"When we set out on this production, I spoke of a piece that would meld art and God and man. Something that would transcend this world and have precious value in the next. Now we're approaching the end! Our audience for this monumental event? You lovely people, a million stars, and all the angels both in heaven and below. I couldn't be more pleased. And I'm so happy you've all joined me for this particular segment of filming. Now, you've spent the last hour or so meeting some of our principal players, as well as a few side characters. And they're all here now to help us continue. Early Pines and Calico Foster have played big parts. They've been kind enough to join us again tonight and even brought some friends along."

Applause.

Calico appeared at Early's side and slid her arm through his. Jake, Monte, and Lucinda took places on either side of them. Wayne's pistol hadn't wavered.

"Seems to me you can't shoot all of us," Jake said to Wayne.

Wayne shrugged. "Nah, but I could probably get a couple. Which ones do you think are expendable?"

Early wiped at a stream of blood trickling into his eye. "How long can you hold that thing? Must be getting heavy."

"I can hold it as long as Mr. Lamont wants me to. I'm thin but wiry. I just picture the beach I'm gonna buy when this is all over. Sorry about hitting you, by the way."

"Let me ask you something, you ever shoot anybody?" Early said.

Wayne's mouth twisted. "I'd rather not. So if you all would kindly stay put, I'd appreciate it."

"What do you get out of this?"

"Money, what else? And that equals freedom in my script. After this I'm out." He grinned. "Seriously, man, after this job look for me under the palm trees. I'll be the one sitting on a boat with a cold drink."

"Ladies and gentlemen," Lamont shouted, "what is the most well-known story of all time? A story both famous and infamous. Think now, the story by which every other story both in heaven and on earth has been, is, and forever more will be judged? Is it *Citizen Kane*? Unfortunately, no. It should be, but no. There is a reason we have terms like *Christ figure* and *devil figure* in literature. It's because all great stories at their heart are tales of conflict. And what greater conflict can there be than that between universal good and evil? Between gods and devils? Ah, but don't forget man! Fleshly, insignificant bags of souls stumbling through this make-believe existence and calling it life. And that is where the real game begins. This is the flash point—the birth—of true art. And this is where we stand tonight, here on our stage. You, me, all of us—the stumblers and the gods and the devils. But who is who? It's up to you to tell." He folded his hands across his paunch. "Now, that original attempt at greatness climaxed in a trial and subsequently bloody but admittedly beautiful punishment scene. I propose, then, so will ours. And you, my friends, will play a great part." *Applause.* "Let there be light!"

He waved a hand and the rocky slope behind him burst into a thousand colors.

The three crosses towered in the brilliance.

"Look familiar, my friends?" Claps and scattered whistles. "But what about our cast, you might ask? Who will play the lead? Who will indeed slip this mortal skin for immortality? Who will be our desert Jesus?"

"Charles Foster Kane!" the crowd shouted in perfect unison.

Lamont lifted his hands high. "Most likely, yes. But no circus worth its salt starts with a main event, does it? Neither shall ours. You all know the story. There are three crosses here as there were on that original hill two millennia ago. And that first great ringmaster had his warm-up acts as well. In that play, two thieves enter the stage. We see immediately these are deplorable, blackhearted people. As should ours be! Two thieves scraped out of the mire of sin and gore to hang at our hero's side. What do you say? Would you like to meet our first thief?"

Clapping, cheers.

"Okay, how about we start with an obvious one? Cue wind, please. Cue Romans. And . . . action!"

Wind rose on the hill, lifting a thick swirl of dust. When it settled, Roxy Parsons stood in front of the right cross, hands bound in front of him, cast on his hand shining bright in the lights and what looked to be fresh blood streaming down from a gash on his forehead. Two Mexican men with automatic weapons flanked him. Roxy spat on the ground. "Lamont! You ridiculous idiot peacock. Stop this insanity right now!"

Lamont shook his head. "I'm sorry, Roxy, but we needed a thief. It's purely a casting decision. You understand casting. And you can't deny you stole my lead actor from a party. There are a plethora of witnesses to the event. You walked right in and took him. You *stole*, Roxy. That makes you a thief. You're guilty as charged."

Applause.

Roxy spat again. "I'll kill you. I swear on my mother's grave I'll do it myself. I'm telling you right now to—" A machine gun pressed to his temple snapped his mouth shut.

Applause.

Lamont held up a hand for quiet. "Well, good people of the mob, what next? Thief number two? To tell you the truth, I'm still mulling that one. So many people to choose from, every one of them vile. No, let's get straight to the center of the Tootsie Pop. Who do we think should play our leading role? Our beautiful sacrifice? The hero for our painful albeit necessary ending? Who will bleed for us? Yes, I know, we've all watched Charles play the part so far, but this is art. It's alive. It breathes. It sometimes changes. We have choices, don't we?"

Applause. Lamont's bright eyes shifted to Early.

"For instance, what do you think of the indomitable yet very predictable Mr. Early Pines? I used to call him Detective Pines, but that ship has sailed. Ladies and gentlemen, what do we think of Mr. Pines for our choice?"

Applause.

"I agree. It would be fun to stick pins in him, especially after our brief but irritating history, but I'm afraid Mr. Pines falls short of fitting our bill. He's no innocent lamb, is he? Beneath his ridiculous hat, he's a troubled and angry person. He's angry with, of all things, a God named Lee, or a Lee named God, it's all foggy, but bear with me. You see, Mr. Pines can be selfless, yes, but that hat on his head shouts out to us all the very definition of introspection and self-absorption. No, we all know it can't be Mr. Pines. Let's let him be for the moment. So I suppose it must be Charles after all . . . cut!"

The lights dimmed. Lamont nodded.

"A scene well-done! Are you ready, Agnes? You have your line?"

A gray-haired woman in a worn cardigan stepped forward from the crowd. "Ready, Mr. Lamont."

Lamont put a hand up. "All right, cue wind. Get ready, Agnes. And . . . action!"

Wind rose. Agnes's voice echoed through the speakers. "But Charles Foster Kane isn't innocent! He's selfish. He's a grifter. He's a con. He's . . . stupid!"

Hammott beamed. "Is he all those things? All eyes on the screen, if you please."

CHAPTER FORTY-SEVEN

THE DRIVE-IN SCREEN EXPLODED TO life.

"You've got a future, man." Wayne's two-dimensional face twenty feet wide. "Mr. Lamont is ready to make you a star, right? So let's up the ante."

Camera pans to Charlie. He looks horrible.

"What if I said you can have whatever you wanted? You tried to steal half a mil? You can have a hundred times that. Your own chopper. Your own mansion—mansions—wherever you want them. Anything."

Camera pulls back a little, revealing a white-clothed table with an ice bucket and a bottle of water.

"The world is yours, all you have to do is pick up that water and live."

Camera pulls back farther. Roxy Parsons stands, hands at his side, an endless desert valley behind and below him.

"But Roxy has to die?" Charlie says.

Roxy groans, sinks to his knees, and starts to cry.

"You can have it all," Wayne says.

"He'll suffer."

Wayne pulls out a pistol and points it at Roxy. "What if we solved that problem right now? Make it easier?"

Close-up of Charlie, then the camera pans back to a half-body shot. Light begins to grow behind him. Brighter . . . brighter . . . The sky on the periphery darkens. A dove appears, lands on his shoulder. Charlie turns and starts walking. He lifts a hand. "See you, Wayne. I know the way back to the cave."

Hammott Lamont's unmistakable voice from off camera, "This is my Charles Foster Kane, in whom I am well pleased . . ."

Scene fades.

Applause.

Early turned to Lamont up on the hill, surprised to find four manned movie cameras on booms now hovering over the stage like mechanical dinosaurs.

Hammott held up his hands, smiling at the crowd. "So, do you believe in miracles, good people? Because you just saw one. Right before your eyes, our selfish leopard has changed his spots. And it wasn't acting, folks, that's the best part! Charles Foster actually made the choice to forgo his life for another's. Like the old script says, 'Greater love hath no man than to lay down his life for a compadre!' Especially if it's a wish-he-was-a-gangster-and-he-wants-to-kill-you compadre. Yes, Charles has become our clear hero of choice. I couldn't be more pleased. And his reward? He will go down in art history. He will win the ultimate game! The world will fall to its knees when they see and relive, over and over and over through all eternity, what's about to happen here tonight."

Applause.

Hammott spun and walked over to Roxy. They spoke, Hammott smiling, Roxy animated with both anger and fear. Hammott put a hand on the producer's shoulder and leaned closer. A slow stain of urine appeared on the producer's pants and his knees buckled. His two guards held him up by his arms.

Lucinda signed something with quick hands.

Monte swallowed hard. "Lucinda says Lamont told Roxy this was for real. Lamont might call it a game. Or art. But he's really gonna crucify these people. We got to do something here."

"Nope," Wayne said, gun shifting back and forth between them. "Nope, nope, nope."

"Wayne," Early said, "this is completely out of control. Hammott's crazy, you know that. Give me the gun and I promise I'll put a stop to it. You don't want this on your conscience."

Wayne's hand trembled the slightest bit. "Look up there, dude. Those guys with the AKs? Lamont can call them Romans all he wants, but those guys are real-deal cartel. I don't know about you but I'm allergic to bullets."

"How does he even know people like that?" Monte said.

Wayne lifted a shoulder. "He knows everybody, man."

"He hired cartel and he trusts them?" Monte said. "He really is crazy."

Wayne smiled. "Maybe they're the ones who're crazy. I bet you a hundred bucks they won't see a dime."

"You'd lose. The cartel doesn't do anything for free," Early said.

"These yokels will. Magic of cinema, man. I know Lamont. He'll wiggle his nose and disappear, and these guys'll be standing here by themselves in the desert. I seen it half a dozen times."

"With the cartel? He can't be that stupid," Monte said.

"Nope, he's that smart. It's not even about the money to Mr. Lamont. It's about the game. You watch."

"They'll find him," Calico said.

"They won't find nothing but the wind, man."

Early held out his hand. "Give me the gun, Wayne. I'd have a chance. You could walk away from this insanity."

"Tempting as that sounds, the answer's still a hard no, man. Look at Roxy. I got no interest in winding up like that."

"Lamont's talking about murdering my brother. Give Pines the gun!" Calico pleaded.

The pistol stayed where it was.

"Ladies and gentlemen," Lamont boomed. "Please welcome to eternal immortality Charles Foster Kane!"

Applause.

CHAPTER FORTY-EIGHT

A CARTEL GUARD LED CHARLIE out of a stand of saguaros. The wind blew on its own now. No effects needed. Calico's brother wore a clean suit, but he looked horrible. Drawn and pale. He stumbled hard.

"Charlie!" Calico said.

His blank eyes shifted in her direction, face registering confusion, but he shuffled on. The guard stopped him in front of the center cross.

"Pines, do something!" Calico said.

"Not happening," Wayne said.

Pines started forward but Jake put a hand on his arm. "Take it easy, amigo. No quick moves. Think it through."

"I'm thinking, believe me," Pines said. "Wayne, I hate to tell you, but if you don't get a whole lot smarter real fast, you're gonna have to actually shoot me. And you better be accurate because if you're not, I'm going right over top of you."

"Ladies and gentlemen!" Lamont shouted. "You all know that glorious old story. You all know what has to happen here. We have a thief. We have our hero. What next?"

"Another thief!" the crowd roared.

"Yes, yes, we'll get to that. But a choice was also put to the crowd that day, wasn't it? We can't forget that part." *Applause.* "That's right! And a choice will be put to you as well. Remember, cameras are rolling, so make it good."

"What's he talking about?" Monte said.

"Barabbas, maybe," Jake said. "In the Christ story, the governor offered the mob a choice. It was Jewish tradition. They were allowed to choose one prisoner to be set free. Anyone they picked. Barabbas was a murderer. A very bad guy. But they chose to let him go and crucified Jesus."

"See? I didn't know that," Wayne said. "You're a handy guy, Jake. All that seminary training, I guess."

Jake's mouth set in a hard line. "If I were you, I'd listen to Early. If this is for real, you'll be a murderer just like Lamont."

The barrel of Wayne's pistol dipped a little, but he righted it.

"So Lamont's got him a Christ. But who's gonna play his Barabbas?" Monte said.

Jake glanced at Pines. "I can make an educated guess."

"Barabbas!" Lamont said. "Who in our cast of characters would make a good Barabbas, do you think? Remember now, he has to be a violent man. A selfish man. Hmm, let's see, who would fit that bill?"

"Early Pines!" someone shouted. Others cheered and repeated the call.

"This ain't looking good at all," Monte said.

"Sure isn't," Wayne said.

Lucinda signed.

Monte watched her, then nodded. "She says when the governor put the choice to them, the crowd decided they wanted Barabbas released instead of Christ. So if Hammott follows the story, Early here'll probably get himself a pardon. But we've still got to do something about Charlie and Roxy."

"You know what? I'm done. You better know how to use that thing, Wayne." Pines started forward.

Wayne stepped up and put the pistol against Pines's forehead. Early lifted a hand to knock it away but the sight of Calico in his peripheral stopped him. Wayne's finger was on the trigger and the thing would probably go off. A big gust whipped across the mountainside, making both of them lift a hand against the blowing sand.

"Have you even looked around, man?" Wayne said. "You can't *do* anything. Don't you wonder where all this came from? Think about it, dude. Don't you wonder why you're even here? *How* you're here?"

"We're here because a pilot saw your helicopter," Calico said.

Wayne shifted the gun and squinted down the barrel at her. "Uh-huh. You wanted to help your bro, and Early wanted you. Well, you and Mr. Lamont's head on a stick. Everybody in this theater knows that, man. But you think you'd be here if it hadn't been planned? Mr. Lamont wouldn't have allowed it. He thinks of everything, always. You can't win against him. Nobody can."

"He didn't allow anything," Monte said. "The pilot—"

"By pilot you mean Gracie," Wayne said. "She did a pretty good job of dropping bread crumbs. Problem was, we have some weather coming up from the Gulf, so we had to push shooting up a day. That's why Caesar had to jump in and get you here on time. I gotta hand it to the little dude, he slid you guys in under the wire. As it is, judging by the way this wind is kicking up all of a sudden, even tonight might be a bit late."

"Caesar," Pines said.

"Yeah, he works for the cartel," Wayne said. "Lookout and unofficial spy. Used to be a pickpocket down in Mexico City. Mean little sucker too. No joke, you shoulda shot him while you had the chance and done the world a favor. Still, turns out he's a pretty dang good actor. So, see? Mr. Lamont wanted you here for his big finish. That's the way it is. Mr. Lamont doesn't lose. And that, mis amigos, is exactly why I'm not putting down la pistola."

Another even heavier gust. Wayne turned his head away from it and squinted, protecting his eyes.

"Lamont did all this so Early can play Barabbas to Charlie's Jesus?" Jake said. "Why?"

Wayne shrugged. "Probably for fun. Who knows what goes on in that dude's head? Half the time he thinks he's Orson Welles, for crying out loud. But you saw the film up there. Early's no Boy Scout. Especially in the violence department. If you ask me—which no one ever does—he's as good a choice as any."

"What's the point?" Pines said. "We know the story. He's going to give me back to the mob, right? Why not get on with it?"

Wayne pursed his lips and nodded as if this were a good point. "Yeah, maybe, but this is Lamont, man. And the game. And he hates you a whole lot. You never really know what direction things are going to take. I'd give you a fifty-fifty chance at best. But that's the whole point. That's where brilliance comes from."

"Early Pines, you say?" Lamont's voice pressed through the wind, rolled across the rocks and brush. "You think he would be the best choice for the part? Yes, Early would be excellent. But maybe . . . just maybe . . . Gather closer, my friends! Can you feel the energy in the air? It's rising like this wind. Here we are balanced between history and the edge of a Gulf hurricane. That old Rainmaker is raging and we lift a fist to heaven and laugh in his face. You know why? Because this is *my* story now. And nothing can stop it!" He tilted his face to the sky, his beard vibrating in the windblast. "Do I finally have your attention, Old Man? How do you like me now? You had your chance. You know you did. Blow all you want! Even you can't stop this." Lamont turned back to the crowd. "Yes, I can see Early Pines in the part. Absolutely. But what if we were to go a different route? Make it even more interesting? I mean, we've established that there must be a trial here. But in the original script, who was actually on trial?" He pointed upward. "Wasn't it really God in the hot seat? I say yes, and he still is. He was judged and found wanting then, and he will be again tonight." He waved to his right. "Amigos, bring him out!"

The wind squalled. Two more cartel moved into the light, pushing a big man along with their gun barrels. The man's hair was dark and heavy and laced with gray. His face hard and lined above his beard. He wore old jeans, boots, and a faded black T-shirt, his arms tattooed and muscled.

"Ladies and gentlemen," Lamont said. "Say hello to our Barabbas, Mr. Lee Pines!"

CHAPTER FORTY-NINE

EARLY'S WORLD SPUN.

"Behold Barabbas!" Lamont had to shout to be heard over the wind, even with the speakers.

Applause.

"But, for our intents and purposes tonight, we'll simply call him Lee. It's easier, yes? Now, let me tell you a little about Lee here. Lee Pines spent much of his early life nursing both a liquor bottle and a grudge. See, Lee grew up getting slapped around by just about everybody he knew. His father, his mother—and later a long string of pseudo stepmothers. Even his older brothers got in on the action. You get the picture. Eventually Lee escaped the violence, fell in lust, and got married. He grabbed his own little slice of the American dream by the hair and yanked. That lust of his led to a single child. Can you guess who that child was?"

"Early Pines!" the crowd boomed in ground-shaking unison.

"Yes, Early Pines! Rodeo veteran, ex-detective, puncher of humans, overtalker, and—worst of all—a man with awful taste in hats! Now, as you've all been previously briefed, our two Mr. Pines have come to an apparent impasse. The younger essentially knocked the elder's head into next Tuesday with a single blow. Lawsuits have been discussed. Careers lost. Hope crushed. Who's to blame for all this?"

"Lee Pines!" The crowd's response obviously rehearsed.

"Correct. Why couldn't he only have stayed on his side of the street?"

Applause.

"What do you want here, Hammott?" Early said. "Let's talk. Just you and me. How can we end this?"

"End it? The way every story has to end. With a big, massive, huge, phenomenal finish. In layman's terms—you being a layman—a climax followed by a resolution. Except sometimes I like to skip resolutions. So boring really. Finish things off with a reverberating boom, if you will. Art! So pay attention, please!"

"Pay attention, please!" Another unison crowd yell.

"Now, good people, we come to the mob choice!" Lamont shouted. "Charles Foster Kane, surprising us all, has shown a tender and good side. He willingly offered to sacrifice his life for another. Will he finish the job today? Will he go meet the angels?" He gave an exaggerated shrug. "Or will you, the people, choose differently than that angry mob in the original script? Will you turn Charles the innocent loose to go back to his lovely sister and put Lee Pines in his place on the tree instead? What say you?"

The drive-in crowd erupted. All trying to outshout each other. Lamont listened to the mayhem for a good thirty seconds before he lifted his hands for quiet.

"Well, we have a varying array of opinions, don't we? Honestly, I'm not surprised. That original mob was much more unified in what it was after, you know. And then there's the fact"—he winked at the camera, huge close-up on the drive-in screen—"that you were instructed in your read through to do exactly what you just did. And you played it perfectly!"

"What in the world is going on?" Monte said.

Early shook his head.

"Hammott Lamont is going on, kids," Wayne said. "Buckle up and hang on. Please keep your hands and feet in the car at all times."

"Why were you so instructed, you ask?" Lamont continued. "Because, when it comes right down to it, it's not your decision at all, is it? After all, you're only extras. You're living mannequins in makeup and costume. Excellent at what you do but ultimately completely uninvested in the outcome of the eternal work we've set out to create. No, the decision here comes down to one man!" He looked down. "Let him come up, Wayne. It's time."

Wayne lowered the gun and gave Early a grin. "That's your cue, dude. Break a leg and all that. Not mine preferably."

Early didn't hesitate, his long legs making quick work of the distance between him and the director. He lifted a fist.

Lamont met him eye to eye. "If you do that, Calico dies first. The men are already instructed. Then the rest of your friends and then you. I'd do it that way so you could watch it happen."

"What do you want, Hammott?"

"I want what we're here for, of course. I want art. I want the game. The universe brought me you. And now you have to play your part. You have to make a choice."

"A choice between what?"

"Between who will live and who will die, what did you think? It's crucial to the scene. And when it's done, it will eat you alive, kill you slowly over years, which is the best part."

"Your scene's over, because I won't choose."

"But don't you see? I've thought of that. Saying you won't choose is making a decision in itself—you kill both Charles and Lee. We *will* have our finish, there's no other option."

"It's murder."

"It's art."

"It's murder plain and simple. You're a sociopath."

Lamont shrugged. "Maybe I am, don't know, don't care. But in art nothing is ever plain, and nothing is ever simple."

"Dress it up however you want, you can't do this and get away with it. There are too many witnesses."

Lamont turned to the crosses. "You'd be amazed at what I get away with. The masses will literally worship me when they see the final cut. Even you. Still, no matter what you think, it's not about getting away. It's about getting the shot. Tell you what, we'll start by crucifying Roxy. Get a feel for the whole thing. It'll definitely be some nice B-roll. What do you say, Roxy? You ready? Have you made your peace?"

The guards moved in.

"Lamont, you idiot, no!" Roxy shouted.

Lamont's eyes found Early again. "So you have a little time to think while Roxy goes up. What's it going to be? Charles or Lee in the starring role? I really am leaving it up to you, you know. It's an undeserved honor in a way. Believe it or not, your decision will ring through the heavens for eternity. You will be immortal."

"I'm telling you right now, I won't let you kill anyone."

"Why do you have to suck all the fun out of everything? I'll bet you were better when you were drinking. Face facts, you're unarmed and outnumbered. The only power you have right now is the power of decision. So, decide."

"What's going on here, Early?" Lee said. "This guy really wants to kill somebody?"

Early looked at Lee. The man who had once been his father still had purple moons under his eyes and an angry orange-yellow bruise on his cheek from where Early had decked him. "So it seems."

"He gonna kill me?"

"He's not gonna kill anybody."

"Wishful thinking on your son's part, Lee," Lamont said, eyes still on Early. "The truth is, yes, if your son goes the way I know he will—true love and all that nonsense—I'll definitely be killing you."

Lee spat toward one of the cartel guards. "You're Hammott Lamont? One that sent the lawyer?"

"I am."

"So why don't you shut your fat mouth and do it then? You talk too much."

Lamont studied him the way a sadistic kid might study a bug he was about to pluck the legs off of. "As tempting as your offer is, it's still not your choice."

"It's not too late to walk away from all this, Hammott," Early said.

"Your desperation will be so beautiful on film."

"Stop."

"It can't be stopped. It's in motion. The stars have spoken. Heaven is waiting. The script is the script."

He waved a hand. Men stepped into the light and began working ropes and levers to tilt the crosses back, down onto the ground.

CHAPTER FIFTY

THE WIND GUSTED, LIGHTENED, THEN gusted again. One of the big boom cameras hovered just feet from Early and Lamont. Early turned his back on it, but it swiveled and repositioned.

Lamont's eyebrows knit for a close-up. "The time has come for blood and beauty. But we're still missing a thief, aren't we?"

"We need another thief!" the crowd shouted.

Lamont tapped his lips with a finger. He scanned the group, then the crowd, as if considering the problem. An act, surely. Early could see a dark and resolute anticipation far back behind the man's eyes. Lamont knew what he was about to do, and he relished it.

"A bit part really," Lamont continued. "But then again, I like to say there are no bit parts. How about Calico Foster? She certainly stole my heart."

"Calico Foster!" the crowd shouted.

Early tensed his legs, ready to swing no matter the consequences.

Lamont shook his head. "I hate it. Much too cute. Plus, who knows what the future holds for the lovely Miss Foster and me? No, I have a better idea." He steepled his index fingers. "How about Wayne? Yes, Wayne, I think!"

"Wayne the thief!" the crowd yelled.

"What?" Wayne said. "What are you talking about?"

"Come here and give me your pistol, Wayne."

"Mr. Lamont, Please! I—"

"Come here," Lamont repeated.

Wayne approached. "No way, man. I'm not—"

"Your pistol," Lamont said.

"Mr. Lamont—"

"I'll have them shoot you down where you stand if you don't give it to me. You know I will."

"Don't do it," Early said. "Give it to me instead."

Wayne searched Early's eyes, face a storm of terror.

Lamont held out a hand. "Wayne. Now."

A last look at Early, then Wayne's shoulders sagged. He handed Lamont his pistol with trembling hands. A guard dragged him to the cross on the left.

Lamont beamed. "Perfect! I feel good about it. Now, onward and upward. Early, have you ever seen DeMille's *King of Kings*? Brilliant for its time, it truly was. Made in 1927 if you can believe it. No sound, but my opinion is that the silence added to the power of the piece. I personally thought Gibson's *Passion of the Christ* was decent, but then again, look what technology he had to work with compared to DeMille. So how can you really compare? Dozens of Christ pictures. All pale wisps compared to what we're about to accomplish."

"Why?" Early said. "What is it you want to show the world? Blood? Murder? What's that going to change? They have enough of their own."

"It will change everything. I'll show them immortality! I'll show them what a lie it's been that they've all been salivating and arguing over for two millennia. I'll show them art and flesh and spirit. I'll show them *me*, Early. You're blinded. You don't understand the immediacy of God. Of heaven. Of hell. You're hard. Immovable. You're like all the rest of them. The barrier between you and anything spirit is as impenetrable as that old temple veil. But even your eyes will lose their scales, because this film will tear that veil in two again. From the bottom to the top this time, because I'm the one doing the tearing, not the Old Man."

"You're out of your mind."

"And yet you're the one who hears the sun."

"You're not putting anyone on a cross."

"Why not? Why not take all of it—violent fathers, snakes, and dead friends—and shove them right in the Old Man's face? Make him pay. Wasn't that God-slash-Lee's original trick?"

"Because it's sick and it's demented."

"Tell that to the Old Man! He started it. Tell you what, Early Pines, to protect your suddenly sensitive disposition, let's do a slight rewrite."

Lamont lifted the pistol. The muzzle flashed.

Wayne screamed and crumpled, blood pooling onto the packed earth beneath him.

The wind gusted, pulling at Lamont's suit.

Early looked at Wayne and shook his head. "Hammott . . ."

"Did it bother you?" Lamont said. "Why? After all, the man was holding you and your friends at gunpoint two minutes ago."

"Will you stop now?"

Lamont winked. "Just getting started. Make no mistake. Wayne was as big a thief as they come. He stole everything. Time, petty cash, occasionally the odd pharmaceutical. He didn't think I was aware, but he should have known better. What am I not aware of? I'm everywhere, always. He might not have known it, but he was earmarked for nails and wood from the start. I confess, though, our rewrite was fun. Art is a constant surprise, isn't it? And sometimes we deserve a little immediate gratification. Hey, good news! Now we have enough crosses for all three—Charles, Lee, and Roxy. But don't worry. You won't have to watch them die. You'll be watching Calico watch them die. We'll stage close-up shots of both of you. The universe writes and we perform. I like this so much better."

Early looked down the hill to Calico's pleading eyes. He turned to Lamont. "You won't stop?"

"Not until we have our climax."

"Then I'm about to do something I've never done before. Something I think will make you very happy. Those cameras still rolling?"

"Always," Lamont said. "But don't try to—"

"I'm going to beg."

"You're going to what?"

"You heard me. I'm going to beg."

"Ha! I don't believe you."

Early took his hat off and held it in front of him with both hands. "You said it yourself, I'm outmanned and outgunned. I don't have a choice. Let these people walk out of here right now."

"Early Pines begging . . . The thought is attractive, don't get me wrong, but the climax still has to happen. It's simply out of my hands. Still, yes, there has to be something we can do with that in editing. This piece is so full of twists already. I love it. All right. Lights! Cue begging. And . . . action!"

Lamont's eyes looked confused when the *Kiss Me, I'm Baptist* hat went back to Early's head. Widened when he saw the bullet in Early's left hand. Went round when Early pulled his pistol with his right in a smooth motion. Narrowed to slits when the bullet went into the gun, the chamber spun, and the barrel touched the end of his nose.

"Now," Early said. "Tell them all to drop their guns and back away. You get rid of Wayne's cannon too."

"You had a bullet in that stupid hat?" Lamont said.

"The magic of cinema. Along with the magic of duct tape."

Lamont arched a brow. "You spun the chamber. You don't even know where the bullet is."

Early grinned. "Nope. And neither do you. I know how much you love games."

"I don't think you'd shoot me."

"You think very, very wrong."

At that moment, a wall of wind pummeled. It rattled and howled and lifted great billows of dust off the valley floor. The world narrowed. Only Early and Lamont and the unblinking eye of the camera.

Lamont's jaw set. "I actually thought you were going to beg. I should have known better."

"Oh, I'm begging," Early said, talking over the wind. "I'm begging you to give me a reason to pull this trigger."

"All right then. What now?"

"Now I'm gonna hit you. Hard. Cameras rolling?"

CHAPTER FIFTY-ONE

"DUDE, WOULD YOU HAVE REALLY shot him?" Charlie said.

Early answered around a mouthful of pizza. "Don't know. I woulda pulled the trigger for sure. But he had a five out of six chance."

"Five out of six. I should have used Wayne's pistol." Lamont was handcuffed to the snack bar popcorn machine, beard crumpled into his chest, eyes black and swollen to slits, both cheeks deep purple, and his moustache crusted with blood. His heavy body slumped against the candy counter, legs splayed out in front of him. "You have any idea how much work went into setting up this shoot? Why didn't one of the Mexicans open fire? What did I pay them for?"

"Word is you didn't pay 'em," Monte said.

"Wayne had a big mouth. One more reason to shoot the little rat," Lamont said.

"You killed a man in front of all of us," Calico said. "Doesn't that even register with you?"

"What registers with me is that my rear end is asleep. At least give me a piece of pizza. Something to drink. I'm dying here."

"You're already dead," Roxy said. "Wait till we get back to LA."

Lamont shrugged, leaned his head back, and closed his eyes.

With Lee, Charlie, Roxy, and Lamont added to their initial group, there were nine of them waiting out the storm in the little building. They'd seen others running for shelter during their sand-blasted scramble, both extras and cartel, but none had come here. Then again, they'd come from somewhere else in the first place. Outside, the wind was doing its level best to uproot the little shack from the ground.

"All that wasted time," Lamont mumbled.

"Hey, you're the one who invited us," Jake said. "If there's one thing I know from experience, it's that it always pays to think twice before bringing Early to a party."

"All the reports said he was predictable," Lamont said. "He was supposed to rush me. Do something rash. But a bullet in the hat?"

Early walked around the counter, opened the cooler, and pulled out a Mexican Coke. Calico joined him. "When did you come up with the hat trick, Pines? You have a bullet in there all this time?"

Early popped the top off his bottle, then opened another for Calico and handed it to her. "Nope. A friend suggested it recently."

Calico sipped. "What friend?"

"The old woman at the trading post."

Calico touched her necklace. A corner of her mouth quirked up. "That was her big secret?"

"One of them."

"I don't believe it. What else was there?"

"Why do you think they're called secrets?"

The tempest proved short-lived as far as tempests go. Early woke to dawn, still and warm, Calico's head on his shoulder. He rubbed his eyes with his free hand. Roxy and Charlie were both snoring. Monte and Lucinda asleep also. Lee and Jake were gone.

So was Lamont.

Only a set of cuffs hanging on the popcorn machine where he'd been.

Early extracted his arm and stood. Lamont had drawn a happy face in the dust that coated the glass candy counter. Next to it, spelled out in jujubes and Milk Duds—THE MAGIC OF CINEMA, AIN'T IT GRAND?

Early stared at the candy, then picked up a Milk Dud, popped it in his mouth, and moved across the room in his socks as he chewed. Outside, he eased the screen door closed and bent to pull on his boots.

Empty desert stretched to the hills. No cars, no marquee, no projector screen, no crosses. Other than the snack bar, nothing but empty borderland and sky.

Jake and Lee sat on top of one of the picnic tables, feet on the seat, gazing out at the nothing. Early took a spot next to them.

"Surprised?" Jake said.

"Nope. I had a feeling the guy was gone before I even opened my eyes."

"He could've killed us in our sleep, man."

"Then who would've read his Milk Dud message? Guy like Lamont needs an audience above all else."

"How in the world did they get everything out of here? In a sandstorm?" Jake said.

"Got me. But nothing about this surprises me anymore."

"Early," Lee said, "what was this all about?"

"If I figure it out, I'll let you know."

Lee ran a hand through his thick hair. "They sent that lawyer. Man pressed and pressed. But I want you to know something—not for a minute was I ever gonna sue you or make trouble."

Early looked at him. "Why not? You could've named a price. Had whatever you wanted. You would've been set for life."

"Nah, I wouldn't have had what I really wanted. Couldn't have taken me back in time and let me change all the stupid things I did. You're the one good thing that came out of my rotten life. You remember the day you threw me out on my ear?"

"I remember."

"I've never been so proud of anybody as I was of you that day. Told all my friends my son was a man. More of a man than I'd ever be. I ain't saying I've been an angel or that the planet wouldn't be a better place without me on it, but I've at least tried to be a man. A man more like you. So, no, I'd never do nothing to you if they offered me the world, I don't care how hard you hit me."

"I did hit you pretty hard."

Lee grunted a laugh. "You put some shoulder behind it, no lie."

They sat in silence, morning sunlight soft as feathers falling around them.

"Hey, Lee," Early said after a few minutes.

"Yeah?"

"Thanks for that, I guess."

"You can call me Pop if you want. Don't have to or anything, but if you want."

"You might want to give that some time."

Lee pulled a pack of cigarettes from his pocket, lit one, blew a stream of smoke toward the mountains. "Fair enough. I gotta hit the head."

When Lee was gone, Jake glanced over at Early. "Gonna be a long walk back."

"At least we have pizza for breakfast. Every cloud and all that, right?"

"You okay?"

Early shielded his face with a hand and gazed out toward the east where the sun was getting down to its daily business on silent, greased tracks. "It's quiet, isn't it?"

"Yeah."

"You think Gomez Gomez can see us down here?"

"I honestly don't know."

Early looked at his friend. "Yeah, I'm okay. You know what? For the first time I can remember in a while, I think I'm okay."

CHAPTER FIFTY-TWO

THE DAY LAY WARM AND very still, pillars of cloud motionless above the trees. Birds flitted and chirped, protesting strangers in their midst every time a boot snapped a twig beneath the pine-needle carpet. This was a broken land, but whole too. Whole the way only broken lands can be. Because broken lands call in the dreamers, a hearty and uncommon people who will stuff even the widest, emptiest sky full of hope. And hope, by nature, heals. Whether in heart or land, hope makes straight the crookedest roads and fills the deepest canyons. Those who understand this never question the eternal truth that winter inevitably gives birth to spring. And death, frightening as it might be in the moment, always gives birth to life.

The old woman had been right on that count.

Which was why, as they made their way down the slope, Early couldn't shake the feeling that he walked the path of ghosts. But these ghosts didn't haunt. They swirled, smiling and singing, their faces radiating the fact that they were the living ones and Early was the wraith. That they were flying free and wild through the bright, eternal story while he was still a looking-glass-dimly man marooned in a temporary reflection. They might have felt sorry for him had their joy allowed any room for it.

And he was sure he heard Gomez Gomez's irresistible, raspy laugh among them.

"Where are we going again?" Calico spoke softly as if she sensed it too. As if the very air around them demanded reverence. She'd taken his arm, though she didn't need it. She moved with ease and grace through the pines and rocky outcrops.

"There's something I need to do," he said. "And it'd mean more if you're with me when I do it."

She looked at him like she was about to say something but didn't. Just as well. For a change he wanted to be alone with his thoughts.

At length they came to the edge of the trees. Calico sucked in a breath. "Early! It's beautiful."

A hundred feet or so past the trees, the mountain slope ended with an abrupt drop. Far below, the desert spread to the horizon, broken only by the distant Chiricahuas. A memorial stone had been erected partway down the path.

GOMEZ GOMEZ AND ANGEL
FOREVER MEANT TO BE

Calico squeezed his arm as they approached it. "It's amazing. It really is."

"Gomez Gomez loved it here," Early said. "He kept the fact to himself, but it meant something to him."

"I can see why."

Early pointed. "The snake got him over there. We found him sitting up, still facing the desert. When I think about it, I've been facing the desert for a long time too."

Her grip tightened.

"We let his ashes go right here. Seemed like the whole town came. We watched the wind take him and Angel together. It was beautiful in a way. And it was what he would've wanted. I must've come up here a dozen times since to resay my goodbyes to the little maniac. He was really something."

"You loved him."

"I should've done more for him. I loved myself more."

"Even Early Pines can't control snakes."

"I mean before that. No excuses, it's who I am. Or who I was, hopefully."

"We can't live backwards, Pines. Or forwards, even. In the end, right now is really all we have."

"I'm good with right now."

"Is that why we're here? Another goodbye?"

He tried to read her eyes. Which wasn't hard—she was open to him. Which thrilled him because it was something he hadn't seen before. "I think so, yeah. But not to Gomez Gomez. I've been riding that horse too long. It's getting tired."

She nodded. "Are you saying goodbye to me then?"

"I've never for a second wanted to say goodbye to you. I think that's a well-established fact."

They watched the desert while the day held its breath. Early took the Baptist hat off his head and looked at it. "Gomez Gomez told me about pouring out his liquor here. Dumped it and threw the bottle as far as he could. It was only a symbolic thing, but it meant something to him. Gomez Gomez finally let go, you know? It couldn't have been easy for him."

"It never is with us imperfect believers, right?"

"No, I guess it isn't."

"There's nothing wrong with symbolic, Pines. And nothing wrong with hard either."

Early moved to the very edge of the cliff and held out the hat over the abyss. "Nope, there's not."

"What are you doing?"

"A little experiment, old trading post woman secret number two."

"Be careful."

He smiled as the words played back in his mind. Crazy how he remembered every one of them.

Out there in some forgotten valley, God breathes. Can you see it? A tiny tendril of dust stirs from the floor of the desert. God imagines, and the tendril swirls and grows and pulls dust into its vortex. It circles and dips, picks up speed and strength and bits of tumbleweed. It chases a game trail across the valley floor. On and on it goes, bigger and bigger until it bursts into a full-fledged wind, spreads its arms, and tumbles up and over the mountains, bending trees, banging doors, dropping birds . . . It strips us, bares us, even scatters what's left of our lifeless ashes. And why? All because God let out a little breath. Because God wants it so. Do you believe in God, Detective Pines?

"You had no idea, Hammott . . . I think the Old Man was playing you that day, pal. Talking to me."

"What are you mumbling about?" Calico said.

"This, I think."

The gust came up from the valley with a rush, lifting dust and flattening brush against the cliff face. The hat hung loose in Early's fingers, but even had his knuckles been white the wind would have taken it. Because nothing stops the wind when the time has come. The hat whipped upward, spinning, flipping in the sunlight. It took a wide arc outward, then, as the wind waned, began its long descent to the valley floor.

Early could have sworn he heard an echoed, fading laugh.

Calico smiled. "I can't believe it. You let it go."

"I guess I did. But somehow I don't think I had much to do with it at all."

"We gotta have a party. *Kiss Me, I'm Baptist* is actually history."

"No Baptists invited. I'll bring the Coke."

"You know what?"

"What?" Early said.

"I think I might kiss you now."

That time he definitely heard a laugh.

CHAPTER FIFTY-THREE

THREE DAYS AFTER THE WIND took his hat, Early stood in front of his adobe watching a dust trail tumble and dissipate as a distant car approached. Too far away still to make it out. Jake was supposed to be coming but the dust was all wrong for Jake. Jake dust was more deliberate. This dust had an edge to it. It was Calico dust, and Early's heart picked up a few beats per minute. She did that to him. Probably always would, even from a million miles away in One Horse. Five minutes later, her sunburned Tempo skidded to a stop two feet in front of his legs.

She climbed out and stretched, the car's engine ticking. "Looks like I made it in time for the sunset."

"Hey," he said.

"You look surprised."

"I am a little."

"I told you I was coming back."

"Uh-huh."

She took his arm. "Let's go out back. We need to talk. You got any Mexican Coke? You got me drinking the sludge now."

As they sat on the patio, bottles in hand, watching God paint, the coyote trotted out of the brush and curled up next to Early's leg.

Calico shook her head at the sight. "Are you serious?"

Early sipped and lifted a shoulder. "I told you he was a terrible judge of character."

She smiled and looked back at the western sky. Early ignored the celestial paint job and watched her instead.

"So the car's running all right thanks to Ray," she said.

"I did notice that when you almost ran me over."

"Charlie's back in Los Angeles. Would you believe it? He's doing a movie with Roxy Parsons."

Early laughed. "No joke?"

"Word is it's gonna be awful."

"Maybe we'll get invited to the premier."

"Do they have premiers for straight-to-cable stuff?"

"Probably not."

"Anyway, no thanks. I've had enough Los Angeles for a while."

"You wanted to talk. Why do I get the feeling you're stalling?"

She sighed. "Can we watch the sunset first?"

"If you want."

A playful wind stirred the sage, touched her hair. She turned to him. "All right, here goes. I'm sorry. I know we've been through a lot, and I care about you, I do, but I still don't believe in long-distance relationships."

He scratched his neck. "One Horse isn't that far."

"I told you from the start—"

"You did."

"It'd be too hard, you here and me there. And the thing is, I've gotten very attached to you, Pines. Against all better judgment. It's not healthy."

"I've found bad judgment often works in my favor. At least 'attached' is a step in the right direction."

"Yeah, but—"

"What if I find something to do in One Horse? How about that?"

"There's nothing to do in One Horse. Besides, that'd make it worse."

"Worse why?"

"Because I bought the Venus Motel today."

Early set his Coke down, not sure he'd heard right. "You did what?"

"You need to get your ears checked."

"You bought . . . How?"

"I got a check in the mail two days ago. For six hundred thousand dollars."

"Charlie?"

"Yup."

Early grinned. "The little punk had the money the whole time. I knew it."

"Yup."

"What about Bob's?"

"I sold it to Jube. It's practically his anyway."

"I can't believe you bought the Venus. So you're going to be here?"

"You're smiling. I was a little nervous to tell you."

"Why?"

"I don't know. I just was."

"I don't think this smile's ever leaving my face."

"That might get awkward in some situations."

"People will have to deal with it."

"Least they don't have to deal with the hat anymore, so there's that."

"True story."

"Anyway, I kinda like your crooked tooth. Wait, I forgot. I have something for you. I'll be right back."

Early listened as she moved through the house—a sound he could get used to. The front screen door creaked, and the Tempo's door opened and closed. Then she was back on the patio carrying a large box and a thick manila envelope.

"Is that what I think it is?"

"It's about time."

Early took the box and opened it. "Stetson. Headwear of kings."

"Put it on. You're gonna make Jake so jealous."

Early did. Checked out his reflection in the window. He eyed the coyote. "What do you think?"

Yellow eyes blinked.

"I think he likes it," Calico said.

"So do I. But not half as much as I like that you bought the Venus."

"It's an eight-track place. And that sign—I couldn't help it. I loved her from the minute I saw her." She stood. "I wish I could stay longer, but I need to get going. I'm meeting the old owners at Spur's for dinner to iron out a few details. I wanted you to know first. I'm glad you're happy." She handed him the manila envelope. "Charlie sent this with the money. He said it was for you."

"Me?"

"He said a maid named Isabella gave it to him in the desert. He said she apparently saved his life and something about speaking English all of a sudden and how she was gorgeous. He's pretty hung up on her, which is different for Charlie. I wonder if he was hallucinating."

"What is it?"

"I don't know. He said to open it by yourself."

Early shrugged a shoulder. "All right." He set the envelope on the ground next to his chair. The coyote sniffed it, dismissed it, and laid his head on his front paws. "When do you go back to One Horse?"

"I'll have to go get my things at some point, but I'm taking a room at the Venus until I can move into the owner's unit."

"So you'll be here now?"

"Like it or not."

"You got plans tomorrow night?"

She smiled. "Yeah, the sunset with you."

He walked her to the car. Twenty yards down the road she skidded to a stop and leaned out the window. "Hey, Pines!"

"What?"

"Next time you see me, ask me to dance." She was gone before he could answer.

Back on the patio, he looked out at the darkening sky. Wind stirred, pulled at him.

"Yeah, yeah, I know, we're talking now. You're not Lee. Although I guess I'm talking to him too."

The coyote stood, cocked his head, then padded off into the gathering darkness.

Early's phone vibrated in his pocket. He pulled it out and swiped the screen. "Hey, Monte."

"Hola, kid. How's the weather in Arizona tonight?"

"Pretty decent. Raining Stetsons."

"I have no idea what that means."

"It means Calico's buying the Venus and she's gonna be local."

"Well, we'd better get an invitation to the wedding then."

"She's of sound mind and body. I doubt that's gonna happen anytime soon."

"Try not to be more of an idiot than you already are, okay? Listen, on another note, I just saw something I think you'd be very interested in."

"Yeah?"

"Uh-huh. So Lucinda was making me watch one of her real-life crime shows she always has on. You know, the ones where they use no-name actors to reenact the crimes and all that?"

"Yeah."

"Well, I'm sitting here in my recliner, almost asleep, when Lucinda punches me in the arm. Hard, by the way. Guess who's playing a dead guy lying there all scatterwampus and bloody?"

"I'm waiting."

"At first I thought it was stinking Orson Welles."

"Hammott Lamont?"

"One and only. The episode was several years old. We looked it up on the internet. Found the cast. Guy's name wasn't Hammott Lamont, it was Maury Walker. Lucinda got on Google right away. Not much on him. He did a couple commercials and had some small parts on stuff you never heard of. No agent mentioned, then disappeared and hasn't been in anything for a long time. At least nothing I can find."

"Because he became Hammott Lamont."

"What I'm thinking. Has a more upper-crust ring to it than Maury Walker. Weird, man. One more bizarre turn in a carnival fun house of mirrors. I'd keep poking out of pure curiosity if I knew where to poke."

Early studied the distant horizon. He could just make out the mountains. "Yeah, hard to poke at ghosts. Thanks for the call, though."

"You know me, kid, anything I can do to keep you from sleeping at night."

After Early hung up he went inside, letting the screen door slam behind him. He grabbed another Coke from the fridge, went out to the patio, and sank into his chair. The coyote was back. It lowered onto its haunches next to his boots and watched him.

Early eyed it, took a swig of Coke, and picked up the manila envelope. He tore open the end and turned it over. The first thing that dropped out was a smaller envelope, *Early Pines* written across it in flowing female script. Something hard inside. When he opened it, a ring fell into his hand. Silver, delicate, with a clear sky-blue stone. He recognized it immediately. There was a note with it.

Early Pines,

How about that bullet trick? You're welcome.

I told you I'd save one of your secrets. Here it is—the ring is for her so you can stop threatening to buy one. I know she admired it when she saw it at the trading post. She's tough but beautiful. And a beautiful soul should have beautiful things. Besides, it goes with the necklace I gave her.

Be nice to Charlie if you have the opportunity. It's true he's a clown, but deep down his heart is sound and I've gotten rather attached to him.

As for you, don't worry anymore about your friend Gomez Gomez. I can tell you with certainty and joy he rides the wind even better than he rode bulls. Early Pines, you aren't only chased, you are loved. Now, please, go rest your legs.

Isabella
PS: Suck it up and call your father Pop.

Early pulled the remaining item from the original manila envelope and turned it over in his hands. He eyed the coyote.

Smiled.

And started to laugh.

CHAPTER FIFTY-FOUR

An onshore wind blew and the palms above the parking lot rattled and wheezed. It was late, the parking lot almost empty. Air thick with low tide and yesterday's catch.

Hammott Lamont stood in the shadows and watched the harbor lights bob and dip. He was tired. The kind of tiredness that always lasted for days after a shoot. And now there would be reshoots. And then edits. And then more reshoots. Then one day, finally—history. Hey, even Orson himself wasn't immune to a few project hiccups. That was part of the journey. But now, at least for the moment, it was over. He sighed a day-after-Christmas sigh. Then again, what journey ever ends? There was a lot of world out there. And a million roads. And a million frames to link together to form the ever-glorious whole.

A good night's sleep, a good meal or three, a little whiskey, then plan and regroup. Rework the script.

Out in the channel, a fishing boat made its way home. Music played somewhere. A planet full of people. Normals. Unexceptionals. Plebeians. Each of them thinking their lives meant something in the cosmic plan. It was almost funny.

Almost.

Hammott made his way along the docks on autopilot, lost in his thoughts. The shoot had had some promising moments. And they'd left with some decent footage. Still, Pines had blown the ending and that was unacceptable. Well, Early would be dealt with. But tonight, food, drink, and sleep.

He should move the boat. After all, there were endless harbors, a million coves out there. He'd been here too long. Tomorrow he'd let the crew take it somewhere else. San Diego, or Kauai, or maybe South America. He'd spend some time at the downtown penthouse. Rest. Think. Let his mind and emotions settle. He'd eat at Spago and Petit Trois and In-N-Out. He'd have Liz wait on him and toast Pines's imminent suffering with a glass of Balvenie Fifty Year.

The dock creaked and shifted as the ship tugged at its lines. Late-night dew coated the rails. He headed to the expansive back deck and stretched, still tired but feeling good to be back.

Then he saw the door.

It stood half open, as if in invitation. Liz would never have left it like that. None of the crew would. "Hello?" he said. He knew then, and he had to laugh.

The room inside was large and opulent. Comfortable furniture. Brass. Lots of wood. Low lamplight gave the space a warm, comforting glow.

Early Pines waved from an overstuffed chair, long legs stretched out in front of him, boots crossed. That scar. And that incessant, idiotic crooked-toothed grin. He had a Mexican Coke in his hand.

"Heya, Wayne. I gotta say, you're looking pretty good for a dead guy. Man, this whole identity thing is fascinating. Hiding behind an actor the whole time? Pulling all the strings? Do I call you Wayne or Hammott Lamont?"

"So you found Maury Walker."

"He was sitting at the bar in the Brown Derby. Cliché enough? Although now he's in Paradise being held for assault and battery. Unfortunately for him, they don't serve gin and tonics at the jail."

Wayne shrugged. "If you want to check my birth certificate, it says Hammott Lamont. But I've used Wayne so long even I think of myself as that now. Anyway, I always hated the name Hammott. One of my father's cruel jokes. He was like that."

"So you hired an actor to be you and gave yourself the name Wayne? Why not Rhett or Jet or something?"

"Nobody notices a Wayne. Besides, names are temporary, it's the soul that counts."

"Why hide at all?"

Wayne grinned. "It makes the game more interesting. Plus, when push comes to shove, a fall guy is always handy. Maury spilled it all, huh? I'm a little surprised."

"Nope, Maury's tight as a clam."

This gave Wayne pause. "Then how'd you know? That death scene was flawless."

Early tossed a thick, dog-eared book onto the coffee table. *Citizen Welles.* "Welles's biography. You ever read it?"

"Of course I have."

"You said it yourself, out there in the desert when you were holding that cannon on us—it's all about misdirection, right? *F for Fake*, *Touch of Evil*, heck, even *Citizen Kane* . . . Rosebud was a sled? Orson was the king of misdirection and you pathetically want to be like him."

"No, I want to be better."

Early held up his hands. "And yet here I am."

"Okay. Still, why come here? Why the boat? I could have gone anywhere."

"To start with, *Magic Trick*—the name of your tub—is also the name of Orson's 1953 film. But mostly because you told me you'd be here."

"I told you?"

"*After this job look for me under the palm trees. I'll be the one sitting on a boat with a cold drink.* That's what you said, word for word."

Wayne smiled. "Oh yeah. I couldn't help that one."

Early took a drink of Coke, picked up the book, and thumbed through it. "Speaking of misdirection, did you know some guy figured out the card trick Orson pulled off on *The Merv Griffin Show* the night before he died? Then he posted online how Orson did it. Where's the fun in that?"

"It only means Welles is still relevant. He'd take it as a compliment."

"Maybe. I doubt anyone will ever do that for you. Too bad."

"Of course they will."

"Come on, man, in the end you're no Welles. You're not even close."

"I'm better."

"Nah. I've read the book."

"Say what you want, eternity will judge."

"It sure will."

"So what now? We play Go Fish? Have a pillow fight? Paint our toenails? This has been fun, but frankly—and I certainly do mean to be rude—I'm getting a little bored. It's time for you to exit stage left. Don't worry, though, we'll see each other again."

"Ah, c'mon, is that any way to treat a guest? Hey, did you finish all that caviar? I've never actually tried it."

"Goodbye."

"Wayne-slash-Hammott, you don't seem to get it. You've played, now it's time to pay."

"Pay for what?"

"Kidnapping, torture, assault with attempt to commit murder. I'm sure we could think of more if we put our heads together."

"Even if those things were true, what can you do about it? You were fired."

Early tossed a badge onto the table next to the book. "Surprise."

Wayne shrugged. "Congratulations, but so? It was a movie. Make-believe. Nobody was really ever going to get killed. Just look at me, right?" He walked to the liquor cabinet, opened it, pulled out a bottle of the Balvenie and a crystal tumbler. He looked at Early. "You're already drinking, do you mind?"

Early shook his head. "Your boat."

Wayne poured, drained half the tumbler, gave a satisfied sigh he hoped was especially irritating, and poured again. He brought the bottle with him when he sank onto the couch opposite Early's chair.

"The thing is, Charlie and Roxy were actors. They knew what they were getting into. It's a method thing. And besides, Maury was calling the shots out there. There are a couple hundred witnesses who will attest to that."

Early reached down and came up with a third item for the coffee table. "Box number three. Your script says different. That's your handwriting on practically every page, isn't it? We've checked, it's not Maury's. You spell it out pretty clear. You were going to kill them, absolutely. Far as I'm concerned, you're a sociopathic lunatic."

Wayne smiled. "Where did you get that script?"

"Charlie."

"Old Chuck finally got his script, huh? Good Lord knows he asked for it enough times. How?"

"Isabella gave it to him."

"Who's Isabella?"

"One of your maids."

"I know all my employees, and I don't have a maid named Isabella."

Early laughed. "No, you don't, which is the best part. There's also no old lady who sells jewelry at the Chiricahua Trading Post."

"What are you talking about?"

"I'm talking about the game. Not your game. The real game."

Wayne killed off the whiskey in his glass, refreshed it from the bottle, and leaned forward. "I *am* the game. How can you not see that by now?" He frowned. "You were entertaining for a minute or two, I'll admit it, but you've been a problem. At first I thought the universe brought you, but now I'm thinking you crawled out of hell just to wear me out. And you are wearing me out because I'm tired. And now you think you won somehow? Everything I do has a thousand layers to it. And don't think you can record me saying this either—which I'm sure you're doing and feeling like a genius doing it—because that's called entrapment. My lawyers will tear you to shreds."

"No doubt about it. I wouldn't stand a chance. Who would against your money?"

Wayne studied him. "All right. Why are you still here?"

"You never should've hit Calico."

"Maury hit her, not me."

"On your orders."

Wayne leaned back, weary to the bone and done with the conversation. He needed sleep. Wasn't even hungry anymore. Who did this guy think he was? "So? What are you going to do, punch me?" He laughed a slurred laugh and tried to put his hands up but the stupid things just sat there on his lap. Then the one holding the tumbler let it fall to the floor. "What the . . . ?" The room dimmed and from somewhere far away he heard the deep thrum of a motor. His body slumped to the side. "No . . . How?"

"Balvenie Fifty Year. It's what the gods drink, right?"

Wayne's voice came from the other side of the harbor. "You kidding me? The whiskey?"

"What can I say? You went for the hooch so, no, I'm not gonna hit you." Early lifted his Coke bottle. "But I can't promise the same for the hombres in that boat out there."

The motor thrum grew louder. Then a heavy thud against the side of the yacht. The room tunneled. Wayne could only manage a croaked whisper. "Who?"

That stupid, stupid crooked incisor tooth. "You're right, no court would ever be able to touch you. But, man, in what world did you think it'd be a good idea to stiff the Mexican cartel?" Early stood. "Hey, by the way, you hear all those birds dropping out of the sky?"

"Early, please . . . no . . ."

"Can you believe it? They say that boat of theirs can make Tijuana in under seven hours. I'm guessing you'll sleep for at least ten."

"Early . . ."

Early set his now-empty bottle down on the coffee table in front of Wayne's face. It looked bigger than life. It looked like cinema. Wayne could see Early's distorted legs through the glass.

"See ya around, Wayne," Early said from another world. "Thanks for the Coke."

CHAPTER FIFTY-FIVE

Jake was leaning against the hood of the old Chevy when Early got back to the harbor parking lot. "Did you say goodbye for me?"

"Forgot."

"Oh well. Couldn't have happened to a nicer guy."

Early looked at the water. "He hurt Calico. What did he expect?"

"Not a midnight cruise to Mexico, I bet."

"Life's full of happy little surprises."

"How you feeling?"

"Top of the world actually."

"Yeah?"

"Yeah."

"How about the sun?"

"Quiet as a nun in socks."

"I'm glad to see you back. I missed you."

"Thing is, I think Gomez Gomez is all right. And I'm pretty sure he's happy where he is."

"I think you're right. What are you gonna do now?"

"I don't know. Still a few legal hoops to jump through before they let me go back to work. Someone recently told me to rest my legs. Sounds like a good idea."

Jake smiled. "So you're still at large? At least for a few days?"

"Why don't I like the sound of this?"

Jake walked around to the passenger door of the Chevy. "I hear there's a pretty good rodeo about to get rolling down near Ensenada. Straight shot south. What do you say?"

The breeze picked up off the water, but the new Stetson held tight.

"Seriously? You're standing there talking to me about another rodeo with a straight face?"

"I don't joke about rodeos. Sacred ground. Quiet as a nun in socks? Where in the world did that come from?"

"My brain is a beautiful and fascinating place. You're saying Ensenada as in Old Mexico?"

"Not to be confused with New Mexico."

Early fished in the pocket of his jeans, pulled out his keys, and slid into the driver's seat. "Straight shot south, huh?"

"Nothing but freeway. Not a back road to be found."

Early turned the engine over, threw the truck into gear, and grinned. "Wanna bet?"